MONSTERS
Peter Cawdron

thinkingscifi.wordpress.com

First published as an eBook by Peter Cawdron
using Smashwords

ISBN-13: 978-1480258754
ISBN-10: 148025875X

US Edition

Dedicated to

National Year of Reading

http://www.love2read.org.au/

Table of Contents

Prologue

For those that could still read, for those that dared, newspapers were the best source of information about the collapse of the Old World. It had only been a couple of centuries since Comet Holt first appeared, but Nature was quick to reclaim her jewel given half a chance, undoing tens of thousands of years of human progress in what seemed like the blink of an eye.

Nature was vengeful. After billions of years of evolutionary pressure, she was not one to stand idly by while man re-created the world in his own image. She had taken her licks, she had endured earth-shattering asteroid impacts, the eruption of super-volcanoes that spanned hundreds of miles, and severe glaciation that had threatened to engulf the entire planet, transforming Earth into little more than a snowball, yet somehow life always endured. Homo sapiens were just another emergent species with a fragile hold on a span of a few million years at best, a few thousand if civilization was any measure. Life had flourished on Earth for billions of years, and would continue for billions more, regardless of mankind, regardless of Comet Holt.

Newspapers were a surprising link to the past. They had been intended as a disposable medium and were out-of-vogue when the comet arrived. The broadsheets, or tabloids as some of the more salacious papers were called, were a passing snapshot into the affairs of any given day, hurriedly printed on cheap, low-grade paper. Far from their heyday, when the daily print-run toppled presidents and spoke *Vox populi, vox Dei*, with the voice of the people echoing the sentiments of their God, newspapers had faded to little more than pulp-status in most countries, yet it was the daily periodicals that captured the fall of civilization in a roughly chronological sequence.

Newspapers provided a glimpse into the consumer desires from a bygone age, the distractions and hype that once seemed so important, and they cataloged news from far flung corners of a planet most would never venture to cross. Buried deep within their black on white print, scattered across days, weeks, months and years, lay the fragmented story of how the reign of mankind ground to a halt following the appearance of the comet. Among their petty advertisements for skin cream and new cars, among the frivolous reviews for local wine shows and the jaundiced opinion pieces on federal politics, lay the fragments of what happened as society collapsed under its own weight.

Comet Holt was billed as the celestial show of the millennium. Fifteen times larger than Halley's comet, its twin V-shaped tail lit up the night sky for months as it approached the sun from the outer reaches of the solar system. At first it was little more than a smudge, but its long, blue and white tail spread out more and more as it approached the sun. Space telescopes measured the tail as reaching over six hundred million kilometers in length, a staggering four times the distance from Earth to the sun.

The distinct V-shape drew considerable attention from media commentators, although professional astronomers pointed out that all comets had twin tails. NASA explained that the dust and gas streaming away from the glowing nucleus of the comet projected outward on slightly different angles. The dust tail, they said, was brighter and curved, revealing the orbital path of the comet, while the ionized gas was fainter, streaming directly away from the sun in a straight line. The public was entranced.

At its height, the comet's tail stretched across forty degrees of the night sky and was breathtaking to behold. Holt was a splash of white paint daubed on a starry sky. Van Gogh, it seemed, had been brought back to life.

Although it had never been seen before, scientists said Holt was a short-period comet, but one that originally orbited within the Oort cloud for billions of years before being unseated. At some point, the comet's cosmic ballet became perturbed and Holt drifted out of the Oort cloud, starting its long, slow fall toward the sun with a highly elliptic orbit that for hundreds of millions of years barely crossed the path of Neptune.

Scientists said Holt's initial planetary orbit was measured in tens of thousands of years. From there, it was just a matter of time before the gravitational attraction of Neptune either threw Holt out of the solar system or sent it plunging toward the sun. NASA calculated the stability of this orbit and the newspapers spoke of an age that saw the rise of mammals, the fall of dinosaurs, and the advent of bipedal apes before Comet Holt crossed in front of the oncoming Neptune and found itself flung toward the inner planets.

Comet Holt grew in intensity as it approached the sun. Each night it appeared earlier in the evening sky, lower, longer and brighter, until it looked like Holt would collide with the radiant reds and yellows of the setting sun. Holt rounded the sun, breaking up as it passed too close. The comet lost over half its mass in the process, with the majority of the comet breaking up and falling back into the sun. The flare of volatile materials unleashed during the comet's disintegration was visible only to orbiting astronomical observatories.

Although the comet's fiery death throes never competed with the brightness of the sun, the heavily-filtered photographs looked sensational in the newspapers. The science editor for the New York Times called the fragments that escaped the sun's fiery grip a 'necklace of pearls.' At first, they were barely visible in the dusk, soft specks of light moving away from the sun along the ecliptic. As the days passed, the fragments appeared later in the evening sky; a string of pearls, each with its own tail, each tail blurred as it stretched away from the horizon.

After a month, in the dark of a moonless night, the pearls shone with a radiance never before seen by the races of man. It was as though seven separate comets had been painted on the backdrop of the heavens, and the comparisons with Van Gogh were replaced with those of Michelangelo and Rembrandt.

The public fell in love with the pearls. Cities across the world would dim their lights on Sunday and Monday evenings so residents could enjoy their stunning beauty at its height. Like diamonds on black velvet, the comet fragments were mesmerizing, putting mankind's petty troubles and earthly contrivances in perspective for a while. Crime rates fell, as did acts of suicide. An age of romanticism swept the globe, transcending cultures, with the awe and wonder of nature being given a place of prominence and prestige, if only for a few short months.

Although comets had long been seen as the harbingers of doom, few saw any danger looming. Those that did were labelled crackpots and were ignored. The newspapers belittled them, calling them superstitious, paranoid, but even the naysayers couldn't have foreseen what was to come.

The pearls were no threat to mankind, at least that's what the newspapers said. NASA calculated their orbit and determined they would pass harmlessly into the outer solar system, with a periodic cycle of over a hundred years. The next time the family of Holt appeared, they would have spread apart, forming distinctly separate comets, each with a slightly different periodic cycle, returning up to three years apart.

NASA said Holt would never appear the same again, that this generation was privileged to witness an astronomical spectacle like no other. They told the world the pearls were continuing to break up, leaving tiny fragments in their wake.

NASA predicted Earth would pass through this fine cloud once a year, giving the public an annual meteor shower thousands of times more sensational than the Leonids. Although meteor was too strong a word, they said, as the shower would glisten high in the atmosphere like sparkles on the Fourth of July. Being micro-meteorites the fragments were millimeters in size, just dust particles and flecks of snow and ice. None of them would ever reach the ground, so there was no danger, at least that's what the papers said.

The Sparkles, as they came to be known, were every bit as magnificent as NASA had predicted. Flashes of light rippled across the sky, appearing first in the constellation of Virgo, but slowly stretching out to span two other constellations as the month progressed. At their height, thousands of streaks of light were visible every few seconds. For a couple of weeks, it was as though the planet were under the constant gaze of a full moon. Some claimed it was bright enough to read a newspaper beneath the stars, at least that's what the media reported. For almost two months, the Sparkles continued. Then, as quickly as they had come, they were gone.

The aerosol-like remains of the Sparkles soared high in the jet stream, interrupting international air traffic for nine months. Several transatlantic flights were crippled by the fine ash, each of them hobbling in to London on a single engine. After two passenger jets crashed near Sydney, Australia, killing over eight hundred people, flights across the Pacific were suspended. The military continued to fly, but the loss of several fighter jets curtailed their activities to critical missions. Turbo-prop airplanes were more resilient, and so a fleet of military heavy-lifting aircraft was re-tasked to provide the government with transport, but the wear on engine parts due to the fine grit limited their effectiveness. Within weeks they were spending most of their time on the ground undergoing re-fits. Global travel had ground to a halt.

At first, the majority of people weren't too bothered by the interruption to air travel, and there was even some talk about the good this naturally imposed moratorium would do for the environment. Greenpeace noted that if modern man could live without airplanes for the best part of a year, then perhaps they weren't as necessary as everyone assumed. With romantic sunsets dominating the early evening, and each dawn being announced by sweeping vistas of orange, pink, yellow and purple, Comet Holt could be forgiven for interrupting holiday plans, at least that was the initial sentiment.

Opinions changed as the global economy faltered. Investors got nervous and companies struggled to adjust to life without air travel. The newspapers downplayed the impact, but the reality was air travel had become a form of commute as common as a taxi ride. Without it, companies turned to a virtual presence in remote locations, but it wasn't as effective. Business slowed, efficiency dropped, and inflation raced ahead, dampening economic confidence even further.

Later that year came the first of the drifts, followed by the floods. Eight million people died in North America alone that winter. The snow drifts were abnormal, that much everyone agreed upon, but what had caused them took time to unravel. In New York, the drifts reached heights of eighty feet, paralyzing the city for months on end. With over sixty major US cities affected by the drifts, the United States was helpless to prevent the loss of life on a scale never before seen outside of a world war.

Snow compacted into ice under the weight of the drifts, causing buildings to collapse. The ice was impossible to tunnel through, with demolition experts likening it to granite. Wall St moved to Queens, while the bulk of New Yorkers vowed not to be displaced by nature, but as the years passed it became increasingly obvious they were fighting against an incoming tide.

In Chicago, civil engineers compared the compact of ice to mountains arising suddenly out of the ground. Roads shifted, bridges fell. Interstate ground transport came to a halt. On the northern side of a number of apartment blocks in Boston, large packs of ice persisted through to the following summer, being hidden in the shade for most of the day.

NASA said that dust fines in the stratosphere, the charred remnants of the Sparkles, had led to the formation of these devastating snow storms. The fines, as they were called in the newspapers, were apparently as vaporous as cigarette smoke, but their dominance in the stratosphere upset global weather patterns. NASA predicted subsequent years wouldn't be as bad as the Sparkles reduced in intensity. They were wrong. The newspapers told them so.

The electronic world on which mankind had come to depend was the first of the catastrophic failures that sent Homo sapiens spiraling back into the Stone Age. The winter ice that killed so many crippled the electrical grid. Computer servers had become the bastions of knowledge and communication. Without power they became paperweights.

Few books survived that first winter. In the northern regions of Europe and the US, the dull glow of their smoldering remains kept millions alive long enough to perish in the floods that followed in the spring thaw. In the equatorial regions, heavy rains and sweltering summers caused those books and newspapers not kept in sealed containers to rot. Within a few years, books were a distant memory, hoarded by the rich.

The decade that followed the passing of Holt became known as the Fall. Those fragments of newspapers that survived the Fall were given a status akin to holy relics, as though somehow their preservation kept the past alive and contained a hope for the future. In reality, few read their contents anymore, even fewer understood them. Brittle sheets of typeset paper were sealed behind glass, kept in makeshift safes, wrapped in plastic and hidden under floorboards, their greatest value being found in trade. Some still read them, most didn't see the point, the general populace regarded the papers with almost medieval superstition, thinking knowledge had inflamed man's hubris predicating the Fall.

After a few decades, the wealthy chose to be buried in newspapers, wrapped in loose print pages, taking what precious little remained of the Old World to rot with them in the grave. Like diamonds and gold in a bygone age, the scarcity of newspapers caused even fleeting scraps of newsprint to become objects around which wealth could concentrate. As

7

time passed, the realization that their true wealth lay in the knowledge they preserved became incidental, and then irrelevant.

During the Fall, water levels rose. The sea invaded the land, flooding low-lying areas, submerging coastal cities. The US government built levees around New York and Miami, but they were fighting a rear-guard action, leaving these cities isolated and exposed to the ravages of the sea. The need for a second line of defense to protect these cities in the event of a breach strained construction resources, limiting the area that could be effectively protected.

Environmental scientists said it wasn't just Comet Holt that was at fault, that the combined effect of global warming along with the greenhouse effect caused by the Sparkles had raised global temperatures by an average of four degrees.

In Europe, most of Holland, Belgium and the northern regions of France became a shallow inland sea. China's great rivers, that for thousands of years had sustained the burgeoning population, flooded on a scale that spanned hundreds of thousands of square miles, washing villages, towns and cities out to sea. Indonesia lost entire islands to rising sea levels, while several pacific nations slipped beneath the waves, but that wasn't the worst of the curses brought by Comet Holt.

Four degrees didn't sound like much of an increase, but it wasn't spread evenly around the globe, some places experienced only a moderate increase in the average local temperature. Trade winds shifted, sending warm air over Antarctica and breaking up the great ice packs and glaciers that had dominated the continent for millions of years. Within a few years, the average depth of the glaciers covering Antarctica dropped from two thousand meters to a little over six hundred.

The Himalayas exacerbated the problem, with flood waters flowing down across the subcontinent of India, Pakistan and Bangladesh. The influx of fresh water crippled the coastal ecology of Asia, destroying food supplies and forcing mass migrations in search of sustenance. Those that

8

escaped the floods succumbed to disease and famine, killing 1.4 billion people within the first decade. As tragic and heartrending as this catastrophe was, it too was not the worst of the curses brought on by the coming of Comet Holt.

Drought ravaged Asia, Africa and the Americas, crippling crop production. Hundreds of millions of people starved.

It might have been the climatic changes that brought man to his knees, but it was the rise of monsters that kept him there.

During the first few years, the monstrosities were dismissed as oddities. Mankind was too busy struggling with the natural disasters overwhelming civilization to understand what was happening at a biological level. Those scientists that had the luxury to investigate the gigantism arising within dogs, cats, wolves and bears struggled to understand the cause.

Birthrates dropped among domesticated farm animals like cows and pigs. For those that remained fertile, complications arose during birthing as sows, ewes and mares struggled to bear oversize stock, often proving fatal to both mother and child. The number of stillborn farm animals and complications during birthing resulting in death reached alarming levels, but the primary concern of scientists was the impact on food production, not the implications of rapid evolutionary change on the distribution of species. Natural Selection was pushing back against artificial selection.

The thickness of eggshells decreased in both domestic poultry and wild birds, reducing the number of offspring to an average of 1.8 per roosting nest in North America alone. At that rate, biologists predicted the extinction of all but the hardiest of bird species within a decade.

So many amphibian species succumbed to extinction in the wake of Comet Holt that scientists initially thought the entire phylogenetic clade had been wiped out, destroying tens of thousands of individual species. The discovery of desert frogs and cane toads surviving in the remote outback of Australia gave hope that some amphibians had survived to continue a genetic line that predated the dinosaurs.

Algae blooms choked the Great Lakes, while microscopic plankton and other strains of cyanobacteria dominated large tracts of the Pacific Ocean, spanning upwards of ten million square miles from the coast of Chile to New Zealand. Although the mechanism stimulating the algae was unknown, scientists hailed the bloom as a carbon sink. They said the bloom acted as a counterweight to anthropogenic climate change, and they thought that atmospheric warming might reverse, but it didn't. They noted that the algae was exchanging CO_2 for oxygen, but the blooms suffocated the oceans, decimating fish stocks. Within a few years, the proportion of oxygen within the atmosphere began to change, creeping up toward prehistoric levels.

Scientists predicted the biosphere would be self-regulating, and expected oxygen levels to peak well below 25%, but even a small increase of less than two percent within the first decade encouraged forest fires to run rampant. The CO_2 released by the fires only fueled the algae further.

It took some time for scientists to recognize the relationship between the devastation of entire families of species and the advent of gigantism, as not every species was equally affected. At first, the enlargement of surviving species was assumed to be a naturally selected response to the rapid loss of competitive pressures from other species, but Natural Selection didn't explain the changes to domestic pets.

Although most cats and dogs had become feral, being abandoned by their owners either through desperation or an untimely death, even the litters of those that continued in the care of humans showed enlargement. Within a few years, cats were reaching four feet in length.

Dog breeds like the German Shepherd reached the size of a small pony within a decade.

Comparisons were made to studies on the recognized changes in feral animals, like the lengthening of the gut and thickening of the intestinal tract, but these had previously corresponded with dietary changes. That these new variations should arise in animals still reared on processed pet food was alarming. Little attention was paid to the issue, though, and it barely registered in the back sections of the newspapers.

The advent of gigantism was gradual. It was an anomaly, a nuisance, nothing compared to the annual cycle of the Sparkles, with their driving snow and spring floods.

Although the newspapers made fun of the scientific name for cats, *Felis catus* and *Felis silvestris catus*, joking about the similarity to Felix The Cat, Sylvester and Tweety Bird, serious research was undertaken using the common, household cat to examine the potential long-term effects of gigantism.

Researchers at Cornell University conducted a controlled study of twenty five generations of cats from five distinct pedigrees over three years, in order to understand the phenomenon more precisely. Their findings were controversial. Not only were cats becoming progressively larger, but the composition of their physiology was subtly changing. Muscle tissue became more dense, nerve endings increased in frequency, hip bones morphed in shape, giving the cats more leverage when springing for prey, but the most controversial aspect of their findings was that the animal's canine incisors were increasing in length and thickness.

Time Magazine picked up on the implications of this research and ran a front page story titled, Our Future? With a picture of cavemen using spears to battle saber tooth tigers, the imagery was inflammatory. Several prominent biologists spoke out against the article, saying it was speculative, that there was no reason to think animals were undergoing genomic regression, and yet there was no doubt gigantism wasn't merely enlarging animals. Life on Earth was being subject to rapid genetic change, but the question was, how? The ability of scientists to investigate the problem was hampered by the seasonal impact of the dust trail left by Comet Holt.

In spite of government warnings, large sections of the population fled to the equatorial regions to escape the extreme winter snow storms. The influx from Europe and the Americas inundated third-world resources. There was an expectation that the government or the military would be able to make everything right, but the scale of migration was unprecedented and quickly escalated out of control.

Tribes formed within the various migration camps, mostly along ethnic lines as they always had, but a few were based on religious affiliation. With millions of people displaced, disease soon swept unchecked through the make-shift camps. Man preyed on man in a struggle for survival that was barbaric and cruel.

Those newspapers that still survived were largely run by volunteers. They reported outbreaks of cannibalism. It seemed once that particular taboo lifted, once it was accepted by one tribe, it quickly became the norm in an area as food and medical supplies dwindled. The army and police were stretched too thin. They had to pick and choose which laws they could enforce, with their preference being to turn a blind eye where there was at least a semblance of civil order, regardless of what evil lay beneath.

Political structures collapsed, leaving local fiefdoms in their place. The presumption of innocence was lost, and bitter feuds broke out between tribes vying for dominance of the camps. In the midst of the chaos, religious groups struggled to maintain their character, pleading with their followers to stay loyal, but the abuse of authority within their own ranks undermined their credibility. It seemed opportunity was the greatest temptation of all. When the animal attacks began, preying on the sick, the elderly and the weak, mankind finally realized gigantism was more than a novelty, a new world order had formed. Man was no longer the apex predator.

Investigations were made into the possible causes for gigantism and a biological agent was identified in the fallout from the comet. Although the structure was simple, being a rudimentary combination of amino acids forming a non-bacterial pathogen, it acted like a virus. It wasn't a virus in the technical sense of the word, as its helical structure was far too small, but the word virus was all the newspapers needed to hear. Comet Holt had brought an extraterrestrial plague upon Earth.

The New York Times broke the story with one word plastered across its cover in letters eight inches high, VIRUS. The Washington Post called it THE FINAL HORSEMAN OF THE APOCALYPSE. There wasn't enough time to study the celestial biological agent, let alone to develop a strategy for containing or reversing its effects. What research could be done focused on the genetic differences between quadrupeds and quadrumana, as mankind and primates were largely unaffected by the pathogen. Investigations were made into the evolutionary genetics of the long-extinct mega-fauna and their relationship to an oxygen-rich environment, but the effort was too little, too late.

Hard decisions had to be made, and those that still held to the authority of the Old World knew their days were numbered. The survival of the human race depended not just on the priorities being set, but the speed with which decisions could be implemented. Governments became ruthless. Martial law was implemented in the camps. Punishment was swift and severe. Looting was a capital offense. That discretion was given to field commanders to determine guilt and innocence became a worse problem. The army found itself as judge, jury and executioner.

Somehow, the newspapers still printed. Even when it seemed doubtful anyone would read them, the major papers felt a sense of obligation to voice the concerns of a populace reeling in shock. In some cases, only flyers were printed, just a couple of folded pages, but someone somewhere understood the importance of the news, someone kept the presses running.

The United Nations called the institution of martial law a tactical response, but that was a clever way of avoiding the truth. Martial law was merciless. What began as disaster response morphed into preparations for the radical restructuring of Western society. Rather than seeking to save all, Western governments adopted the tactics of those in the East. They chose to save only some, but their choices were based on money, power and influence, qualities that were transient and rapidly moving out of vogue. For all the fear and alarm that was raised in those final days, few saw the end coming. There was still a sense that somehow civilization would escape the downward spiral into animalistic violence, but it didn't.

Science was one of many casualties as the civilized world collapsed. Cynics had long attacked science with irrational, emotionally-charged arguments that sought to preserve the status quo. They had attacked the theory of evolution. They had attacked the research on climate change. They spread fear and misinformation about vaccines. There had even been doubts cast upon the great accomplishments of the era, like the moon landing. It was as though the existence of the great pyramids was being called into question. And so, when the fall of man came, the Luddites rejoiced. For them, man's demise was a vindication of their ideals, a moment full of spite and bitter rejoicing.

The economies of scale that had for so many years given civilized man access to technologies he could never build for himself finally failed. The innovations that gave hundreds of millions of people access to foods they didn't have to harvest, access to clothes they didn't have to weave, access to houses they didn't have to build, these all fell into chaos. The supply chain, once broken, could not be restarted. Each cog in the wheel, each link in the chain had been built one upon another over the course of centuries.

Ever since the industrial revolution, civilized man had built upon the successes of previous generations. Relative to the billions alive on Earth, only a handful of people actually understood and could build devices like a transistor or an integrated circuit from scratch. Without the supply chain, mankind was as helpless as a newborn, and so when the Fall came and society collapsed into violence and chaos, mankind was left helpless and alone.

Eastern societies fared better than the West. Their dependence on technology was much lower, so it was easier for them to make the transition back to feudal times, but they were easy prey to the monsters of Asia. Tigers were the first to exact their revenge on mankind. Litter sizes increased. Although it took a century for tigers to reach the size of a horse, by that time they numbered in the tens of thousands. With speed and stealth that belied their weight, they preyed ruthlessly on mankind.

The Asian black bear, brown bear and sun bear eventually grew to the size of a rhino, while the Komodo dragon reached up to thirty feet in length. Mankind was easy prey. Omnivores became carnivores spoiled for choice.

Although polar bears resided predominately above the Arctic Circle, a variant sub-species arose to fill the increasingly empty ecological niches in the relatively warmer, southern climates. With a thinner coat, they ventured south across both Asia and the Americas, reaching as far as Beijing in the East and the Dakotas in the West. Their spread into North America was held in check only by competition with bears such as the grizzly, brown and black bear.

Herbivores like elk were dangerous, attacking anyone that ventured into their territory during mating season. Their aggression was surprising to all but hunters, who had long known a stag in the rut was as dangerous as a mountain lion, but now a fully-grown male could reach nine hundred pounds. Even a fleeting attack was often fatal.

At first, animal attacks and fatalities were considered a rarity, but soon the remaining scientists realized this was due to a breakdown in reporting structures. In reality, for every account that made it to the press there were hundreds of attacks that went unreported. With such abundant food sources, the resurgence of the mega-fauna took a little over a hundred and eighty years.

There were few newspapers in those final days of the first decade, but those that did survive spoke of being abandoned. The last of the papers were handwritten accounts, printed and circulated to as many who would heed their message. They were feeble attempts to dispel the myths and misconceptions that had proven so lethal to so many. There were the lies about Europe surviving intact, the lies about safety in the tropical zones. Rumors spread on the East Coast about the West being a haven for all, and vice versa, but these lies were devastating. Lies were the final plague upon mankind, displacing and killing hundreds of millions who believed in a false hope, that help was around the corner, that salvation was coming. Help never came. A sense of bitterness arose among survivors.

Conspiracy theories abounded, with blame being apportioned everywhere, but no one had any answers. Survivalists fared better than most in the early days. Their paranoia had them hoard supplies that could feed hundreds for years on end, but even they found themselves overwhelmed by the ferocity of man reduced to the state of a wild animal. Their attempts to defend themselves and their caches only drew more attention to their supplies and they were inundated by hordes of devious, vicious men and women struggling to survive.

The buildings of man still stood, and would probably stand in one decrepit form or another for millennia to come, but the societies that founded them faded like the early morning mist drifting across a lake.

Once the newspapers came to an end, the New World began, a world in which survival was the only virtue. For those in the New World, the reign of Homo sapiens, the wisest of men, became but a legend, a fable lost in the mists of time. It seemed fantastic that once people had flown above the ground in silver birds that roared through the sky.

Concepts that had been taken for granted were like the fairy tales of old. The ability to talk to someone hundreds of miles away through a small metal box, or to capture the view one saw in front of them, freezing it on a glass screen or printing it on paper seemed fanciful. Pictures and images of the Old World survived, but they held no more meaning than hieroglyphics. They were a novelty, an amusement, something to argue about or trade for equipment, but never something to understand. Slowly, the Old World was forgotten, except by those that kept the newspapers.

Monsters roamed the cities. These weren't the monsters of myth and lore, but they were every bit as deadly. Packs of wild dogs, wolves, mountain lions, rats as large as domestic cats, and they all bred profusely.

Guns, which had so long been the means for mankind to project power, failed to stop the monsters. Even high-powered rifles did little more than aggravate a Grizzly standing twenty feet tall on its hind legs. Military squads could have taken out most of these animals, but their ranks were decimated by famine and disease.

As the New World took shape, new priorities arose. Reading was lost. At first, there was no time to read. Then there was nothing of any substance to read, just fragments of information, often completely irrelevant to the harsh reality of life. Most people understood basic numeracy, just enough to barter in the markets. Some grasped simple words, but only if they needed to keep a ledger. Few understood enough to read properly.

Suspicions arose. Survivors sought to blame someone for the calamities. Science was an easy target. Science had failed. Science had underestimated the implications of Comet Holt. Science couldn't save mankind from the drifts and the floods. Science had missed the rise of monsters. Science had made mankind soft, vulnerable, weak. Some said scientists had created the monsters, like Frankenstein in his lab.

Knowledge was seen as something akin to arrogance. Superstitions prevailed because they were easier to justify than reason. Readers were persecuted like the witches of old, with a sense of vengeance being laid upon them for the sins of the past. Those that wanted to hold on to the Old World with its knowledge of atoms and stars, footballs and cars, were seen as dreamers at best, or as subversive at worst.

There was no equilibrium between the tribes of men. In some countries, mankind managed to maintain a level of sophistication like that of the feudal Dark Ages, in others, they were thrown back into the Stone Age, existing as subsistence farmers, hunters and gatherers.

In the New World, monsters reigned.

BOOK ONE

READERS

Chapter 01: Readers

Bruce Dobson was a reader. He hadn't always read. It wasn't until after the battle of Bracken Ridge that he first sought out a reader in much the same way as men once sought out a prophet or a soothsayer, only his interest wasn't in divining the future. Bruce wanted to read about the past.

For Bruce, the past was an enigma, a dark secret, a puzzle he had to unravel. Somehow, intrinsically, he understood that life moved in cycles, repeating time and again with only minor variations. Summer always followed spring, the moon waxed and waned, crops grew, harvests came, seed was gathered, and life would begin anew in the coming year. There was much to learn from the cycles of the past.

His father thought he was mad. Why bother with the past? The past was gone, never to return. What could the past offer? It was the future that was important. Whereas the past was static, the future was whatever he wanted to make of it, so why bother with the past? His father had a point, Bruce understood that, but, he argued, the past determined the future, in the same way as the autumn rains preceded the heaviest snows. Try as they may to deny it, their lives were shaped by the past.

Bruce Dobson died on Bracken Ridge, at least that's the way he felt. His innocence, his excitement for life, his zeal and enthusiasm were casualties in the war with the northern tribes. Seeing his brother fall before him was too much for young Bruce.

Jonathan was the older of the Dobson boys. Jonathan told his mother he'd look after Bruce. The two boys, barely eighteen and twenty, thought they were indestructible, as countless other young men had before them, misguided and sent to their untimely deaths across thousands of years of senseless tribal warfare. The cause had changed, the faces were fresh, but the heartache and tragedy was just the same as it had always been.

Pockets of snow lay on the frosty ground, slowly melting as the days grew longer. Birds returned from the south, anticipating the break that had come in the weather. The bright sun was refreshing.

The arrow that felled Jonathan came in the first wave. It was surprisingly quiet, like the wind whistling through the trees. Neither of them saw it coming. The thin shaft with its twist of feathers seemed to materialize from nowhere.

The arrow struck Jonathan's collarbone and glanced up through the side of his neck, tearing open his jugular vein. Jonathan sank to his knees, his hands grasping at his throat. Bruce was still trying to process what had happened as Jonathan fell to one side, slipping into the furrows that scarred the muddy ground. Blood soaked into the worn, tired tracks that wound their way up the steep ridge.

Bruce had never seen so much blood. The splash of crimson was jarring to his mind, such a violent contrast to the dark woods still devoid of leaves. Brilliant streaks of red sprayed out across the white snow. He tried to stem the flow. He tried so hard as Jonathan lay there speechless in the bloody mix of ice, snow and mud. His brother's lips were moving but no words came out, just a sickening gurgle as he gasped for air.

It was Jonathan's eyes that were the hardest to accept. In that moment, as Bruce knelt in the muddy track, pressing his fingers hard against the wound, trying in vain to stop the bleeding, it was the look in his brother's eyes that said so much more than any words could articulate. Jonathan couldn't believe what was happening to him, he couldn't believe his life was ending so quickly, so suddenly, so painfully. Just moments before, they'd both laughed, joking around with the warmth of the sun on their faces, a delightful contrast to the brisk cool in the air. They were marching to glory, or at least that's what they'd been told, that's what they believed.

Blossoms grew on the trees along Bracken Ridge, buds opening out into the first flowers of spring. It should have been the start of a new year, a better year. Hundreds of young men had marched forward with excitement, now a ragged line of boys screamed in agony. In the months to come, Bruce learned that the first wave had fallen in much the way the generals had expected, exposing the enemy's position and allowing for a flanking maneuverer. Their sacrifice was called noble, but that was a lie, one that depressed Bruce and left him crying out for answers.

Jonathan looked pitiful as he lay there. No words were spoken, none were needed. Bruce understood. He could see it in his brother's eyes, a plea for mercy, a desire to unwind the moment and escape this cruel blow. Jonathan's eyes shouted out in agony as he gripped his younger brother's hand. Those tender brown eyes couldn't understand what was happening to them, they couldn't accept such a violent and brutal death, and yet death marched upon them regardless.

Volley upon volley of arrows rained down on the muddy track in which the two boys lay. Bruce was struck on his arm and thigh, but he barely felt any pain as he watched his brother die.

Within a few minutes, Jonathan fell limp. His eyes lost focus, seemingly looking through his transparent younger brother, looking up at the brilliant blue sky above. Bruce cried. Whereas once he'd felt like a man, ready to take on the world, now he realized he was still just a child. He wanted the war to go away, to leave him and his family alone, to return them to their innocence, but time ignored his pleas.

Bruce had no idea how long he sat there in shock, cradling his brother's head. The battle raged around him as he sat slumped in the mud, trying to straighten his brother's hair, to clean the mud and blood from Jonathan's face, but his hands were dirty, everything he did made things worse.

Bruce sobbed with anguish. Jonathan grew cold.

Soldiers fought with swords and spears. Men fell around him. The mud and blood obscured their uniforms. Enemies in life, they were indistinguishable in death.

Bruce barely noticed the clash of swords. His mind was as numb as his legs soaked in snow, slush, mud and blood.

A dark shadow cast over the sun and he looked up. One of the northern soldiers towered over him, his legs set on either side of the muddy rut. He held out a sword, bringing the blade to Bruce's throat.

Bruce looked into his eyes, wondering what he was waiting for, wanting him to end his torment, but the soldier lowered his sword. In the midst of hundreds of other fallen soldiers, this young man seemed to sense the personal tragedy Bruce had endured and had no heart to kill him. The soldier ran on, swinging his sword and fighting to kill someone else.

Bruce cried.

The hours of that day seemed longer than any other Bruce had ever known. As the sun set, someone grabbed Bruce, dragging him from the field of battle, dragging him away from his brother despite his screams. With the fall of darkness, monsters rose, claiming the carcasses of those that had died in battle.

Bruce limped away from Bracken Ridge, unable to watch. Technically, he could have been charged with desertion, but those that would have executed him lay dead alongside his brother. It was in that moment, as he cradled his wounded arm, as he limped away from the campfires of his troop, that Bruce decided to become a reader.

Life was shallow, hollow, just a fleeting fragment of what he'd imagined in the excitement of growing up on a farm. Life was precious, wasted on those brute beasts that thought sacrifice was the highest virtue. For Bruce Dobson, those men were the monsters, not the wild animals with their razor sharp teeth and bloodied claws. Those men, that sacrificed the lives of others like pawns on a chessboard, those were the real monsters.

Reading was a mystical art, the refuge of charlatans. There were many that pretended to read, that knew just enough to fool others, but Bruce wasn't interested in them. Long ago he had realized they were con-men. Bruce wanted to find someone who understood, someone who could teach him reason.

Readers, those who read for the love of knowledge, stayed hidden, and with good reason. Tribes had gone to war over readers. There were those that wanted to abuse their knowledge, to use it for their own ends, to manipulate others. Most of those in authority could read, but what they read was strictly defined. Knowledge was considered dangerous. Like a fire, they'd say, if reading isn't kept under control, it will burn down the house.

A reader, a true reader, wanted only to set people free, or at least, that was the assumption Bruce carried with him. He knew freedom had always been a dangerous concept, and now more so than ever. Freedom meant having the confidence and conviction to know right from wrong for one's self, and no tribe could abide such insolence. Tribes needed loyalty, submission, unity and dedication, not doubts and questions. Tribes needed heroes, not dreamers.

Over time, suspicions arose around readers. Superstition said they were alchemists, wizards, witches. They were different, they were feared. They sacrificed children to their gods, or so the villagers of the plain said. They drank the blood of those they seduced. They were the monsters that attacked in the dark of night. For Bruce, that was absurd, but such madness prevailed in the valley.

Bruce found his reader by accident. She was older than him by at least ten summers. A couple of years had passed since Bracken Ridge, but the emptiness he felt inside longed to be filled. He had been trading at the southern markets in the village of Amersham when he first saw Jane.

Amersham sat on a low hill surrounded by open meadows and cultivated fields. Wooden ramparts enclosed the original village, giving it the appearance of a garrison, but over time the population had outgrown the walls and the village had sprawled. Log cabins and thatched huts lined the roads and alleyways, with stone buildings being reserved for the wealthy or industrious.

Bruce rode into the village on the back of his pack horse. The monstrous animal lumbered down the dusty road, the span across its hindquarters loaded up with a dozen barrels of Indian corn and several crates full of chickpeas and dried insects. Bruce rocked with the steady motion of the horse. Although its steps were slow its gait was long, giving it a fair pace, faster than a man could walk.

As he entered the outskirts of the village, with its roads paved with fragments of stone, Bruce could see the circuit magistrate and his men collecting taxes at the roadside tollgate. If he'd known they were there this month he would have headed east to one of the other villages to avoid their thieving hands, but it was too late. To pull out would have invited unwanted attention.

The magistrates could read, but for them reading was a ceremonial function, with little or no meaning involved. Whatever they read was only ever used to oppress others. With pomp, they would profess their disdain for all but the laws of the land. For them, reading was tightly controlled, and only ever as it suited their dominance over the villagers. Bruce wasn't fooled by their hypocrisy.

The guards were armed with rifles, but they had bayonets attached, because even if the rifles worked they probably didn't have any ammunition. Guns were useless against monsters. Bullets tended only to inflict pain and were rarely fatal to the huge beasts. And if there was one thing worse than a monster on a rampage, it was one that was fueled by the anger of being stung with bullets. Nah, he thought, this is just for show. They're trying to look good for the villagers.

Bruce pulled up behind a number of other travelers mounted on their steeds, each waiting to pay for entrance to the markets. One of the judges was preaching, taking advantage of the captive audience. He stood on a raised wooden dais.

"We need to stay vigilant, my brothers," cried the aging man. "There are those that would try to destroy our way of life, that would see us turn back to the old ways, those that put their trust in the knowledge of science. But what has such knowledge ever done for us?"

It was a call/response sermon, and the villagers knew the drill. Those that were around the gate responded mindlessly with rumblings of assent as the judge continued. Bruce didn't buy it. This wasn't about science, it was about control. These guys would sacrifice their own mothers to ensure submission to their rule, and he knew it.

"We trusted science. We trusted its promises, but where did that take us? What good did that do us?"

Again, the crowd provided the obligatory answer in the form of a barely recognizable murmur, "Nothing."

Most of them weren't interested, they were just going through the motions. It had always been that way from what Bruce understood, even in the old days when the knowledge of science prevailed. Back then, most people gave lip service to science but they didn't understand it, they didn't appreciate it. Science was just a means to an end, allowing man to live life to the fullest with his moving pictures and flying machines. And now, in the new world, authoritarian rule had become the means to the end of survival. Without banding together, man would have been driven to extinction. And yet in both cases, the common man just wanted to get on with his life and took the course of least resistance. If agreeing with the magistrates allowed him to trade and feed his family, he'd agree.

"We have to work together, not against each other. Our greatest value is in our loyalty to each other. Never forget that, never forget that alone we are nothing. Together we can defeat even monsters."

It was the same dull, boring lecture, replete with pious platitudes. Bruce hated it. Even before he learned to read he could see through these rants, realizing they were nothing more than propaganda. Bruce could see through the fallacies. Two plus two equals four, he thought. Everybody knows that, no one needed to be reminded of it, but the supposed dangers of knowledge, the insidious evil of free thinking, the canker of written words, this apparently required constant repetition.

Their insistence on repetition struck him as inherently wrong. Ever since Bracken Ridge, his distrust of authority had grown and now he despised the judiciary.

A tax collector approached him as his horse shuffled forward. "Thirty credits," cried the collector, his outstretched arm barely reaching Bruce's foot as he sat high on his massive horse.

"What?" cried Bruce, looking down at the collector. The man was resplendent in his fine clothes. Dressed in scarlet, with polished brass buttons running down the side of his uniform, he looked out of place in the small town, with its drab clothing and young population.

Thirty credits was highway robbery. Bruce would be doing well to sell all his produce for forty credits at most. He pursed his lips, holding himself back from swearing, knowing it would do no good to draw undue attention to himself. He'd come to town seeking a new plow but would have to settle for something second-hand after paying for access to the markets. Thirty credits out of pocket would leave him with little in the way of money until he sold his corn and chickpeas. He paused, mentally assessing whether he could inflate his prices to recoup the loss, wondering if that would be counterproductive and kill off sales. His hand reached into his purse, fingering the coins reluctantly. He went to say something but stopped as a commotion broke out in front of him.

"This is extortion," cried the woman sitting on the horse ahead of him. She was talking to another tax collector, arguing over the fee. "This is not a tax. This is robbery. How am I supposed to conduct business and earn enough to pay for your bloody taxes if you keep stealing from me? Taking my very livelihood?"

"Come now," said the tax collector below Bruce, seeing he was distracted. "Pay up and move along."

The stout man reached up and slapped at his boot, but Bruce was fascinated by the high-spirited woman in front of him. She had the courage to say what he was thinking. She swung her legs around and slid down off her horse, sliding over the edge of the beast and falling the last eight feet to the ground, surprising the tax collector. That was a dangerous way to dismount, thought Bruce, but he liked her style. A fall like that had to hurt, she could have twisted or even broken her ankle, but what an entrance. And it clearly had the desired effect on the tax collector standing before her. She was in his face, intimidating him, yelling at him.

"You're a thief and a scoundrel. This is not a fair price! I will not pay."

The judge preaching on the dais, resplendent in his black robe, fell unusually quiet. The chief justice came over, having heard the commotion. He tried to calm the woman but she would have none of it and refused to lower her voice.

"This is an outrage. You have no right to triple the tax. Who do you think you are? What gives you the right to bully us like this?"

The tax collector standing below Bruce suddenly didn't seem so intimidating anymore. Even the armed guards on either side of the gate seemed befuddled by this woman. No one had challenged their authority before. A moment's hesitation on their part had undermined their credibility and they seemed to realize that the longer this went on the less sway they held over everyone else. The chief justice must have sensed the unrest as well as he was trying to appease the woman and get her to move along. Bruce watched as she settled with five credits, which was barely half the regular tax. She had some moxie. She yelled abuse at the collectors as she stormed off, pulling her horse along behind her.

The tax collector tapped Bruce's boot again, saying, "Come on. Pay up."

"Sure," Bruce replied, and he tossed a couple of coins through the air, deliberately sending them wide of the collector so they landed in the dust. He wasn't even sure how much he'd tossed, it certainly was no more than ten credits and may have been less than five, but that didn't matter, Bruce was riding the wave. "And that's all you'll be getting from me this fine day."

Behind him, he could hear other traders calling out similar sentiments. The magistrates had their hands full. With a chuckle, Bruce prodded his horse, sending it forward, smiling at the guards as he passed through the gate.

He lost sight of the feisty woman and spent the rest of the day wondering about her. He'd only seen her from behind, but he was sure he'd recognize her voice if he heard her again.

By mid-afternoon, Bruce was down to two barrels of corn and one crate of chickpeas, having made forty nine credits. The dried insects had been the first thing to sell, and he regretted not bringing more, having underestimated the interest in them. He'd told a couple of the women at the markets about the incident at the gate and they said it was probably Jane, the blacksmith's daughter. They rolled their eyes, saying she was trouble.

Bruce had his head down when Jane walked up to his stall, but her presence demanded his attention. As he looked up, he recognized her from the way her hair was pulled back in a ponytail and the soft flower pattern on her dress. He wanted to say something about the morning, but she got straight down to business.

"I'll give you six credits for the lot," she said, pointing at the two barrels and the remaining crate.

"Six credits," he cried, somewhat offended that she hadn't asked for a price first and had just assumed she could impose one of her own. "I can't sell you all this for six credits. I'd be running at a loss."

"Make it five," she said sternly, folding her arms tightly across her chest.

"Now, wait a minute," he said, pointing at her, both his voice and his ire being raised. "You can't just come at me demanding an absurd price, and then drive an even lower one. What do you think this is? The tollgate? I'm not some tax collector you can push around."

"Four," she said without a hint of emotion on her face. With narrow eyes and pursed lips, she looked as though she were ready to take him on in a fight.

"Hang on," he said, holding his hand out, appealing for her to let him speak. "You can't keep going down. That's not the way bartering works."

"Three credits. That's my final offer," Jane said, her hands set firmly on her hips.

"Oh, you are infuriating," Bruce said, running his hands up through his hair. "How on Earth do you think you can get away with offering me three credits?"

Jane went to say something, but Bruce cut her off. "No wait. I don't want to know."

"You were behind me at the gate," Jane said, regardless. "So I figure you owe me at least twenty credits."

"You are outrageous."

"Three credits," Jane said, repeating her offer.

Bruce figured she probably came late to the stalls knowing sellers would want to offload their stock so they could leave early the following morning. Most of the traders he'd spoken to wanted to get a full day's travel in before the weather turned bad. He certainly did. Damn, she's good, he thought, a tinge of resentment eating away at his mind.

"Four," he said, making a counteroffer.

Jane held her hand out and dropped three coins in his hand, saying, "Deliver the barrels to the blacksmith forge before dusk."

The audacity! Bruce started to say something, but she walked off, saying, "It was a pleasure doing business with you."

Bruce didn't like Jane. She wasn't pretty, her face had been badly scarred by pox as a child and her hair was thin and straggly. To him, she looked sickly and unhealthy. Her hard demeanor only reinforced that impression. A thousand comebacks started flooding through his mind as he watched her walk away. He'd been weak, and she'd sensed that and pounced like a mountain lion. He should have ignored her and driven the price toward ten credits. At the very least he could have wrestled her back to six! Bruce turned, kicking one of the barrels in disgust, but a deal was a deal. He was a man of his word, or so he told himself, the truth was, he had to get rid of these barrels and with the sun sitting low on the horizon buyers were thinning out and heading to their homes. He didn't want to be stuck with any leftover produce, so three credits was better than nothing.

Bruce borrowed a hand-cart from one of the other traders, loaded up the produce and made his way across town to the blacksmith. As he approached, he could see Jane upstairs, but she didn't see him, she was facing to one side, looking out across the open fields at the dark forest beyond the village. She had the wooden shutters open and was airing out some blankets, draping them over the side of the windows.

Below the rickety one-room hut lay the forge. With four walls of stone held together with thick layers of mortar, the forge was the sturdiest building in the village. A red glow emanated from within as smoke rose from the chimney, drifting to one side in the cool breeze. Bruce could hear the sound of metal being pounded.

The old blacksmith saw him approaching and came out to meet him, leaving his apprentice at work inside the smoky building. Bruce pulled the cart up beside the cellar entrance on the western wall of the forge, immediately below Jane. He was sure she'd seen him, although she didn't acknowledge him, disappearing inside the second-story room.

"Ah," said the old man, reaching out and shaking Bruce's hand. "Jane said you'd be around before sunset."

Bruce responded to the old man's warm greeting. Jane's father was frail, but his handshake was firm. He smiled, revealing several missing teeth.

"She said you were there at the tollgate and saw the fiasco with the tax collectors."

"Yeah," Bruce replied sheepishly. He hadn't come for a conversation and so was a little taken aback by the man's jovial, chatty nature.

"She's a fiery one, my Jane, full of vinegar, isn't she?" said the father, slapping Bruce on the arm. Clearly, that ran in the family, thought Bruce. Jane's father laughed, adding, "Oh, I'd love to have seen the look on that bastard's face when she dropped down beside him. I bet he went as white as a sheet."

"Yes, he certainly did," Bruce replied smiling, warming to the old man.

"These pricks think they can push us around," the old man said. "Sometimes they need a reminder that life is a two-way street."

The old man smiled, reaching into his pocket and pulling out a few coins. Dropping them into Bruce's hand, he added, "There's the balance that was due you."

The look on Bruce's face must have revealed that something was wrong as the aging man quickly added, "It was six credits, right? Three to secure the purchase. The balance on delivery."

Out of the corner of his eye, Bruce could see Jane leaning out of the window above them, a smile on her face as she leaned forward on her elbows. He acknowledged her with a slight wave, returning the smile.

"Ah, yeah. That's right. I guess."

"Well, good," said the man, throwing open the cellar doors and picking up the first barrel. He disappeared down the wooden stairs. Bruce glanced up again, but Jane was gone. He felt silly standing there with three credits in his hand. He was so sure he had Jane figured out, but she'd surprised him. Bruce turned and walked away, pocketing the coins, smiling at how she'd played him twice, like a cat with a mouse. She may not have been pretty, but she was intelligent and mischievous, and that intrigued him.

That night the air was unusually cold. Autumn was giving way to winter. Soon snow would fall and within days the trails would be impassible. Bruce planned to return to his farm the following day so as to finish his fortifications against the coming ice storms. For several days there had been reports of wild dogs, but no one took them seriously as the village was surrounded by crop fields, with large gates barring the major approaches. Wild dogs had never come up to the village before. The huge beasts tended to stick to the wooded areas, so there was no cause for concern.

Bruce heard a woman scream over the jostling and singing in the bar. He and several of the locals rushed out into the main street to see a woman lying on her back at the end of the dusty road. A wild dog stood over her, dwarfing her with its immense size. Somehow, he knew it was Jane, even at that distance. He wasn't sure how. Perhaps it was her silhouette, or maybe her clothes as she was still wearing the same dress he'd seen her in that afternoon, or it could have been the pitch in her voice as she cried out for help, but in the low light, he knew it was her and a chill ran through him.

The monster was savage. Dark brooding eyes stared down at Jane with malice. The creature's fur was matted and tangled, as black as the night beyond. With paws the size of a man's outstretched hand, the beast pinned Jane to the ground with its weight.

The events of the day flashed through Bruce's mind, her brashness in the gate, the way she teased him in the market, but all that was about to come to a tragic end as she was torn to pieces by a wild animal.

The beast bared its teeth, growling at Bruce as more locals ran into the street behind him.

The dog snarled, saliva dripping from its jaws.

The men of the village grabbed poles and sticks, swords and axes, anything that was handy, and charged at the brute, shouting and screaming to drive it away, but the monster held its ground.

Jane rolled to one side, scrambling to get away as the men of the village surrounded the animal and began beating it with rods.

The creature was rabid, mad with disease. Each stab, each cut and wound only infuriated it further. With the strength of a horse, the wild dog wheeled, knocking wooden carts around, breaking fences and hitching posts as it reeled from the pikes and spears of the villagers.

The massive dog lunged at one of the younger men, grabbing his lance with its teeth and whipping its head, sending the man flying some forty feet through the air.

The older men brought flaming torches, knowing fire was all the monster feared. They surrounded it, striking only at its hind quarters, forcing the dark beast to circle.

Jane crawled away as the men wore the animal down, using their numbers to confuse it, never having more than one man strike in succession as they kept their wary distance.

The wild dog wheeled to face each attacker, growling and snarling, only to be struck from behind again and again.

Bruce caught sight of Jane fleeing down a dark alley. Her dress was torn. Blood dripped from a cut on her arm. At the time, he was astonished she'd survived at all, let alone with barely a scratch on her forearm. A single bite from the dog would have crushed her bones like matchsticks.

The animal reeled from side to side, never sure which villager to attack as lances and swords slashed at its hind legs, cutting at its underbelly, stabbing behind its ribs. The monster snarled and lunged, snapping at the air, risking the fire for a chance to kill a man, but the villagers were well trained, they knew they had to keep moving, keep weaving as they surrounded the giant dog, constantly changing their position as the beast fought against them. In that way, they confused the animal with their numbers, making it seem as though there were hundreds of them.

Somehow, no one died, and when the monster finally succumbed to its wounds, the men of the village took it as a sign of good fortune to come.

They found Jane on the outskirts of the small town, down by the river, bathing her arm in the water, madly scrubbing at her wound. She'd been bitten, although bite was too strong a word as a bite would have severed her arm completely, or worse, taken a portion of her torso. The deep gash on her arm was little more than a graze by the giant brute.

Bruce waded down into the river to attend to her wound. He had no reason to, it just seemed like the right thing to do. The water was bitterly cold. Bruce was surprised to see Jane wasn't trying to stem the blood. She was rubbing at the wound.

"Give me your knife," Jane demanded.

Bruce was stunned. He handed over his knife, unsure what she would do.

Jane cut into her wound, grimacing as she enlarged the tear in her flesh, stripping back the muscle on her arm. She was crying. Her hands were shaking.

The river turned red with her blood.

"What are you doing? Stop!"

"Get away," she cried, turning the knife on him. Moonlight caught on the blade. Her eyes were wild.

Bruce held his hands out, saying, "Please, don't do this."

"Stay back," Jane cried, shivering in the cold night air. Her dress floated on the waist deep water. Whereas once the fabric had been white now it was scarlet.

The villagers knew.

"It is better," said one of the men standing on the muddy river bank.

"Let her die now," another cried.

"No!" Bruce replied, turning to face them.

Jane returned to cutting her arm.

Bruce stepped toward her, gesturing toward the knife, almost losing his footing on the loose stones lining the riverbed.

The current was swift.

"Don't do this," he said.

Jane backed away from him into deeper water, saying, "You don't understand. I'm dead already."

Her hand shook so much she dropped the knife. She staggered in the water, weakened by the blood loss. Bruce caught her, pulling her out of the river. She felt so light, so frail, as though she were a doll rather than a person. In the moonlight, her pale skin looked lifeless.

He bound her ragged forearm with his shirt as she moaned, slipping in and out of consciousness. Bruce clambered up the muddy bank and carried her back into the village.

Why did he care? Why did he care so much about this strange woman? It was a question he asked himself many times over the years to come, always thankful that he had cared on that cold, dark evening. She was too old for him, too worn, or at least she seemed to be to his young mind. He figured it was the cruelty of the villagers that made him care. No one else had gone to her aid, so he had to, he had to show her the kindness due to one in distress, be they a man or a woman, rich or poor, young or old, beautiful or not. The more she suffered, the more intensely he wanted her to survive. Perhaps it was Jonathan, he thought, not sure of his own motives. He hadn't been able to save his brother, perhaps saving someone else would repay that loss.

Bruce carried Jane to the blacksmith's forge. The old man was beside himself when he saw his daughter hanging limp in Bruce's arms. He must have thought she was dead.

Jane slept for most of the next day. When she awoke, Bruce was sitting by her side, whittling away at a stick, hollowing it out and shaping it into a flute. It was something his mother had done whenever he'd been struck with fever. It had been her way of biding time.

"How are you feeling?" he asked, his knife shaving thin strips off the wood.

Jane touched her arm, feeling the bandages covering the gaping wound where once muscle had shaped her forearm.

"You took quite a chunk out," he continued. "But you didn't make it to the bone. Given time, you'll get some use back, but you'll never throw hay-bales."

"I never could," she replied, her voice coarse, her throat dry. Bruce handed her a water bladder.

"Pretty dumb thing you did there," he said, watching as she sipped some water.

"Pretty smart," she replied curtly, not in any mood for small talk.

"And how is that?" he asked, blowing the dust out of his short flute.

"It's called rabies," she said, turning to one side on the bed of straw. "The infection, the madness of the wild dogs. The villagers think rabies is spread by blood, but it's not, it's spread by saliva. If I hadn't done that, I would have died. Not then, perhaps not for weeks or even months to come, but I too would have gone mad. I may still."

Bruce was fascinated. How could she talk about herself with such detachment? How did she have such confidence in what she knew? How could she be so sure?

"Once, they had a cure, long ago."

That got him to be quiet. How did she know what they had in the Old World?

"If I am to die, it will be on my own terms," she said, her fingers lingering, touching gingerly at the bandages wrapping her wound. He wondered how she could be so cold toward her own flesh.

"Most women would say, thank you," Bruce said.

"Most women would," she agreed. "Where is my father?"

"He's downstairs, working on the forge."

"Could you send him up on your way out?" Jane said coldly.

Bruce couldn't understand Jane, perhaps that's what drew him to her. There was something dark, something mysterious, something rebellious within her. He sighed, getting to his feet. Jane turned to face the wall.

Bruce didn't know it at the time, but several years later she told him she was crying. She felt so protective of her identity that she had to put up walls to keep others out. But here, with Bruce, she felt some genuine kindness, something she'd never known outside of her family, and she didn't know quite how to react. She turned to the wall to hide her tears.

Bruce placed the flute on the chair and left without a word.

The next day he returned. He wasn't sure why, perhaps it was the challenge of breaking through her cold exterior that forced him on, but he felt intrigued by Jane. He should have left town, but he was curious. Could she read? Is that where she got her confidence? It was dumb, silly, he thought, and he felt if he said something he'd come out looking like a fool. He should have left for his farm. The driving snow could arrive at any day on the brooding gray clouds, and yet it could equally be a couple of weeks away, he convinced himself.

Bruce was smitten. Jane wasn't pretty. She was feisty. Her father thanked him profusely. He told him he was always welcome at the forge, but Bruce wanted to hear that from her. She wasn't the only one that could be stubborn, and stubbornness had many forms. With a bunch of dried wild flowers in hand, he knocked on her door.

"Why?" came the curt reply from the other side of the door.

Bruce smiled. How did she know it was him? Thinking about it, he realized, who else would knock? Perhaps she saw him walking up to the forge. If nothing else, she's consistent, he thought.

"Why not?" he called out, being sure to speak with an air of confidence. The more this played out, the more intensely curious he became about Jane. He was beginning to understand something his mother had told him, something all mothers tell their sons, that beauty is more than skin deep, that beauty is in the eye of the beholder.

"That's not a reason," came the reply, but the words weren't terse. If anything, they had a soft ring to them.

He ignored her, looking at the flowers in his hand and asked, "Are you dressed?"

"Does it matter?" Jane replied, although she sounded closer to the door than before. Whereas when he'd first knocked she sounded distant, as though she were lying down, now she sounded as though she were standing next to the rough-hewn wooden door.

"Well," Bruce replied, thinking about it further. "A gentleman would never walk in on a lady undressed."

"Then I'm naked."

"And I guess I'm no gentleman," Bruce said, lifting the wooden lever slowly and opening the door.

Jane was fully clothed, standing just a few feet from the door, holding her bandaged arm in front of her. She was wearing a dress that once must have been pretty, but the pattern had faded and the frayed edges spoke of hard times.

"You're rather persistent," she said.

"And you're rather dressed," he replied with a grin.

"Disappointed?"

"A little," he said, winking at her as he handed her the wild flowers. Being autumn, all he could find were dried flowers in the market, colored husks of a former summer glory, but he'd scented them with a few drops of lavender oil, hoping they were a substitute for real flowers. She sniffed them. The look in her eyes was something he treasured. He no longer saw her scarred skin, her pale features or her straggly hair, he saw her dark eyes, so warm and intelligent.

"Thank you," she said, her face lighting up with a smile.

"I knew there was a thank you in there somewhere," he replied.

She blushed, which surprised him. He was so accustomed to how she hid her emotions that such an open display was refreshing.

"How are you feeling?"

"Much better, thank you."

"There, you see," he added. "Thank you isn't so hard to say now, is it?"

She reached out with her good arm, punching him lightly on the shoulder. "No, it's not."

Bruce sat down on a chair by the table as Jane placed the flowers in an empty wooden jug. He noted she took some care in arranging the flowers, playing with them, teasing them into just the right shape, pretending they were alive and vibrant. He figured it was her way of signaling her approval. He liked her smile. She may not have been pretty, but when she smiled she lit up the room, at least that's the way he felt about her.

"What are you looking at?" she asked, realizing he was staring at her.

"It's nothing."

"Oh, no you don't. I know the wheels are turning inside that little head of yours. What are you thinking?"

Bruce laughed. "Seriously, it's nothing."

"It's something now," Jane protested, her good hand resting on her hip.

"It's silly," he said. "Your smile. I really like your smile."

She laughed.

"And your laugh."

"OK, Bruce Alexander Dobson. Why did you come here? Why did you bring me flowers?"

Bruce raised his eyebrows. She'd done some homework on him. He wondered what else she knew about him, not that there was anything to hide. In some ways, it was quite flattering to hear her say his whole, formal name aloud. Bruce swallowed the lump in his throat and figured now was the time to be blunt, just like her.

"I came here because I'd like you to teach me to read."

She paused, only for a split second but it was long enough for Bruce to see her mind running, weighing his request, wanting to understand his motives. She had to be thinking about denying being a reader, but as the moment lingered, it became harder and harder to deny. To lie, you had to be quick, and he knew that better than most. She'd been caught off guard, she wasn't quick enough.

She stuttered in defense. "I—I."

As one second stretched into two, he could see the anguish on her face, the sense of being trapped. It was too late to deny it. For better or for worse, she'd have to come clean with him and he knew it before the words left her lips.

"How did you know?" she blurted out.

"I knew," he replied, "because you're so confident in what you know."

"Who have you told?"

"No one," Bruce replied, raising his hands in his defense. "I haven't told anyone, and I won't tell anyone."

"How did you," she stopped mid-sentence, and he understood this was scary for her.

She looked at him with suspicion, as though she were trying to figure out whether he had an agenda, whether he was fronting for someone else.

"I guessed. You... You were so assertive at the tollgate. You knew about rabies. You knew what to do. I figured the only way you could be so confident was from reading."

Jane pulled up a chair, sitting down at the table, her hands just inches from his. Her visage changed, her smile dropped.

"This is bad. This is very bad. I've been too careless—reckless. You cannot tell anyone," she pleaded. "Men are scared of women who read."

Bruce reached out and held her hand, saying, "Not all men."

Her fingers were warm, soft to touch. He should have let go, but he couldn't. Somehow, by reaching out, he'd broken through an unspoken taboo.

He ran his fingers up over her hand wanting to reassure her of his intentions. She breathed deeply as his hand ran around her wrist. Her skin felt as soft as fine silk. She flinched, and he could feel her sense of hesitancy. Jane clearly wanted to pull away, and yet she did not want to let go of the moment. He could see it was too much for her, too soon, so he pulled back, saving her from a decision either way.

Jane laughed, relieving the tension.

"Why now?" she asked. Her eyes cast upwards looking at the roof. She wasn't talking to him. He wasn't sure who she was talking to and figured she was speaking metaphorically. "After all these years, I finally find someone that wants to learn, and yet I probably only have weeks to live. Why now? Why not five years ago?"

She looked him in the eye, as though she were trying to read his very soul. "You want to read? Do you know what you're asking? Do you understand the burden you're taking on?"

"I want what you have," he replied.

Jane breathed deeply in response to his comment. She ran her good hand through her hair, ruffling it as she thought for a moment.

"I'm dead anyway," she said with a sigh.

"You'll survive," Bruce said.

"Now, look who's full of confidence? Lesson number one: when it comes to knowledge, there are two kinds of confidence. The confidence that comes from understanding, and a fool's confidence, the bliss that comes from ignorance."

"But you will survive," Bruce said. "I'm sure of it. I can feel it."

43

"I appreciate your sentiment, really I do, but lesson number two: your feelings are irrelevant. This cold world cares not for what you believe, for what you think, or for what you feel. There's no magic, no wishful thinking, no earnest desire that can bend nature to your will.

"You want to learn to read? OK, I will teach you to read. In the days I have left, I will instruct you, but I warn you, with every privilege comes a burden. It will take you years to learn to read properly.

"Reading is far more than picking words off a page. It is to breathe in another's soul, to walk in their shoes. When you read, you lose yourself and inhabit another's life, the life of one that went before you on this Earth."

"Sounds fascinating," Bruce replied. "When do we begin?"

"Hold on, cowboy. It's not that easy. This isn't something you can pick up in an afternoon. At first, you'll struggle. For months if not years. You'll wonder if it's worth it. You'll lose patience. You'll lose interest. You'll think it's not worth the danger of being caught by the villagers, but if you push your mind, drive it hard like a plow horse breaking the frozen ground in spring, then you'll learn what it really means to be a reader."

She paused before continuing, looking deep into his eyes and he felt as though she could read his very soul.

"This isn't a game. This isn't some curiosity or hobby. To read is to understand the mind of the past. To read is to open your mind to another. For all your life there has only been one, there have only been your thoughts, your will, your reason, but all that will change.

"When you read, it is more than simply looking at words on a page and knowing their meaning. To read is to see inside the heart of another human being, to hear their thoughts inside your own head, to think as they thought, to see the world through their eyes.

"There was a time when everyone could read. Well, not everyone in the whole world, but at least here in America, and yet even that was short lived, just a few hundred years.

"For most of history, there were just a handful of people that could read in any generation. And those that could read often abused that power, manipulating others. History abounds with those brave souls that stood up to this abuse: Socrates fought the Senate, Christ fought the Scribes, Luther fought the Pope."

Socrates, Christ, Luther—Bruce knew these names. He'd heard them talked of in legend, sung of in nursery rhymes, but he'd never met anyone who actually knew something about their lives. He was electrified to think of all Jane could teach him.

"Make no mistake," she continued. "Words are powerful, they drive agendas. Words mold people. A handful of words can bring about more change than all the years of a man's life. Words have the power to bind or to set free. Here in America, slaves were lashed for reading. Books were banned or worse, burned, such was the fear of what could be wrought by the written word. Who would have thought such scribble, the dark marks of type on white paper could stir the soul, rouse the slumbering masses to action?

"Nations have fallen to the power of words. Do not be deceived, words cast a spell far greater than any conjurer could ever imagine. Their magic lies not in the supernatural, not in some mystical power, but in moving the hearts and minds of men. Knowledge is alchemy, turning lead into gold, turning letters into words, words into concepts, ideas into power.

"Reading is both a blessing and a curse. Once this door is open, it cannot be closed. Once you know, you cannot forget. Oh, you may try, but once you have drunk from the well of knowledge, there is no turning back. Once awake, you can never sleep again."

"I'm not afraid," Bruce said, holding his gaze on her eyes.

"Ah," she said, laughing. "You should be. These peasants, they have no idea. They hide behind their superstitions. Just a few years ago they killed poor Helena because she could read, thinking she could conjure up some dark curse. If only they knew the curse they already bear, the curse that befell this world from outer space, the curse that humbled the strong and the mighty, the curse that turned their cities into a wilderness."

"Who was Helena?" asked Bruce, sensing Jane's comments about her were more than factual.

Jane wiped a tear from her eye. "Helena was my friend. She taught me to read."

"I'm sorry."

"Don't be. Helena lived a thousand lives. Helena soared among the planets, she climbed the highest mountains, descended into the depths of the ocean. She traveled back in time. Helena sat at the feet of Aristotle. She watched as Rome fell. She saw the wars of men devastate this world time and again, but through it all, words survived. For Helena, though, there was no greater treasure than the dawn of reason, the rise of science. She spoke with Newton, struggled with Einstein, watched as Darwin sailed the Galapagos."

"And as they burned her at the stake, after torturing her for days on end, she spoke no ill of them. She bowed her head, refusing to cry out in anguish. Hers was a life like no other I've known."

Jane paused, and Bruce could see she was lost in thought, reliving her emotions in that moment. Tears ran down her cheeks.

"Will you teach me to read like that?" he asked softly.

"I will teach you," she said. "Even if I have only days left to live, I will pass on what I can. I will teach you for Helena's sake, because that is the way of readers."

Chapter 02: Library

Bruce approached the crossroads beyond the village as the dark of night gave way to the first hint of the coming day. A faint orange glow sat on the horizon. At first, he thought Jane hadn't come, but she was there, dressed as a man. In the low light, he didn't recognize her until she came up to him and spoke in a harsh whisper.

"You're late."

Bruce was taken aback by her appearance. Somewhat surprised, he didn't say anything in reply. He followed Jane, fascinated to see her wearing a baggy shirt and farming trousers. Her hair was bundled up beneath a broad-rim hat. He was walking his horse, just as she had recommended, and had to hurry to keep pace with her as she marched off along the southern track. Although he doubted anyone would overhear them in the dark forest, he whispered in reply.

"Where are we going?"

A fine mist hanging in the cool air as they spoke.

"It's called a library," she said, signaling with her hand for quiet as they marched along the path. "Once we clear the borders we can mount up, until then it would attract too much attention."

Jane wasn't taking any chances. They walked in silence as the sky lit up in blood red hues, slowly softening as the sun crept over the horizon. Birds called in the breaking dawn, which was a good sign as birds tended to be quiet when some large beast lurked nearby.

After an hour, they reached the old raised highway with its slabs of concrete slowly separating with each winter. The slabs had once been continuous, with just the narrowest of gaps between them, but over the decades the ground had shifted, moving the slabs on various angles,

47

allowing grasses to spring up between them. Occasionally, the rusted hulk of a car or truck sat to one side, or off in the ditch, a casual reminder of a long, lost world that seemed more of a fairy tale than a past reality.

Bruce climbed up first, using a rope ladder to mount the huge horse. He reached down, helping Jane climb with her injured arm. She sat behind him with her arms resting gently on his hips. She didn't have to, the saddle was large enough for several people, with leather hand-holds spaced on either side, but he had no complaints.

"There was a time," she said, pausing for a second, distracting herself with some other thought and he wondered what she was going to say.

"A time?" Bruce asked, curious about the past.

"There was a time when horses were small enough to fit through a doorway."

"Really?" he replied, trying to get his head around the concept.

"Our horses are closer to the elephants of old, both in terms of their size and their nature. They can gallop a few hundred yards, but once they would run for miles and miles."

"What's an elephant?" asked Bruce, unsure what that creature was.

"I'll show you some pictures. But they were big, lumbering beasts, with tusks like a wild boar, only their tusks extended out in a curve over ten feet long. They were like spears on either side of their heads. And they had a nose that was anywhere up to fifteen feet long. Imagine that, a nose with the dexterity of a hand, a trunk as thick as your leg that could pluck a single blade of grass. Elephants used their noses to pull on branches and pick fruit."

Bruce laughed. Such an animal was preposterous, unimaginable, like the fabled Griffin, the lion with eagle's wings.

"Surely, you're making this up?" he said. "Next you'll be telling me that dragons are real, flying through the air and breathing fire."

"Oh, but they are. Or at least they were. They were called pterosaurs, and they lived hundreds of millions of years ago. There was one with a wingspan of 36 feet."

"So these things were bigger than a bat?"

"Easily twice the size."

"And they breathed fire like a dragon?" asked Bruce, incredulous, looking up at the sky, trying to imagine a bird with such a broad wingspan.

"Oh, no. Silly," Jane replied. "But these were the real monsters, far more dangerous than anything we see today."

"Oh, I don't know about that. I once saw an eagle carry off a farmer. The poor man screamed, but there was nothing we could do for him. The monster took him up high, probably over a hundred feet in the air, and then just dropped him, watching him plummet to the ground. Then it swooped down and carried off the bloody mess that had once been alive. I've seen them do the same thing with goats. And I've heard of bats that have taken women and children in the still of night. Were pterosaurs as fierce?"

"Probably," Jane said. "But there were no humans around when pterosaurs flew the skies. They ate fish, I think. But I'm not sure."

"No humans?" Bruce asked. "How is that possible? Where were the humans?"

"We didn't exist. We hadn't evolved yet," Jane replied. "Back then, there were no birds, no horses, no men. I know it's hard to imagine, but science has shown us that all the life we see came from a few simple forms billions of years ago, slowly branching into different plants and animals."

Such a concept was mind boggling.

Bruce said, "It's no wonder people are scared of you."

Jane laughed, saying, "And why is that?"

"You speak of science, but it is as though you speak of witchcraft," Bruce replied.

"Oh, it's not witchcraft," Jane said. "It's reality. The problem is, we're fooled by our own eyes."

"How so?" Bruce asked.

"Ever see a full moon rising over the forest?" Jane asked. "Looks bigger than when it's high in the sky, right?"

Bruce nodded.

Jane said, "If you get a bit of stick and measure what you see at arm's length, you'll find the moon is always the same size, but our eyes fool us into thinking it's bigger.

The villagers are scared of science, but science keeps us from being a fool."

"I'll have to try that," Bruce replied, surprised by the notion.

They rode on for a few minutes in silence as Bruce marveled at the realization that there had once been monsters even bigger than those they faced.

"So if elephants were once as big as horses," he asked. "How big are elephants now?"

"I don't know," Jane replied. "Elephants were around six tons in weight, but once there were dinosaurs, monsters over a hundred feet long, over a hundred tons in weight, so I guess elephants could be the monsters among monsters of our day."

"Where are they?" asked Bruce. "Why don't we see these elephants?"

"They're native to a land across the sea. A continent called Africa."

"I'd like to go to Africa some day."

Jane laughed, saying, "It's over a thousand miles away across the ocean."

"We could build a boat."

"Sure. We could build a boat," Jane said, still laughing.

"No?" he asked.

"No," she replied. "It's just too far."

"But once, they could get there?"

"Yes, once they could. But not now. Too much has changed. Too much has been lost. See these highways? Once they powered the nation, allowing metal carts to travel hundreds and hundreds of miles in a day. They called them cars. They had engines, powered by the decayed remnants of life from hundreds of millions of years ago."

"I'd heard that," Bruce said. "But I thought it was a myth."

"Oh, it's no myth. As fantastic as it seems, it is our day that is the surprise, not theirs. It is our day that should have never happened. We should have continued on to new heights. We should not have been humbled by the elements."

"It all seems so fantastic, like a made-up story," Bruce said, being honest. "I mean, it sounds like the fairy-tales my mother would tell me before I fell asleep."

Jane sat back, taking a sip of water from an old wineskin.

"Oh, it's real all right," she replied. "Reading will open new worlds for you, worlds that defy the imagination."

They rode along for hours, chatting idly as the miles passed, their brute horse shuffling on relentlessly. They stopped for a light lunch, allowing the horse to drink from a stream. Bruce was taken by Jane's confidence. He was sure other women were just as confident, but he'd never noticed this trait in anyone else before. They talked about their families and their backgrounds growing up, but Bruce didn't mention Jonathan's death. That wound was still raw.

By late afternoon, they approached the outskirts of an abandoned city. Looking down into the valley, seeing the wreckage of the buildings in the distance, Bruce became nervous. Cities were dangerous, the haunt of monsters. It was ironic that the habitat of man should become the refuge of animals.

"Are you sure about this?" he asked.

"Do you want to read?" Jane asked in reply.

"Yes, but ..."

They stopped, tying the horse up in the crumbling brick ruins of a broad, low building well shy of the city. Jane said the surrounding brick walls had once marked the inside of a vast, sprawling factory, its roof long since having rotted away. Sunlight streamed in around them. Trees had sprung up, forming a sheltered garden accessible only through a metal door set on a series of large steel rollers. Unlike the road, the concrete slab within the factory was mostly buried in dirt and organic debris. Grass grew on the lumpy, irregular ground. Leaves lay scattered across what little was left of the sparse factory floor.

"Are you sure this is a good idea?" he asked as they dismounted.

"I've been here many times before," Jane said, reassuring Bruce the horse would be fine. He wasn't so sure, but learning to read was his idea, and he felt he had to follow through with it.

"Take off your clothes," she said, gathering together a bunch of grubby leaves and loose bark. The prevailing wind had caused the copper-colored autumn leaves to pile up waist-deep against the wall.

"What?" he asked.

Jane pulled off her shoes, followed by her pants, saying, "We need to mask our smell."

"Are you serious?"

"Yes. Otherwise the animals will smell you long before you see them."

Bruce mumbled something, but even he wasn't sure quite what he said.

"What are you afraid of?" Jane asked, pulling off her top. She grabbed a handful of leaves and began scrubbing her bare skin, rubbing them across her belly and around her groin. She raised her arms, rubbing leaves under her armpits before rustling her dirty hands through her hair.

Sheepishly, Bruce removed his boots. He averted his eyes, surprised both by her brashness and his modesty.

"Come on," she said, throwing a bunch of orange and yellow leaves at him, laughing as they fluttered around him. "What's your problem? Haven't you ever seen a naked woman?"

"No," Bruce replied, turning to one side as he took his shirt off. "Not like this."

"Really?" Jane said, her surprise hanging in the air. "Well, you have now."

She reached out with a handful of leaves, rubbing them in his hair.

"Stop that," he said, wrestling with his pants as he staggered to one side.

"Why?" she asked, playfully tossing leaves above him. They fell down around him like golden snowflakes. "What are you going to do about it, naked man?"

Oh, how those words struck at him. He wasn't that much of a prude, but the context surprised him, taking him off guard. He'd slept with a woman once, a prostitute, just before his troop marched on Bracken Ridge, but in the dark of the tavern he'd seen nothing as flamboyant, as proud and defiant as Jane standing there naked.

She laughed. To his surprise, he didn't feel ashamed or embarrassed by her. He was embarrassed by himself, but Jane lightened the air around him. Her laughter was playful, warm and inviting, not intimidating. He could laugh at himself, he decided, and chuckled as he rubbed handfuls of leaves over his body. Turning away from her, he raised his arms, rubbing dirty leaves up under his armpits, only to feel her hand slap his backside playfully as she said, "You missed a spot. Right there."

Now it was his turn. He picked up a large handful of leaves and tossed them over her, watching as they fell like confetti around her.

"That's the spirit," she cried, looking down his body and getting her first good look at him naked. "I see the squirrels have buried their nuts and gone into hibernation for the winter."

"What?" Bruce replied, a little confused. He looked down and realized the cold had caused his penis to look small and stunted.

"You are outrageous," he cried, barreling into her playfully and tackling her. Bruce was mindful of Jane's arm and tried not to get too carried away in the moment and end up hurting her. The two of them fell into the knee-deep pile of leaves, disappearing into a poof of red, yellow, ocher and brown. Leaves flew around them as they rolled naked, laughing. Jane tickled him, and he felt helpless, calling out for mercy, trying to tickle her back, but his tickling didn't seem to bother her. She just laughed playfully.

"Oh," she cried, as his body pressed against her. "I see someone's woken up before spring." And Bruce was overcome with a sense of embarrassment at how his body reacted to hers.

He rolled away, kicking up more leaves and sat there waist deep in the soft, autumn leaves, staring at her.

Jane's smile was intoxicating. He wanted to dive back over to her but thought better of it. She was older. She wasn't as old as his father, but she was roughly as old as his sister, and that was hard to shake from his mind. He'd like to have taken things further, but the timing didn't seem right, and he was worried she'd reject him. Jane was larger than life, and that intimidated Bruce, at least, she intimidated him when he was naked. He felt silly sitting there among the leaves.

"Come on," she said, getting to her feet, grabbing her clothes and rubbing leaves inside them. She tossed his trousers over to him as he sat sheepishly in the leaves.

They covered the last two miles on foot. Jane was surprisingly nimble. She'd let her hair down, allowing it to blow in the breeze. They jogged alongside crumbling walls, over bridges and through the outskirts of a suburb. Most of the houses had been decimated by the fury of summer storms, but a few still stood.

Bruce wanted to hang back as they moved deeper into the town, unsure of the territory. He had his bow and a quiver of arrows over his shoulder. He would have had his sword strapped to his side, but Jane said they needed to keep noise to a minimum, so he held it wrapped in a cloth as he ran along. Jane carried nothing more than her backpack and a long wooden staff.

Bruce felt uneasy, as though a wild dog or a bear would jump out at them at any moment. Wolves tended to stick to the hills, but dogs had been known to claim towns as their territory, using the grid of streets to mark their ground.

The collapsed buildings and fallen street lamp posts provided wild cats with a chaotic hunting ground, with plenty of room to stalk their prey. Whereas dogs would normally announce their presence from afar, barking and charging, providing just enough time to shoot off a couple of arrows, the big cats preferred an ambush. The arrows Bruce carried wouldn't kill either a cat or a dog, but they'd give them cause for thought. Wounds weakened animals, making them easy prey for others, leaving them open to infection, and the dogs seemed to sense that. Just a few arrows would normally deter a dog. Bears were another matter altogether.

Jane knew exactly where she was going, that was obvious. She led him across fallen rooftops, through rusting chain fences, past buildings that had collapsed in the street and cast their bricks in all directions. She paused behind the rusted hulk of various cars and buses, darting over the debris in the road, her hearing finely attuned to the slightest rustle in the trees lining the streets. Bruce kept pace with her, focusing more on her than where they were heading, trusting her judgment.

As they approached one of the taller buildings in the downtown region, Jane held her hand out, signaling for him to stop. Without saying a word, she pointed at the ground and then upwards. Bruce knew what she was pointing out. He'd seen this before, but normally only around cliffs and at the entrance to natural caves.

Guano covered the ground.

The rancid smell stung his nostrils. Bat droppings extended out away from the building, scattered liberally across the ground on a scale he'd never known. There must have been thousands of giant bats inside the crumbling remains of the skyscraper. Bruce was terrified by the faint squeaks and the rustle of thick leather wings flexing in the darkness. These monsters were waiting for dusk to fall. His heart pounded in his chest. Jane continued on.

At the next intersection, Bruce came up quietly beside her as she peered around the corner into a side street.

"Bear," she whispered.

Bruce peaked around the corner. A black bear lumbered down the road. It was late in the season for bears, most of them had hibernated by late autumn.

"This is good," she said. "He'll keep the mountain lions away."

The bear raised its head, sniffing at the wind, catching the subtle scent of their sweat on the breeze.

"If he doesn't kill us first," Bruce replied in a whisper.

Jane crept across the intersection, moving behind the crushed remains of a truck and semi-trailer. Rust had eaten through the thin, sheet-metal panels of the crumpled hood and cabin, leaving only the hollow frame. The engine block and axle were exposed to the weather. The rear trailer was little more than a broken shell, with gaping holes exposing the frame. The tires were flat. Their vulcanized rubber was frayed, exposing the reinforced nylon/steel belt to the elements. Bruce came up behind one of the wheels, using it for cover.

The bear roared, bellowing into the darkened sky, its head reached up toward the gray clouds.

"Quick," Jane said, darting across to the other side of the road and into a doorway.

Bruce went to move, but the bear had reared around facing him, barely a hundred yards away.

"Run," Jane cried, trying to keep her voice low. She was beckoning with her hand, urging him on.

Bruce froze. The bear was lumbering toward the shattered remains of the semi-trailer.

In the bitter cold, his hands felt sweaty. Perspiration broke out on his forehead. Bruce tried to move, rocking forward on his legs, but his instinct got the better of him, crying out for him to stay put, to hunker down and let the danger pass. He looked up, Jane was gone. Panic seized his mind. She'd abandoned him.

Bruce looked around. The brick building she'd been standing beside had once reached up at least ten stories in height, but the upper half had fallen into decay, collapsing into the alleyway behind the main street. Only one of the four walls stood over three stories high. The other walls had crumbled in a heap. Bruce tried to think rationally. Shooting arrows at the bear would be suicide. If he could get up high, perhaps by doubling back to the crumbling ruins behind him he might stand a chance, but the bear would see him and bolt after him. The monster would be on him before he made it more than twenty yards.

The bear roared again, rising up on its hindquarters, its massive paws stretched out wide. Bruce pulled out an arrow, thinking he could strike at its stomach, but his hands were shaking. The bear dropped back on all fours. It had seen him. It ran in hard toward him, its paws pounding on the crumbling pavement.

Bruce dropped to the ground and rolled under the rusting remains of the semi-trailer, shimmying under the engine block. Behind him, he could hear the bear growling as it came bounding up to him.

The bear roared, its claws tearing at the concrete under the truck, trying to dig him out. Bruce reacted, pulling his legs up, wanting to stay out of reach.

The rusting hulk shifted with the weight of the bear, groaning as the bear climbed up on the shell of the cabin, trying to reach its prey from above.

Bruce rolled on his back, looking up as the bear struck out, tearing the radiator away with a single swipe of its claws.

The chassis groaned, collapsing under the massive bear as one of the wheels broke off. Bruce turned to one side as the axle dug into the concrete, missing his leg by inches.

"Hey," came a voice crying out from above him. "Pick on someone your own size."

It was Jane.

The bear turned to face her. Rising up on its hind legs as it straddled the crushed cab of the semi-trailer, the black bear roared, baring its teeth as it bellowed.

Jane was standing in the third floor window of the adjacent, collapsed building, throwing bricks at the bear. Blood seeped from her bandaged arm as she hurled bricks, catching the bear on the side of its head. The monstrous animal roared in defiance as a brick caught it on its snout, breaking a tooth.

The bear charged the building, rearing up on its hindquarters and thumping the wall, shaking the bricks. The monstrous beast was trying to knock Jane out of the window, but that made the bear an easy target. With both hands, she threw a clump of three bricks at the bear and caught it on the bridge of its nose, catching the corner of its eye. The bear dropped to the ground with a thud.

Wounded, the bear loped away down the street. Jane managed to get one last brick to land on its back. It wouldn't have hurt the animal but it was enough of a reminder that this meal was too difficult and the bear roared, somewhat annoyed at resigning in defeat.

Bruce scrambled out from under the semi-trailer and over to the building. Jane came downstairs and picked up her bag, throwing it over her shoulder without saying a word.

"You saved my life," Bruce said.

"And you almost cost me mine," Jane replied rather passionately. "Next time, I'm leaving you to the bear. Have you got that?"

Bruce wasn't used to a woman speaking to him with such authority. He didn't know quite what to think. On one hand, he was excited. The adrenaline flowing through his veins filled him with energy. They'd just taken on a bear, just the two of them, and they'd won. That was unheard of, but Jane clearly wasn't impressed.

"When I say run, you run," she said sternly. "If I say fly, you flap your goddamn wings. Are we clear?"

"Yes," Bruce replied, feeling scolded. He looked at her bloodied arm as she cradled it in front of her. She was grimacing in pain.

"Thank you," he said, and he meant it. The parallel to her apology the day before was accidental, but Jane seemed to pick up on that and her demeanor changed. He could see she wasn't annoyed at him so much as annoyed at herself for taking a risk with the bear, one he wasn't ready to take. She pursed her lips, getting ready to say something and Bruce wondered about the options running through her mind.

"There," she said, cracking a slight smile. "Saying thank you wasn't so hard, now was it?"

He laughed.

"Come on," she added. "Let's get out of here."

They continued on, weaving their way toward the town center, staying to the broad streets as much as possible. It was a couple of miles before Jane stopped silently and pointed at a building in the next block.

"There it is," she said, pointing at a broad stone building, one that had fared better than most.

Somewhere in the distance, a dog howled. The sun was sitting low on the horizon, casting long shadows down the street. The wind picked up, causing shadows to dance within the thicket of weeds and shrubs breaking through the aging concrete road.

As they approached the intersection before the library, Jane said, "Stay here. Don't move. I'll be right back."

"What? Why?" he asked, but she was already creeping forward through the long grass growing out of the cracks in the road. She was heading toward the ruins of a fast food restaurant on the opposite corner of the intersection, with the library looming large beyond. The cracked remains of a giant yellow M sat high on a rusting pole.

Jane turned to him, mouthing the word, "Stay." With her hands out, she gestured for him to stay put, reinforcing the notion.

Bruce waited impatiently as she disappeared through the tangle of weeds and bushes, catching only a brief glimpse of her from time to time as she moved through a thicket of young saplings, already denuded of leaves, ready for the winter.

Bruce kept his back against a low brick wall. Every couple of minutes, he peered around the corner, nervous, afraid some wild beast would sneak up on them. Jane was nowhere to be seen. It had probably only been ten minutes, but he felt like she'd been gone for the best part of an hour. As the cold shadows grew longer, Bruce grew uneasy.

A wild dog trotted down the road. The animal was moving toward the intersection, its tail wagging casually as its tongue panted. His heart raced. Had Jane seen this monster? He looked for her, but she'd squeezed through an overgrown hedge near the library and had disappeared from sight. Any thought for his own safety vanished. He couldn't stand the thought of seeing her attacked by another dog, and this time without the aid of the villagers to fend it off.

The mongrel had long, scruffy hair, much like the one that had attacked Jane in the village, only its coloration was motley. The dog paused no more than fifty yards away, sniffing the ground, looking around, but Bruce was downwind. For the moment, at least, he was safe. Silently, he willed the brute to change direction, to wander off along one of the alleys, but the dog kept coming.

The building across the street to his left must have collapsed recently, perhaps not more than a few months ago, because the weeds hadn't yet worked their way through the long pile of broken bricks stretching out across the street.

Bruce pulled back and crossed over behind the bricks, using them for cover before the wild dog rounded the corner. Crouching, he peered back toward the intersection, watching, waiting. Nothing happened. Could it be that the dog had wandered off in some other direction? He'd like to think so, but he doubted that.

Quietly, Bruce rummaged through his pack, laying four arrows out on the broken bricks. He tore strips of cloth from an oily rag and wrapped them around the arrow shafts, using a fine twine to tie them tight behind the arrowhead. With a flint, he lit the cloth and a thin trail of black smoke wafted into the air. He wasn't worried about the dog smelling the smoke, as that might give it cause to change direction, thinking there was a fire somewhere ahead. If it came to it, a flaming arrow into its thick, oily hide should cause some panic and buy them some time.

The dog padded into view and crossed over toward the crumbling remains of the restaurant.

Bruce weighed his options based on the animal's movement. To shoot early would give him the opportunity to get off at least two or three of his arrows. With burning heads, they'd set patches of fur alight and give the beast a nasty surprise, hopefully a fright that would see the monster turn tail and run.

If he waited though, allowing the mongrel to pass by on the far side of the road, he could line up for a heart and lung shot, striking at the animal from behind, catching it up under the ribs. A good shot would be fatal.

Even a poor shot would cause significant blood loss and the animal would flee. At least he hoped so.

If the beast turned to face him, he'd have to use his sword, so he laid it on the ground beside him, readying himself for battle.

Not seeing where Jane had gone, Bruce settled on the second option as even a poor shot should see the animal react by running away from him, not towards him, and that would give him the opportunity to take more shots if needed.

Peering over the chaotic pile of bricks, he watched as the mongrel moved through the far side of the intersection, its head down, its ears pricked. It was surprisingly quiet for such a large animal, sniffing at the ground as it sought to pick up Jane's trail.

As the beast turned away from him, Bruce pulled back silently on the bow string, feeling the tension build under his fingers. Mentally, he equated that to the rate of fall over what he figured was roughly forty yards to give him an offset of about three feet.

He breathed in as he brought his aim down on the animal, sitting slightly above its shoulder blade, allowing for the natural fall of the arrow to guide it down, under the rib cage. He was shooting into the wind and needed to account for more fall than usual. Exhaling, Bruce prepared to release, steadying his body, allowing his aim to drop naturally into position, timing the shot, going for accuracy over power. The release had to be smooth, barely a conscious thought, just a natural outflow at the bottom of his breath.

A low growl, deep and resonant, caused his blood to run cold.

Bruce froze.

Bricks shifted under the weight of another wild dog approaching from behind, and from the crisp sound Bruce realized the beast was almost on top of him.

In that moment, Bruce flinched, his muscles clenched. If he fired now, he'd miss the dog tracking Jane. Just the slightest twitch at this distance would send the arrow several feet off target.

His mind raced.

Should he fire on the beast stalking her, or turn and try to fend off the brute bearing down on him?

In his heart, he wanted to be valiant, to protect Jane, but his head told him the moment was gone, to fire now would be to waste the opportunity and miss.

The muscles in his arm quivered. He had neither the time nor the nerve to fire with precision at the dog stalking Jane before the monster behind him was upon him.

Bruce spun around, the burning oil on the end of his arrow flared as he turned. There, barely five feet away, was another wild dog, its teeth bared. Bruce fired. He missed. The arrow sailed off over the shoulder of the massive beast, soaring high and clipping a tree. How could he miss? The wild dog was so close, and yet his trembling arms had failed him.

The dog crouched low, the muscles on its broad shoulders twitching, ready to pounce. Saliva dripped from its white canine teeth. With dark eyes locked on Bruce it swayed with him, reacting to his slightest move.

Bruce stepped back slowly, his feet catching on the loose bricks. The dog growled, shifting its weight. Shattered bricks crunched beneath its paws. His heart raced. With his arms out in front of him, Bruce crept backwards, bending down slowly and reaching for his sword.

The dog snarled.

Bruce dared not break eye contact with the beast. As much as he instinctively wanted to turn and run, he knew the monster would be upon him in a heartbeat. With its lips pulled back and its teeth bared it inched closer, growling at him. The dog's breath stank of rotten meat.

Bringing his sword up, Bruce backed away as the dog pressed slowly forward. It was being overly cautious. Why hadn't it attacked? The massive beast could have ripped him to shreds, tearing him apart like a rag doll, but it hadn't. Why was it herding him? His foot knocked one of the smoldering arrows. He picked it up, using the arrow head to snag the larger, oiled cloth which caught fire as he raised it up.

Bruce was so focused on the vicious dog in front of him he was barely aware of the others.

Another dog joined from the left, while out of the corner of his eye he realized a third dog was pacing toward him from the right, snarling as saliva dripped from its jaw.

All three dogs had their ears pulled back, almost flat with the side of their heads as they moved in for the kill. They stepped with deliberate precision, coordinating their attack so he couldn't anticipate which would lunge first.

Waving the arrow with the burning rag to the left, and the sword to the right, Bruce made a show to keep the monsters at bay, trying to appear larger and more dangerous than he was. With dark eyes, the beasts poised, ready to strike.

"Back, back," he cried, not knowing what to do next.

The massive dog immediately before him responded by barking savagely, deafening him with a wall of sound. Bruce waited for the end, hoping it would be quick, hoping he'd at least bought Jane some time to flee. That was when he saw her. Jane was standing on the roof of the crumbling restaurant on the other side of the intersection.

She called out, yelling, "No."

"Run," he cried, seeing her. "Get out of here while you still can."

Jane dropped from the roof into the long grass as Bruce found his back press hard against a concrete wall. There was nowhere left to go. The dogs were growing in confidence. The last remnants of the burning cloth fluttered from the arrowhead, drifting on the breeze. The dog to his right lashed out, snapping at him, knocking the sword from his hand, and Bruce sank to his knees, waiting for the inevitable.

He could see Jane running through the weeds, but she was running toward him.

"Run away," he cried, but she was running hard in toward the dogs, yelling at the top of her lungs.

Suddenly, the dogs backed away, for some reason responding to her call. Leaping over the mound of bricks and sliding on the loose gravel, she came flying in toward him, almost knocking him over. Jane was saying something, but he couldn't make it out over the shock resonating in his mind. She turned away from him, shielding him from the dogs.

To his surprise, the massive beasts lowered themselves, crouching down before her. Their demeanor changed.

"I'm sorry," she said. "I should have warned you, but I didn't want to scare you. I thought I would find them in their den and bring them to meet you. Please forgive me. I wanted to impress you."

"I ... I don't understand," Bruce stuttered.

"Dogs have not always been wild," she began. "For tens of thousands of years they lived with mankind as companions, as pets and workers. Although they have reverted to the wild, something of their former instinct still remains and they can be subdued."

"I ..." Bruce was speechless.

"We use the dogs to guard the library."

"But how?"

Jane stepped forward, scratching one of the huge beasts behind the ear. The dog responded, rolling its head to one side and lifting slightly, encouraging her to scratch a little lower. Jane was surprisingly rough, using her fingernails to get below the dense fur as she scrubbed back and forth.

The dog Bruce had first seen stalking Jane came running over, panting as it approached. Jane moved over to one of the other dogs, a scruffy mongrel lying on its side, exposing its belly. She ran her hand up and down the dog's broad chest.

65

"They particularly like a belly rub," she said, running her hands roughly back and forth.

Jane had moved away from him, so Bruce stepped toward her, and the giant dog she was patting rolled into a crouched position and growled.

"Stop that," Jane said, striking the animal on the snout.

Bruce had never seen anything like this in his life. The dog could have torn her to shreds. Its jaws were large enough to take her upper torso in a single bite, but the monster dropped its head, lowering its snout.

"Behave," she cried sternly, and she reached up and gave the animal an affectionate rub on the top of its head, between its ears. The dog sniffed at the bandaging on her wounded arm, its tongue touching the bloodied strips of cloth, but Jane didn't seem bothered by the beast's attention.

She turned toward Bruce, holding out her hand, saying, "Come."

Bruce looked at his sword lying there on the pavement.

"You really think that will make any difference?" she asked. "Come. Let them smell you. It's how they get to know you. Groom them and they will trust you."

Against his better judgment, Bruce edged forward.

Jane held out her hand, taking his hand and pulling him toward her. She pulled his hand up to the monster's mouth. Bruce tried to pull away, but she would have none of that and dragged him forward, surprising him with her strength. She held his hand there as the dog sniffed. Bruce could feel the animal's hot breath on the back of his hand.

"It's OK," she said. "She won't bite."

"She?" Bruce asked.

"What? Did you think all the dogs were male? The best fighters are the girls. The males tend to run when wounded, but the bitches will fight on to the death."

"Ah, that's not quite what I wanted to hear," Bruce replied, as she put his hand on the neck of the monster.

Bruce could feel blood pulsing through the animal's arteries. She rubbed his hand back and forth, mimicking what he should do.

"They need to get to know you," she said. "So they'll let you through next time."

"So, in the village?" Bruce asked, wondering about the rabid dog that had attacked her.

"That was Nero," Jane said. "He didn't understand. Even with the virus destroying his brain, inducing madness, I think he wanted help. He didn't mean to hurt me. He couldn't help himself."

Jane was sad, Bruce could see that. She tried to shrug it off, giving the dog before her a good hard rub. One of the other dogs came up, nudging her gently, wanting to be patted.

"For Nero to abandon the pack and track me to the village shows he knew something was wrong. He must have been bitten by another rabid animal in a fight. Nero must have sensed the change, the slow degradation eating away at his brain. But there was nothing I could do. He was frustrated, angry. I think he knew he was dying."

She changed the subject.

"A couple of the other readers are hunters. Occasionally, they'll take a stag, drag it into town and give it to the dogs. But, for the most part, I think it's the desire for companionship that keeps the dogs friendly. They seemed genuinely pleased to see me each time I visit. Even though I'm only here every couple of months they miss me between times."

"How did you tame them?" Bruce asked, his hand running over the massive brute before him, feeling the coarse texture of lean muscle beneath its fur coat.

"I didn't. They were tamed years ago, long before I was taught to read, probably several generations ago, but how, I know not. Each litter has been introduced to the readers ever since, continuing the association since birth. And they're loyal, incredibly protective."

"You're not kidding," Bruce said.

Jane led him between the dogs, making sure they each got to smell him. One of the dogs licked his hand, covering it with saliva, its tongue pulled against his skin like wet sandpaper.

"They probably thought you were coming after me, and were trying to protect me," she said.

One of the dogs came up to her, towering over her, its head bending down to within a few inches of her face. Saliva dripped from its mouth. Jane grabbed the dog's cheeks with both hands. She moved her head to one side, so the dog's jaw rested on her shoulder as she shook its head playfully, talking to it in soft, warm tones. The dog responded fondly, enjoying the rough play.

"We've got less than an hour of natural light," she added, turning back to Bruce. "We'd best get inside and get settled before nightfall."

As they walked down toward the library, one of the dogs paced beside them, its back rose just above Bruce's head. It was unnerving for Bruce, but Jane held her hand out, keeping contact with the beast, and it seemed to reciprocate a feeling of friendship.

The library had been built from large sandstone blocks and so had withstood the worst of the weather over the past few centuries. The outer glass doors had been smashed, with one of the doors ripped half off its hinges and hanging to one side, but the inner doors were intact.

The dog made itself comfortable, sitting down in the portico as they walked inside. A steel bar was pushed through the handles of the inner door, preventing any animals from wandering within the building, although if they wanted to, Bruce thought, they could rip the inner doors open. Jane removed the bar, opened the door, and put the bar back through the inside handles, explaining it was always good to avoid surprises, even with the dogs around.

Once inside, they headed up a broad, dark stairwell to the top floor, where skylights allowed the gloomy half-light to filter through. Several of the skylights were broken. Water damage marred the floors. Broken bottles and rusting cans of food lay up against the walls. The roof had collapsed in one area, crushing desks and chairs and breaking through to the floor below.

The shelves were bare, having been stripped of their books. A few torn fragments of paper lay on the ground, but nothing larger than a few inches.

Jane led Bruce past row upon row of empty bookshelves to the back of the building. Sheets of plastic had been hung from the ceiling, sectioning off a small corner of the library.

"This is where we keep the books and newspapers," she said triumphantly, a sense of pride carrying in her voice. Jane pulled back the plastic and they slipped inside.

Bruce looked around. To one side, newspapers had been stacked in clear plastic boxes, sealed against the elements. There were books as well, in groups of ten to twenty in each plastic container. In the center of the room lay the back seat of an old truck, bolted to the ground. Jane tossed her bag to one side and sat down, patting the seat beside her with childlike enthusiasm.

"Sit. Sit."

Bruce sat down and she rested her hand on his knee. The look in her eyes filled him with joy, something he hadn't felt since long before Jonathan died. The dark clouds that had hung so heavy over his heart lifted.

"This is one of four libraries scattered throughout this town. Actually, this is the only library as such, but we've split the contents into three other safe houses, so if one of them is discovered by the ignorant, we won't lose everything. There are five readers in this part of the state, along with two apprentices, not counting you."

"Oh, so now I'm an apprentice?" he asked, raising his eyebrows. He hadn't thought about any designation as official as that, but it made sense that readers had some means of covertly spreading their craft, handing it on from one generation to the next.

"Who are they?" he asked.

"I don't know. We don't use names, or talk about where we're from. It's too dangerous. We use pseudonyms, pretend names, either the name of a famous author or a name picked from a book."

"What's yours?"

"Elizabeth Bennet, after one of the characters in the novel Pride and Prejudice."

"It must be hard," Bruce said. "You can't trust anyone, even those that share your passion for knowledge."

"What would you like to read?" she asked, switching the subject, clearly not wanting to go into it any further, and Bruce wondered if he'd touched on a sore point. What had happened to Helena? Had she been betrayed by someone she trusted? He wanted to ask, but he doubted Jane would go into it with him.

"What is there to read?" he asked.

"Oh, we have Shakespeare, Oscar Wilde, Jane Austen, Rudyard Kipling, Mary Shelley," she began, but the look on his face must have spoken of his ignorance. "The names are not important, but you will come to love their writing, as they reveal the heart of men and women in the most remarkable of ways."

"Read something you like," Bruce said. "And I'll listen."

"OK," Jane replied, and she slipped on a pair of cloth gloves. The gloves were dainty, not the sort of gloves that would be worn by a farmer, as they would have torn too easily. Small details like this fascinated Bruce, and he got the impression that there were particular protocols followed by readers, protocols he'd have to learn.

Jane got up and picked a plastic box with three older books visible within. Their covers were worn and ragged, the pages yellow with age. Jane handled both the box and the books with reverence, carefully picking out one book in particular. As she sat beside him, he noticed how she handled the book, opening it slowly and allowing it to fall open where it may. From there, she used the lightest of touches to turn just a handful of pages at a time, slowly turning back to the start of the book.

"This is A Tale of Two Cities, by Charles Dickens," she said rather formally. "It was the best of times, it was the worst of times, it was the age of wisdom, it was the age of foolishness, it was the epoch of belief, it was the epoch of incredulity, it was the season of Light, it was the season of Darkness, it was the spring of hope, it was the winter of despair, we had everything before us, we had nothing before us, we were all going direct to heaven, we were all going direct the other way - in short, the period was so far like the present period, that some of its noisiest authorities insisted on its being received, for good or for evil, in the superlative degree of comparison only."

His furrowed brow must have told her he didn't understand Dickens. She smiled, excited.

"Don't you see," she said. "This is true for all time. All we have is now, for better or for worse. Ours is a time of wisdom and foolishness, of light and darkness. Dickens is telling us that the way we see ourselves defines reality. We have everything before us and we have nothing, the choice is ours."

Bruce appreciated her passion. Slowly, he became intoxicated by her presence.

"Would you like me to read on?"

"Yes," he replied, and she did, reading for almost an hour before the light faded.

Jane pulled a kerosene lamp from her pack and primed it, pumping a small lever to build up the pressure within the base before the silk mantle cast out its radiant light. Bruce had seen lanterns like these before, but only in the hands of the wealthy. Jane explained that her father traded for kerosene, mined from the shale to the north.

They ate thin strips of beef jerky and cold vegetable mash for dinner.

"Why is there such opposition to reading?" asked Bruce, chewing on the tough, dried meat.

"Knowledge is more dangerous than any gun, more dangerous than a sword or knife. Even in Eden, knowledge was forbidden."

"But why?"

"Knowledge shapes decisions. Limit knowledge and you limit the choices people can make. Knowledge has always been about power, for better or for worse, for good or for evil."

Jane got up and shifted several boxes, looking through the murky, aging plastic, trying to make out the contents. She found what she was looking for, and put one particular box aside before neatly stacking the other boxes.

"Reading has a sad history," she said, opening the box and carefully rummaging around for a book. She pulled out a small, worn booklet. It was much smaller than the other books Bruce had seen. Its pages looked brittle. The cover was stiff. Thin strands broke free from the binding. Jane took pains to handle the book with care, opening it but not reading from it.

Bruce was confused. She seemed in awe of this book, with its small typeface. The print was coarse, the letters were rougher than the clean, clear-cut, crisp sentences he'd seen inside the Dickens' novel.

"This is Foxes' Book of Martyrs," she said with reverence in her voice. She closed the book, putting it back in the box and sealing it.

"You're not going to read from it?" Bruce asked, not sure of the book's relevance.

"No," Jane replied. "I read it once, long ago."

Bruce was surprised. He could see her mind casting itself back as she weighed her words, thinking about what she was going to say, which intrigued him.

"How old is it?"

"The Martyrs was originally written in 1563, but this version is a reprint, dating from the 1800s."

She paused.

"Of all the books here, this is the oldest. It may very well be the last copy in existence."

"I don't understand," Bruce said. "What does it say? Why won't you read it to me?"

"Foxes' Book of Martyrs is not important for what it says so much as for the history it preserves. It's not like Dickens, with broad, sweeping prose that captures the imagination. It is raw, detailing the cruelty of man to those who desire the freedom to learn. Martyrs chronicles those that died so the Bible could be read in the common tongue."

Her eyes were glassy. Bruce could see her reaching back mentally, somewhat lost in thought as she spoke.

"Their days were much like ours. They would burn men, women and children at the stake, burn them alive for simply reading the Bible aloud in a church. But it wasn't infidels or madmen carrying this out, it was Christians killing Christians. And it wasn't just the Bible they feared, they burned thousands of books, anything that dared stir the imagination, anything that challenged their authority."

She looked him in the eye.

"You see, nothing changes. Everything is the same. Across thousands of years, across countless cultures, across all religions and every nation, they've always burned books. Make no mistake, knowledge has always been dangerous.

"When the pharaohs ruled in Egypt, they would carve mighty tablets of stone, trying to preserve their knowledge for future generations, but those that followed after defaced them, carving their own stories over them.

"When the Persians took Athens they burned the Acropolis, destroying the writings of the Greeks. Alexander retaliated, sacking

73

Persepolis and razing the city to the ground, burning thousands of manuscripts.

"When the Roman emperor Aurelian conquered Egypt, he burnt down the great library of Alexandria, destroying almost a hundred thousand books, most of them lost forever in the mists of time."

Bruce had no idea about the names and places she described, but he was in awe at the magnitude of destruction. From her words, he got a sense of the vast time scales involved.

"Such mindless waste," she said, reflecting on her thoughts, thinking aloud. "In Nazi Germany they burned books, saying they were cleansing the country, ridding it of filth, but that's not the worst of it."

"What could be worse than burning books?" Bruce asked, curious at her reasoning.

"Replacing them. Substituting them with counterfeits."

"They did that?" he asked.

"Yes. Once there were schools in every town, places where children were taught to read, to write, to reason. But when it came to biology, there were religious factions that changed the textbooks. Instead of teaching kids about how life branched out from the humblest of origins, they spread lies. Oh, they didn't see it that way, but that was the effect. Instead of spanning billions of years, they said the Earth was just a few thousand years old, that all of nature sprang forth miraculously in just a few days."

"Why would they say that? Why would they lie?" Bruce asked.

"Why indeed," Jane replied. "And this cuts to the core of the problem that has plagued mankind since he first stood upright on the grassy plains of Africa.

"Knowledge is power, the power to craft the lives of others, the power to direct and control. It probably sounds strange, but there is a base instinct in man, a desire to dominate, and knowledge is a tool to that end.

"Knowledge, by itself, is harmless, but knowledge can be used either for good or evil. And so here we are, still burning books."

"You really love books, don't you?"

"Oh, yes. For me, books cheat time."

"What do you mean?" he asked, chewing on the jerky in the soft light of the lantern.

"Think about Charles Dickens. What do we know about him personally? Nothing really. Oh, there are facts and figures in the forward to the book telling me he was born across the ocean in a land called England, that he married a lady called Catherine, that he had ten children, that he wrote dozens of books, short stories, poems and plays, but what does that really tell me about him as a person? Nothing.

"Millions of people lived in that era, and all that they are has perished with time. But here, in these pages, I have the soul of Charles Dickens poured out on paper, perfectly preserved in that moment. His words are as fresh as if he finished writing this tale yesterday.

"I've often wondered what it would be like to go back in time and meet Charles Dickens, but the reality is, I understand him far more through his writing than I ever could meeting him in person. To shake his hand, to sit with him over dinner or to walk through the woods with him, listening to him talk, would not give me as much pleasure as reading this book."

Such concepts were heady for Bruce. He could see Jane drawing upon her vast knowledge as easily as he would fire an arrow or build a fire. He wanted that same confidence.

"Why would anyone not read?" he asked.

Jane smiled, "Oh, Bruce. If only they all did, how different our world would be. If only we could stop for a moment and read about others instead of thinking about ourselves, the world would begin anew."

"Perhaps it can," he said. "Perhaps given time, the world will see reading is no threat and we can change the world."

Jane laughed. "You're so sweet," she said. "No. We are cursed. We live such short lives. Our view of life is so narrow, so shallow. We are like plow horses with blinkers shaping our view, keeping our sight on the muddy field ahead. We are so focused on keeping our row straight that we are ignorant of everything else around us. Man is not a pack horse. Man should not be harnessed with a bridle and bit. Even in the days when everyone read, the world would not be changed. Life is not so simple.

 "Think about everyone that went before us. How many lives were there? They say there were billions. I don't know what that means, as a number it is too large for me to comprehend, but I know each of them was as real as you. And yet what became of them? I know not, for it is lost. But here, in the pages of Charles Dickens, there is a shimmer of light, a glimpse into life from another era."

Her eyes were staring straight ahead, looking at the flickering light. Jane looked and sounded lost in thought.

"Our lives burn bright like a lantern, and we think all this will continue forever, but the truth is our lives are like the flowers in the field. We bloom in summer, and the summer sun seems eternal, but all too soon the autumn winds blow and winter descends quickly, far too quickly. And all these lives that have gone before us, all the lost memories, the love, the heartache and triumph, they crumble like the buildings around us. Even these printed words will fade one day."

She was sad. Bruce couldn't understand why, he was entranced by her reading. This was more than he imagined. Being here in the library, with the plastic sheets flexing in the changing draft, he felt like he was in another world.

The cool of the night descended and darkness fell around them, closing in on their one dim light. Outside, monsters roared in the distance. The lantern flickered, casting long shadows out into the pitch black beyond the plastic sheets.

"I want to read like you," Bruce said.

Jane looked into his eyes, the light of the gas lantern reflected off her dark brown pupils. She had tears in the corner of her eyes, not enough to roll down her cheek, but enough to glisten in the soft light. Bruce reached out, wiping them away. She touched his hand. Her fingers were cold.

"We should get some sleep," she said, dropping her hand away from his.

Bruce leaned in, making as though he would kiss her on the cheek.

"You can't do this," she said, pulling back.

"Why not?" he asked, taking her hand in his.

"You're lost in a dream."

Jane gestured to the stacks of plastic containers around them, adding, "All this is just a fantasy to you, a brief respite from slaving in the fields or hunting in the forest, but the moment will pass and reality will return. I'll go back to the village, and you'll winter in the hills. Spring will come and the fields will call and all this will be but a novel memory."

"It doesn't have to be that way," Bruce said.

"I will not be your conquest for a night," Jane said. "I will not raise a child alone."

"You won't have to," Bruce said, resting his arm on her good hand.

"Bruce Alexander Dobson," Jane cried formally. "Do not play with a woman's heart so lightly."

"Jane Blacksmith Jane," Bruce replied, with mock formality in his voice. "I would not dare."

"My name is—"

Bruce put his finger over her lips, saying, "Your name is Lisa Jane Smith. Although I'm not sure why you prefer Jane over Lisa. Or should I call you Elizabeth Bennet?"

"I need to talk to my father," Jane said, as Bruce ran his hand over her cheek and down her neck.

"I already have."

"Oh, have you now?" she said, sitting bolt upright.

"Yes," Bruce replied, mimicking her posture. "Although, I must say, he's much easier to talk to than you."

She slapped at his thigh, realizing he was mocking her. A grin lit up her face.

"And what if this is not what I want?"

"Then you would not have brought me here," Bruce said, smiling. He paused, the tone of his voice lightened. "Marry me, Jane. Be my wife. Teach me to love reading, just as you do."

Tears streamed down her cheeks. She reached out, touching his face. Her fingernails reached through his beard, scratching softly at his skin. He rested his hand on her lap, gently touching her thigh, running his fingers over the coarse cloth. She started to speak, but stopped herself. He wasn't sure what she was going to say, but he knew what he wanted to say. The words were burning inside his mind.

"I've been looking for more than just someone to teach me to read," he said. "For years, I thought I knew what I wanted, but I didn't think I'd ever meet someone like you, someone that understands not only the facts and figures, the theories and concepts, but the heart of what it means to read. I've fallen in love with you, and for all the right reasons."

Bruce leaned in, wanting to kiss Jane but she pushed him away, saying, "Hold on, Romeo. Let's see if I make it through the winter first. Nero may yet have condemned me to death."

"Oh," Bruce replied, somewhat stunned at the thought she could be so cruelly taken away from him. He looked down at the blood-soaked bandages on her arm. The prospect of losing her to some hideous disease he barely understood seemed incongruous with reality, and yet he knew she was right. That their lives could be overruled by some unseen, creeping sickness was a curse, it was dark magic, something cruel without reason.

Jane laughed, reading the sense of concern on his face. She ran her right hand through his hair and around the side of his beard.

"You're very sweet. And, yes, when spring comes, I will take your hand in marriage."

Bruce smiled.

As the cool of the evening settled inside the library, creeping in through the broken skylight, they huddled together under a couple of blankets. They talked idly before falling asleep in each other's arms.

Chapter 03: Caught

In the morning, Jane picked out a few books to take with them so she could teach Bruce to read back in the village. They'd have to be careful, discrete.

"What is this book about?" he asked, picking up a flimsy paperback and looking at a cartoon drawing of an animal he didn't recognize. Why would this imaginary creature have a red bow tie and a striped hat? Although Bruce couldn't read the words on the cover, he could see there were simple words in the title, none more than three letters in length.

"It's The Cat in the Hat," Jane replied, smiling as he flicked through the pages. She must have read his change in mood, perhaps from the slight scowl on his face.

"This is for children," Bruce said, feeling indignant.

"Oh," she said, seeing his pride was wounded. "This book was loved by both children and adults alike. It's one of the classics."

Bruce glanced at her sideways, not convinced.

Jane took the book from him, saying, "Everyone has to start reading somewhere, and Shakespeare is probably a little beyond you at this point."

She read the first few pages, running her finger beneath the words as she read so he could follow along.

"It's silly," Bruce replied.

"Yes. I think that's the point," she offered, trying to lighten the mood. She picked up another book. "This is The Grinch Who Stole Christmas. Listen carefully to the cadence, the natural rhythm that comes from each of the sentences."

Jane began reading, slowly at first, immersing herself in the narration, gradually increasing her tempo until she was rushing through the prose. She continued until she began tripping over her tongue, stumbling and stuttering as she came to a stop, laughing like a child.

Bruce laughed as well, appreciating how the rhyme and rhythm had driven her on.

"Oh, reading is so much fun," she said. "Wait until you read this to a child. Wait until you see their eyes light up with excitement."

Jane packed the books carefully in plastic, wrapping them and placing them in her backpack.

Bruce looked around at the fallen, empty shelves stretching to the end of the floor.

"How many books were there?"

"Oh," Jane replied, pulling her hair back into a ponytail. "This library probably held around ten thousand books and magazines, not to mention the music discs and moving pictures. And all of it was free."

"Free?"

"Yes. Free to anyone that desired to learn."

"They didn't charge for any of this?" Bruce replied, trying to imagine row upon row of shelves filled with books, magazines and newspapers.

"No. So long as you brought your book back within a month or so there was no charge."

"So knowledge was free?" He had to ask again. He had to be sure he'd heard her correctly. The concept seemed so radical.

Jane smiled. "Yes, knowledge was free."

Bruce was silent. Jane could see his eyes flickering around, his mind processing that realization.

"There were even larger libraries in the major cities, and universities that held anywhere up to a hundred thousand books and research papers."

"Get out of here," Bruce exclaimed. "Are you serious?"

"I'm serious," Jane said, picking up her backpack and walking to the central stairwell.

82

Bruce followed along behind her. "So how many books were there? I mean, in total?"

"Oh, well that depends on how you count them. If you tried to count every copy of every book that has ever existed, there would be more than all the leaves on all the trees you've ever seen. I once heard there were over three hundred million different books, but some of them had print runs that would run into the millions as well."

"Really?" Bruce replied. "You're saying there would be millions of copies of just one book?"

"Yes. It seems quite remarkable, doesn't it?"

Bruce barely realized they were walking down the stairs, past fallen roof beams and crumbling internal walls.

"How could there be three hundred million different books? Who could write so many books?"

"I don't know."

"Who could ever read them?"

Jane laughed. "Not me."

"It's sad, isn't it?"

Jane listened. Bruce figured she knew where his train of thought was leading him and was happy to hear him reasoning through this for himself.

"Hundreds of millions of books reduced to just a few small stacks squirreled away in run-down buildings. Will we ever get it back? The past, I mean. Will we ever recover what was lost?"

"No," Jane said as they walked through the lobby. "Those books are gone forever. But we can write new ones. We can build a new future."

"How many books are there?" he asked. "How many are left?"

"In this town?" Jane replied, thinking about it. "Roughly four hundred, plus the magazines and newspapers you saw upstairs."

It was a beautiful day outside. As they walked out into the warmth of the sunshine, a couple of young dogs played in the overgrown weeds. They pounced and snapped at each other, rolling over and growling.

"Aren't they cute?"

Bruce tried to force a smile like hers, but the concept still jarred his mind. "As cute as little carnivores can be."

They returned to the village that afternoon and arranged to marry in the spring.

Throughout winter, Bruce ventured from his farm in the hills down to the village to visit Jane. He braved the cold, the storms and the monsters to be with his fiancée, and that drew Jane even closer to him. She told him he was silly, crazy to be taking such risks, but he assured her they were calculated risks, that he'd meticulously planned out all the possible routes, that he carried survival equipment and only ever traveled when the cirrus clouds high overhead spoke of fair weather.

Jane asked Bruce to stay in the village. He had nothing to prove, she said. He wouldn't admit to the pride involved, and yet it was there. He was showing off as he courted her, but he couldn't admit that to himself even when she tenderly pointed it out. Jane told him there was nothing more he needed to do to win her heart, and yet his instinct said otherwise, and so he braved the winter.

Jane taught Bruce to read. He was a quick learner, eagerly devouring books and content to listen to Jane read aloud those books that were beyond his grasp.

Her father was supportive, although he'd never bothered learning to read for himself. During a particularly windy snowstorm, old man Smith asked Bruce, "Why read?"

His question took Bruce off guard. Bruce had been helping out on the forge for most of the day while Jane baked upstairs. The two men had talked about so much as they worked with the glowing red steel, talking about everything from his background in the militia to his hopes for the farm. On retiring for the evening, Bruce had been bringing in firewood when the old man asked, "Why would you bother to learn to read when Jane can read for you?"

"Well," Bruce replied, thinking about it for a moment. "That's a good question."

Jane was quiet. Bruce looked over at her, noticing she was struggling to suppress a smile as she stirred a stew over the fire. She clearly wanted to hear what he had to say.

"I guess it's personal. Reading is something you do for yourself."

"Does that make it selfish?" asked the old man.

"No," Bruce said. "At least, I don't think so. Reading is solitary. A writer may control the words on a page, but what those words mean is up to the reader. It's all about context. Writers may control the context within a novel, but they cannot control the context of life in which a book is read. Life has its own twists and turns. Writers don't make a book great, readers do. No two people will get the same thing out of the same book. They'll both see something different, they'll take something different away from it, and what they take with them will enrich their lives."

The old man mumbled something under his breath. Jane couldn't help herself, Bruce could see that in her smile. Jane had to jump into the conversation. She must have been trying to get her father to read for years.

"Think of the most beautiful flower you've ever seen, Papa. You could describe it to someone else, but until they see it for themselves they'll never really know quite what it's like. The same is true of books. You have to read them for yourself."

"A man should be tending the fields," her father said. "Planning for the future, not dreaming about the past."

"My dreams are only of the future," Bruce said.

Jane wiped her hands on her apron and began dishing up dinner. She must have sensed this wasn't going anywhere as she changed the subject and started talking about the wedding. The following day, once the storm lifted, Bruce insisted on returning to his farm.

They married in spring, with wildflowers dotting the countryside.

The villagers remembered how Jane had been attacked by the wild dog and survived not only the attack but the possibility of contracting rabies. They took the couple's nuptials as a sign of a good year ahead. The mood of the villagers was raised further by light rains on the day Bruce and Jane married: a good growing season lay ahead.

Bruce and Jane spent their honeymoon in the library. Shakespeare and Sherlock left presents for them, a fruit cake and a copy of Carrying the Fire, the story of Michael Collins' exploration of space in the Gemini and Apollo spacecraft. Bruce was fascinated by the concept of traveling to the Moon, the thought had never crossed his mind before, but now he was electrified by the idea. Jane half-heartedly complained, saying she'd have preferred something by Charlotte Bronte.

"Tell me about them," Bruce said, cuddling Jane as they sat on the leather bench seat inside the top floor of the library.

"Who? Shakespeare and Sherlock?" Jane asked. "I don't know any more than you do, other than that they're older than me. Or, at least I assume they're older. I don't really know. But they've been coming here longer than I have. We exchange notes. Nothing of any real substance. We're not supposed to even do that, but I can't help it, and I suspect they can't either."

"It must be hard," Bruce said. "Not being able to talk openly with the only people you feel you can really trust, those that share your passion for reading."

"It is," Jane replied. "Whenever I come here, the first thing I look for is a note in the ledger. We treat it as a diary of sorts, cataloging our fleeting correspondence. Most of the comments are general, not directed at anyone in particular. They're notes about incursions by hunters into the city, circulating books between locations, a list of the books someone has borrowed and when they'll return them, stuff like that. But, occasionally there's something personal, and that's nice."

"Don't you think we're a little exposed?" Bruce asked. "I mean, how many other people in the territory got married this spring? There can't have been more than half a dozen at most. If they figure out the village we came from they'd realize there was only one marriage, ours."

"They wouldn't betray us," Jane said, quite adamant in her assertion.

"You don't know that."

Looking in her eyes, he could see she knew he was right. "They wouldn't want to, but no man can tell how he'll bear up under torture. Just be careful, Jane. Don't say too much."

Jane's head drooped slightly as she nodded, agreeing with him.

"So," he continued. "If they've got elaborate names like Shakespeare and Sherlock, what's my nickname going to be?"

"Oh. You don't get to choose your pseudonym. It gets chosen for you."

"Really? So what's mine?"

"Promise you won't get mad?" asked Jane.

Bruce was silent and a little nervous. He didn't want to promise anything. His curiosity was getting the better of him and he gestured to her with his hands, prompting her to carry on.

"You're The Cat."

"The Cat?" he asked.

"The Cat in the Hat."

Bruce laughed. "You told them, didn't you?"

Jane smiled sheepishly.

They spent three days at the library. Bruce was curious about the town so Jane took him for a couple of walks with the dogs, using them for protection and early warning about any predators in the area. They explored the surrounding factories and rundown houses over several days, collecting trinkets and anything that might be of some value. After that they returned to his farm and settled into married life.

The farm stretched out over almost five square miles and would have been impossible to manage alone, but several other families on the outskirts pitched in to help for the right to catch insects in the fields and share in the harvest. During spring, they could be seen in the early evening, walking through the new growth of wheat and barley, swirling poles around them, catching crickets and grasshoppers in their vast nets. With cockroaches reaching the size of a man's foot, and the largest grasshoppers being the size of a man's hand, they were good eating, providing plenty of protein.

Bruce preferred his roaches deep-fried in vegetable oil, but Jane was more economical, boiling them and making mash from the leftovers. Dried crickets would keep for months on end, making them ideal for a snack-on-the-go. Although the summer harvest of crickets tended to go a little moldy through winter, they were still edible well into the following spring.

Bruce would bring in hired help for a month or so at a time, but he was hard working and tended to shoulder more than his fair share of the load. He had one beehive, on a hill in the northwest corner of his farm. It was well fortified, as much to keep the bears away from the main homestead as it was to farm honey.

Spring tended to bring the bears, but they quickly learned there was no easy meal to be had and would return to the forest.

The hive was located in a small thicket of trees on the brow of an exposed hill. Like everything on the farm, it was the result of generations of work being handed down.

Deep pits had been carved into the rocky ground and lined with spikes to deter any critters from raiding the hive. Being exposed, the winter winds tended to keep the snow from building up within the trench. Drainage channels allowed the spring thaw to wash away.

Bruce would swing a drawbridge across the moat to reach the hive, using smoke to keep the bees subdued when harvesting honey. He'd once snagged a bear cub that had fallen into the pit and impaled itself. The bear skin lined his cabin wall, taking a place of pride among his possessions.

The bees were the size of his palm. If they got beneath his heavy clothing, a sting could ache for weeks. Depending on the health of the colony, Jane would have him bring back honeycomb with immature larvae as a special treat, but Bruce didn't like to weaken the hive. Jane thought they should have more hives but for Bruce, honey was secondary produce. There was more money in wheat, if he could keep the locusts at bay.

If a mild winter passed, Bruce would switch tactics, planting only a thin crop, knowing the locusts would come in strength and decimate the fields. Instead of focusing on wheat that year, he'd plant just enough wheat to draw the locusts in to the area and would use the empty silo as a trap. The smell lured them in. One year, before his father passed away, Bruce caught thirty tons of locusts in a single season. Unfortunately, some of the capture spoiled before he could prep it for the markets, but he still made more that year than he did from both wheat and barely the previous year.

Although the southern markets were almost thirty miles from his farm, Bruce and Jane made the journey down to the village of Amersham several times a year, if only as an excuse to follow up on Jane's father.

After a couple of years, Bruce was starting to read some of the classics, but his interest lay with the newspapers and the fleeting glimpses they provided of the Fall. Life had never been so good, at least from his perspective.

Jane was melancholy. As spring bloomed and color returned to the landscape, with wild flowers dotting the fields and birds singing to fill the days, Jane remained moody. Bruce knew something was wrong.

"What's troubling you, Honey?" he asked, as they sat outside their log cabin in the early evening. Streaks of pink sat high in the stratosphere. Sunset cast long shadows on the ground, lighting up the sky in golden hues.

She turned to him rather absently, still processing what he'd said. Jane paused before speaking, and he could see she was weighing her words.

"I can't lie to you, can I?"

"Nope," Bruce replied, smiling. "You're a terrible liar anyway."

"I'm too slow off the mark," she confessed.

"You think too much. You over complicate things."

Jane sighed, leaning against him as he put his arm around her.

"What could be bothering you on such a beautiful evening?"

"I'm not with child." It was an awkward sentence, which surprised him. That alone spoke volumes, revealing a glimpse of her inner torment. For someone so eloquent, with such an appreciation of English literature, it was a guttural, coarse statement, baring her soul.

Bruce pulled her in a little, giving her arm a rub. He didn't know what to say. What could he say? A lump formed in his throat. He tried to swallow, wanting to push the emotion away. Looking at her, there were tears in her eyes. They rolled down her cheeks, leaving glistening tracks in their wake. She was looking for him to say something that would make this better, but there was nothing to be said. Words couldn't console her, and he knew it. The cry of a newborn babe was all she wanted to hear.

"Well," he said, forcing his voice to sound upbeat. "We'll just have to try harder."

"Oh, you'd love that, wouldn't you?" she replied, tickling him.

"Hey," he called out in his defense. "It was your idea. We should double our efforts and get started right away."

Jane laughed.

They didn't talk about children after that evening. Bruce was tender, considerate, but it became an unspoken barrier between them. As much as Jane tried, it seemed she couldn't put this behind her, and he felt her anguish.

Months passed, seasons came and went, and still she remained barren. Bruce could see she put on a brave face, not wanting to trouble him, but in the quiet moments he could see beyond her facade and longed to see her with child.

After a particularly harsh winter in which the prevailing winds shifted, causing the drifts to bury the countryside for months on end, Bruce and Jane were anxious to visit Amersham.

Spring brought the Sparkles in the early evening. For the villagers, the annual flickering flashes of light high in the sky were unnerving. Bruce had read about them in the newspapers. He understood they were nothing more than grains of sand, tiny specks of dust striking the upper atmosphere, but he couldn't say that. To explain what the Sparkles actually were would be to dispel superstitions. Showing he understood would raise questions about how he could be so sure. If tradition said the Sparkles were the spirits of the dead returning each year, if folklore spoke of streaks of light carrying evil intent, who was he to argue? Bruce hated that. Jane kept him in his place, making sure he understood how dangerous intolerance was when fueled by fear. For Bruce, the Sparkles were fascinating.

Having read about the exploration of space, Bruce longed to know what it was like to fly so high in the sky. He'd read about the re-entry of the Apollo capsules and how they glowed like the surface of the sun, lighting up the daytime sky like a comet, just as the Sparkles did at night. Bruce tried to imagine what it must be like to enter the atmosphere in a ball of fire and survive unscathed. Such thoughts were incredible to his mind, schooled by images of metal forged in a blacksmith's fire. How could the astronauts survive when their capsule glowed red hot? Jane told him their heat shields were made from a special kind of glass that vaporized into a gas under intense heat, slowly peeling away behind the plummeting spacecraft. Whenever Bruce watched Jane's father at work in the heat of the forge his mind would wander to visions of space capsules blazing through the sky, glowing red-hot.

While staying at the forge, word came that a reader had been caught to the east. The village chief announced that an audit was being conducted and that the reader would be brought to trial in the market square.

Jane was beside herself. Bruce understood her anguish. Visions of Helena burning at the stake still marred her mind. It was something he'd never seen, but Jane's description was as vivid as anything he'd ever read. Even before he met Jane, he couldn't understand how people could be so cruel.

Jane wanted to leave, to head back to the farm. Bruce was firm. He wouldn't run. To leave suddenly, when they'd intended to be there for a month, would have aroused suspicion. Besides, it was a trial, it was a public debate, a chance to air concerns. Jane pleaded with him not to get involved, but Bruce couldn't help himself. The injustice ate away at his soul.

When the day of the trial arrived Bruce took his place on the bench seats arranged in the market square. Under a blazing sun, the circuit judge called out the charges.

"Hugo Travers, you are accused of fomenting subversion by dabbling with knowledge beyond your ken. Through these dark arts, you have brought famine and pestilence on the villages of the east, a curse upon our crops and animals. How say you?"

Hugo had suffered enough already, that was clear. The trial, if it could be called that, had already been staged in three other villages. At the conclusion of each, Hugo had been beaten to the verge of death, the fearful animosity of an ignorant people having been exacted on his body.

Sitting there slumped in the judgment seat, Hugo was but a shadow. His hair was matted with dried blood. Scabs seamed his face. Dark blue bruises lined his neck and shoulders. Boils and blisters marred the skin on his bare chest, weeping yellow pus. He'd lost his left eye. A deep, dark recess was visible where his eyelid had been cauterized and sealed. Hugo's other eyeball was hideously swollen and deformed. He looked like a monster, but Bruce understood the real monsters were those that did this to him.

In the time he sat on trial, Hugo's one, remaining eye never moved, staring blindly ahead.

Looking at him, Bruce knew Hugo had suffered more than any man should for any crime, and yet he'd been kept alive as long as possible as a show to others, a freak to be paraded as far and wide as possible, a vivid warning against the supposed evil of reading.

Hugo winced under the heavy metal collar around his throat. The rusting metal bit into his neck, drawing blood. A chain led from the collar to the troop of six guards escorting the judges.

The villagers feared him, that was obvious. Hugo looked more like a beast than a man—a wounded, crippled animal. The look on his face spoke to Bruce. He'd seen that expression only once before, sitting in the mud on Bracken Ridge. Hugo had the resigned, sunken features of a man whose life was waning. Through swollen lips, Hugo answered.

"Guilty."

Although this one, incriminating word was spoken in a whisper it carried on the wind, haunting the market.

A scribe noted Hugo's response with a quill, writing in the Book of Judgment. The oversized, leather-bound book acted as both the register of laws and a ledger of prosecution.

"There is a natural order for mankind," the judge cried, his voice bellowing out through the marketplace. "There is a natural place for man. We have neither wings with which to fly in the sky, nor gills with which to breathe under water. We have our place in nature. To usurp this, to steal the fire of knowledge from the gods, is folly.

"Reading unsanctioned books is evil. But it is the nature of man to become intoxicated with knowledge, to become drunk on his own ego, to think he can ascend into the heights like a bird or to have mastery of the deep like a whale. It is knowledge that brought the Fall upon man. Knowledge is a tree laden with forbidden fruit, poisonous and noxious.

"And why would a man partake of that which is evil, of that which will only ever bring misery? Once man thought he could have mastery of this world and billions died because of his arrogance. The hubris and presumption of man has brought nothing but suffering."

Jane held Bruce's arm, her fingernails dug into his skin. He went to move, to stand and say something but she held him back, growling at him under her breath. The villagers around them murmured.

"Let this be a lesson," the judge continued. "We cannot abide such egotism, such delusions of grandeur that cause a man to forsake the common good, to think he is above the rest of us, that he can determine for himself right or wrong.

"And there are others. This man, this Socrates as he called himself, he told us of several others, of Shakespeare and Sherlock, and of a woman, Elizabeth Bennet. If you know who these people are, save them from themselves, save them from the blindness of arrogance that compels a man to seek the deceit of forbidden wisdom."

The villagers spoke among themselves in hushed whispers. Jane spoke softly in Bruce's ear.

"Please, don't. Don't do anything foolish. There's nothing we can do for him."

Bruce shifted in his seat, anger welling up within him.

"He knows," Jane whispered. "He's taken the oath. He's part of the pact. If any of us are caught, we know we're on our own."

"This isn't right," Bruce replied, struggling to keep his voice down. Around them, villagers stared, their beady eyes picking the two of them out of the crowd.

"It's too dangerous," Jane said, her words barely audible. "Not for us. For the books. If they find the library they'll burn the books. We have to preserve that knowledge for future generations, even if it costs us our lives. Hugo knows that. He accepts that. There's nothing we can do."

Bruce stood, pulling against her, rising above the sea of heads seated around him.

"Hasn't he suffered enough?" he asked aloud, his voice carrying through the market.

Bruce couldn't contain himself. How could any of these people live with themselves? He had to speak up, and would have spoken up regardless of whether he'd learned to read or not. It was not right.

Bruce hoped his few words were tactful enough to make the point without undermining judiciary authority. It was a good question, or at least he thought so. It needed to be said.

"No," Jane whispered. "Don't you understand? This is what they want. They are trying to goad you. It's a trap."

Bruce spoke under his breath, saying, "Reading is not a crime."

The villagers around them stared, catching their words and murmuring among themselves.

The judge took his time before addressing Bruce.

"You disagree with our ruling?"

"I am nothing but a lowly farmer," Bruce replied. "I mean no disrespect. I see here a man punished beyond anything I have ever seen before, even in the bitter heart of war."

The judge was silent, as was the crowd, and Bruce felt as though he were slipping a noose around his own neck.

"If a man steals from me, I would seek recompense from the court. If a man were to argue and fight, I would want a fair trial, that justice may be done. If he were to kill one of my kin, I would not exact my own revenge, I would seek a judge to rule and mete out judgment as appropriate."

A murmur of agreement rippled through the crowd. Bruce was stalling, trying to gain agreement from both the judge and the villagers as to what was appropriate, hoping they would see how barbaric they were. For him, this wasn't about reading or any other crime, imagined or real, this was about rousing slumbering morals. Such brutality was not seen among beasts. These people were worse than monsters. Bruce didn't dare say what he was thinking. He tried to appeal to reason.

"In my ignorance, it seems this man has neither stolen from me, nor hurt my family, nor struck down my kin, and yet he has suffered intensely for his crime."

Looking at the judge, Bruce could see the old man's eyes narrowing as he listened intently. Whether it was to trap him in his words, or whether he was genuinely considering his arguments, he wasn't sure, but it was out of character for a justice to let a commoner talk so freely in a public forum. By seeming to acknowledge Hugo as a criminal, Bruce hoped he was addressing his grievance without attacking the judgment.

Jane sat beside him, rocking back and forth slightly, saying, "Sit down. For the love of all that is sacred, please sit down."

"And what would you have us do with this man?" the judge asked. "Would you have us set him free?"

"If he has murdered a man or raped a woman, we would execute him," Bruce replied.

"Oh, but we will execute him," the judge said. "He will burn at the stake."

"But don't you see," Bruce cried, pointing at the shell of the man quivering in fear. "He is twice dead. You may not have killed his body, but you have destroyed his soul. Is there such a crime that deserves such punishment? More than we would mete out to a murderer?"

A murmur resounded through the crowd, growing in volume as the villagers agreed with his logic.

"I ask only that the court consider his crime on balance with his punishment. I am but a simple man. For me, there is hunting and fishing, tilling the fields and harvesting a crop. I mean no disrespect. I mean only to be honest before the court. This wretched man has lost his sight, he can no longer see, he can no more read than I can fly to the moon. I ask the court to consider an appeal for mercy. I ask that the court shows leniency."

With that, Bruce sat. Jane gripped his arm. "What have you done?" she whispered. "What have you unleashed?"

"I'm sorry," he replied softly so only she could hear. "I just couldn't bear to sit by without saying something, anything. What if that were you? What if that were me?"

The chief justice conferred with several other judges, talking intently with them. At least one of the judges seemed to agree, debating quite passionately with the others. The noise of the crowd rose as the villagers talked about what had been said. Some agreed, some disagreed. No one, it seemed, was impartial. Several people sitting near Bruce reached out, patting him on the back and on his shoulder, showing their support.

The justices finished their deliberation. The chief justice brought his gavel down, calling for order. He signaled to the guards and they moved in from both sides, pushing their way down the row of peasants before grabbing Bruce. They lifted him up and dragged him back to the aisle.

"No!" screamed Jane. "No, you can't do this."

Bruce felt a lump form in his throat. He'd never experienced such violent authority being so roughly imposed by another. Even when he was at war, authority had been more of a threat than reality. Here the judge's authority was arbitrary and brutal. At the mere wave of a hand, these soldiers had carried out their unspoken orders without a moment's hesitation, forcibly imposing the judge's will. Bruce felt powerless. He looked back at Jane. She was screaming at the guards, pulling on one of their arms.

"Let him go, you monsters!"

"Shut up, wench," cried the guard, grabbing her and throwing her violently backwards into one of the benches.

"Please no," Jane sobbed as she lay there on the dusty ground, her dress torn in the scuffle.

"All is well," the judge called out above the commotion. "Bring him forward."

The guards brought Bruce before the judge, releasing him and standing back to one side. The crowd was restless. Voices cried out in anger. Again, the judge brought down his gavel, calling for order, demanding submission. Bruce stood there silently, expecting to be struck down from behind and brought to his knees, but the blow never came.

"You chose to speak for this man? For this reader who can never read again?"

"I did," Bruce said, looking the judge in the eye. He was trembling, which surprised him. His right leg was shaking, his hands twitched involuntarily, and he found his mind racing, wondering what would transpire over the next few minutes. Bruce wondered if he'd live to regret those words spoken in haste. He wondered what would unfold, wondering if these few minutes would plague him for the rest of his life, but in his mind he was defiant.

Reason told him these were just men, no more or less a man than him, but emotionally he felt they held the power of life and death over both him and Jane. Bruce may have been bold enough to speak up, but the quiver in his voice betrayed the fear welling inside. Those two brief words, admitting to nothing more than his conviction, left him feeling as though he'd confessed to murder.

The chief justice set his face like a stone. Hard lines ran down his aging cheeks. With down-turned lips he spoke in an even tone, and Bruce felt goose bumps rising on his skin.

"It is in the interests of this court to see that justice is carried out impartially and without prejudice. We cannot tolerate evil in any form, be it theft or murder, rape or reading, and yet it is the opinion of this court that this commoner has a valid concern. Punishment must be weighed against each crime, and Hugo Travers has suffered for his crime. It is the decision of this court that a public spectacle be made of this man."

The justice motioned his head toward one of the other judges standing to one side.

"Justice Chambers notes that to kill such a one as this is akin to making him a martyr—a hero to a cause that knows no scruples. In this regard, with due consideration being paid to the punishment already inflicted, it is the decision of this court that Hugo Travers live as a lasting testament to the folly of reading. He is released into your custody. You have spoken for him. You shall bear his burden. He shall be an example of madness."

The judge brought down his gavel, sealing his judgment.

"This decision is binding."

Bruce stood there stunned as the guards brushed past him. They struggled with the metal collar around Hugo's neck, prying it open.

"Guilty," Hugo mumbled. "Please, I am guilty, guilty, guilty."

Bruce rested his hand on Hugo's shoulder as the guards pulled him to his feet. Hugo flinched, expecting to be struck again, trying to absorb the blow. By moving in sync with what he must have assumed was another savage beating, Hugo still had some semblance of self-preservation demanding he survive a little longer. Even with all he'd been through, his instinct for life drove him on. Bruce found himself overwhelmed by a sense of pity.

"Guilty," Hugo whimpered.

"It's OK," Bruce said. "Everything is going to be all right."

He put his arm around Hugo's shoulder, helping the man as he stumbled forward.

The judge brought his gavel down, silencing the unrest in the crowd as he cried out, saying, "The case of Evan James verses Timothy Clarance, in the dispute over lands in the Forest of Dross will now be heard."

Bruce led Hugo away, taking him from the market and into a side alley.

"I'm guilty," Hugo continued, unable to comprehend what had happened.

Jane came up beside them, tears streaming down her cheek.

"You're stupid. You are so stupid," she said. Bruce smiled, taking her concern as a compliment.

"Oh, Hugo," she added, seeing the poor man hunched over. "It's going to be all right. We're going to take care of you. You're safe. There's nothing to worry about."

They brought Hugo back to her father's house above the forge. The old man was furious when he saw how Hugo had been treated.

Hugo was still in shock, and Jane was worried about his mental state. She said she wasn't sure if he'd ever recover properly.

Over the next few days, they tended to Hugo's wounds, bathing him in warm water, giving him a bed to sleep in, fresh clothes to wear and fresh meats and vegetables to eat.

Slowly, Hugo responded.

On the third day, Hugo spoke for the first time since the trial. Jane was preparing a stew for dinner while her father finished up in the forge. Bruce had been out working in one of the mills. As he sat down at the table opposite Hugo, the old man sensed his presence and spoke with unexpected clarity.

"Thank you for seeking mercy and saving my life."

Bruce smiled, not that Hugo would have known.

"We were glad to help," Bruce said modestly.

Jane wiped her hands on her apron, left the stew to simmer over the open fire and sat down at the table with them. She reached out and held Hugo's hands. Bruce watched as Hugo's frail fingers gripped her hands, pulling her slightly closer. In his mind, locked in perpetual darkness, he must have relished the touch of another bringing warmth and kindness into his pitch black world.

"You have nothing to fear," Jane said softly.

Hugo must have realized how hard he was gripping her hand. He released his grip. Jane patted his hand gently.

"It's only been a few weeks since I was captured," he said. "But my life seems like one lived by two different people. It is as though there have been two minds inside just one body. Before all this, there are only fleeting memories, dreams of a life that doesn't seem as though it were ever real. Now, I feel as though I am dead already."

"Don't say that," Jane said, troubled by what she was hearing. But Bruce understood. He'd felt the same way following the death of his brother.

"Your kindness," Hugo continued. "Your love for a stranger—it is overwhelming."

"You have been through much," Bruce said, reaching out and resting his hand on Hugo's forearm, understanding the blind man's need for touch, realizing it must have given him a sense of grounding that had been lost with his sight. "They will not hurt you again."

Hugo was silent. Although his one remaining eye was blind, it moved as his eyelids flickered, revealing his mind processing a host of conflicting thoughts and emotions.

"I am a burden," he said.

"You are not," Jane replied emphatically.

"I am blind. There is nothing I can be but a burden."

"You have read," Jane said. "You have seen more than those with sight will ever know. It is those ignorant souls afraid to read that are blind. They may see the blue sky and the green fields, but they will never see the clarity of reason."

"But I will never read again," his chest heaving as he spoke.

"I will read to you," Jane said.

Hugo's cheek quivered, his lip twitched.

"It is early days," Bruce said, seeing the emotion welling up within the old man. "Do not trouble yourself with such thoughts. We are honored to have you with us. We will care for you as best we can, as a son would care for his aging father. Give yourself time to adjust, Hugo."

"Your pace of life has changed," Jane said. "But you are alive. Rejoice in that, my friend."

"Thank you," Hugo said, pulling his hands back. "Thank you, Elizabeth Bennet."

Bruce smiled at Jane. She looked shocked, but she shouldn't have been, thought Bruce. It was a guess on Hugo's part, of that he was sure, but there were few that would care for a blind reader other than another reader.

"I've got to get some more firewood," Bruce said, standing up and resting his hand on Hugo's shoulder. "It's good to have you with us, Hugo."

Jane got up and tended to her stew, talking with Hugo as Bruce went outside. At the bottom of the stairs was a small piece of paper, folded and stuck into one of the gaps in the wood. Bruce opened it and took it to Jane.

Thank you for saving my friend,
Shakespeare.

"What do you think it means?" Jane asked, having read the note aloud to Hugo. "Did you know him? Did you know who Shakespeare is?"

"No," Hugo replied. "Perhaps he lives here in this village? Or maybe he is one of the judicial group."

"Justice Chambers?" Jane asked. "He spoke up for your release."

"I don't know," Hugo replied.

"He's too young," Jane said. "I'd always thought of Shakespeare as older."

"Either way," Bruce said. "We are exposed, far too exposed. We need to get back to the farm and lay low."

Chapter 04: Hugo

Hugo journeyed with them back to the farm.

As the days passed, Hugo grew stronger and more confident, adjusting to life without the aid of sight.

Hugo had been a baker in the village of Eigerville. He'd been betrayed by his own son. After his wife had died of typhoid, his son had grown more distant, blaming Hugo and his reading for the death of his mother. When Hugo's grandson fell ill with fever, his son blamed him and turned him over to the authorities. For Hugo, there was nothing to go back to in Eigerville.

Hugo was passionate about remaining active. After little more than a week, he was getting around the farmhouse by himself. He walked with the side of his hand brushing gently against the walls, the bench, table and chairs, lightly touching them as he moved, giving himself a point of reference from which to locate himself within his mental map of the cabin.

Having returned early from the fields one day, Bruce watched Hugo silently from the open doorway, but somehow Hugo knew he was there even though he hadn't said a word.

"Do you pity me?" Hugo asked, turning roughly toward where Bruce stood with the sun warming his back.

"I don't know if pity is what I was thinking," Bruce replied, being honest in response to the old man's candor. "More surprised at how well you negotiate yourself around all our clutter."

"Don't you pity me either, Jane," Hugo said, and Bruce turned, surprised to see Jane standing behind him in the doorway. Her shadow cast inside the cabin, and Bruce wondered if Hugo had some sense of light and dark. Either that or there was some subtle creak in the wooden floor that he'd missed, not being as attuned to his other senses as Hugo.

"We'll get rid of some of this junk," Jane replied, ignoring the old man's comment.

"Don't you worry about me," Hugo said. "I enjoy the challenge. Keeps the mind sharp."

"Worried about you? I'm worried about me," Jane said in reply. "I skinned my shins on the kindling box by the door a couple of weeks ago while moving around in the dark. I've been pestering Bruce to get rid of a lot of this clutter for months, so please, don't take away my excuse now I finally have one."

Hugo smiled.

It was good to see him smile. He must have felt he was a burden, as he went out of his way to help around the cabin, making beds, working with his fingers to clear the bench, washing clothes and dishes. Jane assured him he was anything but a bother.

Bruce spent most of his time out in the fields or working in the barn. Jane would join Bruce in the afternoons after finishing up her chores. Hugo would tag along with her, using a wooden cane to provide him with some independence. He'd learned the layout of the farm and seemed to relish those times when Jane would ask him to fetch a water bladder or a spade from the shed.

Jane kept a vegetable and herb garden for the house beside the woodpile. Hugo proved himself adept at determining which plants were weeds by the texture of their leaves, their growth between the rows, and comparisons with the other plants. Often, Bruce would return from working in the back fields to find Hugo sitting in the garden, facing the sun, enjoying its warmth on his face as his hands glided over the soil and plants, picking at the weeds.

Bruce built a loft within the farmhouse to give him and Jane some privacy while opening up the downstairs area for Hugo. They said they'd been planning to add a second story within the cabin anyway, but Bruce suspected Hugo knew better.

Hugo had a brilliant memory and a mind that loved to reason, to think in depth and discuss concepts from new angles. He taught Bruce about physics in the evenings. It seemed Bruce was destined to learn about physics whether he wanted to or not, which brought a smile to Jane's face.

In the soft crackling light of the fire within the cabin, Hugo spoke of his love for science.

"It was Galileo who said, mathematics is the language with which God has written the universe. Mathematics allows you to read nature like a book."

Bruce was sure he was right, even though he wasn't that good with mathematics, but Jane had taught him to take up opposing positions so as to avoid any bias in his reasoning. He hadn't been game to try that with Jane, but he figured he'd give the concept a whirl with Hugo to see what he could learn.

"I can't see it," Bruce began, suddenly becoming acutely aware he'd used a term inappropriate for Hugo. He tried to catch himself, but once that word was spoken it could not be recalled. Bruce tried to go on without putting his foot in his mouth again.

"I can understand how mathematics is needed for bartering in the markets and buying equipment, but there are no numbers governing my plow, or guiding my arrow to a deer. I don't mean to sound like one of the judges, but I'm not sure how much help physics can be out here on the farm. I mean, we don't have cars and computers, airplanes or submarines. We've just got axes and spades."

"Oh, on the contrary," Hugo replied. "You are so familiar with nature, you take physics for granted, just as I once did. You shoot your arrows and instinctively appreciate the rate at which they fall, but it is a rate that can only be properly expressed using mathematics. Our world is ordered by numbers, my friend, whether we realize it or not."

Bruce could see Hugo's face lighting up with the prospect of an intellectual challenge.

Jane took Hugo's hand, guiding it to a cup of herbal tea she had made from soaking dried apple and crushed almonds in boiling water. She had allowed the tea to cool before giving it to Hugo. He raised it to his lips, sniffing and then sipping, savoring the taste.

"Even though I know you're right," Bruce said. "There seems to be too much chaos, too much noise and confusion to find any simple, clear-cut ways of using physics on a farm or while out hunting."

Hugo smiled.

Bruce could almost hear his thoughts before he spoke. His eyebrows were raised, his cheeks were flushed, and his posture was straight. Even with the horrible scarring on Hugo's face, he looked excited. As shocking as his appearance was, Jane and Bruce looked past that, seeing the beauty of his heart.

"It's in the finer points," Hugo replied. "You'll find physics in the subtleties most people overlook. Physics is an old Greek word, it simply means nature, and that's all physics is, a way of describing the world around us. There's nothing hard or mystical about it. We instinctively use physics all the time without realizing it. I'll show you an example."

Hugo turned toward where he could hear Jane cleaning up and asked for a broom. She handed the coarse wooden broom to him, taking time out to watch his example.

Bruce and Jane exchanged silent glances with each other, curious as to what Hugo had in mind. For his part, Hugo was oblivious to their unspoken communication. In the time Hugo had been with them, they'd learned to say more with gestures and facial expressions than they ever had before, not that they were trying to exclude him, it was that they were a married couple and they felt the need to be expressive with each other in some private way. For Bruce, it was fun to be intimate in a variety of manners. Having Hugo around accentuated that aspect of their relationship, and Bruce loved it.

Hugo held out the broom for Bruce, saying, "Can you balance this broom on just one or two fingers?"

Bruce took the broom, lifting it up, feeling it naturally weighted toward the bristles. Holding the broom with one hand and trying to position his fingers in the right spot, he quickly realized he was going to run out of hands and laughed, giving Hugo an audible cue.

"Hold out your arms," Hugo said, taking the broom from him with the confidence of one that had sight. The fire crackled with warmth. "I'll show you how easy it is. This is a simple experiment, but it demonstrates the notion of a center of gravity."

Hugo ran his fingers along the broom, gently taking Bruce's arms and stretching them apart. He rested the shaft of the broom on one finger from each of Bruce's outstretch hands. Bruce was amused by the novelty of having Hugo so actively involved in something that would normally require sight.

"Now, if you keep your hands level and start moving them together you'll find the broom stays balanced. It won't fall from your fingers even though it is heavier at one end. The broom will stay balanced because you already have it in balance. As you move your fingers together you'll naturally find the center of gravity."

Bruce went along with the old man, more out of politeness than anything else, but he was right. As Bruce moved his hands together they ended up close to the bristles, but the broom remained balanced on his two fingers.

"And how is this going to help me sweep the floor?" asked Bruce with a lighthearted voice.

"Oh," Hugo replied. "It won't help you keep the cabin clean, but it will help your hunting."

That got Bruce's attention.

Hugo reached out and took the broom from him. Bruce was fascinated to see how confident the old man was, instinctively grabbing the broom even though he couldn't see the shaft. Hugo leaned it up against a wall that was just out of reach, confident of his position within the room.

"All right, Mr. Physics," Bruce said. "I'm sure this is going to be good. Tell me, how can balancing brooms improve my hunting?"

"By helping you make better arrows," Hugo replied. "You can take this principle and apply it to your arrows. Imagine the bristles of the broom are the arrowhead. The arrow should always reach a point of balance well beyond the halfway point between the flight feathers and the arrowhead.

"Now, this is where the physics kicks in. Sort through your arrows. Divide them into those that have their center of gravity closer to the middle of the arrow and those that balance closer to the arrowhead.

"Those arrows that balance close to the arrowhead are going to be heavier overall. As they whip through the air they're going to tilt down and fall shorter than an arrow with a more central balance. These weighted arrows are best for use at close range, as they'll pack more punch. If you use them at distance, you'll find them inaccurate as well as inconsistent with each other.

"Arrows that balance closer to the middle of the shaft will gain lift as they fly through the air, much like an eagle soars without flapping his wings, gliding on the breeze. These arrows will be more accurate at long range, but they're not going to have as much penetrating power. They're ideal for bringing down birds."

Bruce nodded, mumbling in agreement as Hugo spoke.

"But get too close to the middle of the arrow shaft and the flight characteristics will be unstable. It will take a bit of experimentation to find the right compromise. If your center of gravity is behind the middle of the arrow, your shot will fail entirely, flipping the arrow over in mid-air."

"Oh, yeah," Bruce said. "I saw that hunting rabbits with my brother. We'd make our own arrows, but without too much care, and the rabbits would look at us befuddled as our arrows toppled to the ground."

Hugo laughed as he continued.

"If you separate your arrows like this, marking them with reds and yellows to tell you how they rate according to their center of gravity, you'll find your consistency between shots will increase."

"Huh," Bruce replied, genuinely surprised.

"You see, something as simple as understanding the physics around the center of gravity is important."

"Yes," Bruce said, agreeing with him. "I'll give that a try."

And he did.

Bruce spent the next morning carefully comparing his arrows, refining them so they were more consistent with each other and separating them into the two categories Hugo suggested. Some practice shots confirmed the old man's theory and Bruce couldn't wait to try the arrows on a hunt. He went out that afternoon, down by the swamp and caught a pheasant. Hugo was visibly proud to have been some help.

"Not bad for a blind man, hey?" Hugo bragged, biting into a juicy piece of breast meat that night.

"Not bad at all," Jane said.

"Hey, Bruce. I've been thinking. We should make a steam engine."

"A steam engine?" Bruce replied. "What exactly is a steam engine? And why would I want one?"

Hugo laughed. He was clearly enjoying Bruce's easy-going nature and willingness to try new things.

"Well," Hugo began. "Think about your fireplace. All that wood burns, throwing out a nice warm heat, but most of the heat is lost as it goes up the chimney. A steam engine is a way of capturing that heat as energy and harnessing it to do some work.

"Think about the steam that comes off a boiling kettle, it is energetic, whistling as it rises out of the spout. We can control that thermodynamic change from a liquid to a gas and put the steam to work to help us."

"What kind of work?" asked Bruce, curious.

"Well, there are a number of things we could do. I reckon we should go with a turbine steam engine. Yes, that's what we should build. Pistons would be too difficult. They'd require a level of machining precision we just don't have."

"Now, hold on," Bruce said, seeing Hugo had already jumped two steps ahead of him. "What's the point of this thing? What is it going to do for us?"

"Oh," Hugo said, getting back on track. "Steam engines are wonderfully diverse. We could use it to pump water from the stream. We could use it to grind grain in the mill. If we got really sophisticated, we could even use a steam engine to power a cart, pushing it along without a horse."

"Sounds fascinating," Jane said, sitting down beside them.

"But they're dangerous," Hugo said, as though he were recounting some adventurous tale from his youth.

"What isn't?" asked Bruce.

"Oh, we have to be careful," Hugo continued. "We'll need Jane's dad to help manufacture the parts, as the pressures need to be carefully contained or they could blow apart the house."

"OK," Bruce said, chuckling. "You've talked me into it. Sounds like fun."

Jane swatted him. Hugo sensed their banter and laughed.

Nothing ever came of the steam engine, but plenty of planning and discussion surrounded the concept over the following months as Hugo explained the laws of physics to Bruce.

Hugo spoke of Archimedes and Newton as though he'd known them personally.

For Bruce, the idea that technology from the past could be revived in the present was fascinating. He was torn. On one hand, he wanted to build a steam engine out of a sense of nostalgia, if not for practical reasons. On the other, he didn't want to fail. It seemed the vision was too fragile, too precious to risk, and so the engine remained little more than a dream, a tantalizing possibility.

Chapter 05: Autumn

Jane fell pregnant late in the spring, which gave the new year a lift. Hugo was as excited as Bruce. As the months wore on and summer slowly turned to autumn before descending toward winter, Jane glowed with excitement. Her maternal instincts kicked in as she prepared for the birth of their child.

Hugo said she was nesting, slowly tweaking small aspects of the cabin for the arrival of the baby, knitting baby clothes, converting a wooden crate into a crib and clearing out any musty old bedding. Being pregnant, Jane couldn't help out as much on the farm as she once had, putting the burden of preparing for the snow drifts on Bruce.

The past year had been kind. The thick deciduous trees bordering the farm to the north had held the monsters at bay during summer, but with their leaves covering the ground, Bruce had to reinforce the berms and spike pits protecting his fields before winter set in.

A mountain lion had been stalking deer nearby, spraying to mark its territory, leaving the smell of musk drifting across the back plots near the forest.

Bruce was worried the massive beast would find a way through the pits, over the berms and approach the farm buildings. Although the cabin sat in a depression near a stream they had a clear field of view of the various approaches over the low-lying hills. At night, though, a big cat would be dangerous. If a mountain lion got inside the corral or the barn it could kill the livestock. More than likely, a lion would go for the chickens in the pen as the smell probably carried on the wind for miles.

"Be careful," Jane said as Bruce hoisted a saddle from the loft of the barn, positioning it on his horse with a pulley.

"I'll be fine," he said, and he believed it, even though he knew his beliefs made no difference at all. Deep down, memories stirred of the sense of invulnerability he and Jonathan had while marching on Bracken Ridge. They thought the world would fall at their feet, but they were wrong. As Bruce strapped the saddle in place he shook off any doubts, knowing what needed to be done.

"Take one of the farm hands with you," insisted Jane, her arms wrapped around her waist in the cold autumn air. "If you run into any monsters you'll need help."

"The hands are all to the south," Bruce replied. "I'll lose too much time. Don't worry. If I have to, I'll split the work over a couple of days so I'm not exposed around dusk."

"I could go with you," Hugo said. Bruce turned around. Hugo stood slightly to one side of Jane, his blind eyes staring into the distance.

"No offense, Hugo. But if I do run into a mountain lion, what could you do? Act as bait?"

Bruce laughed, resting his hand on Hugo's shoulder and giving it a squeeze. "I've done this a thousand times. It's no big deal. Any cougars in the area won't be too active until winter sets in and they can track deer by sight, following their hoof-prints in the fresh snow."

Bruce hitched the horse to a cart carrying sharpened stakes and pikes.

"I'll be careful."

Jane was silent. He could see her lips pulled tight, her features somber. Bruce kissed her, rubbing his hand through her hair. "I'll be back before you know it."

Although he was heading for the back fields, Bruce took the main track south, heading up the hill before circling around to the north to avoid the cart getting bogged in the soft, muddy ground. The farm stretched for several miles over the rolling hills, hiding the cabin from view, but Bruce was armed with lances and a crossbow.

Lances were particularly effective against the big cats. Much like the wooden stakes, they were sharpened to a point but they were built with barbs, sections intended to snap off once embedded in a monster. Each lance could be used five or six times against an animal, each time inflicting painful wounds before snapping off, leaving the head embedded in the beast. Wounds became infected over time and so the big cats had learned to stay clear of the lances. Unlike wolves and dogs, mountain lions tended to stand off rather than charge in. They preferred to look for an opportunity to pounce and attack swiftly and decisively. One jab from a lance was normally enough to convince them deer was easier game.

Bruce worked through the day, tracing the ditch around the back acres, bolstering and reinforcing any loose spikes, ensuring they faced out at the forest. He kept a wary eye on the trees beyond the fields, watching how the growing shadows flickered with the wind.

It was late afternoon when he found the breach. He was about to head back to the cabin when he spotted a collapsed section of bank. The earth mound had slid into the pit, burying the wooden spikes. The rains must have weakened the soil, causing a mud slide.

The wooden spikes, each of them over ten feet long, had been buried in mud and rocks. Looking at how the ground had settled, Bruce figured the mud slide must have happened a few weeks ago during the heavy rains, but it was the tracks in the soft dirt that caused a chill to run through him. There, in the loose gravel and dirt, were fresh paw prints.

Bruce scurried up the berm, wanting to see where the lion had come from. He could see tracks pacing along the muddy edge of the forest, weaving in and out of the trees. The monster had been circling the farm, looking for a point of entry. Those bloody chickens, thought Bruce. He'd told Jane they weren't a good idea, but she wanted the eggs. He was sure they had attracted the beast.

Bruce unhitched the cart, leaving it partially blocking the muddy track to bar the path of any more wild animals. He mounted his horse. A sense of panic welled up within him. Whereas at first he'd been calm and detached, looking at the intrusion from a practical perspective, now his imagination got the better of him and he worried about Jane. That big cat could be anywhere. With hedgerows separating the empty fields, there were plenty of places for a mountain lion to hide.

Bruce rode hard, whipping his horse, driving it on. He figured the lion would have entered under the cover of night. Mountain lions may have been bigger than man, they may have lost their fear of mankind, but hundreds of thousands of years of evolutionary instinct had honed their hunting habits, demanding stealth from them.

After less than a mile, his horse faltered. Horses might have once been endurance animals, with the ability to sustain a gallop over a mile or more, but that trait had been lost with their increased bulk. Oh, what he would give for a horse from centuries past, one that would carry him on the wind, one that could fly across the fields, but his horse tired, slowing to a walk.

Frustrated, Bruce dismounted and ran on, his crossbow slung over his shoulder, his lance out in front of him.

The horse instinctively followed its master, but Bruce knew that wouldn't last. As soon as the horse got a sniff of that big cat it would flee, probably down to the lower fields. But that was OK, he could retrieve it later. For now, his concern was Jane and Hugo. They should be inside, he told himself. They'll see the big cat coming from a mile away, at least that's what he hoped. Everything will be fine. And yet on he ran, his lungs burning in the still, cold air.

It was a beautiful autumn day and, deep down, Bruce knew they'd both be outside soaking up the last rays of the sun before the winter storms blew down from the north.

Already, a light dusting of snow lay in the shadows, hidden from the failing heat of the late-autumn sun. The tracks of the mountain lion meandered, appearing in the soft mud, disappearing on the hard-packed paths, reappearing for a moment and then fading again. Before long, Bruce had lost the trail, but it didn't matter, he was making a beeline for the farm house. If the mountain lion caught Jane and Hugo in the open they wouldn't stand a chance. Bruce didn't worry about where the cat was, he worried about where it was going. He was sure it was following the scent of the fowl. He had to get back to protect Jane.

Bruce ran hard. His leather boots were not supple, causing blisters to form on his heels as he ran. His boots were fine when farming, but the constant flexing and pounding caused his skin to wear. He told himself it was no more than three miles back to the cabin, but his muscles were sore. The leather strap from his crossbow and quiver cut into the side of his neck. He tried to tuck his collar under the strap, but as he ran the weight continued to wear on his shoulder, rubbing his skin raw.

Mud caked on his boots, weighing him down. The very fields fought against him, holding him back.

In the distance, he could see smoke rising from the cabin. As he approached the brow of the tabletop, coming up to the gentle slope that led down to the farm, his horse bolted to the south, neighing in panic, and Bruce knew the cat was close.

The undulating land had dead spots, dips and contours that could hide a monster. Was the creature ahead of him? Had the animal crouched behind one of the hedgerows? Could it be slinking forward in one of the shallow gullies? His pace slowed. Fatigue set in as a twinge of cramp flickered in his calf muscles.

Bruce paused at the top of the rise, breathing deeply, sucking in the cold air. Barely half a mile away he could see the cabin and smokehouse, the barn and poultry coop, the corral and woodpile.

Hugo was sitting on the porch, facing the warmth of the sun. Jane was walking between the barn and the chickens. Even from where he was, Bruce could hear the animals crying out with anguish in the barn. Jane must have been trying to still them. They could smell the monster, but where was it? Bruce jogged down the hill, hoping he could make it back when his blood ran cold. He could see the mountain lion moving up on Jane from behind the woodpile.

"Get back in the cabin," he yelled, waving his arms as he ran on. "Run! Get back in the house."

Jane turned. She had to have heard him, to have heard something, but his voice must have been indistinct, just a faint cry carrying on the breeze, an echo off the surrounding hills. She looked around without looking up at him. Jane peered along the main trail Bruce had taken to the south that morning. She hadn't seen him coming down the steep hill behind the farm.

The monster stalked her, creeping in from behind the woodpile, keeping her in sight.

"Jane," he yelled, struggling for breath. "Get in the house!"

Hugo was standing. He had stepped off the porch and was facing Bruce. With his keen hearing, he must have recognized both Bruce's voice and the direction he was coming from.

"Hugo. Get her inside." Bruce bellowed.

Jane turned, seeing Bruce running down the hill. He waved toward the house, trying to gesture for her to run, but she seemed relaxed. She could not have known how close the danger was. Jane waved back, frustrating Bruce.

Hugo moved briskly along the side of the cabin, his hand running along the wooden logs, using them as a guide. Jane called out to Hugo. It was impossible for Bruce to know what they were saying, but by facing Hugo, Jane had her back to the mountain lion.

The beast crept closer, stalking its prey, sensing the weakness.

Jane seemed confused. She must have recognized Bruce's voice but not understood his words. For his part, Bruce was struggling to run. His pace had turned to more of a hobble, which may have looked casual and relaxed at that distance.

"Get inside," he yelled. Bruce was trying not to panic, not to say too much and confuse things further. The last thing Jane needed was to panic. If she walked briskly, without running, she just might make it, he figured. At this point, if she ran, the lion would bolt after her instinctively. He could see its tail twitching, its shoulders crouched, its eyes fixed on her.

Bruce dropped the lance. The bulky wooden pole was slowing him down. There was no point in being armed if he was too late to stop the attack. The crossbow would have to suffice.

Bruce slipped and slid on the loose ground as he hobbled down the rough slope, urging his body on, trying to push through the pain and run.

The mountain lion leaped out from behind the woodpile, roaring.

Jane froze.

For a moment, she stared down the big cat.

With fangs bared, the monster dared her to run.

Jane couldn't make either the cabin or the barn, Bruce could see that. His heart pounded in his chest. She did the only thing she could and darted toward the other end of the woodpile, trying to outwit the beast.

The lion pounced, lashing out with its claws, coming within a few feet of her as she scurried between the log piles.

Snarling, the mountain lion swung around behind her, but the muddy row was too narrow for the big cat so it leaped up, straddling the loose wood.

Jane slipped in the soft mud, falling as the lion reached down between the rows, trying to snare her with its claws. Wooden logs fell in on her as the wood pile toppled.

Bruce ran as hard as he could, with his crossbow out in front of him in one hand, ready to bring it to bear as soon as he was in range. With the slope dropping away beneath him, Bruce struggled to keep his footing, feeling the muddy ground slipping out from beneath him. He wasn't going to make it. Deep down, he knew she couldn't escape. He was too far away to help. The lion was on top of her.

The woodpile collapsed under the weight of the monster, sending logs crashing down into the narrow row, pinning Jane beneath the crush of wood. She screamed in agony. The sound of her voice carried on the wind, sending a chill through him as his heart pounded in his throat. His legs faltered. Tripping and stumbling, Bruce struggled not to fall as he leaped down the hillside toward the farm. He was too late, and he knew it.

The big cat reached down with its paws, pulling the logs away to get at Jane buried under the wood. Bruce forced back a lump in his throat.

Hugo yelled, bellowing incoherently at the top of his voice.

The mountain lion reared its head, looking around, growling wildly, baring its teeth.

Bruce wasn't sure what happened next. He reached the corral and ran behind the barn, losing sight of the big cat for a few seconds, but he could hear Hugo yelling over the noise of the cattle panicking in their stalls, lashing out with their legs, trying to break free and flee.

As Bruce came around behind the woodpile, he could see Hugo. The old man had walked out into the open grassy paddock between the cabin and the barn. He was throwing something at the lion, an assortment of small stones and rocks, distracting but not hurting the monstrous creature. Hugo had to be throwing at the sound, as he couldn't see the massive beast before him.

The lion turned on Hugo, leaping from the woodpile, causing another row of logs to collapse in on Jane. The savage beast swiped at Hugo, tearing open his chest with its claws and tossing him across the grass like a rag doll.

"No," Bruce yelled, firing the first of his arrows.

His aim was true, catching the lion up under the ribs, but the brute barely noticed. Taking his eyes off the monster for a second, Bruce loaded a second arrow as he ran, staggering to one side under the pain in his legs. When he looked up he saw Hugo hanging from the monster's mouth, its teeth piercing his abdomen.

Hugo screamed.

Bruce fired again, hitting the beast in the throat, and the lion turned on him, blood dripping from its jaws.

Hugo's body fell limp to the ground as the mountain lion charged at Bruce, its paws digging up clods of dirt as it pounded toward him. There was nothing between them, not more than thirty yards separating them as Bruce struggled with another arrow.

His fingers were cold, his movements clumsy.

The arrow slipped from his trembling hand.

As the arrow fell, tumbling toward the ground, Bruce grabbed at the air, his fingers catching the briefest, fleeting touch of the flight feathers as the arrow slipped out of reach. Before him, the lion roared.

The mountain lion leaped, flying through the air as Bruce ducked, dropping to the ground and rolling to one side. He felt the monster's claws race through the air as the huge beast soared just inches above his head. With deft motion, the big cat turned as it landed, wheeling around on its paws and facing its quarry.

Bruce scrambled to his feet, pushing off the ground and running for the barn. He made for the corner, knowing the giant beast wouldn't be as nimble at turning.

Rounding the side of the barn, Bruce pulled at the wooden door.

The big cat came charging after him.

Bruce ducked inside as a huge paw struck out through the doorway trying to grab him, its claws tearing up the hard wooden floor.

Inside, the farm animals howled in fright. One of the horses had kicked out a support beam, causing the building to sway as the mountain lion charged at the doorway. Wooden planks buckled and splinted as the monster fought to get inside.

Bruce grabbed a pitchfork and drove it hard into the lion's paw. The animal roared in agony, pulling its arm back and yanking the pitchfork out of his hand. The pitchfork caught on the door jamb and came loose, falling to the ground.

The lion was infuriated. Turning its head sideways, it tried to squeeze through the doorway, its teeth biting at the air, trying to break into the flimsy building.

Bruce grabbed a wooden lance and thrust it into the lion's mouth, driving up under the soft palate and twisting, snapping off a barb.

The lion roared in pain, pulling back and shaking its head, trying to free the splinter of wood embedded in its mouth.

Bruce cried out in anger, consumed by rage.

He yelled as he charged at the monster with his lance out in front of him. Bruce aimed for the neck but caught the beast under the shoulder, snapping off another barb under its winter coat, and the mountain lion turned and ran, howling as it vaulted through the farmyard.

Bruce charged off after the animal, screaming incoherently at the top of his lungs, but the lion quickly out-paced him, galloping up the hillside and disappearing over the fields.

Bruce dropped the broken lance.

Exhaustion set in as the rush of adrenalin faded. His hands were trembling. An uneasy quiet fell over the farm. He limped back toward the barn.

A lifeless bloodied arm protruded from beneath the fallen woodpile. The rows in the pile had been stacked over eight feet high, now they lay scattered in a crush of thick logs. There had to be roughly a ton of wood pressing down on Jane's body, and the thought of the pain she endured as she died jarred his mind.

Bile came up in the back of his throat and Bruce fought against the urge to vomit. His body ached, but it was more than physical. A sense of loss overwhelmed him, choking him. Bruce couldn't see her face beneath the press of logs. He couldn't face Jane. He couldn't face seeing her broken body mutilated by the weight of hardwood.

Hugo lay to one side, his body twitching. Somehow, the old man was still alive, barely. Bruce knelt down and took his hand. As much as he was steeling himself for the grim task of recovering Jane's body, he couldn't walk past Hugo.

Bruce felt his body tremble, but he couldn't let go of Hugo's hand, he couldn't leave the old man to die alone in his world of cold, bitter darkness. Bruce hadn't left his brother, he would not leave Hugo. He understood the tragedy of death, the futile struggle in those final moments, the panic and the fear. Life was too precious. He would stay with Hugo until the end. He owed the man that much at least.

Hugo was trying to speak. His lips moved but no words came out. His chest heaved, blood seeped from his wounds.

"It's OK, my friend," Bruce said softly, patting his hand, trying to reassure him. "The monster is gone."

Hugo squeezed Bruce's trembling hand. His fingers were frail and weak. Although no words were spoken, Bruce knew what the old man wanted to hear.

"She's fine."

Bruce lied.

A faint smile came to the dying man's lips. With his life fading, he believed Bruce.

"Jane is OK, she is going to be fine. You did it, my friend. You saved her life."

Bruce felt his mouth run dry. Tears fell from his eyes, running down his cheeks. Looking across at the collapsed woodpile, there was no movement, no sound. Blood pooled in the mud, having run out from beneath the wooden logs. Jane was dead, but he didn't have the heart to tell Hugo his sacrifice had been in vain. Bruce struggled to control his emotions, his chest heaved as he sought to compose himself.

"It's going to be a cold winter," he said, feeling he owed Hugo more than silence. What could he say to a dying man? What comfort could there be? Words failed him. All he could think to talk about was how life would continue on. Perhaps that would be of some comfort. "Next year I'll raise corn in the southern fields as well as the west. The price has been good for corn. If the winter is long and deep it will keep the locusts from coming with the spring."

He swallowed the lump in his throat.

"I'll use the money to bring in some hired-help from the village. We'll fell the woods to the east. Open them up for grazing the following year."

The old man squeezed his hand, signaling his approval. Hugo's breathing was labored. Looking down at his bloodied body, Bruce felt inadequate. What words could ever make up for the loss of a life? What could ever be more important than the sum total of a man struggling against his own death? And yet Bruce felt he had to keep talking, if not for Hugo's sake then for his own. With the world collapsing around him, he had to draw upon something.

"There's been talk of peace with the northern tribes. They say trade will open up again. There's talk they've taken a city and held back the monsters for two years now. Sounds like there could be change in the wind."

Hugo's hand twitched and fell limp. His head sank to one side as his body succumbed to the blood loss. Bruce rested his hand on the old man's forehead, feeling his wrinkled skin already cool to touch. Gently, he lay Hugo's arms by his side.

Shaking, Bruce got to his feet. He stood there for a moment in shock. Slowly, he walked toward the woodpile, his mind set with grim determination to recover Jane's body.

Flurries of snow drifted on the breeze. The sweat that had once cooled the furnace of his body now sent a chill through him. There was no rush, though, no sense of urgency, just a sense of duty. He had to give Jane the respect in death she had earned in life. The task of uncovering her body was daunting, but he owed that to her. He owed both Jane and Hugo a proper funeral, either burial in a pit deep enough that no monster would unearth their remains, or on a funeral pyre, one that would burn for days in memorial. Thinking about it, Bruce decided he'd rather cremate their bodies than bury them, but if the winter was long, he would need all the wood he had. Still, their lives must be honored. It was only fitting.

Bruce began pulling the heavy wooden logs away. His muscles ached as he shifted the wood, carefully selecting each log so the pile didn't collapse any further. It took almost ten minutes to work his way down to where Jane's forearm protruded from between two bloodied logs. Gently, he moved her cold hand to one side, noting how she had fallen, with her arm twisted behind her, almost pulled out of its socket.

Her body lay sideways beneath the debris. As he cleared the logs around her head and shoulders he realized several of the larger logs had fallen above her, wedging themselves across the narrow aisle. Bruce felt like he was going to be sick, but he kept clearing the wood.

The sun slipped below the hills and the cold wind stung his face but Bruce was beyond caring. His broken heart hurt more than any physical pain. He couldn't rest until they both lay safely in the barn.

In the morning, he'd light a bonfire. The thought of a raging fire, defiant against the bitter cold, seemed more dignified, more ceremonious than a burial, a celebration of life rather than a capitulation to death. Besides, the ground would be frozen within a few feet of the surface. It would take days for Bruce to dig a hole deep enough for the two of them. His body was shattered and the thought of so much exertion caused his heart to sink further.

After clearing the logs away from Jane's hips, Bruce gently repositioned her, moving her with care.

Jane groaned.

Bruce faltered, almost collapsing at the sound of her whimper. He staggered, overwhelmed with emotion.

Several of the larger logs had been upended in the avalanche, digging into the soft ground around Jane, forming a crude triangle across her upper torso. They must have borne the brunt of the collapse, he thought, shielding her from the worst of the weight. Another log supported the remaining low-lying portion of the wood pile, forming a shallow bridge over part of her legs.

Jane moaned. Her head rolled slightly to one side.

With a surge of newfound energy, Bruce threw the remaining logs onto the grass, pulling her bloodied, battered and bruised body out from beneath the woodpile. He lay his jacket over her, tears streaming from his eyes as he brushed her matted hair gently to one side.

"Oh, Jane. Jane," he sobbed, repeating her name over and over.

Bruce carried Jane to the cabin. Her body felt frail, fragile, as though the slightest bump would cause more damage than all the wooden logs.

He laid her on Hugo's bed, dragging it over near the fireplace. The fire had gone out, but the glowing coals still radiated warmth.

A sense of feeling returned to his cold hands, and they stung from hundreds of tiny cuts and cracks in his skin, but that didn't matter.

Bruce ran his fingers gently over her arms and legs, checking for broken bones. Skin had been peeled off her leg, revealing her bloody shin. Her right hand had been crushed, with several small broken bones protruding out of her torn skin, but she'd escaped without any major bones being smashed. A large welt had formed on her head. Bruising marred her body, turning her pale features yellow and black.

Being six months pregnant, her stomach protruded noticeably. A large dark purple bruise had formed on one side of her belly, and Bruce worried about their unborn baby, but Jane was alive. For now, that was all that mattered. He made a splint for her hand and wrist, and bandaged her arm.

Bruce stoked the fire, stirring the flames as he added more wood. He heated some water and began gently washing Jane's wounds, cleaning dirt out of the cuts and grazes. Slowly, Jane regained consciousness.

Once he was confident she was going to survive, he left her briefly. Taking a blanket, he went outside and wrapped Hugo's cold, stiff body. He moved the body, placing it in the back of the barn. The cattle stirred as he entered, wary of any movement, but he paid them no attention.

When he returned to the cabin, Jane was awake. She tried to speak, but her mouth was dry. Bruce got her some water and helped her sip from a cup. He took crushed willow bark and boiled it, skimming the scum from the surface and mixing it with a little honey and some dried tart cherries to form a natural painkiller.

Jane chewed on the soaked cherries.

"Where is Hugo?" she whispered, wincing as she looked around.

"I'm sorry," Bruce replied. "Hugo didn't make it."

Bruce told her all that had transpired, how he thought she was dead, about his battle with the wild cat and Hugo's bravery.

Jane cried.

Bruce sat, slowly pulling off his bloodied boots. His feet and ankles had been rubbed raw. He soaked them in salt water, grimacing from the pain, but knowing he needed to keep the possibility of infection at bay.

Jane fell asleep listening to the crackle of the fire, but Bruce couldn't sleep. The wind howled around the cabin, causing the roof to creak, setting his nerves on edge as he wondered about the mountain lion, worrying it would return in the dark. They would be safe in the cabin, but the barn was listing and could fall if the big cat tried to get in after the cattle. If the lion went for the chickens the coop would fare better, at least he hoped so. Eventually, his weary body won the argument and Bruce fell asleep in a chair in front of the fireplace.

When he awoke, the sun was high in the sky. Light streamed in through the thin gaps in the shutters. Outside, snow blanketed the ground.

Winter was setting in. There was much to do. Bruce had to fetch the horse that had fled. He had to repair the breach in the spikes. He had to shore up the barn. Jane told him it was too much, too soon, and Bruce agreed to rest.

It took a couple of days before Jane could walk without help, so Bruce tended to the farm animals. He built a bonfire for Hugo, lighting it at dusk so the flames would lick at the night sky. As the funeral pyre burned, he and Jane talked fondly of Hugo, trying to replace their sadness and loss with a sense of thankfulness for his life.

"How long was he with us?" Jane asked, watching as the flames leaped up at the sky, sending glowing embers floating high on the breeze. "At least six months?"

"Yeah, although it seems more like six years," Bruce said, joking.

"Will you be serious," Jane replied, a scowl on her face.

Bruce smiled.

"Hugo would have laughed."

"Yes," she admitted, her good hand supporting her pregnant belly. "I guess he would have."

She leaned against Bruce, snuggling with him as the warmth of the fire radiated outward. The crackle of burning logs filled the air. Smoke drifted lazily away.

"I feel like we should tell someone. His family ought to know. For all that happened between him and his son, he ought to know how his father died. How courageous he was, giving his life for me."

Bruce didn't reply. He nodded, but a knot formed in his throat and he couldn't speak. As it was, he was fighting back the tears knowing just how close he'd come to losing her as well. It could have been both Jane and Hugo on that funeral pyre, and that realization terrified him.

She squeezed his hand. Feeling the warmth of her fingers in his palm, he turned to her, saying, "I'll send word."

Jane reached up and wiped the tears from his eyes.

Sparks drifted up into the night, seemingly joining the stars above. There was no moon, and the light of the fire caused shadows to dance around them.

"Do you know how big they are?" asked Jane, staring up at the stars.

Bruce was silent. He knew exactly what she was doing, and he knew Hugo would have approved. Rather than hearing a somber, deathly tome, the old man would have been happy to know they went on to talk about the wonders of nature around them.

"The stars look like points of light, little more than specks of sand, diamonds glowing in the sky."

She ran her hand up the inside of his arm as her voice carried softly in the cold night air.

"And yet they are bigger than anything we could imagine. Far, far bigger than Earth itself. Our sun is roughly a million times the size of Earth, and yet the sun is small as far as stars go."

Jane pointed at the grain silo, off in the distance behind the barn, its dark silhouette blotting the horizon.

"Take a cup full of grain, and that's all our little old Earth amounts to when compared with the sun."

"And there are bigger stars?" asked Bruce. "How could they be bigger? They all look the same size to me. Are the brighter ones bigger?"

"The brighter ones are probably just closer, not bigger," Jane replied, staring up at the sky. "If the biggest star was the size of our grain silo, then our sun would be the size of a handful of grain, and the entire Earth would be no bigger than the tiniest speck of dust."

"And yet here we are," Bruce replied, "thinking they're so small."

"All this," she said, "everything we see around us, is just a speck amidst a sea of monstrous stars."

Bruce hugged Jane, pulling her in against the cold. They stood there silently for a while, watching the wooden logs slowly collapsing in on themselves. They left the pyre to burn through the night.

Chapter 06: Birth

Snow flurries swept across the countryside, burying the land.

Bruce finished working on the barn and repaired the breach by the forest before the deep snows arrived.

Jane was worried.

Whereas once the baby within her womb had been quite boisterous, moving and kicking, now the babe lay still. As much as this alarmed Bruce, there were so many other things he had to care for that he lost himself in his duty to the farm. Jane, though, grew depressed. She was sullen and moody. Her zest for life faded.

After a few weeks it was clear she would never regain the use of her right hand. The logs had crushed the same arm she'd injured in the village and she'd lost all feeling below her wrist.

Jane told Bruce there were moments, in the early morning, where she'd get the sensation of pins and needles in her hand and she'd think she was getting better, but her hand remained lame.

Bruce could see how dejected she had become. He offered to make a run to the village and from there on to the library to retrieve some of her favorite books, hoping these would lift her spirits. But it was wishful thinking, and they both knew it. Winter had already set in. Jane showed her thankfulness for his attention by being tender and considerate, but he could see she was putting up a front.

The drifts arrived, but not before Bruce had reinforced the barn and stacked hay bales four wide and six high in a line between the cabin, the barn and the chicken coop.

Once the snow mounted up outside and became hard-packed with the plummeting temperatures, Bruce began removing the hay bales, taking them back into the barn and revealing a snow tunnel between the buildings. He used wooden cross-members to shore up the tunnel every ten feet and poked holes for ventilation.

Snow buried the cabin but melted away around the chimney. Bruce dug narrow culverts on an angle away from the windows, leading up to the surface to ensure adequate airflow and natural light reached them in the cabin.

Winter was unusually cruel and cold, making it impossible to venture beyond the farm, but the snow drifts provided a degree of thermal insulation, keeping the temperatures in the barn around freezing while the outside world plummeted to lows Bruce had never seen before.

On those rare occasions when he braved the surface, he found it hurt to breathe. The air was so cold the wind would burn any exposed skin. But they had plenty of supplies and could make it through the worst of the storms.

Jane's belly continued to swell as the baby grew within her. She said it was a good sign, that if the unborn child had been killed in the crush her body would have rejected it as a stillborn babe by now, and yet the child failed to move.

When her waters broke, Bruce was ready. Jane had schooled him in what to expect, making sure he was well drilled in each of the particulars.

Bruce had seen his older sister give birth, so he knew what to expect, and Jane had acted as midwife for several of the villagers. Ideally, it would have been better to give birth in the village, where there were more women to help, but winter prevented any travel.

Jane fortified herself. Bruce was impressed by her focus and deliberation as the contractions set in. Her labor was long, reaching through the night into the next day.

As dusk fell on the second day, they braced for another long night. Bruce had towels and water handy, along with a knife he could sterilize in the fire to cut the umbilical cord.

As her contractions increased in intensity, Jane squatted, using gravity to assist the birth. She was sweating, breathing in short pulses. Bruce knelt before her as she held onto the arms of two chairs he'd placed on either side of her. She was magnificent, he thought, but he couldn't tell her so. She was in no mood for small talk.

Between contractions she sat back on the edge of a chair, her legs spread apart, and Bruce could see the baby's head crowning.

Jane cried in agony as her contractions increased in intensity.

"Oh, Bruce. It feels like I'm burning up inside," she cried.

"Hang in there," Bruce replied, feeling woefully inadequate. "You're almost there. I can see the baby."

Jane panted as she knelt between the chairs, taking up a crouched position. The baby's head came out and she groaned, fighting the urge to push. She had told Bruce what to do at this point. He had to check to make sure the umbilical cord wasn't wrapped around the baby's neck, strangling the child.

Bruce ran his fingers around the baby's throat as Jane pursed her lips and took short, sharp breaths, fighting against the natural urge to push the baby out.

"All clear," he said. "You're good."

That was all Jane needed to hear. With one last push, the baby flopped out into Bruce's waiting hands. His face lit up with a smile. Jane was too relieved to care in that moment. Her head tilted backwards as she breathed deeply. With a warm, damp rag, Bruce wiped away the thick mucus and fluid from around the baby's eyes, nose, and mouth.

The baby didn't breathe.

Jane looked at Bruce with sadness in her eyes. She feared the worst, he could see that, but he kept a brave face. He turned the baby over, resting its chest in the palm of his hand, his thumb and forefinger supporting the baby's small head.

"Come on," he said, his hand rubbing the child's back, gently patting him, willing him to breathe. Him, he thought, surprising himself with the realization that they'd had a son. The baby spluttered and cried, breathing for the first time.

Jane had tears in her eyes. The look on her face was one of exhaustion and relief. She held out her hands and Bruce handed her the baby, kissing her on the forehead. He clamped and cut the umbilical cord.

"Oh, he's so beautiful," Jane said, peering at the baby in her arms.

"He certainly is," Bruce replied, giving Jane a cloth as she sat down on a stool by the fireplace.

Bruce cleaned up as Jane gave the baby the opportunity to suckle.

"So is he a Julian or a James?" he asked, bringing up the names they'd agreed upon over the last couple of days. Bruce wanted to call the baby James, after his father.

"Neither," Jane said, glowing with a smile.

"Well?" asked Bruce. "Don't keep me in suspense."

"I don't know what suits him yet," Jane replied softly. "But I'll think of something."

"Oh, you will, will you?" Bruce said, coming around beside her and resting his hand gently on her shoulder.

Jane grimaced, leaning forward. She had told Bruce beforehand that the contractions to pass the afterbirth were less severe than those of birth, but they looked even more painful to him. Over the next half an hour, she continued to struggle with what looked like stomach cramps.

When the placenta came out, Bruce placed it in a bucket. Jane had him turn it over so she could see the underside. She used a knife to examine the placenta. To his untrained eye, it looked like a large liver or kidney, although it was clearly more complex than either of those organs.

Jane's stomach cramps continued, and she put the baby down in the small crib she'd made for him, keeping him by the warmth of the fire.

"This is not good," she said.

"What?" asked Bruce, not understanding her concern.

Jane doubled over in pain. A thin trickle of blood ran down one leg.

"What is it?" he asked as she reached out to hold his arm, steadying herself.

"I think the placenta may have torn away part of my uterus."

Bruce wasn't familiar with the term uterus. He'd seen the afterbirth of farm animals and had heard his mother use the word uterus on a couple of occasions. He knew it related to reproduction, but Jane's harsh use of the word caused a chill to run through him. He knelt down with her as she rested on the blankets spread out by the fire.

"Oh," she cried, grabbing at her stomach. "Oh, no."

Blood ran freely.

Bruce was flustered, he didn't know what to do. He grabbed a couple of towels and a blanket, using them to mop up the blood.

The color drained out of Jane's face and she sat slumped up against the chair, her legs apart, blood running out on the floor.

"You're the best thing that ever happened in my life," she began softly, running her fingers through his hair as he padded towels against her, trying to stem the flow of blood. Wiping his hands, he reached up and felt her forehead, even though she was in front of the fireplace, she felt cold and clammy.

"Tell me what to do?" he pleaded, a quiver in his voice.

"Oh, my dear, sweet Bruce," Jane began. She was unusually calm. Her eyelids were half closed as she spoke. "There's nothing you can do. Take good care of our son. Teach him to read."

"No," Bruce said, holding her bloodied hand to his lips and kissing the back of her hand. "Please, don't leave us. Don't leave me."

"I don't want to," Jane said softly, her voice barely audible. "Oh, how I don't want to."

Her eyes looked glazed. Her movements slowed. There was a lethargy to her motion, as though she were floating in water.

"There must be something I can do," Bruce cried, looking around, his mind racing through the possibilities. "There must be some way I can fix this, something I can do to help."

"My dear, there is nothing that can be done. This is one monster from which you cannot save me."

"Oh, Jane. Don't say that. You're going to be OK. Please tell me you're going to be OK."

Jane's head dropped. She forced herself up, struggling to stay conscious.

"Promise me you will teach our baby boy to read."

"I promise," Bruce said, shaking.

Jane slumped to one side, unable to hold herself up.

Bruce padded a blanket, making it into a pillow for her, gently resting her head upon it. She looked up into his eyes. He'd seen this look before—a life fading in the twilight. On Bracken Ridge, he'd seen this same glazed look in his brother's eyes.

"Please. Don't leave me alone. I don't know what to do."

"James," she whispered. "His name is James."

Bruce sobbed, holding her hand to his forehead. Jane's eyes flickered as her hand fell limp. He knelt beside her, his chest heaving in grief. With his fingers pushed up gently against her jugular vein he felt her pulse weaken, grow erratic, and finally stop.

"No," he cried, clenching his fist into a ball.

"No," he yelled, staggering to his feet.

Bruce paced around the cabin screaming, "No. No. No!"

He was distraught. He pulled at the hair on his head, feeling the pain from his pulsating skull. The world around him seemed to narrow, as though he were standing in a tunnel. The cabin was small, too small. He wanted to pace, to walk at length, to run. Bruce rubbed his temples, mumbling to himself as he strode back and forth.

"Oh, please, no. This cannot be happening. Please tell me this is a dream. Let me wake from this nightmare."

The more he paced, the more he felt the muscles in his body building in tension. He picked up a log of wood and began pounding the bench top, trying with all his might to either break the wood or to break the bench. With thundering blows, he slammed the wood down, each time screaming, "No." But neither the bench nor the wood had any give. He could rage all he wanted, but nothing made a difference.

The baby was crying, but Bruce couldn't hear its cries until he paused, his hands throbbing from the reverberation of each blow through the wood.

Bruce stood over the crying baby, looking at James so small and helpless. Tears streamed from the baby's eyes as his tiny hands shook with anguish.

"There, there," Bruce said, reaching in and picking him up. "It's OK. No one's going to hurt you. Everything is going to be fine."

The baby continued to cry, so he bent his index finger in toward his palm, giving baby James the opportunity to suck on his knuckle. It wouldn't suffice for long, but it soothed the poor boy, allowing him to calm.

Bruce sat there, rocking back and forth on the edge of a chair, rocking the newborn baby back to sleep as his mother lay dead just a few feet away.

He put baby James back in the crib and tried to compose himself.

"Please wake up," he said, knelling down by Jane. "Please, just like in the woodpile."

But the touch of her cold, pale, lifeless skin told him there would be no miracle this time. He had to do something, anything. To do something would distract him from the haunting reality of his loss.

Bruce was manic.

He arranged a blanket over against the wall and moved her body there, getting her out of the bloody mess in front of the fireplace. With considerable care, he lay Jane's limp body near the door, placing a pillow under her head.

Bruce wasn't thinking straight, he wrapped her with a blanket, wanting to keep her warm. He turned her face toward the wall so it seemed as though she were sleeping. Then he returned to the fireplace and began cleaning.

Using soap made from animal fat and several buckets of water, he worked fastidiously, with close attention being paid to each subtle detail. Bruce soaked up the blood, cleaned in between the cracks in the floorboards, wiped the bloodied handles of the chairs. It was all he could do. For Bruce, it was either work hard or lie down and die. Through it all, he sobbed, his chest heaving with grief.

The baby stirred.

The water Bruce had boiled earlier was lukewarm. He took a small cup and crushed up a little bread, mixing it with a few drops of goat's milk. Bruce stuck his finger in the milky mixture and tasted. To him, it tasted like nothing more than dishwater, but he hoped it would give baby James something to sustain him.

Bruce changed his son and fed him, dipping his finger in the mixture and letting James suck on his finger. The baby wanted to suck constantly, and sought for his father's finger whenever he pulled it away to get more fluid. It took a while, but the mixture seemed to satisfy the child.

Between feeds, Bruce sat there rocking James, talking with him softly, telling him how wonderful his mother had been and how he would care for him.

At some point in the early hours of the morning, after settling the baby and returning him to his crib, Bruce fell asleep, only to wake with baby James crying as dawn broke.

Hours seemed like seconds. Had it not been for the light slipping between the cracks in the shutters, Bruce would have thought not more than a minute had passed.

Bruce changed James and fed him again, marveling that life could start from such humble beginnings. As a newborn, James was unusually content, such a stark contrast to the turmoil and hurt Bruce felt inside. As he sat there cradling James, he felt the urge to talk, to express his feelings and try to work through the pain he felt tearing at his heart.

"Why has the sun risen?" he began, his rough fingers gently stroking the baby's forehead. "How can a new day dawn while my nightmare continues? Why does light break forth when darkness still surrounds me? Is there no mercy in this world? Is there no compassion?

"The night should not have ended. The day should be dark, black with clouds, not vibrant and bright, ignoring my heartache and tragedy. Am I mocked? Is my heartache ignored? The day dawns, ignoring my pleas to stop and mourn."

Tears fell from his cheeks.

"I should have died on Bracken Ridge ... Jonathan was stronger, faster and braver than me. I guess I was the little brother, always a few years behind. When we marched through the leafless winter trees, neither of us knew how that muddy ridge would change our lives.

"The woods looked so peaceful. Buds broke forth from the twigs. Blossoms awoke, defying the winter.

"We thought we were invincible. We thought the world would bow before us, that our days of laughter and fun would never end.

"Just a foot to the left, and that arrow would have struck me. If they had fired a split second later it would have been my life that ended in a pool of blood and mud that day. And what would Jonathan have made of this world in my stead? Would he have had a desire to read? Would he have courted your mother?"

Bruce sobbed quietly for a few seconds.

"Oh, our lives are as frail as a butterfly in spring. Our days are full of promise and hope, brimming with dreams and joy, and yet there is only ever one end in sight, that of the bitter, cold, dark night.

"I want to return to yesterday. Only yesterday, it seemed as though the sun would never set. Yesterday, I laughed, looking forward to this day, to the day you would first feel the warmth of life. Now, I would give anything to have not seen this sunrise."

Bruce played with his son's hair, gently stroking it one way then pulling it back another as he talked softly to him.

"We pretend things are important, but things never are. It is people that are important. So little really matters in the long run. We live, we work, and we die, but for what? For the chance to allow some light to shine through into this dark world, to brighten the path for those we love.

"Nothing else really matters. Nothing else counts for much. My horse cares not for anything other than its feed. These buildings care not who lives within them. 'Tis you, baby James, it is you that counts for the future.

"Time is cruel. One day blends into another. Days become weeks, months become years. We waste time. Oh, we don't mean to, but we don't realize its true worth. 'Tis no fine painting that is priceless, no marble statue of some lost former glory, no, not even the writings of Shakespeare can be counted as beyond reckoning.

"Time is all there is in this world, but time cannot be bought with the instruments of man. There is no treasure-house crafted from gold or chest full of diamonds that could buy back just one day with my beloved.

"And yet those days, when we frolicked in the leaves, when we huddled to read by a flickering light, shivering in the cold, when we danced and laughed, talked and cried, those days seemed like they would never end. When they were common, they passed with barely a thought, but now, just a fleeting moment is worth more than kings could command. In a moment, those days are gone, while my agony lives on."

Looking into the baby's eyes, he spoke softly. "If it were not for you, I could not go on. For your sake, I will be strong."

Tears streamed down his cheeks. Bruce kissed baby James and settled him back in his crib.

With the winter drifts upon him and the snow piled deep outside, Bruce knew it would be a couple of months before he could cremate Jane's remains. He couldn't stand to see her like this, ravaged by death, an empty shell before him, so he built a wooden coffin, lining it with blankets.

As much as it pained him to do so, he kept the coffin in the barn, up against the north-facing wall where it was coldest. Each day he would check on the coffin, making sure it had not been disturbed, but he could not bring himself to open the lid.

As the snows began to melt, Bruce dug out the corral fence and used the wood as fuel for Jane's funeral pyre. By early spring, the days were warm, but the nights were still below freezing, with the snow still knee-deep on the ground.

The warmth of the fire he lit for Jane did nothing to ward off the chill he felt inside. In the still air, the flames reached up over forty feet, lashing out against the dark, gray sky. Wood crackled as it burned. Sparks drifted on to heaven, yet the cold remained within his soul.

Bruce was numb.

As spring bloomed, Bruce took young James to the village. There was no easy way to deliver the heartbreaking news of Jane's death to her father.

The old man Bruce said should stay with him and work on the forge. The money was good, but Bruce felt committed to the farm. Somehow, deep inside, he felt he owed that to Jane and Hugo.

The next few years were a blur.

Bruce went about his routines with his usual vigor and determination, but at night he felt hollow and empty.

Raising a young child alone seemed to double the workload, and Bruce took James with him everywhere, out into the fields, mucking out the barn, tending to the animals.

The farm hands and insect gatherers living on the fringe of his property were kind, bringing him meals and checking up on him. Bruce wasn't cynical. He appreciated their kindness, knowing they didn't have to drop by, but nothing could fill the emptiness inside.

One day, to his surprise, Jane's father appeared at his door. He'd brought a young couple with him, saying they'd agreed to work on the farm if they could build their own cabin and take a share of the land.

At first, Bruce was taken aback by his father in law's brashness, protesting that the farm had been in his family for generations, but the old man had a point. Bruce had gone from farming thirty fields to raising crops in just seven. Even with the seasonal help in the spring and extra hands during the harvest, Bruce hadn't been able to farm like he once had.

Jane's father said it was important for him to have someone living there with him at the heart of the farm, someone to help repair the barn and break up the fallowed ground in the back acres, or he'd risk losing the farm to the wild. Reluctantly, Bruce agreed.

Simon and Martha initially moved in with Bruce and James, staying with them over the first winter. By this time, James had turned four and was growing more independent and in need of better supervision. Having a woman around the house helped.

In the spring, Bruce and Simon built a second cabin by the stream. Bruce found solace in a sense of purpose and enjoyed the extra work required to build another log cabin.

Simon and Martha were good folk. They had none of the superstitions of the villagers.

Simon would gladly talk with Bruce about the library, and Bruce often found himself lost in his recollections of Jane and Hugo, and the wild

142

and fanciful idea to build a steam engine, and the flight of an arrow, but he was careful not to give too much away about the location of the library.

For Bruce, their friendship was a shallow consolation for his loss as neither Simon nor Martha had the inclination or aptitude to read. They seemed in awe of what little knowledge he had. It was only then, in the fifth year since Jane's death, that Bruce realized he hadn't read anything since the day she died.

There were a couple of books in the house, but they were Jane's books. Bruce had a book on physics that he'd been reading to Hugo, but nothing of his own.

Bruce determined the following year to return to the city library, but somehow he never had time. He'd forget, and then a vague longing would eat away at his mind and he'd find himself daydreaming of the times he spent with Jane and Hugo.

Bruce had to make time to read, he knew that, and yet the journey seemed daunting without Jane. Perhaps there was a little fear there, he thought. He knew the crumbling highway would be haunted by the ghosts of painful memories stirred up from within.

By working hard on the farm, he could crowd out the ghosts and lose himself, lose sight of his anguish and despair. And so Bruce stalled, finding excuses to plan the trip for some other time.

James was nine years old before Bruce realized he'd not kept his promise to Jane. Was it selfishness that had kept him from taking the boy to the library? Was it because he couldn't stand the thought of facing up to his own personal loss? He wasn't sure, but he wanted James to learn to read so he knew he had to push through his lethargy. Jane was right, he thought. Once you read, once you really read and understand, there is no turning back, there is no forgetting. No matter how badly he wanted to, he couldn't let go of the light. Reason was always there, shining in the darkness, even when he didn't want to acknowledge it.

That summer, Bruce set out with James for the village of Amersham. They stayed the night with Jane's father, in the room above the forge.

Young James loved his grandfather. For his part, the old man looked exceptionally healthy for his age and spoiled his grandson.

The journey from Amersham to the library was unusually quiet. Normally, birds filled the wilds with noise, while insects fluttered through the air, but a forest fire had moved through the area a few days beforehand. Smoke drifted lazily from smoldering tree stumps. The smell of death hung in the air. For once, Bruce was glad to reach the outskirts of the city.

Walking through the run-down city with James at his side, Bruce felt none of the apprehension he had during previous visits.

Giant bats hung inside the skyscrapers, rustling and fighting with each other, but that didn't bother him. A bear growled somewhere in the distance, but he felt no fear.

James was excited by the journey, and Bruce became swept up in that excitement. A whole new world was opening up for James, and Bruce could see it in his eyes. For James, the city was the stuff of fantasy and legends.

Although it had been the best part of a decade, the older dogs still remembered Bruce and the younger dogs followed their lead.

Bruce brought some of Jane's clothes. The matriarch of the pack, a bitch Jane had called Cleo appeared to recognize the smell before he opened his backpack. With gray hair around the animal's snout, the old dog sniffed at the bag, nudging it gently.

Bruce pulled out an old dress and rubbed it on the dogs, they seemed to like the scent. Cleo, though, whined. Could it be that Cleo knew? Could it be that from Jane's absence or from the age of the scent she understood Jane was dead?

Several of the other dogs stood off to one side, looking around as though they expected Jane to arrive from further down the road. For Bruce, it was heartrending to see these wild beasts pining for his lost wife.

There were no children's books in the library. Bruce worked his way carefully through the boxes, but someone else must have borrowed them. He left a note, expressing his interest in them, saying he would be back the following month.

James was content to play with a toy truck and a bunch of figurines with movable arms and legs. Any sense of identity had long since faded from the figures, leaving the small dolls devoid of any personality, but that didn't seem to bother James.

Bruce found he couldn't read. Reading held such an association with Jane in his mind that to sit there with a book open left him heartbroken. He tried flicking through the laminated pages from a couple of newspapers and reading about what had once been current affairs, but the names were unknown to him, the places meaningless. "Pope Augustus in Vatican City," it was little more than a jumble of letters arranged in a row. Jane had taught him to become immersed when reading, but now he felt detached. Reading was laborious.

Bruce felt awful. He felt as though he had betrayed Jane, but his eyes just wouldn't run along the page in a coherent manner. When he got to the end of a sentence, he found himself wondering what he'd just read.

Bruce and James slept in the library. In the morning, Bruce determined to make a fresh start, to put the past behind him. He had to stop feeling sorry for himself, but that was easier said than done. He thought about Hugo and his fascination with physics and it gave him an idea.

"Have I ever told you about slingshots?" he asked young James.

"No."

"We're going to make a giant slingshot. You're going to love this. Your mother wouldn't approve. She'd say it was too dangerous. But I suspect even she'd think it was fun if she saw what I have in mind."

With wide eyes, James followed Bruce out of the library. They spent the morning foraging for parts in a rundown department store and a mechanic's garage. It was late in the afternoon before they finished piecing together the disjointed parts.

The sun was low on the horizon.

The dogs had been gone for most of the day, but with sunset approaching, they returned to their den in the collapsed ruins of the fast food restaurant next to the library.

"Perfect timing," Bruce said, cranking the ratchet of a manual engine hoist working a block and tackle. The slingshot he'd devised stretched out between a crumpled lamp post and traffic light. Being comprised of a series of car tires linked together with loops of steel chain, the slingshot groaned under the strain of the pulley.

"Stand well clear," Bruce said to James. "Your Uncle Hugo would have been a bit more precise with the design and would have understood the tensions and pressures involved, but for me, this is a bit of guesswork. All I know is this baby is ready to fly."

One of the dogs was standing nearby, looking on with curiosity. In the center of the slingshot sat a truck tire.

"Here we go," Bruce said, flipping the stainless-steel quick-release.

The dog flinched as the slingshot whipped forward, sending the truck tire flying into the distance.

"Woo hoo," James yelled, caught up in the excitement.

The tire soared sixty feet in the air, clipping the side of a building before falling to the ground and bouncing along the boulevard.

The dog's ears pricked. The hair on its back was raised in alarm. Its muscles tensed as its head darted back and forth between watching the tire skid down the road and turning back to look at Bruce.

"What are you waiting for," Bruce cried, raising his arms in the air. "Go. Go!"

The dog flexed and bolted, chasing after the tire. With its head down, the massive beast ran in hard for the kill, tackling the tire as it slid to a stop in the next block.

James laughed, jumping and calling out with excitement. "Do it again. Do it again."

Bruce smiled. He hadn't had this much fun in years.

The rest of the pack saw the first dog returning triumphant with the tire between its teeth, and began milling around the intersection, sniffing at the slingshot. For Bruce, the attention of so many dogs was still a little unnerving. Jane had always been so confident around them, and they seemed to sense that and respect her. Bruce, on the other hand, could never get used to the stench of their breath, their large canine teeth and lean muscular bodies. They were monsters, not pets, and try as he might, he couldn't drop his guard quite as easily as Jane.

The dog with the tire strutted over toward Bruce, holding the tire between its massive jaws. Bruce reached up and tried to pull the tire out of its mouth, but the massive beast wasn't finished with its artificial prey just yet.

"Come on," Bruce said, pulling on the tire. Saliva dripped from the dog's mouth. A low growl said, mine. That was enough of a cue for Bruce. He let go and started looking around for something else he could fire off down the street only to hear the tire falling to the pavement behind him. He turned, looking back at the dog as it stood there panting.

"I suppose you think that's funny," he said to the animal.

"Come on, Dad," James said, grabbing the tire and dragging it over to the slingshot. "Let's do that again."

A couple of the dogs stood right in front of the slingshot, and Bruce found it difficult to shoo them away. Eventually, he fired again and the dogs bolted, thundering down the street, tearing up the crumbling concrete as they each scrambled to reach the tire first. They fought with each other, pulling at the tire, fighting over it as though it were a bone.

One of the younger dogs made a break with the torn remains of the tire hanging from his jaw. The others followed hard behind. As they pounded down the street, Bruce became acutely aware of how easy it would be for the two of them to be crushed in the stampede. He grabbed James and pulled him behind the sandstone stairs leading up to the library and hid as the dogs came charging up to them, howling and barking. Sure enough, the dogs overran the slingshot in their excitement. They rolled, play fighting with each other, only their play fighting would have crushed a man. Jane would not have approved, but Hugo would have loved it, he thought.

"That's probably enough for one day," Bruce said.

"Aw," James replied.

They retired inside the library for the night, leaving the dogs to play with the tire. A couple of the dogs started chewing on the tires that made up the slingshot. Bruce tried to shoo them away, but they were too pumped up. Oh well, he thought, there were plenty of tires at the abandoned garage. He could always rebuild the slingshot.

That night, Bruce started teaching James to read. Although there were no children's books, he'd pretty much memorized The Cat in the Hat.

During the day he'd found a stack of aging paper inside a broken computer printer. After trimming and sharpening some burnt wood, Bruce and James made their own book, The Dog in the Library, using the charcoal as pencils. Sitting there in the gas light, they drew pictures rougher than any cave painting, writing silly rhymes beneath them. James loved it.

Over the next few days, Bruce taught the young man the discretion and valor of past ages, teaching him about historical figures like Washington, Jefferson and Lincoln, along with the heroes of past wars, General George Patton, Chesty Puller and Hugh Thompson.

James was fascinated by war, as most young men were, and Bruce explained how it was natural to overlook the horrors of battle. He told him about his brother, Jonathan, and the battle on Bracken Ridge, removing any possibility that war was anything other than a waste. War was a necessary evil, nothing more, nothing less.

Back on the farm, everything seemed lighter. Life seemed easier. James still had a glow about him. Bruce found a renewed sense of vigor. In teaching James to read he discovered the joy of learning himself. Perhaps this is what Jane had felt when she taught him to read. If so, he could understand why her eyes would light up when his began to glaze over. There had only been so much he could take at one time, but she had seemed indefatigable, and now he understood why.

The sun was high in the sky.

Sweat dripped from his brow.

A light breeze blew from the west, but it was humid and muggy, giving no relief from the heat of a summer's day.

Bruce was setting a fence post when the eagle struck. He'd been thinking about Jane, but not in a morose way. Since he'd begun teaching James to read he'd seen Jane's life in an entirely new light, appreciating all she'd given him.

With newfound resolve, he dug into the stony earth with his spade, working around a buried rock, trying to pry it loose. Bruce had to dig down a couple of feet before setting the post. Even then, fence posts were more of a guide for the cattle than a cage. The huge lumbering beasts could easily knock them over. But there was something about being fenced in that cattle responded to, somehow they found comfort in being enclosed. They were skittish in an open paddock, but a fence calmed their nerves, even though it was the spikes and pits that kept them safe from monsters, not low wooden fences.

The eagle struck with a sense of ferocity that took his breath away.

The pain that surged through his shoulders caused his whole body to spasm. Somehow, he kept hold of the spade. His fingers locked into a fist around the handle.

At first, Bruce had no idea what had happened. It felt like someone had hit him across his upper back with a lump of wood, but as his head hung down he could see his legs being dragged along in the dirt. Bruce found himself hurtling along parallel with the ground. His feet splayed beneath him, catching clods of dried mud, kicking up dust as he struggled to free himself.

A dark shadow blocked out the sun.

Vast wings pumped up and down, beating at the air.

Blood seeped through where the talons pierced his shoulders.

Slowly, the eagle gained height. Bruce swung wildly, trying to free himself as the hedgerows passed beneath his feet. He could hear someone screaming, but he never realized it was he himself. In some regards, it was as though his mind was operating on two levels; his base survival instinct took over from the sheer paralysis gripping his mind.

Bruce fought, struggling in vain as the eagle banked, turning and climbing higher in the sky, above the fields, beyond the meadows, high over the treetops.

He knew what the winged beast would do next. He'd seen this years beforehand, when one of his father's hands had been taken by one of the monstrous birds. As the eagle reached the low-lying clouds it would release him, dropping him to his death. Then the massive raptor would feast on his carcass, taking his remains back to its nest in the cliff-tops to feed its young.

The wind whipped by him. The eagle fought to climb higher, struggling with his weight. In the distance, Bruce could see the farm buildings.

James was outside, running madly up the hill toward the fields. That he would see his father die in this manner, torn apart by a wild beast, hurt Bruce more than the talons cutting through his back and chest.

Simon was with James. Bruce could see Simon had a crossbow, but at this range he'd never hit the monster. Even if he got close, he was more likely to hit Bruce than the eagle.

With each beat of the massive wings, the ground receded further. Bruce felt a lump in his throat at the realization that this was all his life would amount to, all he would be remembered by. His life, his memories, the love he shared with Jane, the books they had read, the son he had raised, for him, all that would come to an abrupt end.

The barn appeared so small below him. What had once seemed so large had been given an entirely new perspective, as though a doll's house had been laid out before him.

Bruce could see the corral, the wood pile, the silo and the log cabins. Thoughts raced through his mind. How could life end like this? Life was so cruel, so unfair.

Fear welled up inside him.

Vertigo swept over him.

A tingling sensation ran through his legs at the expectation of plunging hundreds of feet to the hard-packed earth.

James was screaming. Although Bruce couldn't make out what he was saying, the boy's voice carried on the wind.

Rage swelled within Bruce. He had no more than a minute to live, perhaps just seconds before the bird dropped him and he plummeted to his death, but he had to go out fighting.

The initial shock of being snatched from the fields passed, and now self-preservation demanded action, regardless of how futile it might be.

Bruce swung the spade up, catching the eagle on the side of its breast. The spade glanced harmlessly off the dense muscle tissue, doing little more than knocking a couple of feathers out of place.

The giant bird responded by squeezing its talons, crushing his collar bone and sending pain searing through his body.

Bruce reached up with his left hand, grabbing the bird's leg just above its talons, and held on tight, striking again with the spade.

The eagle opened its talons, releasing him.

Instead of falling, Bruce found himself hanging beneath the eagle, holding on to the bird's leg. With his right arm, he lashed out, jabbing with his spade, driving hard into the soft abdomen of the giant bird.

The eagle swooped, dropping to one side, and plunged toward the ground for a few seconds, trying to shake him loose.

Again, he lashed out with the spade, striking at the bird's tail and drawing blood. The eagle leaned down, turning its head back beneath itself so it could strike at him with its beak, but Bruce found he could shift his weight. Swinging and squirming, he flexed his body, shifting his center of gravity, causing the bird to struggle in flight.

With its free leg, the eagle scratched at his forearm, tearing long gashes in the skin, cutting into the muscle.

Blood sprayed across his face.

Bruce struck at the free talon with his spade, swinging with all his might. He caught the base of the leg, carving out a clump of feathers.

The bird reacted, stuttering in the air as it twisted and banked.

The massive eagle dropped into a dive, screaming in toward the ground as Bruce struck at its tail feathers, hacking away at the monster with his spade, using it like an axe. The giant bird pulled up just a few feet from the ground and swooped over a hedgerow, trying to catch him in the branches and tear him free. The ground whipped by beneath him, just a blur on the edge of his vision.

Bruce let go as he cleared the hedge and rolled on the ground, kicking up dust. The spade went flying from his hand.

As he lay there, his body racked with pain, a dark shadow blotted out the sun. The eagle screeched as it came in for the kill, its wings outstretched, its sharp, bloodied talons leading it on.

Bruce rolled on the ground, seeing the monstrous raptor descending on him, its eyes dark with vengeance.

The spade was too far away.

With its wings beating at the air, the eagle's bleeding underbelly was exposed. Suddenly, Bruce saw an arrow embed itself deeply in the side of the eagle's ribcage. Another followed, striking its abdomen.

The bird pulled back, flapping its wings frantically as it pulled out of its attack and changed direction. Another arrow struck the eagle in the neck. The bird of prey turned and fled, blood dripping from its side as it sought the refuge of the skies.

Simon was standing less than twenty feet away, reloading and firing as fast as he could, but his last arrow fell short, missing the eagle as it moved out of range. James came running in to his father, smothering him, shielding him instinctively, but the danger had passed.

Simon and James helped Bruce back to the farmhouse where Martha tended to his wounds.

It was several weeks before Bruce felt strong enough to undertake even light chores around the farm.

James was overly protective. For the young boy, the eagle attack was a formative moment, they could all see that.

Bruce assured James he was fine, that he'd recover, but from that day on, James never looked at his father as indestructible again.

Over the next decade, as James grew into his teenage years, he remained focused and supportive of his father but he also became strong-willed and independent. Bruce told him he had nothing to prove, but his words fell on deaf ears.

Bruce tried to assure his son he was fine, but he never recovered fully from the attack. His back healed, but his collarbones never set properly. They became malformed, sloping sharply to his shoulders.

James told his father he struggled with the idea that one day he'd lose him to another monster. Perhaps not an eagle, maybe a bear or a wolf.

Bruce tried to assure James he was fine, but he could see the doubt in his son's eyes. As he grew older, James would defy Bruce and Simon by going off hunting alone.

Bruce feared for his son. He'd seen this level of exuberance and hubris only once before in his life, while marching upon Bracken Ridge.

BOOK TWO

WRITERS

Chapter 01: Fool

James was nineteen. He was breathing hard as he moved onto the ridgeline above the snow-clad forest.

In the crisp cool air his breath formed a light fog as he exhaled, confirming the direction of the morning breeze. He was upwind from the stag and moving around behind it. If the animal continued in the same direction he'd first seen it moving, along one of the rocky paths running parallel to the ridge, then it was following an animal trail west, around the peak, toward the plains below.

It was early spring in the valley, but snow still blanketed the mountains. The trees around him looked like dwarf varieties, barely six to eight feet high, all perfectly uniform, in the shape of a cone. They had been buried by the drifts, the snowstorms that ravaged the land during winter. In reality, these trees were fifty to sixty feet high, James knew that from his summer hunts. But for now they lay buried beneath the treacherous snow and ice.

To stray too close to one of these idyllic Christmas trees was to risk injury or death by falling down through the branches under the compacted snow. Even with his snowshoes on, spreading his weight across the soft surface powder, sections of snow would occasionally collapse beneath him, subsiding two to three feet at a time as the snow settled.

Crossing an open snowdrift was often the most dangerous act of all, as the shorter trees hidden beneath the smooth, flat expanse of snow would weaken the surface. It was like stepping on thin ice, although there was no ominous crack to warn you of the danger that lay below. For James, though, this was the only way to cut off the stag. The huge beast couldn't negotiate a drift. It would have to circle the peak, and that gave him time to set an ambush.

James loved his father, even if he was too conservative. His father taught him to follow subtle indentations running through the snow, as these were the signs of worn animal paths dusted with fresh powder. The wolves in particular, could smell the pine trees beneath the snow and had learned to avoid these deadly traps. There were a few small paw prints crisscrossing the open ground before him, probably from foxes, so James followed these, weaving his way across the open space, keeping his head low as he crossed the crest of the ridge.

Although the temperature was below zero, James was sweating in the still air. The bright morning sun reflected off the snow, causing him to squint. He opened his shirt, exposing the skin on his chest to the cool air. Sweat wasn't good. Any stray scent could betray his presence. He'd had a dry-bath before dawn, rubbing pine needles and dried leaves under his arms and around his groin to mask his smell.

The villagers had already seen at least one black bear in the forest below, but James was counting on the snow to keep them at bay.

The bears were the worst of the monsters. Where once they had rivaled the height of a man when rearing up on their hind legs, now they towered above the tallest of men, reaching up to fifteen feet and weighing in at upwards of eight hundred pounds. And they were deceptively quick, capable of outrunning a man over a hundred yards. Beyond a quarter mile, though, they lost interest, not having the stamina to sustain the chase. The accepted wisdom was that within a hundred yards, they'd run even the fastest of men into the ground. Bears were faster uphill than down, something James found curiously counterintuitive given how quickly he tired on an uphill run.

His father said it was because of their metabolism. He told James he'd seen a bear kill five men after being shot through the heart with an arrow. James had exclaimed, how is that possible? His father told him the bear had been fatally wounded, but its strength and prowess were such that it could fight on regardless, running the men down and killing them before succumbing to its own wounds.

Bears were lazy—opportunistic was the term his father had used. After coming out of hibernation they tended to stick to the valleys. Hunting above the snow line, James thought he should be safe, but by cooling his body and dulling his scent he was being particularly cautious. His father hated him hunting alone and would insist on coming along or would plead with him to go with a group, but James was a loner. Even a small group of hunters made a lot of noise and left a lot of signs, scaring the prey and making the hunt longer.

Long hunts were dangerous hunts. There was something about teaming people up that dulled them down, convincing James he was better off alone. If he was going to die in the jaws of a bear, he'd rather it was through his own stupidity than because of someone else's carelessness. Still, his father would insist on hunting with him, and James enjoyed his company, learning from his forest-craft, but the old man wasn't as nimble as he once had been before the eagle took him. He couldn't venture as far or as wide, and so James would hunt on his own.

James would sneak off alone, terrifying his father, but always returning home after a few days. As far as he was concerned, he was invincible.

As he crossed the snow-bound ridge, James picked up the trail of the stag again. The deer was avoiding the heavy snow laid down by the drifts, following the leeward trails where the snow was thin. He'd seen the beast at a range of several hundred yards, too far for a shot, and had to get closer.

His father used a crossbow that was good at that range, but James preferred a long bow, relishing the tension of the string beneath his fingers, and the subtleties that allowed for greater control and accuracy with each shot.

The long bow took more discipline, required more consistency, but gave greater satisfaction. His arrows were good up to a range of a hundred and fifty yards, but lacked accuracy at that distance, and a wounded animal could bolt for miles, going on for days before succumbing to a clumsy wound. No, unlike the other boys in the nearby village, James wouldn't risk a lazy shot.

The thrill of the hunt lay in stalking prey, in outwitting them and positioning for the best shot, in making a clean kill. And, besides, the spill of blood would attract wolves. With a quick kill, he'd have time enough to field-dress the beast, carve off its hind flanks and leg muscles before the wolves began to circle.

The wolves, though, had learned to leave hunters alone. There was plenty of meat for everyone. No one needed it all, and the wolves understood an easy feed was better than a hard kill, one in which they'd lose at least some of their pack. It was a tacit agreement between species. An easy meal provided safe passage. But like an angry landlord, if the wolves arrived early, before the deer had been carved, they'd demand all they found. Time was of the essence, as wolves were intelligent.

Powdered snow kicked up beneath his snowshoes, spraying lightly in the air with each long shuffle as James worked his way around the peak.

He caught a glimpse of the stag below. It had at least twelve points. It was an old male. The meat would be tough but full of flavor. No one would believe him about the size of the horns, and if he hadn't been so stubborn as to hunt alone he could have had someone else carry them back to gain bragging rights, but it was the meat that was important, not his ego.

The stag stopped at the edge of a clearing below. A large tree had fallen and gouged out the snow on the steep slope, clearing away the hillside for several hundred yards and exposing loose shale. The stag could smell something on the breeze. The animal stood proud, its head erect, sniffing at the air, but it wasn't James it was smelling as he was downwind.

James pulled an arrow from his quiver. Its brilliant red flight feathers would provide him with a visual marker, allowing him to track its flight and understand any thermals or wind in the valley below. The stag was roughly a hundred yards down the slope. James would have preferred to get closer, but the stag skittered and danced, kicking up powdered snow as it trotted, looking around, smelling danger on the wind.

James would have to ensure his first arrow was on target. He'd get time for a second, but not a third.

The stag turned away from him, looking down the valley, giving James a clear line of sight at the heart and lungs. From this angle, he could strike in front of the rear leg, up under the stomach so the arrow could penetrate beneath the ribs and pass through into the animal's chest. The shot would be fatal, but the stag could run for the best part of a mile before dropping.

James steadied himself. Kneeling on a rock, he took aim, pulling back on the bowstring with three fingers. He kept his wrist straight, in line with his hand so as to keep the tension in his hand to a minimum and allow him to relax into the shot. His father didn't like the three-fingered hold, preferring a pinch-grab, telling him the three-fingered approach tended to pull to the right on release, but James found it easier to retain pressure while lining up his shot. He breathed deeply, exhaling and relaxing, releasing the bowstring at the bottom of his breath, while his lungs were empty and his body was naturally still.

The arrow shot out in a flash, sailing away, arcing through the air but the deer reacted, jolting with its feet and staggering to one side.

The deer had been spooked by something else, something on the far side of the clearing, further down the hill.

James watched as his arrow sailed to within half a foot of the startled animal as the deer broke to one side, moving for the cover of the trees. Had the deer remained still, James would have struck the massive animal just in front of its hindquarters, right on target. He already had a second arrow up and drawn, ready to fire, but the stag was gone. He could hear the beast bolting through the trees further down the gully.

James released the tension on his bow and looked carefully into the shaded forest beyond the clearing. There, on the far side of the gravel and ice, he could see the slow lumbering outline of a black bear moving through the tree line.

James pulled back on his bowstring and took aim. At this distance, an arrow would barely penetrate a bear's thick hide, if he hit it at all.

Although the bear's coat was thick, it would have lost most of its fat during hibernation and hopefully would be in no mood for a prolonged chase. At best, James would simply annoy it, but he was mad, this bear had spoiled his hunt and caused him to lose at least two months' worth of cured meats.

With the sun moving high in the sky, the day was lost. James aimed for the bear's ass, wanting to give it a good spanking. It was silly, and he knew it. To fire and expose himself was dumb. Although he was safe enough, he figured, as the loose rock would slow the bear's ascent after him, allowing him to flee, but why inflict a punitive wound? Why exact revenge for his anger? What would it accomplish? Nothing. And so he eased his pull, muttering under his breath before laughing quietly to himself at the absurd notion of even thinking about taking on a bear alone.

The bear sniffed at the breeze. It had picked up the scent of some other game further down the valley. The monstrous animal broke into a gallop, which startled James.

The bear bounded off over the hard-packed snow further down the mountain. James picked his way forward beneath the peak. He was foolish to follow a bear, and yet he was curious at what it was chasing. He moved lower down into the valley, away from the snowdrifts on the mountain top, to where the snow lay only ten to fifteen feet deep. In some places, where the trees were thick, sections of ground could be seen, covered in dead

162

branches and pine needles. James avoided those spots, as they'd damage his snowshoes.

Coming down behind the bear was risky, but he was still downwind and the monster was distracted. Adrenaline pumped through his veins as his mind calculated the risk.

James caught sight of the bear making its way slowly down a rough patch of exposed rock, winding around a low cliff face. It had spotted something in the gorge leading into the valley proper. James figured it had to be an easy kill, as the bear wasn't in too much of a rush, and he wondered if the wolves had brought something down and the bear was moving in to scavenge.

It was then he saw her, lying in the sun beneath a standing dead pine, lifeless branches littering the ground around her. The snow covered rocks were stained red with blood. She was clutching at her leg. Even though he couldn't make it out at this distance, James knew what had happened, she had stumbled into a bear trap. But who was she? Why was she out here alone? What was she doing so far from any of the villages of the plain?

He lost sight of the bear as it disappeared behind a rocky outcrop. The monstrous animal would be upon her within minutes. She didn't stand a chance. But what could he do? He had a long bow, not a crossbow, even if he wanted to help, he couldn't. It would take most of the men in the village to bring down a bear this size, and even then, they could lose several men in the process—it just wasn't worth the risk for one life.

"HEY," he yelled, seeing the bear emerge from behind the rocks, calling out to the animal before his mind had properly processed what he was doing or what he thought he could accomplish. It was stupid, foolhardy. Had his father been there, he would have scolded him.

"Over here," he yelled, waving his hands as he ran out from the trees to the top of the low cliff.

The woman looked up, seeing both James and the bear. She fought to free herself from the bear trap, but with a bloodied leg she wouldn't get far before the monster caught her.

The bear looked around lazily before turning back to its prey. The lumbering beast padded over the snow down toward a small creek running with melting ice. On the other side of the creek, the woman strained to pry open the jaws of the bear trap. In the still air, James could hear her crying out in pain as she fought to open the teeth of the steel trap.

James dropped his pack on the rocks, pulled out six arrows and stuck the arrowheads into the soft snow. He knelt and fired the first, aiming for the armpit of the huge animal, praying his shot would have force enough to penetrate into the lungs, or perhaps to strike an artery.

The angle was wrong. The first arrow glanced harmlessly off the side of the bear.

James cycled rapidly through the rest of the arrows.

The second flew high and to the left, but it caught the bear on the side of the head, just behind its jaw, causing it to roar with pain.

The third was on target, sinking deep under the armpit.

By the time James fired the fourth, the bear had turned to face him. Rising up on its hind legs, the monster roared at him.

James was tempted to go for a heart shot, but the rib-cage and chest muscles were as thick as armor. A neck shot would cause massive bleeding, but this was a male bear, with a thick fur coat protecting its neck from fights with other, rival males.

In that split second, James settled on the groin. The arrow wouldn't kill the bear, but he was never going to be able to kill this bear and he knew it. He was buying her time. At least with a shot to the lower abdomen he was assured of a good hit. The fur was thinner there, and stomach wounds were notorious for infection. The bear might not die now, or in the next few days, but within a month it would be either sick or dead.

His fifth and six shots struck low on the bear's body and the beast roared with anger before falling back to its four paws and pounding up the snow covered hill toward him.

James stood, looking over at the woman. From where he was he could see she was a teenager, not much older than him. She was yelling something, but he couldn't make out what she was saying over the roar of the bear. Finally, her voice registered.

"RUN! RUUUUUUNNNN!"

The bear pounded up the mountain, but not directly toward him. It had to round the rocks before it could cross the top of the cliff to catch him. James dropped his bow and quiver, even though there were four more arrows he could have fired.

With its shorter front legs, the bear made easy time up the slope and had closed the gap to within fifty yards.

James ran.

His snowshoes were cumbersome uphill, demanding wide, long strides when he wanted to pound as hard and short as he could to make more ground. He darted through the trees, and up over a small rise. His heart was pounding in his chest. His lungs were burning as he sucked in the cool air around him.

Behind him, he could hear the bear tearing through the thicket, breaking branches and snapping deadwood beneath its weight.

The black bear roared and James felt as though the monster was already on top of him.

His snowshoes caught on loose rocks and branches, causing him to falter.

At the clearing, James rushed out onto the loose rocks and ice only to lose his footing and slide several feet down the side of the slope.

A deep bellow shook the woods. The bear lunged, seeing its quarry lying helpless.

James struggled with his snow shoes, pulling them from his boots. He looked up as the bear bounded through the trees, kicking up the powdered snow behind it.

James turned and scrambled on, using his hands and feet to clamber over the loose terrain as the bear came crashing through the trees and into the opening behind him. His right leg slipped, pushing a small avalanche of rocks and ice free and causing him to slide again.

James looked back over his shoulder. The bear was no more than fifteen feet away, tearing up the rocks between them. Blood ran from its torn cheek, dripping from its mouth. The monster's eyes seethed with anger, its teeth were bared, snarling. The bear lunged at him, landing on a loose patch of ice that gave way beneath the creature's weight, causing the massive beast to slide down the hill.

James slid helplessly down after the bear, falling with the wave of rocks and stone and ice knocked free by the animal.

He found himself crashing into the huge beast as it fought with its legs to steady itself during the slide.

The bear stank of piss and shit. Its breath was warm and fetid, its fur matted and coarse.

James pushed off the bear's hide, grabbing at the rocks sliding past and scrambling to free himself from the tangle of wild bear. He felt a rush of wind as the bear's paw lashed out at him, trying to grab his head, but that motion threw the bear off balance and it rolled further down the slope.

James darted to one side, scurrying upwards as the loose rocks and shale slipped beneath his feet. He made for the far tree line, hoping to find firmer footing there. For all its efforts to catch him, the bear slid further away.

James made it to the trees and paused, catching his breath. Looking back, he could see the bear had reached the base of the rock slide and gained its footing. It charged around the base of the rocks, intent on coming up the side to catch him. There was nothing James could do but to press on and hope he could out-distance the bear. He couldn't outrun a black bear. His only chance lay in the huge beast wearying itself with the chase. He hoped the monster would use up what little of its winter store of energy was left and lose interest in him.

The slope steepened. The large pines gave way to smaller trees, clinging to the side of the embankment, forcing James to climb hand over hand up the side of the mountain. The bear fought on behind him, roaring after him. With his muscles aching and his hands stinging from the cold, James pushed on, hoping the near vertical climb through a thicket of smaller trees would deter the bear, but it only seemed to enrage the animal more as it fought to stay with him.

James climbed up on the crest of the mountaintop, just below the peak, and looked out across the deceptively dwarf pines spread out before him, buried by the drifts that had fallen with the prevailing winds. Without his snowshoes, it was suicide to cross the deep snow, but the bear would not relent. The monster was barely ten feet behind him, tearing at the trees and rocks as it clambered up after him. On the flat table-top, the bear would easily outrun him, its wide paws spreading its load, allowing it to manage the deep drifts far better than James.

James could see the trail by which he'd stalked the deer. He ran over, wanting to link up with that track, knowing it was a safe path above the treacherous drift.

The snow gave way beneath him, and he found himself sinking into the soft powder up to his thighs. Twisting sideways, James launched his legs up, fighting not to sink more than waist-deep into the soft snow with each bound. Although he was running, the snow reduced his pace to a dawdle and James found himself peg-legging, vaulting up over the surface of the snow only to sink in with each step.

The bear mounted the summit behind him and roared with delight, seeing him barely thirty feet away. It charged, sinking no more than a foot or so with each bound. Within seconds it would be on him and he knew it.

Fear pumped adrenaline through his veins.

The only chance he stood was with the trees.

James changed his tactics, breaking to the right, over toward a clump of treetops barely rising above the deep snow.

The bear pounced, kicking up the fine, white powdered snow as it lunged at him. James was moving too slowly. With each driving step he sank further into the drift. He dove forward, lying prostrate on the snow, spreading his weight so as to not sink further.

James scrambled using his arms and legs, but even this saw him swamped in fine powder. He floundered forward, toward a low treetop as the bear came crashing down just inches from his leg.

They were too close to the tree.

Instead of fifty feet of packed snow built-up solid beneath them, there lay a thin sheet of snow over the burgeoning tree canopy.

Beneath the snow, the mat and tangle of the pine tree spread out, reaching wider as the fall went deeper, leaving the snow close to the treetop as little more than a fragile shell.

The crisp upper layer of snow caved in beneath their combined weight, sending them both plunging through the branches underneath the drift.

As they fell through the snow, the cone shape of the tree opened out below them, as it was comprised mainly of flimsy twigs and leaves. Both bear and man plunged into the darkness.

James reached out, grabbing at the branches and limbs as the bear plummeted past him, falling headlong beneath the tree, roaring as it fell to the ground with a sickening thud.

Chapter 02: Nightfall

Night had fallen by the time James made it back to the cliff face overlooking the girl in the snare. He was bruised, tired, torn and bloodied. His left hand had been impaled by a branch as he sought to break his fall through the snow down the inside of the pine tree. It had taken hours to work his way back to the surface of the drift. The bear had growled and groaned in the darkness beneath him as its life ebbed away.

The snow melted on his clothes, leaving him damp and cold.

Limping, James crossed the cliff. He gathered his bow and arrows, picked up his pack, and made his way down to the stream in the gully.

The girl lay still beneath the standing dead tree. He called out as he approached, but she didn't respond.

James dropped his pack on the snow and stepped over the twigs and dead branches littering the ground. The young woman stirred at the sound, rolling to one side. Her leg looked bad. It was broken. The steel jaws clamped on either side of her leg bit into the flesh below her knee, reaching the bone. James reached out and touched her hand, speaking softly.

"Hello, Sunshine."

Her skin was cold to touch. The sun was setting, leaving them in the shadows as the temperature plummeted.

"Who?" she asked, her voice struggling, breaking up as that one word struggled past her lips. "Who are you?"

"Hey. It's OK. My name is James. I'm from a small farm to the north of Amersham. Relax, I'm going to get you out of here."

"You," she managed, her voice still croaky. "You're a bloody fool."

"Hah," James laughed. That was good. She was thinking, and, yes, she was right, he was a bloody fool taking on that bear alone.

James rummaged around in his pack, pulling out his sleeping bag and wrapping her in it, but he didn't open the sleeping bag, not until he removed the bear trap.

"You're shivering," she managed, her teeth chattering together.

"You too," he replied. "It's cold, and it's going to get colder. I've got to get a fire started."

"What about my leg?" she asked, grimacing in pain as she moved slightly.

James glanced down at the bloody bear trap.

"At this point, it's better on your leg. Believe me, once I start removing it, you're going to beg me to stop anyway."

The girl was quiet.

"As soon as I start to remove that trap your wounds are going to open up and bleed. I need to get a fire going so I can sterilize some water to clean your wound and keep you warm while I bind your leg."

The look in her eyes was one that cried out for pity, but James had to be honest.

"I'm sorry, but with all you've been through, there's worse to come."

James scouted around for some dry pine needles and set out his firewood in order of size, starting with the needles and slowly working up to twigs the size of his trembling fingers. He put aside two long, straight branches to act as splints for her leg, cleaning twigs from the branches with his knife.

The bear trap had been set on rough ground, protected from the wind by the lee of a large rock. A light dusting of snow sat on the twigs and sticks scattered across the frozen ground.

James used a small rock to carve out the snow and ice, making a shallow pit for the fire. After carefully stacking the pine needles so they made the shape of a tepee, he began striking his flint, sending sparks onto the dry kindling. Normally, he'd have started a fire earlier, while the setting sun was still warming the hills, but he had no choice. His fingers were feeling the cold, the slightest bump or slip sent pain shooting through them, but he persisted, bending forward and gently blowing as the sparks settled on the pine needles.

Slowly, a red glow appeared, then the faintest of flames, and he dared not breathe, willing the flame higher as he carefully added pine needles one by one.

Within minutes, James was adding twigs and then sticks to the fragile burning tepee, carefully arranging them to avoid a collapse, allowing the fire to take hold.

The flames warmed his hand. Blood began to circulate more freely and his torn palm throbbed. Blood seeped through the bandage he'd wrapped around his hand. It had taken the best part of half an hour, but the fire crackled as it threw out warmth.

Fire was important, not just for comfort but to keep wild animals at bay, and there would be visitations, he was sure of it. The wolves must have smelt the blood. They'd be merciless, sensing wounded prey.

James collected some larger sticks and branches and sat his steel cup on one side of the fire, melting some snow. Within a few minutes the water began to boil, so he used a cloth to remove it from the heat, sitting it in the snow to cool.

James ran his knife through the flames, fascinated as the metal changed color and the steel became sterile. He knew what needed to be done.

The girl had been silent, but she was sitting up, watching him.

"So what's your name?" he asked.

"Lisa," she replied as he began looking at her leg again.

No surname? No point of origin? Common courtesy demanded that at least, but she clearly wasn't forthcoming. He started to say something but thought better of it. There would be time to learn where she was from later.

"Well, Lisa. I'm sorry, but this is going to hurt."

He handed her a small branch saying, "Here, bite on this."

James grabbed the bear trap with both hands and pried it apart.

"Ahhhh!" Lisa screamed, the stick clenched between her teeth, her hand squeezing his shoulder intensely. James jimmied the trap around, away from her leg and let it snap shut.

Lisa was panting, hyperventilating. She rocked back on the ground, her fingers grabbing at the branches around her, looking for anything to squeeze in response to the pain.

James knelt sideways next to her, anchoring her thigh against his leg to keep her lower leg immobile.

"Lie still. I need to clean your wound."

"Ohhhh," she groaned.

Carefully, he dabbed at the wound with the warm water, washing out grit and dirt. She grimaced, jerking as he rested her knee against his leg, trying to keep her lower leg as straight as possible. In the cold, her leg must have been numb. It wouldn't last.

"Oh, that hurts," she cried. "It feels like you're burning me."

"I know," he replied as he continued methodically cleaning her wound, picking out debris with the tip of his knife.

"No more," she pleaded. "Let it be. Please, let it be. I can't take any more."

"I know," he repeated, continuing on regardless.

"Oh, please," she whimpered, tears streaming down her cheeks, her right hand reaching out and touching him, imploring him to stop.

"Almost there," he said, lying. "You're being brave. You're being very brave."

He rinsed the cloth and used the blade of his knife to scrape away more tiny bits of wood and dirt.

"Please, no more."

"Just a little more," he replied, leaning forward and cleaning another part of her wound. Blood dripped onto the ground with a steady rhythm.

Lisa beat at him feebly with one hand, but he didn't stop until he was satisfied the gaping wound was clean. He lay the splints next to her, looking into her eyes. She didn't have to say anything, he knew what she wanted—pity, compassion, but here in the wilderness there was only life and death.

"Listen," he said. "I need to move your leg again, I've got to align the two halves. I'm sorry, but this is going to hurt even more."

Lisa was doing her best not to roll around in agony, rocking on her back while keeping her leg against his. He could see the anguish in her face, the pain in her eyes. Holding a strip of cloth in his mouth, he pulled her lower leg back below her knee and began strapping her leg to the stick.

"OH, YOU BASTARD. I HATE YOU, I GODDAMN-WELL FUCKING HATE YOU," she screamed into the night.

"I know. I know," he said, wrapping her leg tightly.

With two splints supporting her leg, he bandaged her wound and then opened his sleeping bag and helped her inside, moving her onto a ground sheet.

Lisa was beyond caring. He could see it in the gaunt look on her face, her blood-drained pale skin, her blood-shot eyes, she could have died right then and it wouldn't have mattered. Any fight, any desire for life was gone. She fell asleep with exhaustion.

James restocked the fire for the long night ahead, placing several long branches across the flames, slowly moving them in as they burnt down. He changed his clothes and tended to his own wounds. Stiff and sore, he melted some more snow, making a stew by dropping in cuttings of potato, onion and dried meat. In the distance, a wolf howled and he knew it wouldn't be long.

With their backs to the rock, they were sheltered from the worst of the wind. The large rock also gave them some physical protection, limiting the directions from which they could be approached.

James looked around.

The standing dead tree was surrounded by branches and twigs littering the ground. Any approach by a wolf pack would avoid the uneven, noisy routes, so they wouldn't approach from there.

A stream cut in front of them, but it was unlikely any wolves would risk getting wet as the chill could be fatal. That left the gentle slope leading down from the ridge-line to the right.

James dug out the chain anchoring the bear trap in place and moved it over onto the slope, setting it so as to catch any beast creeping down from above.

He buried the trap slightly below the snow, hiding it from sight, although he knew the wolves would probably smell the blood on it. They might even think it was an old kill, buried by some other animal, and possibly trip the trap while trying to exhume it. James marked the trap with a stick in the snow. It wouldn't do for either him or Lisa to stumble upon the trap in the morning.

Sitting by the fire, James whittled away at a long shaft of wood, fashioning it into a spear. He carved barbs into the wood, staggering sharp sections that he could break off as they embedded into an animal.

Fire was his best option and he knew it.

Wolves may have increased in size, but their dislike of man and their disdain for fire hadn't changed. Once, they had been larger than most dogs, now they were the size of a small horse. But their instincts kept them wary. Their instincts hadn't changed as quickly as their body size, giving James the ability to keep them at bay by exploiting their pack instinct, their desire to move in unison with one another.

Without straying too far from camp, James gathered more wood in the early evening. Snow drifted in the air. It was late in the year for fresh snow, but not unheard of, and James wondered what the morning would bring. If a blizzard closed in on them, it could kill them. They had to get off the mountain.

The moon rose above the ridge, lighting the night, giving James a semblance of time as it passed. He wanted to sleep, he needed to sleep. It was going to be a long day tomorrow. Lisa was in a deep sleep, but he had to keep watch, he had to ward off any wolves or, if it came to it, another bear. If a predator came upon them in the dark, it could tear them to pieces before he had time to react.

With a heavy blanket wrapped around his shoulders warding off the cold, James struggled to stay awake. As the hours passed his eyes felt heavy and he slipped into a deep sleep.

It was dark when Lisa woke him. She was shaking his shoulder, saying something in a whisper. On opening his eyes, James could see how far the moon had moved. At least six hours had passed. Dawn couldn't be too far away, but the horizon hadn't lightened yet.

The fire was low, but still burning. It took a few seconds for his eyes to register the dark shapes moving beyond the flames. Red eyes glowed in the darkness. Slowly, James got to his feet, staying low. A deep growl resonated through the night air.

James picked up one of the burning branches. The glowing embers at its tip flared as he swung it around, yelling at the wolves, trying to startle them, to scare them with the sudden rush of noise.

One of the wolves circled in closer, baring its teeth and snarling at him, demanding its portion of any kill. But there had been no kill, the blood that they smelled was Lisa's. James kicked the logs crossing the fire, stirring the embers, pushing the dry wood in further where it would catch alight. Sparks rose up into the night sky.

Stepping forward, James waved the glowing stick around, threatening the closest wolf. He stabbed at the wolf, making as though he would attack. With each swing the flames flared up, releasing a crackle as the branch swished through the air. The wolf backed away, drawing him out a little.

Creeping backwards, its soft paws barely breaking the packed snow, the wolf snarled, threatening to lunge at him regardless of the puny flames.

James felt exposed, scared. His heart pounded in his chest. He was aware his range of focus had narrowed, fixing on this one wolf. He turned his head, trying to keep the other wolves in view, but they were hidden in the shadows.

He tried to be aware of their movement, but his eyes gravitated back to the beast before him. This was all just a bluff, and he knew it, if they charged there was nothing he could do. He stepped forward boldly, asserting himself, yelling at them, trying to appear bigger than he was, trying to suggest he wasn't worth the effort. It was only then he became aware of the wolf on top of the rocky outcrop beside him, but it was too late.

"Look out," cried Lisa.

The wolf on the rock leaped through the air, howling as it lunged at him. Just one swipe from its mighty paws would be enough to tear his arm out of its socket and that terrified him. He ducked, dropping and turning, striking out at the wolf with the burning branch but he missed. The giant wolf landed with a thud, kicking up a fine spray of snow.

The first wolf turned on him, lunging in at him, knocking the branch from his hand. James scrambled as the wolf danced to one side. Rather than attacking, it was cornering him, backing him up against the fire. He knew what it was doing. He'd seen this before. Wolves would corner an elk by mesmerizing the animal, having one wolf lead the attack, keeping the petrified animal distracted as the rest of the pack closed in on its hindquarters. James knew the real attack would come from the side, coming at him from out of the shadows.

The spear, where was his improvised spear? He couldn't see it anywhere so he grabbed an icy branch from the ground. The wood was cold to touch, but he swung it anyway. The wolf kept its distance, its eerie dark eyes locked on his.

He stepped backwards beside the fire, wanting to use it for protection.

Lisa screamed. One of the wolves had emerged from the darkness and was edging toward her.

As James turned toward her, he caught the motion of several other wolves coming in for the kill. With all his might, he lashed out at the fire with his stick, brandishing it like a club, driving at the glowing coals.

A wall of fire erupted from the ashes, spraying the oncoming wolves with burning embers. Glowing coals scattered in the air, catching one of the wolves in the face while the other had its fur set alight.

James lost his footing and fell into the fire as the wolves howled.

Another cloud of burning embers billowed up into the air, and James rolled away into the snow, trying to put out the fire on his clothes.

Burning coals caught in his jacket, they seethed and sizzled as he rolled in the snow. He'd burnt his hand and had hot ash in his eyes, temporarily blinding him.

In the confusion, James could hear the wolves snarling. Then came the sickening sound of the bear trap snapping shut. It was only then he realized he was yelling out in pain as Lisa screamed in terror.

The wolves fled. As silence fell, he got to his feet, hearing one of the wolves whimpering in the trap, pulling feebly against the chain staked in the icy ground.

There must have been a clean break in its leg as the wolf should have been able to pull the trap loose quite easily. The animal had to have been fighting as much against the sudden shock of the pain as it was against being snared.

James rubbed his eyes, clearing out the ash. The pack had gone, leaving one wolf struggling on the ground, its bloodied hind leg torn open by the trap.

Lisa was hysterical, yelling at him.

"Are you all right? What are you doing? What are you going to do? What if they come back?"

James wasn't sure which question she expected him to answer. As for him, a grim determination swept over his face.

He knew how to keep the wolves at bay. James picked up the wooden spear with its jagged barbs and walked calmly over to the wounded animal. There was only one thing the wolves understood, dominance.

Looking down at the massive beast with its bloodied leg, James could see numerous burns on its fur. It had pulled the chain out of the ground, but the animal was so stunned it didn't realize it could have limped away, dragging the trap with it. Instead, the monster lay there, its legs scraping at the snow as it inched forward, lying on its side.

The wolf was blind in one eye, but that was an old injury. The monster snarled at him, baring its teeth, but this was a hollow threat and they both knew it.

In the distance, on the ridge-line, the other wolves watched as James thrust his spear repeatedly into the wounded animal's neck, severing its jugular vein. Blood sprayed across the ice. There was no mercy to be shown, only a clear message to be sent to the pack.

The wolves would not return, not tonight.

Chapter 03: Laughter

James soaked his hands in the icy cold water running through the stream, soothing his burns.

"They're still out there," Lisa said.

"Yes, they are," James replied, "but they won't return. They'll see that carcass like a scarecrow."

He dried his hands and placed more wood on the fire, ensuring there was enough to burn for hours.

His heart was still racing, pumping adrenaline around his body, but he knew he needed to rest. He wrapped himself in his blanket and lay down near the fire. The cold crept up from the ground, but he was past caring.

"You're going to sleep?" Lisa cried. "Are you serious? We're surrounded by wolves and you're going to sleep?"

"Yes," James replied. "And you should too. It's going to be a long day tomorrow."

"I can't believe you can go to sleep after all we've been through," Lisa said, but her words barely registered.

Lying there, James pictured those things that set his heart at ease—images of Simon and Martha tending to their morning chores, chastising him for being lazy and sleeping in while he laughed in defiance. He pictured his father reading to him or getting him to read aloud. And he remembered the clippings, the pages from textbooks and novels, the fragments of stories, pictures of engineering schematics, the scraps from an old phone book or an invoice from someone's shopping. For his father, it mattered not what was read, but that someone would read. According to his father, there was always something to learn. Often the most mundane of details were the most telling, or so he said. James wasn't so sure.

To James, it was pointless reading a list of names in alphabetical order, or a receipt listing grocery items, most of which he didn't recognize. Chicken and milk were easy, but what the hell was Coca-cola? James would point out that his father's collection of scraps held little real meaning, they were too disconnected in time, they were fragments that made no sense without cultural context. Thinking back to those moments, James distracted himself and soon fell asleep.

When he awoke, the sun was high in the sky, warming the land.

Lisa was chatty.

"I don't know how you could sleep. I couldn't switch off what had happened. My mind has been running a million miles an hour. While you were snoring, I watched the stars drifting west, moving ever so gracefully. I marveled at how the day broke, how the majestic morning arose. Oh, you should have seen the dawn. The sky turned ruddy, then slowly faded into hues of pink and yellow. The first rays of light crept over the mountain, lighting up the snow like it was made out of crystal. It was beautiful."

James yawned, he yawned and started to say something but she kept talking.

"Oh, I hope you don't mind, but I raided your pack for food. It was just in reach."

She paused, stopping herself as she looked him in the eye.

"I'm talking too much, aren't I?"

"No. Not at all."

Breathing deeply, Lisa said, "I guess I just really appreciate seeing this particular dawn. It's one I almost didn't make."

James sat up, rubbing the sleep from his eyes. His back was sore, his muscles ached.

"Thank you," she said.

James nodded. He was still waking.

"Where are you from?" he asked.

"Little Bayless, in the north."

He helped Lisa sit on a rock as he began packing up the camp. With the sleeping bag under her, and the full sun streaming down upon her, she looked content.

After boiling some water, he examined her leg, carefully peeling back the bandages. Being gentle, he cleaned the pus out of her wounds, noting that the edges of the torn flesh were gaining a slight red hue. Infection was setting in. The cuts in her pale skin looked angry. Quietly, he pulled a needle and thread from his pack.

"What are you doing?" she asked.

"I need to clean your wounds again and then close them."

"No, please," she begged, as though she already felt the pain of the needle sewing up her flesh.

"Lisa. Listen," he replied, reaching out and holding her hand. "We have a long way to travel. Your leg will tear if I don't stitch up the wound. Flesh needs to join with flesh, or there can be no healing."

She squeezed his hand briefly before letting go, allowing him to go to work. It was a tacit way of giving her approval without saying the words.

Lisa grimaced, clenching her teeth, trying not to scream in agony as James began washing her wounds with the lukewarm water.

He stitched up the worst of the tears. She panted as he worked with the needle. She was taking short, sharp breaths to stave off the pain.

James tried to be gentle, but he knew his field dressing was crude and would leave horrible scars on her leg. Pressing the needle into her skin, he felt cruel. As her skin gave, the needle slipped easily through the fat and muscle before he had to work it out again. He didn't like this, he didn't like doing this to her, but it had to be done. Lisa held his shoulder, squeezing tight with each stitch.

Although the actual effort only took ten minutes, it felt like hours for both of them. When he finished, he wiped away the blood and left her leg in the warmth of the sun, hoping to dry out the wound before he had to bandage it again.

James fashioned a crutch out of a forked branch and wrapped cloth over the armrest. As he moved around the camp, packing up, he noticed Lisa squirming. He could see she wanted to move, to get up and walk around, but she couldn't. Lisa tried to get up using the crutch, but he told her to stay put, there would be time enough for walking soon.

Finally, she told him why she was antsy. She had to relieve herself, and was unable to do so alone. How is this going to work, he wondered, realizing how impractical this would be for her with her leg strapped straight. He told her to wait while he cleared a section of ground beside the rock, hollowing it out slightly. Then he brought another rock over, so she could position herself between the rocks with her hands, resting her buttocks on either edge. James felt a little embarrassed when she asked for some help with her pants as she couldn't lift herself and pull her pants down.

Lisa laughed at how prudish he was. In some ways, he figured, his modesty probably made this a little easier on her, making it easier for her to deal with by making fun of him.

As she lifted herself up, he reached around her waist awkwardly and pulled her trousers down, followed by her underpants.

He turned his head to one side so as not to look at her naked groin.

She kissed him on the cheek, which startled and surprised him. It seemed such a rash thing to do, and not exactly the most romantic of occasions. But it was opportunistic, he could understand that. Here he was, leaning over her, his arms pulling at her pants, trying to help, trying not to bump her injured leg, trying to avoid becoming tangled in her arms as she held her weight, and with their heads so close she wanted to express her gratitude in a cheeky manner. That rather suited her personality, he thought.

There was nothing else in it, he told himself, as they both laughed at the comical situation they were in. Once her pants were down to just above her knees, he stepped back, turning to one side as she positioned herself between the rocks and relieved herself. That was tougher than tackling the wolves, he thought, as he picked up his pack and pretended to be busy doing something, anything.

A faint smile crept onto his face as he looked away. He didn't dare say what he was thinking lest he incur her wrath, but being chased by a bear was far easier.

Once she finished, Lisa worked her way back onto the rock and began pulling up her pants, but she clearly needed help so with as much care as he could, he helped, trying to respect her dignity as he tugged at her trousers.

"Well, that was fun," she said, wiping the beads of sweat off her forehead.

"Yeah, quite," he replied, unsure as to what the appropriate response should be.

Her eyes were bloodshot. She had a light sweat shining on her forehead, but it seemed to be from more than just the physical exertion of the last few minutes.

James placed the back of his hand against her forehead to check her temperature. "We need to get you off this mountain. I'm going to build a sled, something to pull across the snow."

"Sounds good to me."

Within an hour, James had built what looked like a stretcher, binding two long branches together with cross-members. As there was no one else to help carry Lisa down the mountain, he planned on dragging one end of the stretcher as an Indian sled.

James took advantage of the natural curves and bends within the branches to act as skis at the far end. In that way, the load would be spread as he dragged the sled over the snow. He lined the stretcher with his ground sheet, a canvas tarpaulin that would easily hold her weight.

James busied himself, packing up the sleeping bag and gathering together his rations, pot and knife. Before they broke camp, he gave her some stale bread and a strip of beef jerky to chew on. As they ate their jerky, she smiled. He looked down at his piece. It was moldy and brittle, most of it left over from last year. The bread tasted like the leather from an old boot, but she didn't seem to mind, and he was happy for a bit of protein.

The journey down the mountain was slow. Where the snow was hard-packed he found going downhill easy, but the trek was laborious when wading through the soft, powdered snow that had built up with the prevailing winds.

On the flat stretches of land beside the widening river, James found he could move quite quickly down the gentle decline.

By noon, they were less than two miles from camp. Looking back, James was surprised how little ground they'd covered. It seemed as though they were moving faster, but progress was slow. Numerous small creeks joined the growing stream and were difficult for an able-bodied person to cross, let alone Lisa with her leg strapped to a rough, wooden brace. James lost track of how many times he'd taken the pack and sled across, before returning to help Lisa navigate the narrow gullies.

The stream they followed was surrounded on either side by a broad, flat river bed, a sign of the torrential flooding that came with spring. The high-water mark etched into the rocks above them gave James an idea how forcible and violent the river could be, but that was months away.

By late afternoon, the mountain lay largely behind them, and the wooded lowlands opened up before them, breaking into hills and valleys. With the sun dipping behind the horizon, a chill ran through the air. The snow on the ground was patchy, making it difficult to drag the sled. Birds moved in the trees. James spotted the smoke from a distant cabin, not more than a couple of miles away in the foothills.

It was dark by the time they approached the one-room wooden cabin, with its small stockade shared by a cow and a horse. Row upon row of freshly tilled fields stretched out beside the house.

"See that," he said, pointing at the fields. "That's a good sign. Farmers are much more hospitable than hunters. With hunters, you never know what you get, scoundrels or vagabonds."

"Really?" Lisa replied with mock surprise in her voice. "So which are you?"

James laughed at the irony as he added, "I'm different."

"I bet that's what you tell all the girls," Lisa said, trying to smile as her teeth chattered in the cold. A light mist drifted above the ground, forming an eerie fog.

"Wait here," he said, dropping his pack beside her and pulling out his knife.

James crept forward.

The cabin was off the beaten track, away from the trade routes, which probably meant it didn't attract too much attention.

Approaching from the rear, James took a glimpse in through a small window. There were at least three men and a woman inside. It looked like an older couple with two teenage sons. The oldest son appeared to be a little younger than him, but not by much.

James slipped his knife into its sheath and knocked, wondering what he must look like. If it had been him or his father opening the door, what would they have thought seeing someone in such a ragged, bloody state? Farmers were wary of strangers, but hospitable nonetheless.

The door opened and the light from inside streamed out, blinding him. Beyond the silhouette, he could see a shotgun trained on him. They were affluent, but he doubted they had more than a couple of rounds. No one did. Firearms were more of a status symbol than anything else, a luxury from a bygone era, a means of projecting the perception of power, but more about the show than any real threat. The shotgun was probably loaded, or he wouldn't have brandished it, but whether the firing pin worked was another story. Few, if any firearms were fired in any one generation. Ammunition was just too scarce. And besides, far more men had been killed holding a loaded weapon that failed to discharge than those that had been shot.

James raised his hands.

"I mean you no harm. I'm a lost hunter, separated from his hunting party. I seek only shelter for the night."

The older man stepped forward, while his teenage son kept the shotgun trained on James. For his part, James was more concerned about the other teenager, the one that hadn't shown himself. If they were smart, and it seemed they were, he would have slipped out the front door and doubled around outside, well away from the house, looking for a raiding party. If there was a working firearm in the house, he would be the one carrying it.

"How many?" the old man demanded.

In that instant, James had to decide whether to lie or come clean. Lying would do no good, he had to tell the truth.

"Two, myself and a girl."

"You took a woman hunting?" the old man asked. James blinked in the bright light. It was only then his eyes adjusted to the light and he realized the old man was brandishing a pitchfork. The long, sharp prongs posed a real threat, one far more dangerous than an antiquated shotgun. James stepped back, catching the sharp points glistening in the light.

"I ... I found her on the mountain, rescued her. She's hurt. She needs help. We need your help."

"You expect me to believe you're out here alone with a girl you just found in the mountains?"

James dropped his hands by his side, and the man stepped back, not sure what to expect, but James was exhausted. The prospect of finding shelter for the night was daunting. After all they'd been through he just wanted to rest.

"We are no threat, sir. We mean nothing but to pass on our way at dawn."

"Who are you?"

"Dobson, James Dobson."

"Dobson? From the village of Elmore?"

"No, sir," James said, hoping a little deference would play in their favor. "From a farm north of Amersham. I've got cousins in Elmore."

The old man dropped the pitchfork, saying, "Well, I'll be damned. You're old man Dobson's son."

"Yes, sir."

"Ha. Well, good. Come in, come in. I know your dad. We fought together at Bracken Ridge."

The old man let out a wolf whistle. From the tree line, a voice called out in reply, yelling, "No one else out here. Just a girl by the woodpile."

"OK, bring her in," the man yelled, gesturing for James to enter the cabin.

The old man rocked as he walked on a wooden leg. He noticed James staring.

"The ridge wasn't kind to me."

"My dad lost his brother," James replied.

"Yeah," the old man said, resting against a bench. "Everyone lost something that day."

James took off his boots. A wave of heat hit him as he stepped from the porch into the cabin. He took of his scarf and jacket, surprised by how cold and wet they were. The old lady took his outer clothes, draping them over a chair to dry. James felt his nose begin to run. The heat within the cabin hurt his hands, causing his fingers to sting, but it was a good kind of pain, the kind that made him feel glad to be alive.

The other son arrived at the door with Lisa holding on to his shoulder. She was dragging her crutch, hopping as she entered the cabin. He could see her grimacing with pain. The old lady looked horrified and rushed to Lisa's side, helping her sit on a chair by the roaring fire as the teenager dropped the backpack inside the door.

"So what the blazes happened to you two?" the old man asked, pouring a kettle into two chipped, ceramic mugs. James hoped it was coffee, but it was a blend of chicory and ground milo, poor man's coffee. It was hot, though, warming him on the inside as he drank.

"I was hunting deer up by the north pass when I found her caught in a bear trap."

"Bloody McDonnell," the old man swore. "I've warned him before about leaving traps unmarked over winter."

James looked around. The inside of the cabin was cluttered, with items of every description mounting the walls. Rusting souvenirs from Coney Island sat on the mantle, hub caps from a Cadillac had been nailed to one wall, a faded picture of the New York skyline at night held the place of pride above the fireplace. Horse shoes, advertising banners and a reflective Stop sign were nailed in place on the logs. The chinking between the logs was cracked, but there wasn't any draft.

A row of winning felt pennants, predating the Fall—Middlefield Junior High, track and field, five years running lined the back wall. They probably didn't have anything to do with this particular family, being collector's items rather than a personal achievement.

James suspected neither the old man nor his sons knew quite what the pennants depicted. Their value today was in representing successive, sequential years being displayed from before the Fall. That they were only for a local high school, probably hundreds of miles from here, was irrelevant. They'd been traded as items of value and had accumulated perceived value over the decades. In the years to come, they'd increase in value. They were an investment beyond anything they originally represented.

A computer circuit board had been tacked in place beside the front door. Its black integrated circuits and thin metal lines hinted at a level of complexity lost in the mist of time. His father would have loved this place.

"And you?" James asked.

"Old man Winters," came the reply. "These are my boys, Wilbur and Jonathan, and my wife Amelia."

From the loft above, a face poked over the edge. Brown hair fell curiously forward.

"And Wilbur's wife, Jane."

Jane waved. She mounted a ladder and came down to help Amelia. For so many people in what appeared from the outside to be such a small cabin, the room was surprisingly large.

Amelia and Jane looked at Lisa's leg, bathing her wounds in warm water. The skin on her leg looked pale, like that of dead flesh. The red tinge around the cuts had faded. In the soft light of the fire, Lisa's wounds looked better than they had that morning.

"And what about you, young Lisa? What is your story? Where are you from? How did you come to be up in the mountains?" old man Winters asked.

Lisa hid behind her cup of chicory, sipping it slowly. All eyes settled on her, including James. Up until this point, he'd been so focused on surviving he hadn't wondered why she was in the mountains in the first place, so it was a good question. What was Lisa doing crossing the pass alone, well away from trade routes? And where were her supplies? Who would venture across the mountains without supplies? Such a journey could be done in a couple of days, but only with a fair weather. Only a fool would risk crossing without supplies, a fool or someone driven to desperation. She had to be running from someone, but who? And why?

"Ah," she began. "I'm from Greensburg, just outside of Pittsburgh."

So much for Little Bayless, thought James, and he wondered which location was a lie. Perhaps they both were. That she would lie so quickly and so convincingly troubled him. It said something fundamental about her, undermining his attitude toward her.

"What are you doing this far south?" the old man asked. "Where are your companions?"

"We were set upon by bandits," she replied. "I ran. I was separated from the main party. I became lost in the mountains and got caught in that bear trap."

She was lying. James had found her on the western slope of the peak, well away from the main trade route. And the route was heavily traveled, especially in early spring, with traders wanting to get through before the floods came. Bandits favored the lesser roads, and with good reason. If they were caught they'd be hung.

"Your party must have gone on to Manitou," the old man said. "They'll think you're dead. We'll send word in the morning, let them know you've survived."

Lisa's eyes dropped slightly as she smiled politely. "Thank you."

Liar, thought James. But why? Why would she mislead them? What did she stand to gain from deceit?

Amelia dished up some lentil soup and James forgot about his concerns as he chatted with the men about hunting and fishing. The old lady put some salve on his burns and changed the bandage on his hand.

The two boys wanted to hear about the wolves. James became quite animated, reenacting the encounter, starting with his initial preparation, setting the trap and carving barbs into a make-shift spear. As the fire crackled in the background he described the attack to the rapt attention of the family. Gesturing with his hands, he relived the battle, twisting and turning as he described the fight.

"Oh, yeah," Lisa said, trying not to laugh at his bravado. "Don't forget the part where you tried to commit suicide by diving into the fire."

"I slipped," James protested, a look of horror on his face. "I lost my footing."

"I think they ran off because they were so confused," Lisa replied, tormenting him.

"That's not fair," he protested, forgetting his audience.

"The sight of you rolling around on fire surely scared them to death," Lisa cried. "They didn't know whether they preferred you raw, medium or well-done."

Old man Winters laughed, as did the women. The young men, though, sided with James and clearly considered him heroic.

"Hey," James replied. "I saved your life, remember?"

"Oh, I remember it well," Lisa joked.

"Ah," Winters said, patting James on the shoulder. "Don't take her jests seriously. You were indeed a hero, my friend, and we all know it."

Lisa was smiling. James felt his ego deflate. His grand story of conquest and adventure did seem a little awkward when he thought about it.

"James was very brave," Lisa said, balancing things out. "With one wolf caught in the bear trap, he dispatched it quickly and ruthlessly. The rest of the pack stood up on the hill, watching as their fellow died at his hands. They did not bother us again."

"So it's true?" Wilbur asked. "You really fought off a pack of wolves by yourself?"

James tried to say something, but Lisa beat him to it.

"Yes. It's true. Every detail. Right down to rolling around in the fire."

At that, everyone laughed, including James. He had to admit that it did sound funny.

Wilbur, Jane and Jonathan turned in for the night, climbing up into the loft.

Amelia placed a rug for them on the floor, a few feet from the fire, before she retired for the night and went to sleep on a bed at the back of the cabin. Winters rubbed his hand through James' hair, in much the same way his father would, and then patted him on the back, bidding him a good night's sleep, then he hobbled off to bed, his wooden leg making a dull thud on the floorboards.

James and Lisa lay on the rug, enjoying the warmth of the fire. James propped himself up on his elbows, whispering as he spoke.

"You really thought that was funny?"

"Well, not at the time," Lisa replied. "But now, in hindsight, yes, it was quite funny."

"But–"

"Oh, don't let it bother you. You don't need stories of courage and bravery to define you. You're better than that."

She leaned over and kissed him on the lips, immediately defusing any tension between them. He liked that. He would have been happy to continue kissing her, but she rocked back on her elbows, looking deep into his eyes. In the flickering light, she looked beautiful. Her long hair was matted and straggly, but it didn't matter.

"And what about you?" he asked. "There were no bandits, were there?"

Her body straightened. Her expression went flat as she responded curtly.

"No."

She wasn't going to say any more, that much was clear, but he had an admission from her, and that was a start. Now, though, it was his turn to play the role of tormentor.

"You know," he began. "I saw something quite funny on that mountain too."

"Oh, really," she replied, curiosity hanging on her words.

"Yes. I seem to remember someone straddling two rocks."

"You wouldn't dare," she said, trying not to speak too loudly.

She reached out and punched him lightly on the shoulder. Dropping her head and staring at him with narrow eyes, Lisa made it clear this was not a subject to be broached in public.

James smiled. He leaned in, determined to keep the upper hand as long as he could. Kissing her on the cheek, he added, "Sweet dreams."

James spread a blanket over the two of them and lay back on the rug. Scrunching up a jacket to use as a pillow, he turned away from her.

"James?" Lisa whispered, her hand resting on his neck, her fingers playing with his hair.

"Yes?"

"Thank you."

Chapter 04: Morning

James woke to find Amelia moving quietly around the cabin in the early morning light. Old man Winters was awake. He was grumpy with Amelia. James didn't think too much of it, hoping he and Lisa weren't the object of his annoyance. Winters hobbled around the cabin, favoring his good leg, grumbling under his breath.

Lisa had cuddled up next to James, her head resting on his chest. Gently, he repositioned her and got up. Before he left for the out-house, James pulled back the blanket covering her leg and gently lifted the edge of the bandage below her knee. Her wound looked angry, and needed to be treated, but his bladder was bursting and Lisa was still asleep so James slipped outside.

On returning, James saw Amelia tending to Lisa, wiping her brow.

"She has a fever."

"I'm just a little hot," Lisa replied.

Winters knelt down, looking at her leg. He peeled back the bandages, his fingers pushed gently at the sides of her raw wound. Pus oozed out. The torn edges of her skin looked red, marking where the teeth of the steel trap had sunk into her leg.

"Her leg is infected. She is diseased."

Lisa leaned forward, trying to get a good look herself.

"Get her up on the table," the old man said.

Amelia cleared the rough-hewn wooden table as the two teenage boys lifted Lisa up and lay her gently on the wooden plank surface. Lisa clenched her teeth. Amelia brought a pillow over for her head.

Winters mumbled something and Amelia rummaged around in one of the drawers, pulling out an old leather belt.

"I'm sorry," he said, taking Lisa's hand. "Really, I am. But this is the only way."

He slid the belt under her knee, moving it up on her thigh, but leaving it flat on the table.

"A tourniquet," James stuttered, in shock at what was unfolding. Things were moving too quick, he had to slow this down. "Wait a minute. You're taking things too far, too fast."

For her part, Lisa was struggling to sit up and see what was going on. She grimaced with pain at the slightest movement.

"She's going to be OK," James said. "Her body needs time to heal."

Winters looked up at him with grim determination. He turned to Amelia.

"We're going to need clean bandages and plenty of boiled water."

"No," cried Lisa. She panicked, thrashing with her hands. "Get away from me. Get away."

Jonathan and Wilbur stood behind her, holding the crook of her arm back, keeping her still on the table.

"Let go of me!"

"You can't do this," James protested. "There must be something else we can do. This is crazy. Madness."

The boys held her fast, but their heads were slightly bowed, so they could avoid looking him in the eye. They wanted no part of this, of that James was sure, but must have thought there was no other way, so they reluctantly and silently backed up their father.

James looked at Amelia. She was silent. Tears sat in her eyes.

Winters placed a wood saw in the fire. Sparks drifted up the chimney.

"She either loses the leg or she loses her life. Which is it going to be?"

"I don't want to lose my leg," cried Lisa. She was appealing to James, not Winters, as though the decision was his. "Please, don't let him take my leg."

"You must be strong," Winters said, but he too was talking to James. "She is in no position to make this decision for herself. She needs you to be strong for her."

"You're overreacting," James said, trying to calm things down. He held out his hands, moving them slowly, as though that physical act would result in calming the situation.

Winters stirred the coals in the fire. The tip of a fire-iron glowed red. In his mind, James could already smell the sweet scent of cauterized flesh. He'd seen this before, they all had at one point or another, either when branding an animal or sealing a wound.

"Oh, please, please, please," Lisa moaned.

James found his mind racing. What options were there? Winters thought he was doing what was right. James could force the issue with violence, but where would that end? And Lisa was in no state for a hasty exit. He had to talk the old man down and make him see reason.

"I understand," James said in a calm voice. "I know what happened."

The change of tone caught everyone off-guard. Winters looked at him warily.

"You've been there," James continued. "You've been the one lying there on the table. You must know the terror she feels, but this isn't Bracken Ridge."

The old man's eyes cast down, but not in shame. James could see he was looking at the stump of his knee resting on his wooden leg.

"Hard decisions had to be made," Winters said.

"They saved your life," James added. He was standing beside Lisa as she lay there on the table. She seemed to sense what he was doing and relaxed a little. She held his hand, her fingers barely touching his, and yet he knew he had her support.

"If the infection spreads, she dies," Winters replied coldly. "It's a harsh law, but it is the natural law. You can no more fight it than you can spread your wings and fly."

"And yet man once flew among the stars," James pleaded.

"Wishful thinking," Winters said with a hint of scorn in his voice. "Time is of the essence. We have to act now and save her life before it is too late."

"We need to clean the wound," James said. "Give her body a chance."

"Look," Winters said, pointing at the stitching on her leg. "The wound is red. The infection is spreading, if we act now we can save the thigh. If we wait, she'll lose even that, if not her life.

"Are you willing to risk her life? You look at me like I'm evil, like I'm the bad guy, but you would wait and put her life in jeopardy? Are you honestly that foolish?"

James was silent. He swallowed the lump in his throat. Winters changed his tone. He was sympathetic in his comments, his voice conveyed compassion, not anger. He must have found this as difficult as they did, but felt compelled to act.

"I know how you feel," Winters said. "You did so much to save her, but this is one monster you cannot fight. There is no bear to shoot arrows at, no wolves to chase. There is nothing to be done for the leg. If you care for her, you will let me take her leg—here—just below the knee."

"Please no," Lisa said, sobbing. "Don't take my leg."

"She will understand," Winters insisted. "It may take her time, but she will realize there was no other way."

"But you don't know what you're dealing with," James said.

"And you do?" Winters asked.

"Yes," James said, realizing he'd have to show his hand and reveal what he knew about bacteria. With measured deliberation and his hands out before him, he added, "There is a world that exists beneath ours, so small you and I cannot see it, but it is real."

"You speak like a sorcerer. It is as though you talk of magic."

"Not magic. This is not make-believe or fantasy. Her body is fighting a war against hundreds of thousands of monsters, each of them smaller than the sharp end of a pin."

"But how could such creatures exist?"

"How does the moon not fall from the sky?" James asked, trying to turn the logic around. "That reality defies our expectations is not magic, it simply means there is more for us to learn.

"Think about it. If you dent your plow, does it fix itself? If you break a beam of timber, will it mend? And yet cut your hand and within days the skin has grown back. Why? What's different?"

"I am alive," replied Winters.

"Yes, but it's more than that. If you want a glass of water you make a deliberate decision to get up and get something to drink, but you make no such concerted effort to heal a wound. Why?"

"I don't know."

"Exactly. There are aspects of life that function beyond our knowledge, without our specific involvement, like the beating of the heart.

"There is a microscopic world, smaller than anything we can see, occurring at the tiniest of levels."

"I have played with a magnifying glass," the old man protested. "I have seen nothing of this world you describe. Do you expect me to believe in fairy tales?"

"Don't do this," James snapped. "Don't be like the villagers, caught in their ignorance and superstition. You're better than that."

The old man's patience was wearing thin. The look in his eyes betrayed his feelings. The growl in his voice confirmed his anger.

"It is you who are superstitious. It is you who would have me believe in something without reason."

Outside, birds sung in the warmth of the morning, oblivious to the tension within the cabin. James was losing the argument and he knew it. He looked around, his mind racing, desperately trying to think of some tangible way to describe the world of microbes. His eyes caught sight of a rotund wheel of cheese sitting on the shelf above the kitchen bench.

"Think about mold. Whether it's forming cheese, causing fruit to rot or growing in a damp corner, what you're seeing is a colony containing hundreds of thousands, millions of tiny spores growing and multiplying. You're seeing the microscopic realm explode into our world."

James turned to Lisa, adding, "Her body is fighting a bacterial infection, but we can help her fight back. This is a monster we can defeat. Bacteria are living creatures. They're vicious, but they can be beaten."

"You expect me to believe this?"

"No," James replied, anger rising in his voice. "It matters not what you believe. It's true regardless."

The old man seemed taken aback by his audacity, so James continued, explaining what was happening.

"You're right in that the infection is taking hold and the wound is becoming inflamed. Time is of the essence. We need to clean her cuts with something that will kill the bacteria from the outside, giving her body a chance to fight off the bacteria from within."

"And what will kill these invisible monsters of yours?" Winters asked, mocking him.

"Think about it," James said, appealing to the others. "Think about what you have around you that doesn't spoil."

James turned to Amelia, saying, "Meat rots. Bread goes moldy. What stays fresh? What never spoils?"

"Honey?" Amelia replied.

"Yes."

"What about vinegar?" Jonathan said, a waver of doubt in his voice.

"Bad cider?" Winters asked in surprise.

"Yes," James said. "We might think it's bad, but it's not. We still use vinegar, right? We don't throw it away."

"I use it in cooking," Amelia said, agreeing with him, "And it's good on bee stings, and for getting rid of stains in clothing."

Somehow, from the kindness in her voice, James felt she wanted to believe him. She wanted there to be an alternative to the amputation. He knew he had her on his side, and he intended to use her support to his advantage.

"What about cleaning?" James asked, leading her on.

"Yes. I use it to get rid of mildew and mold, and for cleaning the bench."

"Exactly," James said, ceasing on her point. "Because bacteria and fungus cannot grow in vinegar."

"And you think this will save her leg?" Winters asked. "Honey and vinegar?"

"No," James replied. "I don't think these things will save her leg. I think they will allow her body to save her leg. We need to clean her wounds carefully, washing and treating them, and then give her body a chance to wage war against the bacteria."

"A wish and a prayer won't work here," Winters replied. He took the wood saw from the fire, cleaning the soot from it with a fresh cloth.

Lisa was trembling, shaking with fear, mumbling under her breath as the boys held her down.

"I don't need either a wish or a prayer," James said, refusing to be intimidated. He looked the old man in the eye. "I know you think you're doing what's right. I understand that someone once made hard decisions for your life, decisions against your will, but this is different."

"How is it different?"

"She already fought off a mild fever yesterday. Her leg was far better when I walked through your door than it had been up in the mountains. Her body is responding, but it's fighting a protracted battle, surging back and forth. We need to help it win.

"And we know what we're up against. We know how to treat her. It's not just a case of keeping the wound clean, but cleaning it with anti-bacterial agents, chemicals that will kill germs. We need to give her body the best chance of winning this war. I need time. I need you to wait."

"If you're wrong," Winters began, "she dies. You know that, right?"

"Why did you place the saw in the fire?" James asked, ignoring him.

"To clean it."

"Why not just wipe it clean?" he asked. "And why boil the water? If you start with clean water, boiling shouldn't make it any cleaner. No, think about it. What you're doing is sterilizing both the saw and the water, you're using heat to kill any microscopic organisms that could lead to infection. You just don't know it because this knowledge has been lost."

Winters was silent for a moment. James could see him considering his logic.

"If she gets worse," Winters began.

"If she gets worse, all bets are off," James said.

"If she becomes delirious. If fever sets in ..." Winters didn't need to finish his sentence. James didn't need to respond. He simply nodded and there was an agreement settled between them.

The old man put the saw back by the door and wandered outside, muttering to himself. The two boys released Lisa and followed their father. They avoided eye contact as they shuffled past. Jonathan's head hung low, but Wilbur had an air of defiance. It seemed they didn't agree with each other, let alone with James.

Amelia helped James bathe Lisa's leg, cleaning the wounds while old man Winters and the boys headed out on the farm. Lisa screamed at the pain as the diluted apple cider vinegar bit at her leg. James tried to be tender, but the alternative was worse. Once he was sure the wound was clean, he carefully daubed honey into the exposed flesh.

"I'm sorry," he said, "but we'll need to do this twice daily."

That night, Lisa's wounds looked no better, but they hadn't become worse. By noon the next day, the red tinge around the jagged edges of her cuts had turned to a soft pink.

"Your little magic potion is working," said Winters, sitting down with Amelia at the wooden table for lunch.

He'd been quiet for most of the morning, reshaping a plow over by the barn while the boys had cleaned out the grain silo.

James suspected Winters was as relieved as the rest of them to see Lisa recovering. Lisa, though, was moody, and James could see she couldn't bring herself to be open and warm with a man that almost forcibly cut off her leg.

As they sat there with sunlight streaming in through the open windows, Winters favored his bad leg, resting both hands on one thigh and gently massaging the muscle. James wasn't sure if it was a subconscious reaction to what they'd gone through over the past two days, or if the old man's amputated leg was somewhat tender from the morning's work. Either way, Winters' focus on his bad leg was apparent for all to see.

"How did you know?" Winters asked. The two teenaged boys leaned forward, wanting to catch what was said. James felt cornered. Winters had to know he was a reader, there was no other explanation, but the old man didn't seem threatened, he was curious. It was a risk, but James wanted to come clean. Surely not everyone subscribed to the superstitions of the villagers. There had to be trust, there had to be understanding.

"I read about bacteria," James replied, pulling up a chair next to Winters.

"You're a reader?"

"Yes."

It was good to be honest. James felt he had nothing to be ashamed of except the superstitions that haunted the valley.

"My father taught me to read. He drummed the written word into me from a child."

"Old man Dobson," Winters said, an air of admiration in his voice. "Always was a clever bastard."

James couldn't help but smile.

"So all this," Winters said, gesturing at the walls. "You can read all this? You know what all this is?"

"Yes."

For the next few hours, they sat and talked about the various items displayed within the cabin.

Amelia reminded Winters he was supposed to be plowing the western fields, but he didn't care. The fallow ground could wait. Wilbur and Jonathan were fascinated by the details James could recall as he told them about the Old World and the fall of civilization.

By early evening, Lisa's leg looked healthier. The tissue was visibly pale and the swelling had subsided. James washed her leg again, but she was more tolerant of the pain, taking it in her stride.

As evening fell, Lisa grew restless, saying they should be moving on tomorrow. She asked if one of the boys could take them on to the next town.

Winters said it was foolish to continue traveling, that Lisa needed to allow the bone in her leg time to mend.

Amelia suggested they stay awhile, saying they were welcome to share in their food.

James accepted.

The right side of his chest and back had come out in severe, deep bruising from his fall through the snow. The branches on the pine tree may have broken his fall, but that came at a price. As the days since the bear attack wore on, James was surprised by how sore he felt. The more time transpired, the more his body rebelled against strenuous activity, demanding he rest and recuperate. He could see Lisa was nervous, but she wouldn't tell him why. Having been through so much, he knew they both needed time to recover.

Over the next few days, Lisa's leg improved further. Scabs formed over the deep, jagged tears, hiding the mending tissue beneath a hard outer crust. Her broken leg would take months to heal properly, but Wilbur made a form-fitted brace that strapped to either side of her leg, holding it firmly in place, and she was able to hobble around on her crutch. Lisa was determined not to be a burden and insisted on helping Amelia prepare meals.

For James, those few days were invigorating.

On the fifth day, everything changed.

Chapter 05: North

Sweat dripped from his forehead.

James wiped his eyes with the back of his hand. Although he was wearing leather gloves, blisters were forming on his palms as he dug with the spade, loosening a large rock from the ground.

The two boys, Jonathan and Wilbur, were quiet as they kept up a blistering pace, throwing rocks into the cart as old man Winters hobbled along, leading the horse down the field. They were harvesting rocks, at least, that was what his father called it. Village folk used to make fun of the spring harvest, particularly the teens, but it was serious business, as every farmer knew. With the ground thawing during the day and freezing at night, the dirt would expand and contract, forcing rocks up through to the surface. Given the strength of the horses, any rock larger than a man's hand could damage a plow, so the rocks had to be harvested before seed could be sown.

James bent down, dropping his ass so he could pick up a large rock without using his back. He lifted with his legs, driving up with his thighs, gaining a little momentum so he could hurl the rock into the back of the cart.

A hunk of fractured granite flew through the air, catching the edge of the wooden cart and falling back to the hard-packed earth with a thud. James groaned. Despite his best efforts to lift properly, his back ached. Wearily, he stepped over to grab the rock again when Wilbur called out.

"Looks like we've got company."

A troop of soldiers made its way along the trail toward the farm. Their colorful standards were visible through the deciduous trees still devoid of their leaves. There was an unusual amount of pomp in their scarlet banners, each one trimmed with gold. For a moment, James was in awe.

"Wilbur," Winters said, his voice low and rough. "Get the women and take them out back. Hide them in the cellar under the hay barn. Pile bales on top of the lid, but don't make it too obvious. Be sure the hay bales are messy, so it looks like a staging area."

Wilbur didn't have to be told twice, he tossed his long crowbar into the back of the wagon and ran off on foot toward the cabin.

"Jonathan," Winters said. "You keep going with the rocks. Let's play dumb, like it's no big deal. We've got nothing to hide. James and I'll head them off at the cabin."

James felt a sickening knot form in his stomach. He wasn't sure why, but he thought Lisa was in some kind of trouble, serious trouble if the approaching soldiers were any measure to go by. Winters seemed to understand that too. Jonathan didn't need to be told what to do. He loaded up a couple of the crossbows they carried to ward off animal attacks and lay them in the rear of the cart, out of sight but easily accessible.

"Anything you want to tell me about you and your girlfriend?" Winters asked, hobbling across the stony ground at a fast pace. James kept walking, although his eyes darted back at the dusty road, looking at the approaching troop.

"Ah, no. Nothing." It was the truth, but it felt like a lie.

"They're flying colors from the north. That's both good and bad."

"How so?" James asked, resisting the urge to run ahead of the old man and help Wilbur hide the women. Wilbur, he noted, had not run directly to the cabin, he'd headed down along the hedgerow to the end of the field, using the horse and cart to cover his line-of-sight, allowing him to slip under the hedge and move back to the cabin unseen from the road. James caught a brief glimpse of him darting across between the corral and the cabin, and then heading into the cabin from the rear. They'd done this before.

Winters was breathing hard as he strode over the uneven ground.

"Colors mean they're announcing their character well in advance to avoid any misunderstandings."

"That's good?" James asked, a little unsure.

"Oh, that's good," Winters replied.

"Then what's bad?"

"That they're flying colors means they're confident they're moving in a force large enough that no one can bother them. It's a bit like a cock strutting its feathers in the yard."

"That's bad," James said, helping the old man bend down and pass through a wooden fence. From there he hobbled over to the cabin.

"Yep," said the old man without any emotion. "This is probably just a scouting party split off from the main troop. You sure you don't have something you want to tell me, son?"

James didn't want to lie to Winters. Although he had his suspicions about Lisa, he didn't know who she was or where she was from.

"No, sir."

"Well, seems your girlfriend has pissed off some serious muscle."

The old man was quiet as he hobbled on his wooden leg. He sat on the edge of a watering trough and turned to face the soldiers as they began coming down the worn path between the fallowed fields.

He turned to face James, saying, "I sure hope this little secret of hers doesn't end up costing us our lives."

James replied, "Me too."

Four officers came down the track on horseback. Their armor looked resplendent in the sunlight, shining and glistening. Behind them, a squad of ten soldiers jogged in unison. The soldiers were lightly armed, carrying spears but no armor. The rear two horses were loaded up with extra armor for the foot soldiers. They were laden with shields and pikes, swords and crossbows, all carefully mounted in breakaway baskets, ready for rapid deployment.

As they came up to the log cabin, the soldiers fanned out, moving around the cabin, while the officers came to a halt in front of James and Winters.

"Good day to you," Winters called out.

The lead officer replied. "Yes, it is a fair spring day. The weather is particularly mild for this time of year." James thought it was unusual to see an officer posturing with such pleasantries. "We have come from afar on the business of trade. May we water our horses?"

"Be my guest," Winters replied, standing and giving the lead horse the opportunity to drink from the trough. "But we have nothing to trade. Trade should be done in the villages."

The officer ignored him. The horse lowered its head, sniffing at the water but not drinking.

"What really brings you this way?" Winters asked. The look of concern on his face suggested that while he recognized the officer was polite, he knew the soldiers were searching his grounds without permission. James could hear one of them inside the cabin, knocking furniture around. He must have gone in through the rear door.

"Where are your women?" the officer asked, ignoring Winters.

"They've gone with one of my sons, south to the village of Amersham to fetch seed for our fields."

"How long have they been gone?"

"Two days," the old man replied, moving to one side so the light of the sun wasn't directly in his eyes. The officer nudged his horse, trying to keep the sun directly behind him and making it difficult for either of them to see his face.

"When will they be back?"

"We expect them in a week," Winters replied, lying. James hung back, trying to remain inconspicuous. In the distance, he could see Jonathan still out in the field, placing stones in the cart rather than tossing them in, probably to avoid triggering the crossbows lying on the rocks in the back of the cart.

"You wouldn't be lying to me, now would you?" the officer asked as one of the soldiers stepped out of the cabin behind them. "I don't like liars."

"Me neither," Winters replied. "You wouldn't be lying to me either, would you?" The old man had balls, of that James had no doubt.

The officer smiled, climbing down from the huge beast. One of the soldiers pulled the base of the rope ladder taut as the officer made his way down, making it easier for him to descend.

"We seek a woman, a teenager," he said. "Have you seen any such woman?"

"You're not giving us much of a description to go on," Winters replied.

"I imagine you don't see too many teenage women out this way," the officer replied. "We think she was with a small party, perhaps no more than two or three others, servants of hers."

James got his first good look at the man. He was tall. Despite the weight of his polished armor, he held his back straight and his head erect. His trousers were clean, as were his boots, telling James he had servants waiting on him, which was no surprise given his demeanor.

The officer unclipped his armor, handing it to the soldier behind him and revealing a scarlet vest resplendent with the same crest as the flags and standards carried by the troop. His name and rank were embossed over his heart—Captain McIntyre.

One of the soldiers called out from the barn, dragging Wilbur out into the open. McIntyre marched over with Winters hobbling after him. James followed.

"He's my son," Winters cried. "Leave him be."

McIntyre ignored Winters.

"What was he doing?"

"Mucking out the stalls," the soldier replied.

"Search the stalls," McIntyre commanded. "Turn them over."

Smart, thought James. Jonathan had left the girls in the cellar beneath the hay storage and had returned to the main barn, drawing the attention of the soldiers away from their hiding place.

"What has she done?" James asked. As soon as those words left his lips, he knew it was a mistake. His curiosity was as good as an admission, and McIntyre seized on his words.

"So she has been here?"

Neither James nor Winters offered any more.

"She is the daughter of General Augustus Gainsborough, commander of the northern tribes."

The soldier beside McIntyre stepped forward, making as though he would apprehend James, but McIntyre called him off with the subtlest of hand gestures, just a slight wave of his hand indicating he should hold his ground.

"Where is she?" he asked politely, stepping forward toward James.

"What will happen to her?" James asked, ignoring the officer's question and asking his own.

"We seek nothing but her welfare," McIntyre replied, and James had no reason to doubt him. There was nothing sinister in his motives, of that James was sure.

For James, the charade was stupid. Lisa wouldn't trust him. She hadn't been honest with any of them. What did he owe her? And as for Winters, the old man was putting his life and the lives of his family in jeopardy for both of them, simply out of honor when Lisa had done nothing to prove herself. She'd lied to them, or at the very least misled them. But this was serious. There was no law to govern soldiers other than their own code. Villages had been plundered through misunderstandings, left to burn because of some minor slight. James wasn't prepared to put Winters in jeopardy like that, not for Lisa, not without reason.

212

"She's been hurt," he replied. "She was caught in a bear trap north of the foothills, below Stanton's peak. I brought her here simply because this was the closest farm. Winters and his family knew nothing of her a week ago. They have been good to us, good to her."

He paused for a second, measuring his words, speaking with slow deliberation.

"You'll find her in the cellar, beneath the floor of the hay shed."

McIntyre waved his hand and the soldier by his side headed toward the shed at the back of the farm, calling out to the other soldiers as he broke into a jog.

Within minutes they carried out Lisa, holding her between them, keeping her broken leg with its splint raised off the ground. For her part, Lisa was yelling at them, demanding they release her. She saw James standing by McIntyre and cursed him.

"You ... How could you do this to me? You asshole. How could you betray me? How could you turn me over to them? I hate you!"

Lisa was striking at the soldiers, scratching and hitting them while they did nothing to defend themselves other than to wince under her blows.

"Calm down," McIntyre said trying to placate her, holding his hand up as though he were stilling a wild mare.

"You groveling guttersnipe," Lisa replied with a surge of venom that surprised James. "I should have known he'd send you."

Winters stepped forward, rocking on his wooden leg, trying to appeal to Lisa.

"I don't know what you're running from," the old man said. "But how far did you think you would get on your own? Where would you go from here? How long could you survive by yourself with that leg?"

"At least I'd be free," she cried as one of the soldiers slipped a leather strap under her armpits. Another soldier pulled her up, hoisting her on to the back of one of the horses. He positioned her carefully, strapping her in the broad saddle so she wouldn't fall.

"Thank you for taking care of her," McIntyre said, shaking Winters hand. He tapped James on the shoulder thanking him as well. James was relieved to see there was none of the usual military hotheadedness. McIntyre surprised him.

"Captain McIntyre," James said. "What will become of Lisa?"

"She'll be taken to her father."

"To found a dynasty," Lisa yelled from the horse back. "To be sold off like a slave and bred like a heifer, all so the general can establish a confederacy, an alliance of northern states. You should have left me in that bear trap. At least I would have died with dignity."

James was taken aback. This was a side of Lisa he'd never expected to see. She was fiery, defiant. The bitterness she held caused a pang of guilt to run through him. He'd thought he was doing the right thing by her, even if it wasn't what she wanted, but there was clearly some history between her and her father, something he didn't understand.

"She will be fine," McIntyre said. He turned to climb up on his horse but paused, thinking for a moment before turning back to James. "You addressed me as captain."

James went quiet realizing what he'd inadvertently done.

"You can read."

James felt like he'd been caught stealing, or condemned for murder. McIntyre seemed to sense that.

"We do not share the superstitions of the plains. In the north, we value readers, we honor them. There's a new world awakening. We are restoring the former ways, rebuilding the cities."

He paused, looking to see if James would say anything, but James figured he'd said too much already.

"Come with us," McIntyre said.

James looked up at Lisa and the scowl on her face.

"Come with us," McIntyre repeated. "General Gainsborough would be pleased to meet the man that rescued his daughter."

214

James hesitated. Although McIntyre's words sounded like an invitation, there was something about his posture, his manner suggesting that this was more than a polite pleasantry. McIntyre was being civil, but there was no doubt in James' mind this was not optional. As if in confirmation, McIntyre added, "I insist."

James was acutely aware of the soldiers forming up behind him.

"It's OK," Winters said. "I'll send word to your father."

McIntyre gestured to the rope ladder and James climbed up behind Lisa. She said nothing, but her posture was proud—defiant.

Chapter 06: Downtown

The ride north took three days, during which Lisa barely said a word to James. Any words they did exchange were terse. Her disdain for him was clear. For his part, James understood he was a prisoner, not in the sense of a criminal being shackled in chains, but he was held against his will.

The soldiers were courteous, but always present, never letting him stray when they broke to make camp. There were at least fifty of them. From what James overheard in conversation, the squad that closed in on Winter's homestead were a diversion, the main force had surrounded the farm much earlier in the day. They had lain in wait in the forest in case things went sour.

McIntyre hadn't exposed himself until they were well in place. The outlying scouts were no doubt watching them for hours before McIntyre approached by the southern road. If James hadn't volunteered Lisa's hiding spot, there would have been someone in the trees that saw them scurrying away to hide in the barn. And if they had been caught in a lie, Winters would have lost everything. They would have razed the farm to the ground in spite. Certainly, from what James was able to glean from the soldier's banter with each other, they had a fair idea Lisa was there before they closed in.

James was in over his head. He sat there on the back of one of the broad horses, sitting a few feet behind McIntyre as the troop wound its way over the mountain pass and down through the forest. They were traveling toward Richmond, Virginia. It seemed the rusting road signs were more to be believed than Lisa. Thinking back to what she'd said about Little Bayless and Greensburg, James finally realized she'd lied to both of them.

Winters had never bought into it, he figured, but James still struggled with how she'd lied to him.

After lunch, the order of the horses changed slightly and James found his horse behind Lisa's. Slowly, the trees lining the crumbling road gave way to fields and meadows.

"She told me about the bear and the wolves," McIntyre said, sitting at the front of the group saddle, holding the reins of the horse. It was strange to converse with McIntyre without looking at him face to face, and James wondered how deliberate this was, if McIntyre was hiding this conversation from Lisa who sat astride the next horse.

"And you believe her?" James asked. It was true, of course, he knew that, but his confidence in Lisa was so shaken he was curious to know what McIntyre thought. Don't give away the farm, his father always told him. If you're bartering, you want to trade from a position of strength, keep the buyer off guard. These were lessons that served him well.

"Should I?" McIntyre asked.

"Yes, but you won't. Why would you?"

James was glad McIntyre wasn't looking at him. He never was one for poker and couldn't keep a straight face, so this arrangement suited him. He didn't want to be mean, but he wasn't sure what he owed McIntyre. Why he should be in any way accommodating?

"It's a brave man that takes on a bear alone," McIntyre said, his body swaying with the gentle motion of the horse beneath them.

James replied, "A brave man or a fool."

McIntyre laughed, "Yes. Or a fool."

James was starting to like the captain. There was something about the way he carried himself, as though honor were the highest of morals. James had no doubt McIntyre could dispense his military duties with ruthless efficiency, and yet within that he got a sense that the captain held himself accountable for his actions even if no one else did. In another setting, he was sure he'd find a friend in McIntyre, but this was no place for sentiments. McIntyre answered to General Gainsborough, someone James knew only by vague reputation. Rumor had it Gainsborough was a cold-hearted killer, but rumors took on the fears and prejudices of those that spread them.

What had McIntyre seen in Gainsborough? What was there for better or for worse in the service of a dictator? Looking at the captain's broad shoulders, James wondered what would motivate McIntyre to give his life in service to another. The cut of his uniform, his dark black trousers and polished boots, they spoke of conformity. What had McIntyre given his allegiance to? What had he sworn to uphold, and what jarring contradictions were there between his oaths and reality? It was a jaundiced attitude to assume there were flaws, but the image before James had been carefully cultivated to avoid precisely that realization, and that made James suspicious of what lay hidden beneath the polished veneer. James may have been young, but his father had schooled him well, teaching him to see through the facade of authority and the allure of a fancy uniform.

Shiny buttons and trim, colored ribbons might make a man feel special, but it was what was worn on the inside that defined him. What was hidden inside of McIntyre? What lay beneath the pomp and ceremony? James wasn't sure.

"You could have left her to the bear," McIntyre began. "No one would have thought any less of you. No one could expect you to risk your life to save a stranger. She was as good as dead anyway."

He was feeling him out. As much as James wanted to understand McIntyre, the captain was doing the same with him, probing, exploring.

"I couldn't do that," James replied, not sure what else to say.

"Why?"

"I don't know. I just couldn't. I'm not sure I could explain why. Something within me just wouldn't leave someone to die like that. I had to try something."

"Trapping the bear in a drift was smart."

James laughed. "You're giving me more credit than is due. There was no planning, no noble bravery, no heroic fight. I ran for my life."

McIntyre's head bobbed. He seemed to be considering that in detail.

"And the wolves?" he asked. "Were you saving your own hide then as well?"

James hadn't really thought too much about what had happened, let alone his motives and reasons.

"It just seemed the right thing to do."

"It's that simple?"

"It's that simple," James replied, wondering what the captain was driving toward.

"So you've never met Elizabeth Gainsborough before?"

"No."

"You weren't warned she was traveling through there?"

"No."

"You weren't hired in advance? Paid to scout for her? Told to meet her just off the pass?"

"No. No. No."

"We know she had help escaping. We know someone provided her with a fresh horse."

James was silent. He was surprised by McIntyre's insinuations. He could have denied it more vehemently if he wanted to, after all, it wasn't true, but he was curious. Was this what McIntyre really thought? That James was a mercenary? Would denying that charge change the captain's opinion, or simply reinforce it further? What would McIntyre make of his silence? Hah, thought James, there was nothing he could say, no point of logic he could put forward that would convince McIntyre otherwise.

"So you don't believe any of it?" James asked.

"Nope."

James laughed softly to himself, shaking his head, not that McIntyre saw him. McIntyre kept his eyes forward, looking down the road as the horse plodded on.

"I believe she was caught in a bear trap and that you helped her down the mountain, but beyond that, I don't think you're telling me the truth."

"Well," James replied. "I don't care what you think."

One of the advance scouts came bounding down the road toward them.

"We've got Whiskey Delta, two klicks," the scout said, catching his breath as the horse came to a halt in front of him.

"Break east?" McIntyre asked.

"Affirmative. There's a trail east by north east at 250."

McIntyre rocked in his saddle, turning slightly and signaling with his hands to the rest of the soldiers. His movements were deft, his hand motions crisp. He raised his hand, pulling downward with a clenched fist and followed with a series of sharp gestures using his fingers that finished in pointing to the east. James was fascinated. He'd entered a whole other world. At a guess, he figured the scout had picked up on monsters moving through the valley below and was directing them around the area.

"Whiskey Delta. Wild dogs," McIntyre said, preempting the question from James.

Within roughly two hundred yards there was an overgrown side road branching to the north east. It came as no surprise to James when they turned off and followed it through a thicket.

The soldiers that had once been so relaxed as they jogged alongside the horses spread out, extending forward and behind the main party, pikes at the ready. Their fitness was astounding.

Lisa sat calmly on the horse ahead of them. She seemed disinterested, distracted, only occasionally talking to the officer at the reins.

James looked around constantly, soaking up the subtleties of how the troop worked together but Lisa stared ahead, not even looking at the scenery. She'd done this too often, he thought.

As they rounded a steep corner winding down into the valley, the road petered out into a rough, dirt track.

In the distance, James could see a city looming before them. They were close, much closer than he expected.

Skyscrapers touched the moody clouds. Even from the foothills, it was apparent the buildings had been infected with termites or ants. Reaching up some thirty to forty stories, the downtown buildings had been caked with dried mud. Their elongated rectangular shapes, originally so dominant and sharply defined had been softened. Thick packed mud surrounded the base of each building, spreading out into the streets, burying some of the smaller, one to two story buildings.

Snow sat against the northern face of the skyscrapers. Although the occasional sharp corner of a man-made edifice was visible atop several of the buildings, most of them were dominated by pillars of rock-hard mud. Jagged spires reached up into the heavens in defiance of man.

Another soldier came running alongside their horse. They'd already covered at least ten miles that morning. From what James had observed, the troop wouldn't push more than thirty miles in a day, which he considered a phenomenal distance to cover day in and day out. Their fitness was astounding, but he doubted they could maintain such a pace over more than a week.

"What are you thinking, sergeant?" McIntyre asked.

"We should pull back," he replied, calling out between breaths. "Camp on the ridge-line. Make a run for Richmond tomorrow."

"It's been a good run so far," McIntyre replied. "No attacks."

"Call it in," the sergeant replied. "But my advice is hold off. If we move now, we'll have no time to spare within the city, no room for maneuvering if we get into a fight."

"I'm not keeping her in the wild for another night."

"Understood." The sergeant peeled away, jogging over to the soldiers flanking them and barking short, sharp commands.

McIntyre raised a radio to his mouth. James had seen radios before, but only in books. He knew what they did, but thought that this technology had been lost in time. James understood the need for batteries supplying electricity to such a device, but the very notion of a radio seemed spooky, talking to some disembodied voice, some distant specter, and yet he was thrilled to see a working radio.

"Archangel, this is Rec-Force. Over."

The radio crackled. James found his heart racing. What else had they revived from the Old World? Had they really tamed a city?

"Archangel. Rec-Force. Over."

"Copy you, Rec-Force. This is Archangel." The voice was tinny. James struggled to make out the words and found himself substituting what he thought had been said in the scratchy reply.

"Archangel. We are 15 out. How's the weather?"

James found his mind running with the possibilities. He figured they were roughly ten to fifteen miles from the city center, so he understood that reference, but the weather? That had to be something other than a reference to the clouds or the wind.

"Sighting Golf Bravo Regency. Mike Lima Lakeside. Be advised Alpha Tango collapsed Parkway. Over."

"Copy that, Archangel." McIntyre released the transmit button.

He must have known how much this was eating up James. For his benefit, he clarified the incoming message, saying, "They've sighted grizzly bears in Regency Woods, which is our usual approach. Mountain lions have been seen moving through the suburb of Lakeside, and either the ants or termites have undermined the parkway bridge crossing the river. It doesn't leave us with a lot of options.

"Ordinarily, I'd take Mitch's advice and hold here, wait for tomorrow and circle around to the east before heading in to base, but every night she's out here in the wild she's in danger."

McIntyre was assuming James was interested. He was, but McIntyre never turned around to talk directly with him. James was impressed with his concern for Lisa. As hostile as she was toward McIntyre, he really cared about her, so much so he wasn't willing to risk another night out here.

"So what do we do?" James asked, finding himself swept up in the bravado of the moment.

"Archangel," McIntyre said, talking into the radio. "Advise on Delta Echo, Downtown Expressway."

There was a pause for a moment. James had no idea about the tactics involved, but that McIntyre was exploring possibilities, looking for alternative approaches was thrilling. He sensed the determination of the man.

"Rec-Force. Romeo Mike, Yankee Juliet. Recommend you bravo, box the southern route." The words were barely audible to James, sounding more like the scratching of an animal on a barn door than a man talking, but McIntyre provided the translation.

"Romeo Mike, Yankee Juliet. Rats and mice are active in the downtown region, along with yellow jacket hornets," he said, the radio resting on his leg as the horse rocked beneath them. "They're telling me to cross the river to the south, circle around to the east, then cross back to the north, but that would mean a night in the open on the southern plains."

"We have the package," McIntyre said, talking with as much clarity as he could muster into the radio. "Repeat. We have the package. Running for home. Rec-Force, out."

"Copy that," came the reply. "Archangel, out."

McIntyre slipped the radio back into a leather satchel on the side of the broad saddle. James didn't need any explanation of the last message, the meaning was clear. McIntyre must have sensed that as none was offered.

It took an hour before they began to wind their way through the suburbs on the outskirts of Richmond. Everyone was on edge.

Monsters seemed to sense them coming. Somewhere in the distance a wild dog barked. The soldiers closed ranks as the troop returned to the cracked concrete roads. With their pikes by their side, they ran with a sense of urgency, as if time was the greatest enemy they faced.

As they joined the expressway, with its median barrier separating the two sides of the wide road, McIntyre seemed to stiffen, as though he was expecting to be attacked by something out of the shadows.

James had only ever been into one town, one much smaller than Richmond, and he'd only ever been there to visit the library. The route his father had followed was carefully calculated so that it contained safe-points, places of refuge in case they were approached by a monster, but the route into Richmond felt exposed. If they encountered a pack of wild dogs, there was nowhere to run to.

A giant cockroach scurried beneath the rusted hulk of a car chassis.

The broken slabs of concrete making up the highway had shifted with time, subsiding in some places while rising up in others, slowing their progress. To either side of the road, large banks covered in long grass and trees hid the approaches. They'd have no warning of a bear or mountain lion until it was almost on top of them.

Several of the bridges crossing over the expressway had fallen, forcing the troop to climb over the rubble. The horses struggled with the debris, slowing them down.

To the west, the faint outline of the sun sat low in the sky, hidden by dark rolling clouds. For James, it felt as though the expressway would never end, but McIntyre explained it was easier than risking the suburbs. He said the low elevation tended to hide their scent, making it safer than perhaps it seemed.

James wasn't convinced. As well trained as the soldiers were, his mind began thinking about escape. If a confrontation arose, what would he do? Where would he go? As they journeyed on, he kept a mental note of what he considered the best courses for retreat. He figured he'd let them tie down any monster that might stray across their path while he slipped away in the confusion.

As they moved beneath an overpass, James noted McIntyre had his hand on his sidearm. It had to be loaded, and James wondered what McIntyre might be looking for in the rusting steel girders barely a foot above their heads. Even the horses seemed wary of the bridges. What were they scared of? Whatever it was, it had to be small or the handgun would have been ineffective. Spiders? Ravens? Raccoons? The more he thought about it, the more his mind jumped at the shadows beneath the crumbling bridges.

They made good time on the flat open stretches of road.

With trees dotted along either side of the highway, James was unsure whether they were still within the town. Except for the towering ant hills in the downtown region, they could have been somewhere out in the countryside. He caught sight of a feral cat slinking away through the undergrowth. It had been crossing a pedestrian bridge over the freeway. For James, it was a good sign. The cat had been in the open, it had felt unthreatened until they'd come along. Once, domestic cats had been pets, now they were the least of the monsters. They tended to be overly cautious and careful. If a cat was in the open, there were no dogs within a mile or so, and James breathed easy. McIntyre saw the cat as well, pointing at the animal as it disappeared into the undergrowth, but he never said anything. Although talking wouldn't make any difference, it seemed no one wanted to jinx their transit through the city.

A thick tangle of juniper shrubs and weeds had taken hold in the center strip dividing the highway, forcing them to choose one side or the other.

With a wave of his hand, McIntyre signaled they should stay to the right. James silently agreed with the decision. With the shadows growing long, the western side of the expressway was in the shade, making it more dangerous, allowing monsters to lie in wait without being seen.

James had already noticed movement in the bushes, but he was sure it was from rats. That would explain the cat, as it was probably hunting them. The rats were no danger, not yet. Although they were a couple of feet in length, they tended to be scavengers. They'd scurry along beneath the bushes before dropping away, only for another couple of rats to pick up the trail further along. If the troop ran into a lion or a bear and there were casualties, the rats would be there, feasting on any bloodied scraps.

Slowly, the ruins of low-lying buildings began dominating the embankments. Occasionally, the screech of some wild animal or bird cut through the still air, setting their nerves on edge. As quiet as they thought they were in moving through the city, it was clear the animals didn't think so, and that was likely to attract attention, the wrong kind of attention.

James jumped as McIntyre's radio crackled. The words were harsh, hard.

"Rec-Force. We have visual."

McIntyre reached into his satchel, picked up the radio and replied in the same terse tone of voice.

"Copy that."

Looking at the downtown region rising before them, James wondered where archangel was watching from. Ants and termites traversed the mud-laden skyscrapers. Beyond them, a rusted water-tower sat alone on a hill. That had to be the observation post, James thought. One of the legs had buckled, causing the tower to lean to one side, but it still stood almost two hundred feet in the air.

"Rec-Force. We have Romeo Sierra en-route."

"Copy, Archangel."

McIntyre turned slightly back to face James. "They're sending troop reinforcements to guide us in." It was the first time that day McIntyre had acknowledged him in that way. James felt he should reply and almost said, 'copy that,' in response.

"Great. The sooner we're off these streets the better."

"There's still a way to go yet," McIntyre said. "We'll probably link up just after the city center."

So much for the northern tribes having reclaimed the cities. James was beginning to suspect that particular rumor was nothing more than propaganda. From what he'd gathered so far, he figured they had a token hold on a small portion of the city, somewhere on the outskirts. It was a far cry from driving the monsters out and reclaiming the land, but he could understand their motivation. You had to start somewhere and, for all their faults, the northern tribes had started. It was more than he could say for the raggedy band of villages to the south. And they'd reclaimed technology, not only finding and restoring equipment like radios, but figuring out a way to charge them.

The sun broke through the clouds. Although it was sitting low on the horizon, the warmth on his face was welcome. The horse seemed to appreciate it too, kicking up a little, but not out of fright. The lumbering beast picked up its pace, its hooves clacking on the crushed concrete.

As they approached downtown, the mud-packed nests towered above them. Trails of ants scurried along invisible paths that wound themselves along the edge of the road.

Each ant was the size of a man's foot or larger, carrying twigs, bits of wood, clumps of fur, and the dismembered carcass of a wasp. Their mandibles could leave a nasty bite, easily cutting through skin but not bone. With thick, bulbous bodies, they raced along faster than the soldiers jogging alongside the horses. It was only then James realized the soldiers had changed weapons. Instead of long pikes, carried midway so they were balanced, they now carried crossbows. He turned, looking at the horse coming up the rear behind them. The pikes and lances had been clipped in place on the huge beast, rising up slightly above the animal. Whatever they were expecting, it wasn't a bear or a dog.

James went to say something but McIntyre raised his hand, signaling quiet. The lead horse came to a stop, bringing the troop to a halt.

McIntyre pointed at the built-up layers of hard-packed dirt burying the road. At first James didn't understand. Then he realized what it was that had attracted McIntyre's attention.

There were no ants.

Whereas before, the ants had busied themselves, winding in trails along the road, now they were nowhere to be seen. In the cool air, perspiration broke out on his forehead. The ants had disappeared into underground caverns and tunnels. That they'd forsaken the surface worried him. Something wasn't right.

The soldiers fanned out, spreading themselves across the street and climbing over the thick, caked-mud packed on the ground. The metal frame of a bus protruded from the mud on the far side of the street, below one of the sky-scraping mounds. The rear of the rusted frame disappeared beneath the slope of mud and debris.

Soldiers took up positions, using the bus for cover. It was only now they'd come to a halt that James could hear a hum, a low, pulsating throb, but he couldn't place the direction. The noise seemed to come from all around them.

The soldiers looked nervous. They clumped in groups of three and four, with their backs turned to each other, guarding all approaches.

McIntyre snapped his fingers.

James was surprised by how crisp the sound was in the still breeze. With deft gestures, he used hand signals and pointed at several groups of soldiers. They understood implicitly what he wanted. The closest soldiers climbed up on Lisa's horse, taking positions at the back of the animal.

Lisa looked worried. Their eyes met for a moment and James remembered that look. It was the same expression she'd had on the mountain, one of desperation and anguish. She was afraid. He wanted to go to her, to tell her everything was going to be fine, but he wasn't sure what they were up against, and the soldiers with her looked determined and aggressive. She was in good hands, better hands than his.

The radio crackled. McIntyre switched it off. The two flanking groups of soldiers crept forward. Slowly, the column of four horses moved on, hanging back some thirty feet behind the scouts. James felt sorry for the soldiers out ahead, the six of them were bait, with the majority of the troop hanging back to cover the column of horses.

Although McIntyre hadn't said anything, James had a fair idea what they were up against: yellow jacket wasps. The hive had to be nearby, perhaps in one of the buildings.

His horse followed the lead horses up over the mounds of dirt blocking the road, climbing high above the street lost somewhere beneath the rock-hard dirt. The ground was uneven. The weight of the horse caused it to break through the surface occasionally, its hooves sinking into the brittle clay before it stepped forward again. With each step, James could feel the animal settling into the ground beneath them.

A couple of soldiers climbed up onto his horse, handing James a bow along with a quiver full of arrows. As they had crossbows, they joked about giving him a toy, but James ignored them. He could feel the tension in the bow begging to be fired. The balance was right, the grip tight.

James swung the quiver over his shoulder and pulled back on the drawstring of the bow. His fingers relished the feel of the pressure demanding release. James felt more confident already. Releasing the string slowly, he reached back and pulled out an arrow, examining it closely. The feathers had been set with a slight twist. They'd corkscrew nicely in flight, providing accuracy. The arrow shaft was light, while the head was a sharpened steel tip. Someone had put considerable care and effort into the arrow's construction.

James almost willed a monster to attack. He held both the bow and the arrow loosely in his right hand as he sat swaying in the saddle of the horse. The soldier behind him whispered in his ear.

"Hornets are vicious. If they swarm, wait till they're close before you fire. They'll hover for a fraction of a second before attacking, sitting off from you by about six feet. They like to pick their point of attack. That's when you shoot. Fire too soon and you'll miss. They're just too fast. But fire when they're incoming and committed, and you'll take them easy."

James nodded, thinking carefully about what the soldier had said. He knew there was a tendency to panic under pressure and appreciated the pointers, committing them to memory. These guys knew their stuff. He'd do well to pay heed, and he knew it.

The thick mass of raised clay stretched on for several hundred yards, lumpy and irregular. In the distance, he could see more troops. Reinforcements had arrived. He should have breathed easier but the throbbing, resonant hum around them set his nerves on edge.

Looking at the hard-packed dirt, James could see how it had been built up in layer upon layer by the insects, caked on like cement. The top of several street lamps sat just a foot or so above the uneven surface. Occasionally, signs were visible, their pale letters sticking out of the mud or having been exposed by the weather. They revealed the world lost beneath: God bless America, Taco Bell, Richmond welcomes safe drivers.

The soldiers kept their wary eyes on the buildings, especially the few visible windows not caked in mud.

The still air was broken by what James initially thought was the sound of thunder. He turned instinctively to see the horse behind them drop through the solidified mud, disappearing from sight in a whoosh of dust and dirt.

Immediately, hornets came swarming out of the hole. Soldiers screamed. The fallen horse panicked and struck out with its legs, trying desperately to clamber out of the hole as waves of hornets attacked in their thousands.

"Go. Go. Go," McIntyre cried, whipping his horse.

Looking back, James could see wasps diving in and out of the gaping hole. The trapped horse reared up on its hind legs, throwing soldiers into the nest. Panic seized the troop. Such devastation occurring so quickly was overwhelming. The first of the horses must have weakened the ground, not knowing they were treading on the roof of a winter hive.

James held on as the horse under him bolted forward, its legs slipping on the crumbling clay, and he felt himself falling, as though the hive was continuing to collapse beneath them, but it was the jolt of the horse breaking into a gallop.

The cadence of the run had him bouncing in the saddle, struggling to hold on to the leather straps. At one point, he almost lost the long bow.

The sky turned black. Hornets raced around them, circling back so they could attack from all sides. One of the soldiers on the horse in front threw a heavy canvas sheet over Lisa, wrapping her in it before he found himself fending off a hornet trying to bite at his neck.

The soldiers with James began firing their crossbows, shooting only at those wasps that showed interest in them, leaving hundreds that soared further on. The sound was deafening, an incessant whine drowning out the cry of soldiers being stung to death.

With the wind in his hair and the horse galloping beneath him, James felt he was going to make it. He could see the reinforcements a couple of hundred yards ahead. They had lit fires on either side of the road and were heaping car tires and wood onto the flames. Balls of fire erupted into the air as cans of gasoline were thrown into the bonfires.

A hornet descended on James, keeping pace with him as the horse galloped across the crumbling clay.

The angry insect beat furiously at the air with its wings, its dark compound eyes set intently on him. The stark, black and yellow highlights on its abdomen were striped like a tiger. With its body arched, the wasp closed in, its stinger and jaws poised to strike at his face and neck.

James pulled back and fired with barely a thought to aim, shooting on instinct. The arrow caught the wasp in the thorax, knocking it sideways and causing it to spiral to the ground. The other wasps around him became incensed with the loss, and James found four more wasps darting at him. His footing came loose and he slipped, bouncing in the saddle, sliding over the edge of the massive horse as it galloped on. McIntyre grabbed him with one hand as he slid to one side, giving him the fraction of a second he needed to regain his hold on the saddle before falling to the ground some fifteen feet below.

The rise and fall of the horse's legs, its powerful stride, its muscular frame, they all fought to shake him loose.

James grabbed at the strapping, desperately trying not to fall beneath the thundering hooves of the massive beast. A giant wasp landed on his back as he grabbed at the saddle. James could feel its spindly legs tearing through his coat. The beat of its wings cast a cool downdraft upon him. Its bite tore flesh from the back of his neck, causing pain to surge through his shoulders. He struggled, trying to avoid the monster's poisonous sting. Swinging the bow over his head and behind his back, he struck at the hornet, knocking the insect to one side, but it didn't release him.

Another wasp came down from above, harassing him as he wedged one foot beneath a strap and struggled to get the other in a stirrup. James turned as a fine mist washed over his neck and hair. The wasp on his back fell, an arrow having passed through its side, puncturing its abdomen and sending its body fluids spraying over the back of his head.

James could see one of the soldiers smiling, reloading his crossbow as he crouched at the back of the saddle.

"Look out," James cried, but the soldier couldn't hear him over the drone filling the air.

A wasp came in from the side, striking the soldier with its stinger, catching him on the side of the neck.

The soldier lost his balance. Although his legs were spread wide, riding with the rise and fall of the horse's back, the soldier seemed to drift to one side. What would have been fractions of a second unfolded in slow motion as the soldier keeled over. His face and neck turned blue and then purple with the shock of the poison pumping through his body. James reached out, trying to grab him as he fell. Their hands touched, but James couldn't get a grip, and the soldier's lifeless body fell beneath the hooves of the horse.

Thick, dark smoke surrounded them. James coughed, finding it hard to breathe amidst the acrid fumes.

McIntyre pulled hard on the reins, bringing the panicked horse to a reluctant stop.

The remaining hornets pulled away, fleeing the smoke. James could no longer hold on. Although the horse was still rearing, thumping its hooves and fighting against McIntyre's efforts to keep it still, James let go, falling to the ground. He landed flat on his back with the wind knocked out of him, leaving him stunned for a moment. The horse trotted to one side, mercifully stepping away from him, and several soldiers dragged him into an alleyway.

James reached around behind his neck, feeling blood seeping from the raw wound. Someone brought Lisa over, leaving her with him. Looking around, he could see an outer perimeter of soldiers kneeling with their crossbows at the ready. High above, hornets buzzed through the air. McIntyre staggered over. It was only then James realized these were the reinforcements sent to support them. They were consolidating the survivors.

Peering down the street, James could see soldiers on foot, running hard in toward the smokescreen thrown up by the burning tires.

"Are you OK?" McIntyre asked, his hands running over Lisa's arms and shoulders. She grimaced with pain, holding her leg in the wooden brace.

McIntyre rested his hand on James' shoulder, looking him in the eye.

"Stay here."

With that, McIntyre hobbled out, looking for his men. Blood dripped from his uniform. From what James could tell, he'd been bitten multiple times on the arms and upper chest but had avoided being stung.

The reinforcements tried to recover the injured. James learned several of the soldiers had cut away from the main group on foot, circling around the buildings, avoiding the attention of the hornets. In all, they lost fourteen men and a horse.

It was dark when the troop arrived at the gates of the Richmond compound. James wasn't sure what he expected, but a little over four miles from where they had been attacked, they approached the high-walls of an old prison.

Fires burned in barrels, warding off the cold.

People milled around everywhere, intensely curious about the incoming soldiers. Their clothes were torn and tattered. There was a surprising number of children under the age of ten.

McIntyre, James and Lisa all rode the lead horse. As they entered the courtyard, James leaned forward and asked Lisa, "Why so many children?"

"Orphans," was all she could say in reply.

James felt a knot form in his throat.

General Gainsborough was standing on the concrete steps of the entrance hall. He called out, yelling at the soldiers.

"Hah! Well done. You have succeeded. You have returned my little girl to me."

The soldiers, peasants and children cheered as though they were welcoming them home from some victorious battle. It didn't feel like a victory to James, but he knew Gainsborough was talking more broadly than of the encounter with the hornets. For him, the focus was the return of his daughter, not the loss of his men.

Several soldiers helped Lisa from the horse, carrying her gently. Gainsborough kissed her on both cheeks. He whispered something in her ear, but Lisa didn't reply. The last James saw of her was as several servants carried her inside on a stretcher.

McIntyre reported to Gainsborough as James climbed gingerly from the horse, blood soaking through the bandage on his neck. The general stepped up to James as he alighted from the rope ladder.

"Thank you," he said, grasping James' right hand with both of his hands. "Thank you for all you have done for my daughter. There is much we must talk about, much I need to learn, but you are weary from your journey. I will have my doctors attend to your wounds."

James was silent. He felt intimidated in the general's presence.

Gainsborough walked among the troops, picking out those that had been with McIntyre and greeting them individually. He patted them on the shoulder, shook their hands, asked about their injuries and showed concern, but he never stayed with any one soldier for more than a few minutes. McIntyre remained by the general's side the whole time, talking to him, telling him about each of the men and what they'd endured.

A nurse escorted James up the crumbling stairs and into the prison hospital.

Chapter 07: Prison Life

After having his neck wound cleaned with alcohol and stitched, James found himself in a dark ward, lying on a hard, straw mattress.

There must have been at least twenty or thirty other people in the ward, but they were deathly quiet.

Moonlight streamed in through the rusting bars of the windows lining the far wall, casting a soft light in the long room.

Minutes felt like hours.

His neck stung more now than it did when he was bitten. Lying there, his mind raced, thinking of escape. Part of him wanted to run, while it was still early in his captivity, before they suspected him of being a flight risk, but his rational thinking won the day, and he considered how he needed to plan his route. Getting out of the prison compound would be difficult enough. Surviving beyond the walls was another matter entirely. Besides, as much as he chided himself for it, he was intensely curious about Lisa and her father. James had felt something for her during those days on the farm with Winters. She might be able to switch that off, but he couldn't.

It was late in the morning when a nurse woke him. Startled, James sat up, taking a moment to recognize where he was.

"You slept well," the nurse said, touching the back of her hand against his forehead, checking for a fever. "General Gainsborough has sent for you."

James was still coming to grips with the bright sunlight streaming in through the windows, surprised he hadn't woken earlier. From the steep angle of the shadows, he figured it must be close to noon.

"I've brought you a fresh change of clothes. There's a shower at the end of the hall."

The nurse stared at him for a moment, waiting for a reply. James blinked and said, "Thanks."

A soldier followed him to the shower room, but waited outside while he enjoyed warm water for the first time in days. The soap was gritty, but seemed to work well, and after soaking for a few minutes he felt renewed. James dressed and accompanied the soldier through the prison to meet Gainsborough.

Walking past row upon row of cells, stacked four stories high, James was surprised by the number of people living in the prison.

Clothing had been hung over the railings to dry.

Children scurried about, playing with each other.

Vats of what he assumed were communal soups or stews bubbled away over an open fire. Smoke drifted lazily to the blackened ceiling above before wafting out through broken windows.

The noise was overwhelming, as though everyone was talking at once over the top of someone else, each person vying to be heard. An elderly man squatted in the corner, defecating into a rough hole in the floor. Most of the people look malnourished, sickly and weak.

As they turned into another wing, James got a glimpse of several cells being used as metallurgy workshops. There was a forge of some kind, larger than the one his grandfather had in Amersham, and the sounds of industry drowned out the talking.

Metal resounded against metal.

The wall on one side of the prison had been broken open to allow the engine compartment of a train to fit half in the corridor. Steam hissed. Pistons pumped with rhythmic monotony. Pipes clattered, shaking as the steam passed through them.

Blacksmiths worked on glowing red metal.

They walked into what must have once been a gymnasium. The floorboards were buckled. Soldiers milled around, prepping arrows, repairing armor, stitching up leather jackets.

At the front of the gym sat a large table. Several men worked on turning a suckling pig over a bed of hot coals just outside the double doors leading to the farm.

"There he is," cried Gainsborough, marching over toward James with his arms out wide, greeting him like an old friend. "Our hero. The man who rescued my daughter."

McIntyre was less than impressed. He sat on the edge of the table, stone-faced. James got the distinct impression Gainsborough was overacting, baiting McIntyre, while McIntyre was still undecided about James.

Gainsborough shook James' hand, holding on for a few seconds longer than James would have liked, making him feel uncomfortable. Perhaps that was the point. There was a dynamic at play within the room, of that James was sure, but he was struggling to read it properly. Gainsborough smiled warmly, but James was wary. The old general must have sensed his uneasiness.

"How are you feeling? Did you sleep well?"

James never had the chance to reply, not that he wanted to.

"We have set a feast in your honor. To welcome you to the clan and to celebrate your victories."

Slowly, James found himself warming to the old man. Perhaps he'd been too cynical. But then again, perhaps he hadn't been cynical enough. Either way, he felt swept up in the moment.

"There is much we want to tell you. So many things to talk about. Please, come and dine with us."

Lisa was there. James hadn't recognized her at first. Her hair was up and she was wearing make-up, which surprised him. The jewels on her dress sparkled in the sunlight streaming in through the windows high overhead.

"Sit here, with my daughter and me."

"Thank you," James managed, his eyes overwhelmed with the spread of food before him.

Servants laid out platters of meats, plates of vegetables and delicacies the likes of which he'd never seen. The smell of mushrooms wafted through the air, followed by the sweet scent of braised pork, and James found himself salivating.

Gainsborough had him sit on his right, between him and Lisa, while McIntyre sat on the left. There was so much food. The general used his knife to spear a slice of meat and dragged it on his plate, while servants busied themselves around them, dishing up sides of vegetables.

"Eat. Eat," the general said. "My men wait for us to finish. It would be impolite for us to keep them too long from their sustenance."

McIntyre didn't waste any time.

Lisa helped herself to some dark meat, but James settled on the pork. To his surprise, he saw Lisa's leg had been set in a plaster cast. Gainsborough must have noticed his curiosity.

"My physicians tell me you and your friends did a good job with Lisa's leg, saving her from amputation. They tell me the brace was strong, keeping her leg well aligned. For that, I thank you."

James nodded, still somewhat overwhelmed by the feast.

"Lisa tells me you defeated a bear and a wolf to rescue her. McIntyre doesn't believe it. But I, myself, I think it is true. Huh?"

James looked at the general, resplendent in his military dress.

"Yes, it is true," James replied, talking with his mouth full.

"McIntyre doesn't believe one man could take on a bear and survive, but I believe. And do you know why? Because my daughter hates me. She hates what I have done here. She would do anything to undermine my rule. She would not do anything to help me, not so much as to lift a finger in

240

support of all I have built. And so I believe her because she gains nothing from this being a lie."

Instinctively, James turned toward Lisa, wanting to see the look on her face. Under her breath, she whispered to James, saying, "Don't fall for this. Don't drink of my father's wine."

James was confused.

"You must regale us with your stories of bravery," Gainsborough continued, missing what Lisa had said. James looked at the bronze cup before him. He picked it up, sniffing it before sipping the cold water within. Wine? He wondered what she meant, and realized she was speaking figuratively.

Gainsborough rested his hand on James' shoulder. "I feel like I know you. Your face looks familiar. Have we met before?"

"No, sir," James replied.

"You look like someone I knew once, a long time ago, but I can't quite place where. You've never been to the north?"

"No, sir."

Gainsborough seemed lost in thought for a second, but he quickly got back on track.

"You must see what we are doing here. We are reclaiming the land. Fighting back the monsters. Ours is a humble start, but we progress a little further every day."

Gainsborough was larger than life. He ate with both hands. A pork chop in his right, a torn piece of bread in his left. Grease ran down his full beard. His hair was gray, but slightly curly, giving it a natural wave that swept up and to either side. James found himself being drawn into the general's energetic personality.

"McIntyre tells me you are a reader. This is good. Readers are not criminals. Readers are not wizards or witches. They are not to be feared. Readers are intelligent. They should be shown respect. But I ask you, what is more important than a reader?"

"I don't know," James replied biting into a delicious piece of pork.

"A writer. Without writers, there can be no readers. Writers are the originators, the creators.

"For a reader, there is only the past. All their efforts can only relive what someone else has written. But writers ... Writers command the future. That's what we're doing here, James. We are writing the future of mankind. We are not content to simply read about the past.

"No one ever accomplished anything by looking backwards. We must write the future. And our future cannot be one of submission to monsters. We must make our own future, write our own stories, and chronicle our own exploits, like your gallant rescue of my daughter."

James was excited. As much as he loved his dad and their trips to the library, Gainsborough was right. Readers only ever looked back. There was never any talk of change in the future.

"Help me write the future," the general said.

He had turned sideways in his chair, one arm resting on his knee while the other pressed against the table. His presence was overpowering, intimidating. This was a subtle, almost positive form of intimidation, something James had never known before. Not one that threatened harm or malice, but one that refused no for an answer, one that demanded compliance. James felt himself swept along by the current of a mighty river.

"We need good men. We need writers. We need those that read from the past and apply what they've learned to help shape the future."

Gainsborough snapped his fingers.

"Bring me the table."

A soldier brought over a small wooden box.

"Is it charged?" Gainsborough asked, opening the box.

"Yes, sir," the soldier replied, backing away.

Gainsborough reached in and pulled out a thin, metal object slightly larger than a book but not as thick. He pressed something on the top and a light shone forth from the shattered, glassy surface, surprising James.

"Do you know what this is?" the general asked.

"No."

"It's everything."

Gainsborough handed the flat metal rectangle to him. James was surprised by how light it felt. One entire surface lit up, showing a picture of children running in a meadow. The words "Slide to unlock" flickered and glowed at the bottom of the picture. At the top, the word "Tablet" appeared, and James guessed this was what Gainsborough meant when he said table. But that Gainsborough didn't know the correct, more descriptive term surprised James. Gainsborough couldn't read.

"Go on," Gainsborough said, gesturing with his hand.

James ran his finger over the cracked glass and the image changed, showing a series of colored boxes arranged in rows.

"Hah," cried Gainsborough, turning toward McIntyre. "Never ceases to amaze me."

"What is it?" James asked.

"It is everything you've ever wanted to know. Everything you could ever learn. Touch the word 'books' and see what happens."

James pushed his finger firmly against the glass and the screen before him changed, revealing what looked like a library shelf with a dozen books on it.

Gainsborough gestured with his hand, indicating James should swipe up and down. He did so and watched as hundreds and hundreds of book covers scrolled past his fingertips.

"Pick one," Gainsborough said. He was clearly enjoying the sense of wonder sweeping over James. One title in particular caught James' eye, jumping off the screen at him.

Brave New World, Aldous Huxley.

The book opened to the copyright page. Gainsborough made out as though he were flicking sheets of paper, and James copied, brushing his fingers across the fine cracks in the glass screen and watching as a page appeared to turn, revealing the start of the novel.

"How?" James asked, turning the tablet to one side and examining the edges and looking at the logo on the back.

"It's not magic," the general replied. "It's technology. This is our past, all of it, hundreds of thousands of books, more books than you could read in a lifetime, and all of it on a device that weighs less than a single book."

"So all we've lost," James began, barely able to articulate what he was thinking. "All the books that were burned, all the desolate libraries, we can restore them with this?"

"Yes."

Gainsborough took the tablet back from James, turning it off and placing it in the box.

"This is not just our past, it is our future," he added. "We can reach these heights again."

James was awestruck.

The soldier returned and took the box away, handling it with a sense of reverence.

"You see. We have much to offer a reader like yourself."

James struggled to contain his excitement. "How many tablets do you have?"

"Just one that works. It is a tease, the promise of all that lies out there waiting to be discovered. There are unimaginable treasures like this just waiting to be uncovered in the ruins."

Gainsborough stood. James started to get to his feet, but the older man signaled he should remain seated.

"We need good men. We need those that want to rebuild this world. Stay with us. Learn from us. Help us."

The general didn't wait for a response. He rested his hand on James' shoulder and patted him as he walked away. For his part, James was still stunned by the tablet. He wanted to read those books, all of them, or at least as many as he could.

McIntyre followed Gainsborough. He leaned down as he passed James, speaking softly.

"Don't get too comfortable up here. From tonight, you eat with the rest of the men."

Soldiers formed up in lines according to rank and began crowding around the table, taking their food.

One of the servants helped Lisa stand, bringing her a pair of crutches. James stood as well, not sure quite what he should be doing next.

"You should leave while you still can," Lisa said. "Before you get in too deep."

She turned away from him before he could respond. Leave, he thought. Last night, that had been his intention. Now he wasn't so sure. Part of him wanted to return to the farm, to be with his father, but a whole new world seemed to be opening up to him. And the prospect of getting his hands on the tablet again was too much, clouding his thinking.

Over the next few days, James found himself split between two work groups, farm duties and working in the library. The library was a disappointment. The books were either worthless, trashy paperbacks or technical manuals. Time with the tablet had to be approved by Gainsborough. James had a request in, but the wait was torture.

The farm was well organized. Originally it had been an annex of the prison compound, but Gainsborough and his men had extended it, clearing an adjacent park.

The walls surrounding the farm were made from scrap metal, bound together with wire. They provided an effective barrier against the monsters, keeping them at bay. The overturned, rusting hulk of buses, cars and trucks piled on top of each other held up sheets of metal and corrugated roofing iron over twenty feet in height.

In places, brick walls had been built, but James didn't like the approach. He preferred the spike pits and wooden fences they used in the south.

In theory, the metal fencing and brick walls were more effective, but they also limited visibility. With the open fencing used around his farm in the south, James was able to see the approach of a monster long before it became dangerous. When the fences around the prison farm failed, no one had any idea what would come through because they hadn't seen whether there were mountain lions on the prowl or bears foraging.

In the first month James was there, they lost four men to animal attacks after a loose car frame had been nudged aside by a nosy bear.

James got his tablet time, two hours a week. He had to contain himself, reading quickly but not so quick as to miss the heart and intent of the writers he'd chosen to read.

His father had once told him about the works of Carl Sagan and Richard Dawkins but had never read them to him. Both authors had numerous books in the tablet's electronic library, so James picked the titles that most interested him at first glance: Demon-Haunted World and Devil's Chaplain. Why those titles, he wondered as he pondered what he'd read over the long days between tablet time.

What did his choices say about his attitude? The books themselves were scientific in nature, he'd known that when he'd chosen the authors, and yet it was their defiance that appealed to him. They refused to accept the superstitions and reasoning others took as the norm. Deep down, James wanted to have the same kind of penetrating, critical thinking.

For James, the week between his electronic reading privileges was unbearably long. The rationale behind the delay was that it took eight hours to charge the tablet for just a couple of hours reading, hooking it up to a transformer connected to the boiler. And there were others with higher priority access, those studying engineering and medicine. James was told he should be thankful Gainsborough had allotted him any time at all, and he was, but he wanted more.

He didn't see the general much as the old man kept a close circle of confidants around him.

McIntyre was professionally detached, treating James as just another soldier, which he guessed he was.

Lisa softened in her attitude toward him, but she was still withdrawn, and he only saw her every second day or so, normally at a distance.

James wanted more of everything it seemed, and that frustrated him. He was a grunt, at the bottom of a pecking order he'd never consciously sought out.

McIntyre gave James and another young man an assignment to prepare and paint a harvest bin, a large metal trailer used for collecting corn and wheat. James had never painted anything in his life, let alone a steel structure some fifteen feet high.

Anders was a particularly robust farm hand and was happy to take the assignment. With more experience, he took charge of the task. After two days of scrubbing the flaking paint off the metal frame, they finally got to the point where they could start painting. The frame and axle had been originally painted in a deep green, while the vast empty bin was a dull red.

McIntyre came up behind them as they slaved away under the hot sun.

"Make sure you don't leave any traces of rust on this thing," he said, without so much as an introduction. James had his back to him, scrubbing a support strut with a wire brush and so was taken by surprise by his gruff voice. He turned to say something to McIntyre, but one of the captain's aides was talking to him, pointing something out in the distance. McIntyre had a clipboard and was making notes as the other man spoke.

James wiped the perspiration from his forehead.

Anders was already putting a coat of red paint on the inside of the bin with a roller. He was high on a ladder, leaning into the trailer.

"What color do you want us to paint this?" James asked, gesturing toward the odd assembly of the vast red bin seated on the green chassis and frame.

McIntyre seemed distracted. He grunted, "Paint it the same."

Anders went to say something, but McIntyre was already marching off toward one of the barns.

James and Anders were determined to impress the captain. With six hours of daylight left, they figured they could put their backs into the work and finish by supper. Working from the top down, they ignored the heat, liberally applying a thick coat of red paint to the entire trailer.

The two men finished as the sun sat low on the horizon. There was just enough time to clean the brushes and get back to the compound for dinner.

As they were packing up, McIntyre came storming over. The two young men stood shoulder to shoulder, proud of their work, proud to have finished painting in a single day.

"What in the blazes have you done?" McIntyre cried, his arm out, pointing at the trailer.

James looked at Anders, baffled.

Sheepishly, Anders said, "We did what you asked of us."

"Bloody hell," McIntyre cried. "Do I have to do everything myself? Is it too much to ask for you young bucks to follow some simple goddamn directions?"

"I don't—" Anders began.

James cringed. Suddenly, it was clear what McIntyre had meant, and he felt like kicking himself for being such a fool.

"Why the hell did you do that?" McIntyre yelled. "Are you two idiots trying to make a fool out of me?"

"No, sir," James replied.

"I told you to paint it the same."

"We did," Anders pleaded.

"No you haven't. You've painted it all red."

James felt stupid.

"But you said—" continued Anders.

"I told you idiots to paint it the same as it was," McIntyre cried. "Red on top. Green on the bottom. Get the hell out of here. Go get cleaned up. I'll deal with you two clowns tomorrow."

Anders took the remonstration worse than James. From his sullen look, James could see he was disappointed in himself. James thought it was funny, although he didn't dare say so while McIntyre was standing there.

That night, a cool wind blew in from the north, cutting through the humidity of the past few days. James was walking back from dinner when Lisa called out from somewhere above him.

"Hey, James."

He turned and looked up. Lisa was sitting on a balcony, enjoying the cool of the evening.

"Please tell me that was deliberate," she said, leaning forward, trying not to laugh.

Lisa didn't have to say what she was talking about. James knew. He looked around, not wanting to call out loud in front of the wrong person and say something he might regret.

"So you're talking to me now?" he asked, trying to shift the topic.

Lisa smiled. "Looks that way."

"Can I join you?"

"Sure."

Her leg was no longer in a full cast. Her new cast extended from just below her knee to her ankle, allowing her to hobble around without a crutch.

James climbed up next to her, standing on the rim of a wooden box and pulling himself up on the railing.

"There are stairs, you know."

"Ah, that's not anywhere near as impressive," he replied.

"Or as stupid."

She was still smiling, which James felt was heartening. He sat down next to her on a bench seat and stared out across the fields as a thin crescent moon sat high above the fading glow of the sunset.

"So were you deliberately trying to piss McIntyre off? If so, that was pure genius."

"Oh, no," James replied honestly. "That was pure stupidity."

Lisa laughed. "I don't know. Seems like an easy mistake to make. I mean, from the way it was told to me, and it seems pretty harmless."

"You'd think so, but the captain's taken offense. He thinks we were trying to make a fool out of him."

"Oh, please. He does a good enough job of that himself."

James laughed.

"He's assigned us to the honey wagon tomorrow."

"You know what that is, right?" Lisa asked.

"Oh, I've a fair idea. It's sewage disposal, from what the guys tell me."

"I hope you have a strong stomach."

"What's his problem?" James asked.

"You don't know?" Lisa asked, an air of surprise in her voice. "McIntyre fancies himself as my father's successor. Dad sends him out to find me, to rescue his wayward daughter, only I've already been rescued by some lone hunter. How do you think that makes him feel?"

"Yeah, I guess."

"I'm surprised he didn't start you on the honey wagon."

James laughed. "Hey, how is your leg?"

Lisa's tone of voice changed slightly, increasing in pitch. "It's fine." And James found himself wondering quite how he should interpret that. Something bothered her beyond just the inconvenience of the cast.

Her voice lowered a little, softening as she added, "They say the bone is malformed, that it twisted slightly as it mended, so I'll be stuck with a limp."

"I'm sorry—"

"Don't," she said, cutting him off. "You don't need to be. If it weren't for you I wouldn't have my leg, or my life."

James was silent. For a few seconds, he felt awkward, then the moment felt strangely natural as time moved on. Sitting there, the stars were brilliant. With no clouds in the sky, the heavens shone with a radiance James normally only saw high in the mountains. No words needed to be spoken.

Lisa sighed.

"I'm sorry," she began. "I've been a real bitch."

James tried not to burst out laughing. He hadn't expected her to be quite so forthcoming, but she had always been blunt.

"No. It's OK," she continued. "You can laugh. I know it's true."

Turning toward her, he could see she was smiling.

"Have you figured it out yet?" she asked.

"Figured what out?"

"What all this is about."

"No," he replied.

"Loyalty."

"Loyalty?"

"Sure," Lisa said. "They mean to break you. Break down your sense of individuality and mold you into another loyal soldier. That's the reason for the command structure. That's the reason for sending you to work on the honey wagon. It's not punitive, not really. Who gives a damn what color you painted that stupid trailer? No, it's more than that, it's about exercising authority over you and getting you to submit to their rule."

"I could say I won't do it."

"You could. But you won't. And that's what they're counting on. At each point, you sink further into the mire. At each point, it becomes harder to say no, harder to pull out, and they've got you, they've got your allegiance."

"You really don't like your father, do you?" James asked.

"I hate what he's become," Lisa replied. "I hate how he molds others in his image."

"You think things are that bad? I mean, I look around and I see progress. Sure, it's not perfect, but nothing any man does is ever perfect."

"Listen to yourself," Lisa said. Her voice was soft and dispassionate, as though she were talking to a child. James didn't find that insulting, rather it made him more curious, more determined to understand the issues that caused her such concern.

"That cliche," she said. "The very words you used, those are their words. Without realizing it, you're reinforcing their logic. But think about it, think about what that phrase means, nothing man does can ever be perfect. It's an excuse for shortcomings. Instead of a determination to change, it accepts the status quo. Sure, no one's perfect. But we're not talking about perfection, whatever the hell that is, we're talking about change. We're talking about not putting up with bullshit."

She looked him in the eye as she spoke.

"You see progress. I see slavery. You see the pressed uniforms and brass buttons. I see the widows and orphans toiling away to sustain an illusion. You see technology being revived with the use of radios and computer tablets. I see shiny toys, luring the magpies and crows out of the sky, bringing them in close enough to catch. You see the past being revived. I see monsters lurking in the shadows."

James swallowed the lump in his throat. Lisa rested her hand on his as she spoke. There was something eerie about her words. They held a truth he didn't want to accept.

"You haven't seen the real McIntyre, the real Gainsborough. You've seen the magician's cloak, the rabbit springing forth from a hat. You're enjoying the show without ever going backstage."

"But we have to do something," James said. "We can't just go on running from wild animals. We have to make a stand. We have to do something to try and turn the tide."

"Yes," Lisa replied. "But not this. We should not climb on top of others, using them to get what we want. I have no doubt about the sincerity of my father. He sincerely thinks he's doing what's right, doing what's best. He's going about rebuilding the only way he can, but deep down, there's something else at work. And I don't think even he realizes that. I don't think he understands the forces at work in his own life, the role of pride, ego, ambition, selfishness and the desire to be adored."

The balcony door behind them opened and General Gainsborough walked out.

"I thought I heard voices out here," he said rather jovially.

James stood, feeling like he'd done something wrong, wondering if there was some punishment worse than the honey wagon awaiting this indiscretion.

"Oh, please," Gainsborough said. "Don't stand on my account. It's good to see you two kids together."

James looked at Lisa. Her eyes were full of longing. There was so much more she wanted to say, he could see that. Looking back at the general and his warm smile, James felt a sense of conflict. He wasn't sure what to think. He excused himself politely and walked away, struggling to resolve Lisa's words with the harsh necessity of life around him.

Chapter 08: Promises

It had been almost three months since James arrived in Richmond, and he was getting itchy feet. He had managed to get word out to his father through traders, letting him know he was fine, but it was impossible to explain the complexity of his situation. Three words had come in reply, "Watch your back."

The tablet was a real hook, but so was Lisa, especially now things had thawed between them.

James tried to keep himself aloof from the constant appeals by various commanders for loyalty and dedication. Lisa was right, there was a subtle undertone to so much of what they did. From praise for his work to reproof for his mistakes, there were days where it seemed everything was fake, said only to reinforce the culture of submission. If it hadn't been for Lisa, he wouldn't have seen the spider web, he would have been caught up in it like so many others.

Late one afternoon, word came from McIntyre for James and half a dozen others to gather in the gymnasium. They crowded around as McIntyre addressed them.

"Tonight, the general is going to make an important announcement."

McIntyre stood over them, standing on a low stage, looking out over the heads of those gathered there. "I need you to transform this gym into an auditorium. Clean the floors. Wipe down the chairs. Get someone to scrub the marks by the door.

"I want fifteen rows of chairs, ten on each side. Use a string along the rows to get them straight. Use a block of wood to ensure the chairs are evenly spaced. Then run the string long ways, so each chair is perfectly placed. When the General walks in, I want him to see an orderly arrangement, with nothing out of place."

"Really?" James asked, questioning what he thought was an absurd notion. "But the chairs will move as soon as someone sits on them, so why bother?"

As the words left his lips he realized he was alone on this. The other soldiers stared at him with disdain.

"Discipline is its own reward," McIntyre replied coldly. "Details demonstrate respect."

James had the feeling he was going to end up on the honey wagon again.

"Anders. You're in charge. I want this place to shine. Phillips, you'll coordinate ushers, make sure the first two rows are reserved for the elders."

"There won't be enough seats for everyone," one of the others said, but with an air of deference that wouldn't offend.

"They can stand," McIntyre replied.

The work crew set about cleaning and setting up for the evening meeting. With half an hour to spare they were released so they could wash up and return for the announcement. When James walked back into the hall, he could see someone had hung a banner over the stage that read "Reclaiming the Promised Land."

The gym was packed. Lisa sat near the front, seated at the end of the second row behind the elders. James made his way over and stood near her, leaning against the wall. She looked over at him, hunching her shoulders, and he was surprised to realize she had no idea what this was about.

Outside, the sound of a generator broke through the night. Bright spotlights lit up the stage. Gainsborough walked on stage and the audience rose to its feet, clapping and cheering.

"Thank you," Gainsborough said, looking twenty years younger as he stood there bathed in the bright light. "Thank you. Please, be seated."

It took a few seconds for the clapping to subside.

"As I stand here before you tonight, I cannot help but feel the weight of history bearing down upon us. The importance of our lives, the importance of what we are doing here, of all we are building, cannot be overestimated. For centuries to come, people will look back on these days and marvel, realizing this is where the fight began. They will celebrate our lives. They will honor our lives. They will recognize that we took the fight to the monsters, that we refused to give in, that our lives shaped their future."

"As some of you no doubt have heard, tonight we take a bold step forward into that bright, new future.

"For years, we have dreamed. For years, we have hoped. But now is the time. The future is upon us."

Gainsborough looked around as he spoke. James wondered how far into the audience he could see through the blinding spotlights, but he was personable, as though he were talking to just one or two people, not over a thousand people spilling out into the walkways and corridors surrounding the gymnasium.

"When we started this settlement, the naysayers said it would never last. They said we'd succumb during the first winter. They said the old ways were buried beneath the rubble of the cities, but we have shown them otherwise. They said we would lose sight of the rule of law and would descend into chaos. But I say, they were wrong.

"For seven years now, we have held the prison. We have fought off monsters. We have stayed. We have progressed. We have electricity. We have running warm water. We have sanitation."

That brought a smile to James' face. Working the honey wagon had been torture. Thankfully, pumping sewage was only a monthly chore. James had vomited until he'd been left dry-reaching. It didn't seem to matter how long he was in the tanks, the smell seemed to be ever-present, coming in waves. He'd burnt his clothes afterwards and scrubbed under his nails until his fingers felt raw. Even then, the smell seemed to linger in the background for days. Lisa told him it was psychological, that she couldn't smell anything on him, and maybe it was, but the revulsion he felt was real.

Gainsborough continued, his voice booming through the hall.

"We have shown them that there is a future for mankind. We have shown them that together we can defeat monsters.

"And now we will show them that this was just the start, just the beginning."

He paused, probably for dramatic effect, thought James.

"We have sacrificed much. We've lost friends, brothers, fathers, husbands, wives, daughters, sisters. But their loss has not been in vain. From here, we move on into the Promised Land.

"And so, I've decided. We're going to do it. We're going to take back Washington D.C."

The crowd erupted, standing and cheering. Gainsborough stood there, basking in their adulation, his smile radiating, his arms outstretched.

"My scouts," he began, trying to talk over the cheers. "My scouts have probed the approaches to the city. We will harvest technology. We will establish an outpost. Over time, we will build a second settlement there in the halls of the Pentagon."

Spontaneous cheers and whistles continued to resound from various parts of the hall.

"And we will collect the tribute that is rightfully ours. We will move in force, a thousand strong, bringing in troops from the surrounding villages. We will circle to the north, then out to the west and down to the southern villages of the plain before returning to Richmond with the riches of our spoils."

Again the crowd erupted, getting to their feet and cheering. Lisa got to her feet and hobbled to the side door, pushing her way through the throng. James joined her. He too had heard enough.

They walked out into the compound, leaving Gainsborough in full flight as he continued to stir up support.

"You see," she said, finding a seat to rest on the far side of the courtyard. "This is how it starts, with emotion and excitement. And yet listen to what he's proposing, he's going to plunder the countryside. This isn't about taking back Washington from the monsters, this is about finishing what he started on Bracken Ridge."

That got James' attention. "He was there?"

"He's told me stories," Lisa continued. "I think he was a captain, serving under some other nameless general, some other mindless dictator hell-bent on conquest."

James thought back to his father and the uncle that died in his arms. He remembered the stories his father had told him of those days, words spoken not to instill a sense of adventure in him, but to warn him of the folly of war.

"Leave," Lisa said. "Go. Get out of here. Do whatever you have to, but don't go with him. Don't buy into the lie."

"What about you?"

In that moment, she seemed to realize why he'd stayed so long. It wasn't about the tablet. It wasn't about the camaraderie. It wasn't the promise of a new land. It had always been about her and he could see that realization dawning within her.

Lisa turned away from him, unable to look him in the eye.

"I won't leave without you."

Lisa turned back laughing. Tears ran down her cheeks. She slapped his thigh playfully.

"You never could keep your eyes off me, could you?"

He smiled, feeling embarrassed.

"What is it?" she asked. "Do you get a kick out of rescuing damsels in distress?"

"Something like that, I guess."

"What? A bear and a pack of wolves isn't enough for you? You want to take on my father's army?"

He laughed. "You make it sound almost plausible."

"I can't run," Lisa said. "I ran before, thinking I could put all this behind me, but I can't run anymore. If I run, there will still be widows and orphans. Running will hide the problem, it won't solve it. There has to be a better way. One man should not be the means to another man's success in life. People aren't stepping stones, something to be trodden underfoot to reach your goals. No, I will stay. I will continue to push for change."

James was quiet.

"You should go," she said. Her words were cold, and he knew she was right. He was a fool for staying as long as he had.

People began pouring out of the hall, excited at the prospect of adventure. They told James and Lisa the troop would leave within a week. James found a trader heading south and passed on a short written message to his father. He knew the trader would bring news of the campaign so all he needed to add were the two words his father would understand: Bracken Ridge.

Chapter 09: Forest

James and Lisa walked along one of the prison corridors in the bright sunlight, past windows with rusting wire mesh where once glass had provided a view of the inner courtyard.

"He's dragging me along with him," Lisa said, limping as she favored her walking stick. "He's going to take me on his crusade. I guess he doesn't trust me. He thinks I'll escape again. Listen, I appreciate all you've done for me. I appreciate how you've stuck around, but there's nothing here for you. This place will kill you. Perhaps not physically, but it will suck the life out of you."

James said, "If he's dragging you along, I'm going too. I've already signed up."

"Why the hell did you do that?" Lisa cried. "You don't owe me anything. What is this, some crazy, stupid illusion of love? In case you haven't noticed, I'm no romantic fool. You're a nice guy and all, but think about this, it could cost you your life."

"I know," James replied as they walked past a bunch of kids playing in the hallway, kicking a can around like a soccer ball.

"What if I said I didn't want you to come?"

"You wouldn't."

"So why? Why are you doing this?" Lisa asked.

He'd expected her to call his bluff, but she didn't. That she didn't was telling.

James laughed, trying to make light of the situation. "For the same reason I shot at that bear. For the same reason I waved that burning branch around at those wolves. For the same reason I wouldn't let Winters take your leg."

"And that is?"

"Because you shouldn't have been there in the first place."

"I don't understand," Lisa replied, pausing and turning toward him.

"Your father might be wrong about a lot of things, but he's right about one thing: We shouldn't be here."

James gestured to the walls around them, with large flakes of paint peeling off the aging concrete.

Cracks ran through the support pillars, marking where water-damage was undermining the integrity of the building.

An old lady hung wet clothes over the railing of the walkway above them, oblivious to the rust eating at the bolts anchoring the walkway in place.

Mold crept along one wall, slowly, imperceptibly spreading throughout the building.

A boy of no more than eight or nine dodged between them, chasing after a tin can as it skidded along the corridor. A horde of other children chased after him, yelling and screaming as they played their impromptu game.

"There has to be more to life," James continued. "Your father was right: We can't go on living off the past. As much as I love reading, we need to write a new future. The past is crumbling around us. Sooner or later it will be gone, and then what?"

Lisa tried to say something, but James kept talking.

"When I saw you lying there in the snow, with your leg caught in that bear trap, my heart went out to you. I wondered, how could this happen? What hellish nightmare drove such a beautiful, young woman to be out in the wilderness alone? But then I realized, it wasn't just you, it wasn't just then. How did any of this happen? Once we had mastery of this world. Once we soared through the sky, travelled to the moon, but now we hide in rundown buildings, afraid of the monsters lurking outside. We struggle for life.

"When I released that bowstring, and sent that first arrow hurtling toward that bear, I wanted to change all that. I still do."

"You think you can change this?" Lisa asked, looking deep into his eyes. In that moment, the roar of sound around them faded. The echoes and laughter, the chatter and yelling became but a whisper.

"No," James replied. "But if I am to die, I will die trying. That's what I was thinking when you first saw me. That's why I fired at that bear, because I couldn't stand by and do nothing, even if it cost me my life."

Lisa rested her hand on the side of his cheek and leaned in, kissing him gently on the lips. She was smiling as she said, "You really are the most wonderful of fools."

James started to say something, but she added, "As much as I like you, I don't think you realize how much you sound like my father, and that scares me. Just when I think you're about to sweep me off my feet, you remind me of all that is wrong with this prison."

"You said you want to see change," James replied. "Me too. I don't understand, how is that wrong?"

"Change must come" Lisa replied. "But not like this, not at the cost of your life or any other life. There has to be a better way."

And with that she limped away toward the prison entrance.

Gainsborough mounted his horse, surrounded by almost a thousand soldiers.

Cheers resounded through the decrepit prison.

James lined up with his squad, looking over at Lisa as one of the guards helped her mount her horse. Her rider sat a few feet in front of her, his hands on the reins, ready to move out. There were two guards armed with crossbows sitting on an auxiliary saddle at the rear of the massive horse. Lisa was the only one James could see who wasn't cheering, and he understood why.

The army marched by day, pitching camp in the early evening in carefully selected, defensible positions.

McIntyre worked with the scouts to identify locations in advance, favoring exposed hills with clear approaches. It meant some days they'd march barely five miles while other days they marched twenty-five, with the advance teams going on ahead to set up camp before dark. From what James could tell, they averaged about fifteen miles a day, which was physically taxing on the soldiers, but it was a march, not the more aggressive attacking run he'd witnessed on the road to Richmond. Gainsborough was pacing his men.

McIntyre adopted a rotating flank as they moved through the countryside following an overgrown interstate highway. He kept the officers in the heart of his battle formation, with individual squads spending no more than four hours patrolling the fringes at any one time.

Gainsborough wanted a compressed group rather than one that stretched out over a half-mile. He said this would reduce the possibility of attacks from the rear. The downside, though, was that the force couldn't fit onto the interstate and so the flanks rode the berms on either side of the road, with ground troops spilling into the woods and fields.

Animal tracks, culverts, dried up stream beds and the occasional access road running parallel to the interstate kept the tangle of undergrowth at bay, but the foot soldiers on patrol were perilously exposed.

Against the advice of his troop commander, James selected a long bow for his defense instead of a crossbow. When quizzed about it, he insisted he could cycle through arrows faster and with greater accuracy with a bow. As any conflict would be at close quarters, probably with swords and pikes, his commander relented, so long as he carried a sword as well. For James, it was a simple calculation, his odds improved the more he worked with familiar weapons. The last thing he needed was to deal with a jammed release or a broken crankshaft in the heat of battle.

The sky was overcast. His troop was two hours into a patrol when they came to a bend in the road, forcing them into a light jog to cover the additional ground following the outer rim of the corner. They were running along a track in a dark wood, following the rough contours of the uneven ground.

Through the trees, James could see the main force moving ahead of them on the interstate.

"This isn't good," James said between breaths. "They're moving too quickly."

The soldier beside him grunted in response.

James dropped back beside his troop commander, Davis.

"Sir, we're being followed."

"Nonsense," Davis replied.

"Back there," James said as they both slowed a little. "In our blind spot."

The commander looked over his left shoulder into the dense forest. He stumbled, catching his foot on a root, but didn't fall. The commander slowed to a march and the troop matched his pace.

"There's nothing there."

"I'm telling you," James insisted. "Something's been following us for at least twenty minutes. I thought it would drop off, but it hasn't."

Davis was scared. James could see it in the whites of his eyes. Fear gripped the young man. His pupils were enlarged, but he wouldn't admit what he was thinking and James wondered whether this man's pride would be the death of him.

Was James being paranoid? Over cautious? He checked his own motives. He had been hunting long enough to know when it was his nerves playing on him. Although he hadn't seen a monster, he was sure it was there, pacing along with them, stalking them. James couldn't articulate precisely why he was so sure, but he trusted his instincts, not some irrational fear.

The wind picked up, causing the trees to sway. The rustle of the spring leaves hanging heavy in the trees set his nerves on edge. Over the sound of his own heavy breathing, James swore he could hear the monster growl and he knew he was being hunted.

The smart thing would be to come to a halt, form a defensive position and send in scouts with their long pikes out in front of them, but that would mean pulling the convoy to a halt. There was no way a troop commander was going to make that call, and James knew it.

James felt his heart pounding in his throat. He wanted to stop. He wanted to listen. He wanted to smell the breeze and consider his options, to think about strategy before he was forced into reacting out of necessity. Monsters were defeated with skill and dexterity, not force of arms, and his father had drummed that into him from an early age.

"What do you think it is?"

The foot patrol continued to wheel, following the outer rim of the interstate bend, but at least the commander was listening. That gave James hope.

"I don't know," James replied. "A bear wouldn't have been able to keep pace with us. Dogs move in packs. A mountain lion would have attacked by now."

He was breathing hard. The lead scout some fifty yards ahead slowed as the road they were moving parallel with straightened. That would at least give them a chance, figured James.

"A lone wolf?" Davis asked.

"Wolves tend to stick to the hills," James replied. "Whatever it is, it's in no hurry. It's enjoying the chase, looking for an opening. It's playing with us, like a cat with a mouse. It's got us right where it wants us."

Sweat beaded on his forehead.

Shadows flickered through the thicket of trees and branches. The tall grass swayed in the breeze. Davis whistled, signaling that his troop should close ranks, reducing the spacing between them as they marched along. He turned, looking at the three troops bringing up the rear, but there were only two of them.

"Where's Jones?" No sooner had he asked the question than one of the two remaining soldiers disappeared in a motion so swift he almost missed it. The soldier, barely twenty feet away, was carried into the undergrowth in the jaws of a big cat, just a flash of fur darting between the trees.

"What the hell was that? A leopard?"

"No, it was a jaguar," James replied.

"What the fuck?" Davis cried, his voice breaking in a quiver.

"I've seen them before in the south," James said. "But never this close, never this aggressive."

Davis turned toward the main road, raising his hands to his lips, about to blow a wolf-whistle and bring the convoy to a halt. James raised his hand signaling for him to wait. He was staring intently out into the forest, looking through the thicket of trees for movement.

"Let them go on," whispered James, stepping off the trail slightly and into the thicket.

"What?" Davis cried. "Are you mad?"

James never took his eyes off the forest, his senses were becoming more attuned to the subtleties around him—the creak of a tree moving in the wind, the sound of the soldiers closing in on them from along the track, the breeze coming in short gusts. He shut out every other sight and sound, mentally eliminating anything other than the presence of the big cat.

"We should pull back"

"You don't understand," James said quietly, still looking through the trees. "This is not just any monster. This is probably the most intelligent predator the world has ever known. Flush the woods with soldiers and you'll never find it. You'd lose another four or five men, but you'd never catch it."

"How can you know that?"

"Did you see its fur, the mottled pattern of black markings, almost like daubs of camouflage paint? Pound for pound, jaguars are the strongest

267

of the big cats. Their teeth are like spears, and their jaw strength can crush a turtle shell. They're adapted to low-light conditions, that's what makes them so damn good at hunting. They have strength, speed and stealth. And this beauty took out two of our men before we even knew it was there."

James pointed at a large tree obscured by saplings and new growth. "The jaguar is using the trees. It's as swift as the wind, as quiet as the night." Squinting, he could just make out the dark outline of the large cat some fifty yards away. The jaguar snarled, baring its thick, white, canine teeth. A human arm hung limp from the branch.

"See?"

Davis looked. "I see him."

The jaguar dropped down from the branch, leaving its prey and disappearing into the shadows without so much as a sound.

"We need to get the hell out of here," Davis said.

"No. If we run now, he'll just follow along until sunset, and that's when the real slaughter will begin. He's already killed twice. He's not after meat, he's after sport. He's just playing with us, toying with us. When night falls, he'll be invincible. The darkness will make him invisible."

"You want to go after him?" Davis asked, incredulous. "Are you crazy?"

"Send a runner to McIntyre," James replied. "Tell him we'll rejoin the main group once we've dispatched this monster."

James could see the young commander shaking. The troop of nine remaining soldiers formed up around them, spreading out with crossbows and pikes at the ready, but this was no mountain lion rushing in, this was no wolf pack or bear looking for a full on assault. There would be no attack, not while they were watching.

Through the tangle of bushes, James caught a glimpse of the dark beast staring back at them for a second before it disappeared into the long grass.

The jaguar was larger than a mountain lion, its eyes more intense.

Davis sent a runner, telling him to cut straight back onto the interstate and only then to head up after the main convoy.

James suggested the remaining eight split into teams of two, an archer and a pike-man each. He had them fan out, with instructions to converge on the first sign of attack. Davis covered him with a crossbow while he stalked out into an open patch of ground alone, acting as bait.

James found himself moving through the clearing before he realized quite what he was doing.

With two arrows clenched between his teeth and an arrow half-drawn and ready to fire, his hands were trembling. He crept forward, listening carefully before placing each step. His mind was alive with feedback from the forest around him.

As if in slow motion, he tracked the subtle shadows dancing through the forest, the noise of the leaves rustling around him, paying attention to the shifting wind. He suspected the jaguar would prefer to attack from downwind.

Twigs cracked softly under foot.

Grass waved with the breeze.

There was no sound of life, no talking, no birds, no insects.

In that moment, James felt alone with the devil. The silence set his nerves on edge. The jaguar had already shown the instinct to attack from blind spots, but James hoped that by having Davis and the troop in those regions behind him, he'd force the animal to come at him from the front.

James turned, making as though he were returning to the others while deliberately exposing his flank, hoping to provoke the monster, to give it an opening. The soldiers held their positions some forty feet away. Just far enough so as to make him look vulnerable, but not so far as to be out of range.

Suddenly, James became acutely aware that the grass to his left was swaying, but not in harmony with the wind.

He fired rapidly, cycling through three arrows in rapid succession. No one else fired. They probably thought he was shooting at the wind, but James was sure the massive beast was there, creeping up on him unseen.

Slowly, with an arrow drawn taut before him, he edged through the waist deep grass. Part of him wanted to look around, to check his periphery, to be wary of any movement from the side, but his hunting instinct kept his eyes locked on the shadows swaying across the patch of grass he'd fired upon.

As he approached the edge of the clearing, he could see blood streaks on the grass.

One arrow had lodged into a tree, the others must have hit, but the animal was gone.

The snap of a twig behind him made his heart leap in his throat.

Had the jaguar outflanked him?

He swung around with an arrow drawn and almost killed Davis as the commander crept in some twenty feet away. Without missing a beat, James swung back, looking at the blood smeared trail leading into the dark forest, fearful the wounded beast might return and lunge in attack.

Once the pike-men came up beside him with their outstretched spears, James breathed a little easier.

"You got it," Davis said.

"It's wounded," James replied, releasing the tension on his bow. He rubbed some of the blood between his fingers, feeling the smooth texture, the slightly thick, congealed nature of the blood. "We got lucky."

"So we pull back and leave it to lick its wounds."

James looked around, peering into the woods.

"The only thing that big cat wants to lick is our blood. We have to finish this."

Davis looked over his shoulder and James could see him mentally calculating how exposed they were. They'd strayed a couple of hundred yards from the interstate. The convoy had moved on and was probably a good half mile ahead, if not further. The longer they stayed in the field, the more likelihood there was of being attacked by something else.

"I think we need to go," Davis said, unable to turn his eyes away from the fleeting glimpse of the raised interstate through the trees.

"We stay," Simon said, the youngest soldier in the troop. His blonde hair, small physique and baby face made him look somewhat effeminate, but the determination with which he spoke commanded everyone's attention.

Technically, Simon was on the verge of insubordination, but James was glad to have his support.

"I agree," Anders said. "We stay. We fight. We don't run."

Davis was panicked. He wasn't thinking straight. Fear got the better of him and he ran, not directly away from them, but on an angle, apparently wanting to intersect the highway as close to the main force as possible.

Davis made it no more than fifty yards. That he had run had stirred up something primal within the big cat.

James was shocked by how close the jaguar had been to them and how swiftly it attacked, rising up out of the long grass at full pace and crashing down on the commander's neck and shoulders.

The big cat dragged Davis off into the undergrowth within seconds.

Simon and one of the other soldiers fired short bolts from their crossbows, but they were wide and high of the mark. Whether that was out of fear or a desire to avoid hitting Davis, James wasn't sure, but he got a glimpse of red blood on the beast's speckled fur. One of his arrows had struck the animal on the side of its shoulder.

The troop ran over to where Davis had fallen, only to see his torn body lying lifeless in a dried-up stream bed. His throat had been ripped out.

The remaining soldiers were manic, but Simon and Anders remained calm. James realized his own heart was racing at a million miles an hour.

"We can kill this monster," Anders said. "But only if we work together, or it will keep picking us off one by one."

"At this point, our enemy is fear," Simon said. "If we waver now, we die."

One of the older soldiers spoke. "Who the hell put you two in charge? Davis was right. We need to get out of here before that thing takes another one of us. I say, we work our way back to the interstate and get out of this goddamn forest."

"Don't you get it?" James replied. "They're right. The only chance we have is if we stick together and go on the offensive."

From where they stood, they had a clear view of the raised berm leading up to the interstate. It seemed so close. Even James felt the urge to run, but he knew it was a mistake.

"It's bleeding," Anders said. "It cannot hide any longer. It's own wounds will lead us to it."

Anders was a good man. Ever since they'd worked the honey wagon following the debacle with painting the harvester, James and Anders had got on like brothers. Anders was not prepared to debate the issue any further. He began moving along the riverbed, looking for more signs of blood.

"I've got your back, big guy," Simon said, loading another bolt into his crossbow and moving up on the bank.

James was grateful to see Simon and Anders being assertive. Their action forced the rest of the troop to follow, dragging the others along and finishing all talk of running.

James pointed, signaling for the others to follow along on either bank while he hung back, following Anders over the smooth rocks within the riverbed. He was determined not to lose another man, especially not Anders or Simon.

Anders was a giant of a man, some seven feet tall with a muscular frame, but he moved quietly, like the big cat he was hunting.

James was happy to trust Anders and his instinct in tracking, so he kept his eyes up, looking into the distance. If the monster saw them coming, it would use stealth to attack and James wanted as much forewarning as possible.

The trail led up out of the riverbed, crossing a large rock where the jaguar could have lain in wait without being seen.

Anders stopped short of the outcrop and James instinctively knew what he wanted. He signaled to the men to fan out and approach from either side before Anders and he proceeded up out of the riverbed.

From the top of the rock, James could see patches of blood at irregular intervals—a smear on the bark of a tree, ruddy marks on the long, spindly leaves of a low-lying bush, and the dark drops that had fallen on a rough granite slope some thirty yards ahead.

Anders bent down, running his fingers through the impression of a paw print in the soft mud, looking at how it angled forward betraying the speed with which the jaguar had run.

He continued forward as James held back some fifteen to twenty feet, wanting to use the rock as a vantage point to gain a better view of where the monster was leading them.

As Anders crept forward James noticed something red dripping on his back, running down his jacket. He looked up as Anders passed beneath the jaguar, lying on a branch some twenty feet above the trail, its eyes watching intently as the big man crept on.

James wanted to yell, he wanted to attract the other's attention but without spooking the beast and stirring it to action. The predator had shown cunning, doubling-back on its own tracks. It sat on the branch, its muscles twitching as it waited until they passed beneath before attacking from behind. No one else had seen the monster lurking in the trees. Their eyes were all looking straight ahead, expecting the jaguar to come at them in two dimensions, not three.

James pulled back on his bow, raising it up and aiming at the animal's neck, hoping to hit the jugular vein.

He fired, and the sound of his bowstring snapping cut through the forest. The jaguar turned, taking the arrow just above the sternum.

The soldiers looked up, seeing the beast in the trees and fired. Even bloodied by the impact of several crossbow darts and an arrow, the big cat alighted from the tree with grace, barely making a sound as it landed behind Anders.

The big man fired his crossbow as the pike-men charged at the monster with their spears.

Within a minute, the jaguar was dead.

The soldiers were still celebrating as James leaned down, looking at the magnificent animal. With shorthair fur hiding its lean muscles and its distinct coloration, the jaguar looked magnificent. His father had taught him about apex predators like lions, tigers and jaguars, showing him pictures from books, but he never thought he'd see one up close. As tragic as the death of three soldiers was, James felt a pang of remorse at seeing such an exotic animal die. Its eyes looked hollow, and it was hard to fathom that just minutes beforehand it had viciously sought his death.

Simon cut down a long branch.

Anders strung the jaguar carcass over the makeshift pole and together they carried their kill back to the convoy.

The soldiers were so full of excitement they never thought about burying Davis and the others. James did, although he knew it would be a futile, token gesture at best, as without a deep burial pit their bodies would be exhumed by some other monster within a day or two. For him, this was the harsh realization that had haunted him since childhood, ever since he'd seen his father taken and almost killed by an eagle. Man was part of the food chain. Sentiments were a luxury, one they couldn't afford while on the move.

Gainsborough and McIntyre were fascinated by the jaguar. They had the skin cleaned and cured, and ate the meat. James had proven himself again in their eyes.

"Be careful," Lisa warned him as they sat alone by an open fire that evening. "They mean to win you over with their praise."

As usual, James didn't say too much in reply, but he took her words to heart. She sounded more and more like his father.

Chapter 10: Flight

As they approached Washington DC, James noted how Gainsborough skirted the outer edges of the city. The General ensured his army circled around the city to the north without passing through the former capital. Lisa was right. The campaign was a farce—a theatrical show. They weren't going to take Washington, they just needed the expedition to brush past the city.

"What does the sign say?" Simon asked.

"It's describing the distance to Maryland, 20 miles."

"Merry land?" cried Simon. "What is that? Some kind of joke?"

"No," James replied. "Not Merry. It's Mary, as in the woman's name."

"Mary? You mean they named this area after a woman?"

"Apparently."

Simon seemed a little put out by that, James just shrugged.

The scouts had identified several places of interest and the force headed to a large hangar complex below Washington-Dulles airport. James could see that the thick woods surrounding the hangar made McIntyre nervous, but Gainsborough was intent on exploring inside the derelict buildings.

"Johnson has hooked up a portable generator," McIntyre said after the scouts had moved through the building, checking for monsters. "He says he can bring at least some of the lights on."

"Good. Good," Gainsborough said, walking into the darkened hangar. "Fire it up. Let's see what's in this house of treasures."

McIntyre talked into the radio and moments later lights flickered on the broad, curved ceiling spanning the length of the vast hangar. Some places were better lit than others, but the dark shapes and shadows suddenly took form; whereas before there had been murky, indistinct smudges, now there was an explosion of color.

James bent down and picked up a muddied tourist guide. He wiped the dust from it.

"Oh, my," Gainsborough said, momentarily lost for words as he looked around the vast hangar. He turned to James and said, "Tell me what I'm looking at."

The general's voice carried in the air, echoing throughout the vast hangar. James began describing the various aircraft around them. Lisa limped along beside him.

Over fifty soldiers followed along behind them while the others waited outside. No one said a word. It seemed the grand building commanded reverence.

"Ah," James began, looking at a sea of meaningless names like Concorde, Blackbird, Phantom, Shuttle. He looked up, quickly matching the shapes on the guide with the airplanes before him.

Gainsborough walked over toward a bright yellow plane with no fuselage.

"What is this?" he demanded.

"A flying wing," James replied, reading highlights from the guide.

"It looks like half a plane. Just two wings stuck together," McIntyre said, following a few paces behind the general.

James read from the guide.

"It was developed during World War II and was intended to carry bombs all the way to Germany, in Europe. It could cover 275 miles every hour."

"Fascinating," Gainsborough replied, walking around the brilliantly colored craft, holding his arms behind his back with the formality of one inspecting guards. He walked over to a small metal frame with a large propeller on top. "And this?"

There was nothing on the guide. At a guess, James said, "It's a helicopter, designed for a single man strapped to the seat. The blades whirl around above the pilot's head. Sitting there, it would feel like there was a hurricane beating down upon you. The markings on the tail are German, so this was an enemy craft."

Walking around the fragile frame, James added, "I can't imagine it was too useful. The engine and fuel tank look too small. It probably only stayed aloft for a couple of minutes at a time. It's a prototype, something from which they learnt more about flight so they could build bigger craft."

Gainsborough nodded thoughtfully.

Behind them, soldiers came up and touched the various planes the general had walked past, running their hands over the smooth leading edge of the wings, intrigued by the designs. It seemed they couldn't resist touching, or perhaps it was more likely they couldn't read the 'do not touch' signs, James thought.

A couple of the mechanically-minded soldiers carefully examined the props and landing gear of the flying wing. James could see they were itching to get inside one of these planes. Given their success with the steam engine and boilers, they probably fancied they could get these planes running again, but James knew it was technology hundreds of years more advanced than anything they'd played around with.

"This one has no wings, no propellers, no blades," Gainsborough announced, having walked ahead past several other larger airplanes. James wasn't sure if he was asking a question about the dark capsule in front of him or simply making a statement. A plaque in front of the craft told James this was Apollo 12.

"Men once flew to the moon in this capsule," he said.

"Really?" Gainsborough exclaimed, examining it with curiosity. "It's round. Where is the front?"

The general walked around the sloping sides of the craft, peering in the tiny windows, looking at the tarnished metal and examining the machined handles and pop-rivets. He ran his hand over the dust that had accumulated on the corrugated side panels. Bending down, he examined the edge of the worn heat shield.

"There was no front," James replied as Lisa hobbled up beside him. "Best I understand it, there was no up, no down, no sense of this way or that. Apollo floated in space like a cork on the ocean. When it was launched, it moved up, with the hatch at the top being the front. But when it returned to Earth, it moved down, with this blunt edge leading the way."

Gainsborough said something softly to McIntyre, who then waved his hands, signaling for soldiers.

"This one," McIntyre said, leaning down and examining the wheels on the trolley upon which the Apollo spacecraft sat.

"You can't take it," James protested.

"Why not?" Gainsborough demanded. "It's ours now."

"But you don't understand. This is part of our heritage. That's why it's here, to protect it."

"For what?" Gainsborough asked. "For future generations? We are those future generations."

"But it's of no use to us."

"Man has been to the moon once. He shall go there again," Gainsborough proclaimed.

"But you can't reuse this craft. Even in its day, it couldn't be reused. To launch a spacecraft like this, you need a mighty rocket, you need the technical know-how to cross the unimaginable depths of space. Apollo sent three men at a time to the moon, but only two men in each craft ever walked on the moon's surface, and yet it took over a hundred thousand men and women here on Earth to make Apollo a reality. Technicians, scientists, engineers, pilots, just about every industry was involved in one way or another."

Gainsborough seemed to deeply consider his words. It was in that moment that James realized why they were here—Gainsborough was looking to exploit technology from the past, to cannibalize anything that would be of use to him and his propaganda machine.

"And this?" Gainsborough asked, pointing at the massive delta-wing craft in the center of the floor. "This flew in space?"

"Yes," James replied, checking against the guide. "This is the space shuttle. But it too rode on the back of rockets."

"Rockets like this one?" Gainsborough asked, standing before the Redstone rocket. James nodded.

Gainsborough wandered back out of the annex into the main hangar, having only looked superficially at a fraction of the spacecraft on display. Seeing that the general had lost interest in Apollo, McIntyre and the soldiers left the capsule where it sat.

"And this one?" Gainsborough asked, having walked past several other airplanes to a large bomber raised off the ground in the middle of the vast hangar. There were more modern jet planes and fighters around him, but the General seemed to have a particular interest in the shiny, chrome bomber, and James suspected Gainsborough knew more about the contents of the hangar than he was letting on.

"This is the Enola Gay," James said, reading the name from the guide. He'd heard this name before as a child, it was mentioned in one of the history books his father had read with him. Looking at the plaque in front of the craft he quickly remembered why. Enola Gay had dropped an atomic bomb on Japan in order to end World War II. James doubted Gainsborough's interest was historical.

Standing there, looking up at his own distorted reflection in the shiny metal fuselage of the bomber, James felt intimidated in a way no monster had ever scared him before.

"What did it do?" Gainsborough asked, and James was sure the General knew damn well what the Enola Gay had done.

"It dropped a single bomb with enough power to destroy an entire city."

McIntyre had already walked over beneath the open bomb bay doors. He stood next to a caddy holding a large bomb.

"And this is it?" McIntyre asked. "This is the Little Boy?"

"Yes," James replied, noting McIntyre knew precisely what he was looking for.

Lisa was standing beside her father. "What do you think you're doing?"

"Not now, Lisa."

"You can't do this," she protested. "You cannot use a weapon like this on your enemies."

"It won't work," James added. "It's a dummy, a replica. Even if it was a real atomic bomb, it probably wouldn't detonate after all these years. And how would you deploy such a bomb? Using a horse and cart?"

"You mock us," Gainsborough said. "But we will not stand still. We have recovered a foundry. We will forge new guns. We will make our own bullets."

"And we will have mastery of the air," McIntyre said with confidence. To one side, James could see a couple of the mechanics standing on the wing of a Mustang fighter plane. They'd opened the cowling, exposing the engine and were looking at the various components, while another soldier had opened the cockpit and climbed inside.

"We cannot aspire to jet aircraft," McIntyre added. "But we need not have jets. Even the simplest of airplanes will give us an insurmountable tactical advantage over our enemies."

"And we will acquire nuclear weapons," Gainsborough said. "Perhaps not here, not now. But there are stockpiles. There are naval bases, airfields, army depots. We will find them. We will not need rockets to deliver them, just planes, like the Enola Gay."

James couldn't help himself. He blurted out, "No man should have that power."

"But some man will," Gainsborough replied. "And that demands we hold that power too. You cannot put the genie back into the bottle. Since nuclear weapons exist, we must have them, and we must be the first to have them."

"But, don't you get it? They don't exist, not in practice. Even if you could get your hands on one, you wouldn't know how to maintain it or have the specialist skills to service it. And if you find a damaged nuke, the radiation from an exposed core would kill anyone that handled it. Perhaps not straight away, but within anywhere from six months to a few years."

Gainsborough was silent. James continued.

"Even in their day, nuclear weapons were Pandora's Box, containing an evil so insidious they could never be used. They were so powerful, so devastating that they could not be fired, not without war escalating into total annihilation."

"And yet they ended a war," Gainsborough replied. "They brought peace."

"You're mad," James cried. "Why would you want that kind of power? You don't want to restore the Old World, you want to rule the New."

"Get them out of here," Gainsborough said.

McIntyre signaled to a couple of soldiers who led James and Lisa out of the hangar. Behind them, James could hear McIntyre issuing instructions to take the Mustang, Messerschmitt and Zero—all airplanes from the World War II era. They might be over ambitious, but they knew what was feasible and what wasn't.

"Do you see?" Lisa asked, as they sat in the sun, well away from the soldiers working with ropes to pull the aircraft out of the hangar. "We're all so concerned about our world being overrun with monsters, all this talk about restoring man to his rightful place, but these are the real monsters. My father scares me more than any grizzly bear or mountain lion."

"Come with me," James said rather impetuously. "We can escape this madness. We can live free."

"There's nowhere my father wouldn't follow."

"Not necessarily. If he thought you were dead, if he thought you'd been killed by some monster while trying to escape, he'd have no reason to give chase."

"But I can't," Lisa replied. "I need to—"

"You need to what?" James asked. Although he'd cut her off, her voice had been trailing to a stop, and he knew this was a sentence she didn't want to complete. "You need to change things? Now, who sounds like the general?"

James looked deep into her eyes.

"We can do this. We can escape, but we need to do it now, while they're distracted, while there's enough daylight to put some serious distance between us and them.

"You know he'll never change. You know that, for all your efforts to improve the quality of life in Richmond, your good graces will be abused. And it's not just him, it's the whole system. After Gainsborough will come McIntyre, and after McIntyre, some other lackey they've groomed. And all your goodwill, all your years of toil to help those trapped in that system will simply support a regime you despise."

Lisa had tears in her eyes. James knew her well enough to know that silence was an answer in its own right.

He left her there and headed over to the horses.

There was so much excitement about the aircraft being wheeled from the hangar that no one noticed as he took a water bladder, a satchel filled with dried foods, a couple of blankets and ground sheets, his bow and arrows and a sword.

Looking back at Lisa, he could see she'd moved to the edge of the old administration building, ready to slip around the corner and out of sight. He grabbed some of her clothes from one of the tents set up by the hangar and casually walked towards her. As he helped her stand, they both looked down at her leg. Even with a walking stick, she'd struggle to make more than a few miles in a day.

"Are you sure about this?"

"Yes," James replied as they began working their way around the building, heading toward the forest.

"But my leg."

"We'll use the waterways. Your limp won't matter in a canoe. We'll double back down the river toward the sea and cut inland near Richmond. That'll confuse them. They'll expect me to make straight for Amersham across the mountains, but there's an abandoned town to the south where we can take refuge. My father would take me there a couple of times a year to read in the library. We'll be safe there."

"If he catches us, he'll kill you."

"Well then, we can't let him catch us."

Two hours passed and James was horrified by how little progress they'd made. They'd barely cleared the forest next to the hangar and crossed the adjacent highway.

Moving through the desolate surrounding suburbs gave them a bit more cover and more places to hide, but as soon as the alarm was raised, there would be soldiers crawling all over the place looking for them. What had seemed like a good idea now looked like a deathtrap.

James found a wheelbarrow. The wheel was flat, but he was able to use a bike pump to inflate it to almost full pressure. He helped Lisa lie on a blanket, using it as a cushion for her back.

James had Lisa sit facing him, so her center of gravity was mostly over the single wheel of the barrow, making it easier for him to push. He was able to run at a light-jog pushing the wheelbarrow.

At the top of the rise, he paused, looking back at the hangar in the distance.

"He's too concerned about his precious planes," Lisa said.

Three planes sat outside the hangar, with another having been hauled up onto the back of a wagon using a makeshift block and tackle attached to the roof of the hangar. The prototype helicopter had been dragged out as well, and there was no doubt Gainsborough intended to see it fly again.

"There are still two hours till sunset," James said. "If our luck holds, we can make the river. I'm guessing there's so much commotion back there, they're not going to miss us until nightfall, and by then it will be too late to send out a search party."

They continued on until dusk settled across the land and they were within sight of the river.

An abandoned water tower sat on the edge of a small township so they climbed up, wanting to settle for the night out of any monster's reach. A maintenance platform running around the girth of a rusted steel tank that once held over a million gallons of water, giving them a high vantage point. From the platform, they were safe from predators and could see for miles.

In the distance, they could see the hanger.

Pockets of burning torch light lit up small sections of the forest surrounding the hangar as search parties went out looking for them. James was glad to see the soldiers were evenly spread, meaning they hadn't picked up on their general direction from any careless footprints. Although that could simply be because they hadn't started looking until last light, by morning the scouts would be scouring the area for any sign of their departure.

Hopefully, the search parties would trample over their tracks in the night. Lisa's walking stick would leave a distinct mark in soft dirt, and James doubted their direction would remain a mystery for long.

James rigged up a ground sheet to keep the wind at bay, but he was careful to make their impromptu camp on the far side of the tower so as to not attract any attention from binoculars.

Huddled together under the blanket, Lisa said, "Just like old times, huh?"

"Oh, yeah. This is right up there with being chased by a bear and fighting off a pack of wolves."

"Tell me about your Mom and Dad."

"Well," James began. "I never knew my mother. She died giving birth to me."

"I'm—"

"No, don't be," James replied, cutting her off gently. "She was an amazing woman, from what my father tells me. She taught him to read, and made him promise to teach me to read. He tells me I have her eyes, and I believe him, as sometimes he stares at me like he's lost somewhere in the past."

Lisa moved to get more comfortable.

"My mother was a whore," she began. Her words were coarse, surprising James. "My father kept it from me for the longest time, but these things have a way of getting around. Someone somewhere knew and had loose lips, and so before you know it, a twelve-year old girl is being told her mother is a harlot. I refused to believe it, of course, even though deep down I knew it was true. She abandoned me, I guess. Dad doesn't talk about her or what happened to her. For all I know, she's still out there somewhere."

James was quiet.

"And so I've always put up walls, keeping people out. Life is easier that way. You don't get hurt if you don't let anyone get close enough to hurt you. I found it's easier to be a bitch than a lady.

"I think that's why I hate my Dad. It's the whole rebellion thing, pushing back. It makes it easier if he's the basket case and not me."

She rested her hand on his knee as she spoke.

"Running away with you ... He'll be sure it's to spite him, but it's not. Sooner or later, you've got to choose to live your own life, to stop reacting to others and start living for yourself. I found solace in picking holes in all his plans, in showing them up as shallow, but that's not living my life, that's living his. Running away with you, well, hobbling away with you, that's daring, that's adventurous. It's my choice for my life."

She turned slightly so she could look him in the eye as she spoke.

"You're so confident. I dare say there's no monster you wouldn't do battle with. And you treat me like the lady I'm not. You've got big shoulders, James."

Lisa leaned forward and kissed him gently on the lips. There wasn't much in it, he thought, just enough to let him know where he stood. And for James, that was enough.

"So what about you? What's your story?"

"It's funny you see me as being so confident," he said. "Truth is, I'm winging things most of the time. When that jaguar attacked my troop a couple of days ago, I thought it was going to kill me. I was so scared I couldn't run. I had to fight. I knew if we ran we were dead, but I didn't fight out of courage. I fought out of necessity. And that's always been the way for me. I've never chosen a battle, they always seem to choose me. As for shooting at that bear. Well, up until then, that was the stupidest thing I'd ever done."

"And," Lisa added, "I guess you're counting today as another hall-of-fame entrant under the topic of stupidity?"

"Absolutely. It doesn't get any dumber than this."

Lisa laughed. In the quiet that followed, Lisa said, "Tell me about your Dad."

"His name is Bruce. He's a good man."

That was all James could bring himself to say. In the moment, he was surprised by the upwelling emotions he felt within. He hadn't expected this kind of reaction to her question, but the need to be honest with her stirred something deep within.

"Are you all right?" Lisa asked.

"Yeah ... it's just ... Well, we all have our reasons for running. For me ... I felt I had something to prove. I had to show my father I wasn't a boy anymore. I was a man. Oh, he never expected that of me, and he'd tell me not to be silly, that I had nothing to prove, but by the time he was my age, he'd already fought in the war and had taken over the family farm. It seems like there was nothing he couldn't do."

"Sounds familiar."

"What do you mean?" James asked.

"I'm saying you and your father sound very much alike."

James nodded.

"When I was eight or nine, my Dad was attacked by an eagle. Damn thing picked him up out of the fields like a rabbit. The eagle flew high in the sky and would have dropped him to his death, only he wasn't ready to die. I remember seeing him hanging on to one leg as the eagle soared through the sky. Stubborn old bastard, he refused to fall. He was swinging something, an axe or a spade or something, I forget exactly what, but he forced that old bird down."

James paused, trying not to choke on his words.

Lisa was silent, waiting for him to continue.

"I remember seeing him lying there in the field afterwards. He was a bloody mess. His upper arms had been torn to shreds. His chest and back had been punctured by the eagle's talons. His shoulder blades were broken, crushed by the giant bird."

James took a deep breath. "You think of your father as invulnerable, as though he'll always be there, as though he'll never die, but that day I saw him dying and that scared me more than any monster ever could.

"Somehow, he made it through the day, and through the next week, but he never recovered, not fully. His shoulders didn't heal properly, the bones became malformed, and he has trouble breathing. Although he puts on a brave face, I can see it in his eyes, his confidence is shot.

"So there you were, lying in the snow, running from your father just as I was running from mine. Oh, I love the old fart. But to see him humbled like that, to realize he can't fight back no matter how much he might try ... The thought that the next monster he meets will kill him ... it was too much for me.

"I guess I've been on the run these last few months too. I wanted to be myself. And yet in doing that, I've turned my back on my father. It's just so easy to forget, to get caught up in the drama of the moment and pretend nothing ever happened in that bloody field."

James looked her in the eye and spoke softly. "You're no bitch. I'm the one carrying on like a bastard."

"Hey," Lisa said, rubbing her hand on his chest. "You're a good man, just like your father. I'm sure he'll be proud of all you've done. And not just what you've done, but why you've done it."

James nodded his head without saying a word.

Tears welled in his eyes.

They talked idly for a while, but it seemed neither of them could forget what the other had said, and they fell asleep together under the stars.

Chapter 11: Cat in the Hat

James woke Lisa as dawn began lighting the horizon. He wanted to break camp and descend the water tower before the day broke. The chance of anyone seeing them from the hangar was remote and would have required binoculars, but it was a risk he didn't want to take.

Lisa said she felt silly sitting in the wheelbarrow but James insisted, saying they could make better time that way.

By midmorning James had found a fiberglass kayak in the rundown remains of a Boy Scout camp at the base of Grand Falls.

A strong current carried them down the river, meandering through thick, overgrown forests, under bridges and across shallow swamps. For a while an eagle circled overhead, following them as they drifted down the river. From what James could tell, it had no intention of attacking and was probably being opportunistic, looking to scavenge rather than to catch prey. But it was something a good tracker would note, and James had no doubt Gainsborough's men would have seen the bird of prey.

A broken dam opened out into a section of white water rapids. With two people, the kayak was sluggish and slow to respond to directional changes.

Once they cleared the rapids they pulled over to the western bank, on the far side of the river, and emptied out the water they'd taken on board. Ordinarily, James would have dried out their bedding but the prospect of being caught by Gainsborough forced him on. He wrung out the woolen blankets and repacked them, knowing they'd eventually have to stop somewhere to dry them out.

As they approached Washington D.C., the Potomac opened out into a river proper, with a broad water flow between the wide banks. Something followed them on the riverbank, hidden by the thick trees. James figured it was wild dogs, but they were following more out of curiosity than hunger. That there were wild dogs roaming around gave him cause to think they'd escape the city unseen by human eyes.

A couple of the bridges crossing the Potomac had collapsed sections, but the current naturally carried their kayak through the open spans.

Lisa caught sight of a black bear fishing in the shallows. James couldn't help but feel exposed and helpless in the middle of the river. He knew Gainsborough and his men would never fire on them, but if they saw them and had access to a boat it would come down to an endurance race. Ultimately, escape would be futile as at some point they'd need to return to land and the soldiers would simply wait them out.

By late afternoon, they were still on the river. James estimated they'd travelled twenty five miles, but it was a torturous, circular route. They were probably less than fifteen miles from where they set out on the river, and perhaps only ten miles from the region he'd seen scouts moving through last night. Rather than outpacing Gainsborough's men they could very well come up on them from behind.

As the sun sat low on the horizon they stopped, hiding the kayak on the western bank. James set up camp at the base of a giant oak tree. He would have loved to have had a fire to dry out the blankets and keep animals at bay, but the prospect of being spotted by scouts was too dangerous. He found a clearing and hung the blankets over branches to dry. They were damp, but not soaked, and he hoped they'd dry enough to keep them warm at night, even though he knew they probably wouldn't.

Lisa helped collect several piles of deadwood, scattering them around their camp so any approaching animal would give away its position in the darkness.

The night was cold. James tried to sleep but found himself waking at the slightest noise, just a creak from the branches above moving in the wind. He wrapped the ground sheets around them to keep the wind at bay.

Lisa slept well despite the damp blankets. James found it warm enough beneath the blankets but any time he moved he found himself woken by the cool damp wool.

The next day they continued south, drifting with the current. The tide was going out, which dragged them along at a steady pace for most of the morning. With the warmth of the sun, Lisa grew in confidence, but James knew their escape was anything but assured. By nightfall on the second day, they came across a small fishing village in the ruins of an old naval base. They still hadn't reached the Chesapeake Bay proper, but they were far enough off the beaten track that James felt confident about stopping.

There were only four families in the tiny village, but they were hospitable. They traded regularly with the villages south of Petersburg, below Richmond, and were planning a trip there in the next few days.

James bartered with the kayak to gain their passage to Petersburg along with a small amount of money.

They arrived on the outskirts of Petersburg three days later. Lisa was nervous. Although she wasn't known personally in the town, her father was honored as a visionary.

"They've had word from Gainsborough," James said, sitting down with her on a low stone wall near the market. "He's turned the column around and is heading back to Richmond."

"You think it's true?" Lisa asked, enjoying the warmth of the sun as they waited for their next ride south to depart later that morning.

"Yes. But I don't think his target is Richmond. I'd say he's got wind of our direction."

"So where to from here?"

"We've got to throw them off the scent. If we're going to fool them into thinking we've been killed it has to be convincing. We head south, follow the routes toward Florida, and fake our demise well away from anyone who knows anything about you, me or Gainsborough, then we double back."

As their southern trader mounted up in the village square, getting ready to depart, James heard of an old trader heading to Amersham and the surrounding villages. He introduced himself.

"So you're old man Dobson's boy," the old trader said.

"Yes. Can you get a message to him?"

"Sure," the trader replied, lifting his broad-brimmed hat and scratching his head. "Your father and I go back a long way. I knew your mother. I was there on the night he rescued her from a wild dog."

James said, "I need you to tell him something, a phrase he'll understand. I need you to say The Cat in the Hat."

"The cat is in the hat?" the old man queried. "That's nonsense, it makes no sense. You want me to tell him something that's gibberish?"

"Yes," James replied smiling. He took the man's hat from his head and turned it upside down as he gestured with his hand, mimicking how a small creature might jump in and out of the hat as he repeated, The Cat in the Hat."

"And this will mean something to him?"

"Yes, it's very important. He'll know what it means. Please, you've got to promise me you'll tell him."

"Well, I'm not likely to forget that," the old man grumbled, putting his hat back on his head.

"Thank you," James replied as the man wandered off.

"What was all that about?" Lisa asked.

"The Cat in the Hat is a children's book," James replied. "I've never read it, but it was the book my Mother used to teach my Father how to read. At first, he hated it. He thought it was silly, but she loved the book, and slowly he grew to love it too. Anyway, it became a bit of a joke among the readers and they nicknamed him, The Cat in the Hat, although I don't know that anyone dared call him that to his face."

"I don't get it," Lisa said. "Why pass that along as a message?"

"Because he'll understand what I mean to do. He'll know we're heading for the library. And if that trader is stopped by scouts, he's got nothing meaningful to tell them, just gobbledygook."

"And if the message doesn't get through?"

"We're on our own."

The ride south was slow.

Early floods had swamped the low country, forcing the caravan to the east.

The interstate had been washed away.

Avalanches buried the alternate tracks, and the trader turned back toward Petersburg, hoping to pick up the road to Norfolk.

Rain drizzled throughout the day, increasing to a storm by the evening.

On making camp, James strung his ground sheet between two trees, allowing it to hang down like a tent, secured at the ends. In the driving rain, he and Lisa set up a hammock beneath the canvas sheet, stretching out between the trees. They might not be dry, thought James, but at least they'd stay out of the water. With the two of them and their packs piled into the hammock beneath the ground sheet, a cold, wet, uncomfortable night lay ahead.

"Things could be worse," Lisa said, sticking her legs up beside James' shoulder as she bent around the wet pack in the middle of the hammock.

James laughed. "It's hard to imagine how."

Lisa leaned to one side over the edge of the hammock, wringing her hair out with her hands, watching as the water dripped into the ankle deep water rushing by beneath them. James rested his hand on her leg.

"Any regrets?" he asked.

"None," she replied, without any hesitation. "And you?"

"Only that we didn't steal a horse of our own. But it would have been too easy for the scouts to track."

"I didn't mean about our escape," Lisa replied, nudging him.

"Oh." James wasn't sure quite what to say next. "I thought you weren't the romantic type."

"You call this romance?"

"Life won't always be like this," he said. "We won't have to run forever. We'll find somewhere to settle down and I'll care for you."

"Oh, you will, will you? You'll care for me? How sweet. What if it's you that needs the care? Then I'll care for you. How does that make you feel?"

"Are you always going to be this ornery?"

"Yes," Lisa replied with a grin.

"Good."

There was silence for a few seconds as neither of them seemed to know what to say next.

"Teach me to read."

"What? Now?" James asked, surprised by how Lisa could go from one subject to the next so swiftly.

"No, not now, silly. But promise me you'll teach me to read."

"Sure."

"I want to hear about different cultures. I want to learn about the stars. I want to read the greatest stories ever written, the love stories and tragedies, the stories of heroics and heartache."

"Sure," James said, a little taken aback with Lisa's sudden interest in reading. "Just not all at once, OK?"

"OK," Lisa replied, laughing.

They chatted idly for a while before Lisa fell asleep.

James found himself lying there listening to the sound of the rain pounding on the canvas. He had no idea what the future held, but he was quietly confident. Moving forward into the future with Lisa brought a smile to his face. Life had been rough, but with her, it was getting better. He drifted off to sleep cold, wet, and tired, but somehow content.

Birds were singing when he woke. The early morning sun lit up the canvas tarpaulin. There was no sound of rain or running water. It was going to be a beautiful day.

James was about to get out of the hammock when a hand clamped over his mouth. The cold steel of a knife blade pushed up against his neck.

"Don't try anything funny," came a whisper from behind him.

In a flash, James seized on the arm holding the knife, locking it in place with both hands. He twisted, falling forward out of the hammock, dragging his assailant with him.

Lisa woke startled and screamed.

James flexed with his abdomen and shoulders, propelling his attacker over and onto his back. He wrenched the knife from his hands and was about to plunge it into the man's throat when he saw it was Anders, the soldier he'd saved from the jaguar.

Another soldier grabbed Lisa. She fought him, lashing out with her hands.

Further back, James could see two other soldiers with crossbows covering the attack. His instinct was to plunge the knife into Anders' neck and turn on the soldier grabbing Lisa. The soldiers on the perimeter wouldn't risk firing on her. If he could reach his long bow they stood a better than even chance, but this was Anders.

The big man had landed on a flat rock, knocking him breathless. In that split second, James remembered joking around with Anders while painting the farm trailer. He remembered working together with him on the honey wagon, their march on Washington, and their battle with the jaguar. He couldn't do it.

Anders must have sensed what James was thinking. He had his hands out in a gesture of surrender. He wasn't trying to fight back.

Whatever happened, James couldn't live with himself if he killed his friend.

He dropped the knife.

A split second later, the sharp blow of a club struck him on the back of his head. He'd known it was coming, something had to be coming, and yet the ferocity of the blow stunned him, causing him to black out.

James came to rocking on the back of a horse.

He kept his eyes shut, wanting to learn as much as he could about his predicament before anyone realized he'd regained consciousness.

His head throbbed. His wrists were bound with iron shackles, straps around his waist held him in place, but his legs were free.

James was lying across the horse, with his face against the smooth hair of the animal, blood rushing around inside his head.

Salt stung his face from the sweat of the animal beneath him.

The sun was high above, beating down on his back. He'd been out cold for at least four hours. In four hours, they'd have been most of the way back to Petersburg.

There was little in the way of conversation, but James got the impression Lisa was sitting behind him. He turned his head to look at her, hoping that motion wouldn't be noticed.

"He's awake," came a voice from the ground.

James recognized the voice, it was Simon, another of the soldiers with whom he'd fought against the jaguar.

James looked up at Lisa. She was sitting behind him on the horse, but she wasn't bound. He felt someone undoing the strapping holding him on the saddle. A large hand picked him up, turning him away from Lisa and toward the front of the horse, helping him to sit properly on the animal.

"How are you feeling?" Anders asked as James sat to one side in the broad saddle.

"Sore," James replied.

The big man laughed, "Good."

"So why aren't I dead?"

"Because I wouldn't let them kill you."

James nodded, not that Anders could see him as he sat there with his back to him, holding the reins of the horse.

James felt Lisa's hand on his shoulder. He reached up with both hands in shackles and touched her fingers.

"How did you find us?" James asked.

From the ground, Simon called out, as impetuous as ever.

"We caught a glimpse of you on the river, but you were miles ahead of us."

Anders was more relaxed in his response.

"After seeing you on the Potomac, it wasn't too difficult to figure out where you'd go. You wouldn't hang around the coast. You'd try to get as far south as quickly as possible so we sent riders ahead, asking who was on the trade routes, and started working our way through the caravans."

James nodded, thinking it was the same approach he'd have used. Stupid, really, he should have gone for something more unpredictable, not so cautious.

"And now what?"

"Now, we will return you to General Gainsborough. You will go on trial for desertion. It will be a fair trial, I guarantee you that."

"Great," James replied, trying not to sound too sarcastic.

Lisa had moved closer in behind him. She whispered in his ear.

"My father's taken the main force to Amersham. He means to make an example of a southern village."

James felt his anger rising within him, but there was nothing he could do.

Looking down at his hands, he was glad they hadn't been cuffed behind his back. That gave him some options. He wondered who had the key. He thought about how impractical it would be to fight in chains. If he could get hold of a sword he could adopt a two-handed attack, but it was cumbersome, and no good for defense. He had to get out of the shackles. It seemed the best he could hope for would be for some monster to attack, a mountain lion or a bear, and to take advantage of the confusion to escape, but it was wishful thinking and he knew it. If a troop of soldiers couldn't fight off a monster, what chance would he have on the run in chains?

The troop stopped and made camp well before nightfall, picking a defensible position beneath a rocky outcrop. James figured they were heading due west, looking to link up with Gainsborough somewhere near Amersham. That night, Anders and Simon came over and sat briefly with James and Lisa.

"You should not have run," Anders said. "But Simon and I will testify on your behalf. There's much in your favor. You fought valiantly against that jaguar and saved our lives. That will count for something."

"That will count for nothing," James replied coldly. "This isn't about desertion, it's about Lisa leaving her father, and there's only one way it can end."

James watched as Anders swallowed a lump in his throat.

"Why did you run?" Simon asked. "What did you think you'd accomplish?"

"I thought we'd be free."

"Free?" Simon replied, a hint of surprise in his voice at the answer.

"You're too close to all this," James said, gesturing around them, looking across at the other soldiers setting rusting old bear traps on the approaches to the camp. "You don't see the general for who he really is, an old man living out his dreams through your lives. He has no power over you other than the power you grant him, no authority other than your willful submission.

"You show him respect, and he feeds on that, but the truth is, he has nothing. The army, this campaign, it's an illusion, a construct to make you believe in something that's as fleeting as the early morning mist."

Simon looked crushed.

Anders was quiet.

"There has to be more to life," Lisa said, picking up on James' comments. "We ran because we wanted to be free to live our own lives, not his."

Simon had his lips pursed tight together and James couldn't read the emotion in his face. Was he angry, annoyed, bitter? Or was it that he could see their perspective and was deeply considering their words?

Anders couldn't make eye contact. He seemed uncomfortable with what was being said.

"There must be another way," James added. "Taking back the cities is not the goal we should be pursuing. The cities are nothing but mausoleums for the dead. It's not the cities that are important, it's what they represent, the triumph of mankind over the wild. I say, leave the cities to the monsters. They can have them. We don't want to restore the cities, we want to restore our lives. We want to restore the dignity and quality of life mankind once enjoyed."

Anders breathed deeply. Simon began to say something but the big man put his hand on the teenager's arm, gently signaling for him to hold his peace. "We will consider your words," was all he would say.

Anders and Simon stood and left the two of them sitting by the fire.

"What is there to consider?" James asked, but neither man replied, and James got the impression their interlude with him and Lisa was part of some broader discussion. He hoped his honesty was what they were looking for.

"Don't be too hard on them," Lisa said. "They volunteered to search for us because they didn't want the others to get carried away when rescuing me. In their own way, they're trying to do what's right. If they hadn't been with the troop, the others would have killed you then and there."

"They'll kill me anyway," James replied.

Lisa was silent.

It took another two days of travel before James saw smoke rising in the distance. From the direction, he knew Amersham was in flames. There was no honor in this, just petty revenge, and James wondered how McIntyre would justify this to himself. Those that didn't die in the fighting or the flames would be easy prey for the monsters who would have sensed the carnage and closed in, ready to scavenge. James felt sick.

"He didn't have to do that," James said, knowing Lisa would understand. He was sure Anders could hear him, but the big man didn't acknowledge him. Anders kept the horse plodding along, his back straight and proud as he sat in front of his shackled prisoner. Lisa moved up behind James, resting her hands on his hips.

"I know," she replied softly.

Tears ran down his cheeks, but he made no effort to wipe them away.

"It's not your fault," she added as though she had read his mind.

James gritted his teeth. Down in the valley, he could see a town stretching out before them. They were skirting around the city, passing by to the north, following an old bypass road. James could see the downtown area, but he couldn't make out the library. He desperately wanted to make out the library, somehow seeing that building was important to him.

"You know, I don't even know its name," he said.

"What name?" Lisa asked.

"The name of this town. I've been here dozens of times visiting the library, but it has never occurred to me to learn the name of the town itself."

Somehow, such a trivial detail suddenly seemed excessively important. His mind was manic, still reeling from the shock of seeing Amersham in flames. Now, it was as though just one small concession would bring relief. But names were meaningless, whether it was Durham, Greensboro or Raleigh, what difference would it make? He'd heard of those abandoned cities in this region, but what was in a name? What difference would knowing make? None. Nothing would act as recompense for the loss of Amersham.

James had been defeated.

There was no more fight left in him.

He had thought he was fighting for something real, fighting to do the right thing, but his grandfather, his friends and neighbors had been brutally slaughtered and that realization left him crushed. This wasn't a game. This wasn't a hunt, one-on-one with a monster. His actions had led to the death of several hundred people, most of whom wouldn't even have known who they were dying for.

Although the warmth of the sun rested on his face, James felt cold inside.

Chapter 12: Monsters

By late afternoon the scouting party had rounded the town and James could see the main force of soldiers approaching them on the remains of the interstate.

Anders sent Simon and one other soldier on ahead.

Gainsborough and McIntyre rode out ahead of the troops to meet with Anders further along the crumbling concrete slabs of the interstate, at a junction leading down into the city.

"Well done," Gainsborough cried from horse back.

Lisa was silent.

"Has he harmed her?" the general asked.

"No, sir," Anders replied.

The question was insulting. Based on that, James had a good idea of how the general's justice would be dispensed, with just a pretense of due process before the execution.

Anders dismounted, bringing James and Lisa down with him.

McIntyre and Gainsborough climbed from their mounts and met with Anders.

"You have done admirably," Gainsborough said, patting Anders on the shoulder. "We have need of men like you in the officer corps. Your loyalty shall be rewarded."

Gainsborough stepped forward toward James, saying, "Sword."

One of the soldiers flanking James pulled his broad sword from its scabbard. He turned the sword around, lying the flat of the blade along his palm, wrist and forearm, offering the hilt to Gainsborough. Another soldier struck James behind his knees with the shaft of a spear, forcing him down before the general.

"No," Lisa screamed as a soldier intervened, holding her back.

James felt his blood run cold.

Gainsborough wasn't going to waste time with formalities.

James had expected to die, and yet as imposing as that prospect was, he had been able to think of it in an abstract way, as something detached from the present, but not anymore. Dark clouds swirled overhead, carrying a bitter wind.

Anders flinched, his body seemingly repulsed by what was unfolding. He'd not wanted this, of that James was sure, but his sense of loyalty demanded compliance. Anders was a good man, and James knew he'd regret his part in this. James wanted to say something to him, but he too was resigned to his fate.

Gainsborough admired the blade. James knew what was coming. He bowed his head, not shrinking from the blow, hoping only that it was a clean cut and that death would come swiftly.

The general raised the sword high above his head. James could see the shadow of the outstretched sword cast along the ground by the setting sun. He closed his eyes as his heart pounded in his chest. Every nerve ending, muscle and fiber of his being throbbed with life, as though a mere surge of adrenalin might somehow save him, but not this time.

Lisa screamed.

Anders stepped forward as the sword descended, blocking the blow with the shaft of a spear.

"I'm sorry, sir," the big man said, his arms trembling. "I can't let you do this."

"What?" Gainsborough cried.

James looked up.

"He should face a trial by his peers," Anders said, his voice shaky and uncertain.

"He's guilty. There's no need for a trial," Gainsborough growled.

"Anders is right," McIntyre said, surprising James. "The rule of law should be upheld. Desertion under fire is a capital offense, but we were not in battle. He was absent without leave."

"He's a traitor," Gainsborough snapped, and James was astonished by the dynamic opening up before him with McIntyre and Anders coming to his defense. He wondered about their differing motives. Anders was a friend, conflicted by his allegiance to the north, but a friend nonetheless. McIntyre, though, had no love for him. The captain seemed pleased only to have caught the general on a technicality, and James got another glimpse of the tortured power struggle he'd sensed in the gymnasium when he'd first arrived at the prison.

"And if desertion is the ruling of his peers, he shall be hung," McIntyre said. "But the law is all we have. The law is all that binds us, you yourself have told us that many times. We must uphold the law."

Gainsborough was fuming, his face red with rage. He stormed off, making it no more than ten feet before he snapped and turned back, marching up to within a foot of James. "You will pay for what you've done. You will pay in blood."

James swallowed.

"Take him away," McIntyre said, and Anders dragged James to one side. Lisa ran to James, infuriating Gainsborough even more. The general cursed and swore, pushing his way roughly through the soldiers milling around the fray.

As the rest of the soldiers approached from the west, someone pointed further down the road to the east. There, at the bottom of the off-ramp, a lone figure approached, holding a flag raised high on a standard.

"Who is that?" McIntyre asked. He sent a runner out to meet the stranger while he went after Gainsborough.

James sensed Anders didn't know what he should do with him. Where was there he could take him other than out of the general's sight?

"I will talk to my father," Lisa said. "I'll tell him whatever he needs to hear to spare your life."

"It won't work," James replied.

"I've got to try."

Gainsborough and McIntyre were in the middle of a heated exchange. Lisa went to walk over to her father but James put his cuffed hands out, gently touching at her arm. She turned to look at him and he shook his head. Now was not the time.

The soldiers seemed excited about something. Looking down the road, James could see a flag fluttering in the breeze, it was the old standard of the south. It was only then he realized it was his father standing there roughly a hundred yards away on a rough concrete slab.

"That's my Dad," he said, without thinking about what he was saying too deeply.

"What?" Anders asked. The big man had his hand on James' shoulder, ready to direct him away from Gainsborough and McIntyre, but he paused. He must have been as confused as James was in that moment.

The runner came back, coming to a stop beside Gainsborough and McIntyre. The soldiers around them went silent, wanting to hear what was being said.

"Who is it?" Gainsborough demanded.

"He's a soldier from the southern armies," the runner began. "He seeks the terms of our surrender for the massacre at Amersham."

"Our surrender?" cried Gainsborough, yelling at the top of his voice. "Who the hell does he think he is?"

James wanted to run to his father. He pulled away slightly, but Anders held him firmly in his custody. McIntyre, standing beside Gainsborough, had been watching James. He must have sensed the connection. He tapped the general on the shoulder and pointed at James, whispering something in his ear.

Gainsborough stormed off toward the lone soldier while McIntyre marched over and grabbed James by the upper arm, dragging him over with Gainsborough. Anders and Lisa followed closely behind.

Bruce stood proud, with one end of the fifteen foot flag pole resting on the ground as the standard mounted high above rustled in the breeze. The southern flag, with its deep blues and greens, fluttered proudly before the approaching northern troops.

"Is this some kind of joke?" Gainsborough yelled, still a good twenty feet from Bruce as he marched down to him. "You stand here before me, a full general, while you wear the insignia of a private? State your purpose."

Bruce held his posture upright, but the crippling injuries he'd sustained almost a decade ago were plain to see in his lopsided shoulders.

"You have attacked and pillaged a village of the south without provocation, without any formal declaration of war. That places you in breach of the treaty forged at Bracken Ridge."

McIntyre pushed James behind Gainsborough. Bruce ignored his son. His eyes never left the general's gaze. James sensed his father didn't want to give away any hint of weakness.

"Bracken Ridge," Gainsborough said, turning toward James. "Why, yes. Now, it makes sense. I thought it was James I'd seen before, but it wasn't him, was it? It was you. I remember you from Bracken Ridge."

James could see the bitter intensity in his father's face. With his eyes narrowed and his head tilted slightly forward, Bruce had his face set like a flint.

"You sat there the whole day," Gainsborough continued. To James' surprise, the general's mood seemed to lighten with the recollection. "You sat there in the mud, blood and piss. You sat there crying, cradling the head of a fallen soldier. Who was he? A friend? No. Your brother?"

Bruce would not be goaded. James had never seen such determination on his face. In that moment, he had no doubt about his father's ability to kill a man.

"How pathetic," Gainsborough continued. "And after all these years, here you are, a single man standing before an entire army. And you have the audacity to demand my surrender?"

Bruce would not be mocked. "There shall not be a man among you that will survive this night," he said coldly. "You will surrender, or you will die."

"Hah," Gainsborough cried. He slapped his sides, laughing. Gainsborough turned to McIntyre. "Can you believe this? Even in defeat, they have balls of brass and iron."

Gainsborough turned back toward Bruce, staring up and down at him, examining his old, ragged uniform, such a contrast to his own crisp battle dress.

"You come to me under a military standard with terms for negotiation," he continued. "I respect that. For the sake of the laws of war, I will allow you to return from whence you came, but make no mistake about it. Any attempt to interfere with my troops or my course will be met with a lethal response."

James admired his father's audacity, and he knew his father well enough to know he was following some kind of methodical plan. That Bruce wouldn't bring up James and his captivity in the discussions, even though it was obvious for all to see, was typical of his father. Bruce never was one for blackmail. Gainsborough might have thought he held something over Bruce by having James in chains, but Bruce didn't play emotional games.

"There will be no further warnings," Bruce said, his eyes locked on Gainsborough.

"Who do you think you are?" Gainsborough demanded, his voice rising in anger. "Where are your troops? With what will you wage war?

You come to me without so much as a soldier in support, let alone an army. Look at me. I am a general. I command thousands."

Bruce pulled his lips tight with disdain. He spoke softly, but with depth and resonance in his voice as he said, "I am a reader. I command monsters."

Gainsborough stormed off with McIntyre following close behind, pushing James along with him. The general muttered under his breath as he strode back up the hill. For all their animosity a few minutes ago, Gainsborough and McIntyre now had a common enemy.

Gainsborough was furious.

"You think reading can save you?" he demanded of James. "You think words on a page can stand up against the might of an army?"

James was silent. He tried to look back at his father, but McIntyre forced him on roughly.

"Ready the troops," cried Gainsborough. "We move out in ten minutes."

"But night falls," McIntyre protested. "We should make camp, set defenses."

Gainsborough spun around with his finger just inches from the captain's face, yelling at him. "I will not be made a fool by this village idiot. I will not dignify his ludicrous threats with a defensive posture. He's bluffing. He means to make us look stupid. We will push through the city tonight."

"But sir, there is less than an hour of light," McIntyre argued. "Regardless of his posturing, the city will be swarming with monsters in the dark."

"Then we will kill them," Gainsborough snapped. "We move in a force so large no monster can withstand us. What will a bear do? How many could he kill before we skewered his head on a pike and raised it up as a warning? Or a mountain lion, are you telling me a thousand troops

311

can't dispatch a lion? What are you afraid of, McIntyre? Are you afraid of an old cripple from a lost war?"

McIntyre was silent.

Gainsborough began barking orders at the troops. He grabbed a set of handcuffs from a storage box on the side of one of the wooden trailers and marched over to Lisa.

"You, young lady. You are not going anywhere tonight."

Gainsborough grabbed a nearby soldier and slapped one of the cuffs on his left wrist. He grabbed Lisa's right hand and fought to secure the other cuff to her wrist.

"Let me go, you bastard," she screamed. She slapped him with her free hand.

"You are just like your mother," Gainsborough replied angrily, securing the handcuffs, and James understood precisely how targeted that comment was and how it was intended to hurt her far more than any physical act.

The general turned toward Anders and James. "If he tries to run, kill him." With that, Gainsborough turned away and continued to organize his troops.

McIntyre was back with the main body of soldiers, marshaling the squads, assigning defensive roles for the flanks and the rear, while Gainsborough set a phalanx of soldiers in front of the army.

The phalanx consisted of ten rows of twenty five men holding pikes and spears. The back rows held their long, barbed pikes like flag poles, keeping the center of gravity almost directly above them, while the front couple of rows held their spears level, ready to engage man or monster.

Every couple of hundred feet, the front row would pause, allowing the row behind to take the lead. Once they fell to the rear, they would raise their spears like flags and rest their muscles. The effect was that the swarm of soldiers advanced with a sense of rhythm, with each row staying on the front line for no more than ten minutes. As they rotated, they raised their pikes and got to rest their muscles from fatigue for upwards of fifteen minutes at a time. Gainsborough meant to roll through the town with a show of unstoppable force.

The phalanx was impressive. James had never seen anything like the discipline of these soldiers. It was no wonder Gainsborough was so confident about moving through the streets of the town. He meant to show he was afraid of no man, no beast. Any bear or lion would be skewered by the pikes before they ever got close enough to attack a single soldier.

The army was on the move, marching down the broad junction into the town. The sun sat low on the horizon, casting dark shadows along the boulevard.

"I want another phalanx behind the lead," Gainsborough bellowed. "And we need to have a third ready to deploy at the rear if the march comes to a halt, so make sure we have troops there, held in reserve."

McIntyre was running from one battle formation to another. The army bristled with pikes and spears.

Anders took James to the rear of the logistics group, behind the horses. There were so many troops running about the formation, grabbing equipment and forming squads that it took the best part of ten minutes to reach the rear of the force as the army marched on.

Gainsborough kept Lisa nearby. James could see her in the distance, roughly a hundred yards ahead. The General had the standard bearers on either side of his command group, ten of them flying flags of the north, resplendent in their blues, golds and purples.

"Did he mean it?" Anders asked. "Your father, can he really command monsters?"

James was silent. His eyes looked out at the dark outline of the tall buildings in the distance, mentally calculating how close they were to the library. He figured the army was no more than half an hour from the city center with its run down restaurant and sandstone library. Somewhere in the distance, a bear roared. As if in response, wild dogs began barking.

"He doesn't stand a chance," Anders said, as though James had answered his question in the affirmative. "Gainsborough will tear that town apart looking for him."

"And that's exactly the kind of hubris my father is counting on. He's goaded Gainsborough into doing something stupid, and the old general is playing right into his hands. You have no idea who you're up against."

Simon came running up to them, out of breath as he spoke.

"Logistics are in. We've got the scouts and maintenance troops, but Phillips says you'll hang."

James was confused. Simon was talking about Anders hanging, not him.

"Will he act against us?" Anders asked.

"Not while we're going through the city." Simon had his hands on his hips, sucking in the air as they marched on. "But he will betray you. You're going to have to act now."

"That's less than a hundred men," Anders replied. "I'd hoped for more."

Anders turned to James and unlocked his cuffs.

"I don't understand," James said.

"I didn't sign on for murder," the big man replied. "The general has exceeded his mandate, and we all know it. Most of the troops don't want to admit that, but they all know the south will retaliate for the sacking of Amersham. It's one thing to demand tribute, it is another to start a war."

"And you?" James asked, surprised by Anders.

"I'll hang beside you, old friend."

James slapped him on the shoulder and laughed.

"There are many that hold you in esteem," Simon added, speaking to James. "No one doubts your courage. Give the order, and we will follow you into battle."

"But you're outnumbered, ten-to-one," James replied. "No. I can't do that. I can't send you to your deaths."

"But we have the element of surprise," Anders said.

"Not for long enough to effect any good. Without an assault troop on your side, you don't stand a chance."

Ahead of them, James could see the tall office blocks looming over the boulevard with their darkened, smashed windows. Even from where he was, he could see shadows moving within, bats flexing their wings in the twilight.

"You've got to get your men out of here," James said. "Anyone that continues on will die."

"Are you serious?" Simon asked. "Your father is actually going to take on Gainsborough in open combat?"

"Never underestimate a reader," James replied.

From where they were at the top of a rise, James could see down along the boulevard.

The troops were spread out over almost half a mile, which was unusual, Gainsborough was normally more disciplined in his troop formations.

The lead phalanx had passed the tall buildings and was entering the ruins, the downtown region where buildings had collapsed into the street. They continued their precise drills, with the front line extending their fourteen foot long pikes out in front of them as they marched forward. Damn, they were impressive.

In the distance, fires burned in front of the library.

"Like a moth to a flame," James said to Anders. "When the fighting starts, get your men out of here. There's an old factory on the outskirts of town, about a mile or so behind us. The roof has collapsed, but the four walls will provide protection from any monsters."

"You're serious?" Anders replied. "He's really going to attack single-handed?"

"Oh, he's got help. Don't you worry about that."

"And what about you?" Simon asked.

"I'm not leaving her."

As he spoke, a flash of light erupted from a low rooftop between the advancing troops and the library. They watched as a ball of fire rose high in the air, traveling in an arc, sailing over the troops and into the side of one of the tall buildings. Flames burst out across the aging concrete structure.

"What the hell was that?" Anders asked.

"Slingshot," James replied as another fiery ball erupted from a rooftop on the other side of the road, flying high and striking another building. Flames exploded, showering the street with burning debris.

"But he missed."

"Oh, no," James said. "I think he's right on target."

As he spoke, swarms of bats began pouring out of the windows, with some of the dark, winged monsters on fire, screaming at the night.

The still of twilight was pierced with the sound of screeching bats. Their black, leathery wings thrashed at the air and they turned on the soldiers.

Another ball of fire erupted from the first roof top, only the trajectory was lower, landing in the second row of the phalanx and exploding in flames that burst out in a fan, encompassing the next eight rows.

James could see the dogs running in hard, chasing a burning tire that skidded across the road. With their discipline broken, the soldiers didn't stand a chance.

"That's my cue," James said, holding his hand out. Anders handed him his sword as James added, "Get your men out of here."

Already, bats were flying overhead a quarter of a mile from the towers, swooping down and attacking the troops.

James ran forward, running past soldiers preoccupied with firing their crossbows at the giant bats.

The horses were spooked, rearing up and throwing their riders. Several of them panicked and stampeded through the troops, crushing soldiers under hoof before bolting down the side streets.

Simon stayed with James, running along with him.

A bat swooped down at them, its leathery wings with their spindly fingers beating in unison as it descended upon the two men. With large, white incisor teeth, perfectly honed for shredding small prey, the bat lunged, snapping at the air as James ducked.

As quick as the bat had come, it was gone, beating its wings and then gliding further down the line, harassing other soldiers.

Another bat banked before them, turning sharply to one side, its ten foot wingspan outstretched as it grabbed at a soldier with its feet. The monster dragged the soldier along the street as he screamed and fought against the beast.

The bat struggled to gain height but was determined to hold onto its prey.

As the bat cleared the remaining horses, James could see the monster turning toward the buildings. The massive bat disappeared into the dark, open windows of the sixth floor as the soldier struggled in vain to free himself. In the midst of the noise and chaos, James could make out his screams.

James and Simon ran hard.

The bats seemed more interested in those soldiers that stayed still, picking them off one by one.

Ahead, James could see one of the massive dogs, surrounded by soldiers plunging their spears into its side. Ordinarily, the soldiers would have had the composure and focus to finish off the huge beast in a matter of minutes, but another dog came running in, causing the soldiers to scatter. As soon as the soldiers stopped working together, they became easy prey for the massive beasts.

Fiery projectiles continued to rain down on the army every few minutes, setting their defensive positions in disarray.

Bats carried off soldiers.

The wild dogs ran riot through the troop, causing the soldiers to scatter, running for cover. Ahead, a lone standard of the north still stood, rising out of the carnage, and James knew that's where Gainsborough, McIntyre and Lisa would be.

Night fell.

Darkness descended.

Throughout the chaos, soldiers retreated, trying to find any place of refuge, carrying their wounded from the field of battle. Bats swooped in, darting and weaving, their needle-sharp fangs bared. The speed with which they moved made the crossbows largely ineffective.

Lisa screamed.

James couldn't see her.

She was somewhere ahead of him, but he picked her scream out of the confusion of noise around him and doubled his efforts, pushing past soldiers, ducking beneath the black, leathery wings of bats wreaking havoc on the army.

Pockets of fire blocked his path. His father must have used some kind of gasoline or propellant as the flames consumed the green grass and saplings breaking through the cracked street.

James slipped on some loose bricks scattered across the road, catching himself before he fell. Simon grabbed him with one hand, helping him to his feet.

Ahead, a giant bat struggled to gain height, a soldier clasped firmly in its claws, and that was when James saw her, being dragged along the street behind the soldier. Lisa was screaming for help, being dragged backwards, her right hand still cuffed to the soldier's left arm. The soldier wasn't struggling. His body hung limp beneath the dark monster, blood running from a bite to his neck.

The bat dodged to the left, then to the right, beating its wings furiously, trying to knock Lisa loose. For her part, Lisa was trying to get to her feet as she was dragged on with her arm outstretched toward the vast, black monster.

Simon knocked into one of the soldiers, ripping a crossbow from his hands. He fired at the bat, catching it in the chest, but the monster didn't seem to notice the injury.

James ran on, his heart pounding within his chest, his lungs screaming for oxygen, his legs aching under the strain. He pushed himself to go faster, to run harder, but his body just couldn't comply.

The rusted remains of a car blocked his path. Without breaking his stride, he jumped, clearing the frame and using the engine block to propel himself on further. Beyond that lay the crushed remains of an overturned bus. With his momentum, James bounded up a pile of bricks and jumped up onto the bus, rushing along its length, praying he wouldn't fall through the rusted panels.

The bat pulled Lisa off the ground, slowly gaining height as it struggled with the combined weight of both her and the soldier. Even from the height of the bus, he couldn't reach the monster. The bat was already too high, its wings thrashing at the air as it cleared the lamp posts. Within a fraction of a second, it would be over. Lisa would be out of reach. He'd failed. There was nothing he could do. The bus came to an end beneath his pounding feet and he found himself jumping, flying through the air, but he was going to fall short, he'd end up nowhere near the bat, missing it by almost four feet.

James swung his sword, putting every ounce of strength into his blow, aiming for the soldier's arm just above the handcuffs, praying he didn't miss.

The sword severed the arm just above the wrist and both he and Lisa fell back to the rough concrete. The bat, free from the extra weight, lifted high into the sky, its wings spread wide as it soared around toward its nesting tower, carrying its hard-won prey with it.

James rolled as he landed. His shoulder caught on a curb and pain shot through his right arm. He got to his feet and ran over to Lisa, his right hand still gripping the sword even though his arm lay limp against his side. James was shattered, physically and emotionally. He pushed through the pain, realizing Lisa needed him to be strong.

Lisa was still screaming.

Blood had spattered across her hands and legs, but it wasn't her blood.

"Hey," he began, shaking. "It's OK. You're going to be OK."

She grabbed him, hugging him tight. It hurt to hug her, but he needed to hold her. He'd come so close to losing her.

Above them, another fiery projectile soared through the darkness, sailing into the distance and exploding in a burst of flames further down the street.

James stepped back from Lisa. He pulled the soldier's warm, severed hand from Lisa's handcuffs. He dropped it on the ground, trying not to feel the dead fingers slip from his hand. Emotionally, he didn't want to think about what he'd done. But as much as he wanted to, he couldn't transform that searing memory to some intangible, impersonal act. He couldn't look at the hand, he had to look into Lisa's eyes.

They were both in shock.

James felt sick.

He wiped the tears streaming down her cheeks. Her hair was matted with blood and he could feel a lump on the back of her head.

Her eyes cast down at the bloodied hand lying in the gutter, and she stepped away in revulsion.

He looked around. They were within fifty yards of the library, and James thought about taking her there to hide. He knew the layout well, and figured they would find refuge in the basement.

"Let her go," Gainsborough said.

McIntyre came up beside them and pulled Lisa from him.

"This is between you and me, now," the general said. Above him, bats soared through the air, but their level of agitation had waned. They were no longer willing to risk injury by dropping down and attacking the soldiers.

The battle was swinging away from the monsters, with squads of men firing their crossbows in unison, targeting individual bats and bringing them down in a volley of arrows. After the initial confusion, discipline was being restored and the soldiers were gaining the upper hand.

The old general stepped forward, swinging his sword at James, surprising James with his vigor. James stepped back and the first blow passed harmlessly before him. Gainsborough lunged again, and James parried feebly. His right shoulder was broken. The force of the general's blow reverberated through his sword, causing pain to resound through his arm.

"It's over," James said, his feet slipping on the loose gravel. "Your army is in ruins. Your men are deserting."

"Oh, it's over, all right," Gainsborough said, coming down with a strike from above. James deflected the blow with his sword but he could barely hold onto the hilt. His shoulder throbbed in agony, sending pain shooting down his arm. He switched the sword to his left hand. Gainsborough was playing with him, enjoying the moment.

"Father, No!" Lisa cried, kicking and struggling against McIntyre's grip.

Gainsborough struck again.

James was clumsy, his left hand lacked dexterity, and he struggled not to be hit by the glancing blow.

Gainsborough jabbed, catching James on the left shoulder, puncturing the muscle with a clean thrust.

Blood seeped from the wound.

The old general moved with deceptive speed. He spun around, driving at James with a forceful blow.

James blocked, but the sword was knocked from his hand and he slipped to his knees.

James tried to reach the fallen sword, but the general placed the blade of his sword under James' chin, ignoring Lisa's screams. McIntyre put his hand over her mouth, forcing her to watch.

"You should not have crossed me," Gainsborough said, pulling back the sword, ready to strike a lethal blow.

The musty smell of wild dogs wafted on the breeze.

A low, resonant growl filled the air, causing Gainsborough to freeze momentarily.

"Step away from the boy."

James turned and saw his father walking toward him out of the misty, smoky haze.

Bruce was flanked by two massive dogs, towering above him, their dark outline silhouetted by the distant flames. The sound of their claws striking the concrete struck fear into the hearts of the soldiers around Gainsborough.

James could see grown men cowering, slinking backwards, wanting to melt into the streets and disappear.

Gainsborough froze at the sight of these monsters coming out of the dark of night.

Bruce walked forward calmly.

The dogs kept pace beside Bruce, snarling at the soldiers. Saliva dripped from their twitching jaws. Their ears were pinned back. With their teeth bared, they growled, itching to attack, struggling to contain themselves.

McIntyre loosened his grip on Lisa and she broke free, running over to James and dragging him to one side, away from her father.

The dogs tensed, ready to spring, awaiting the command from Bruce.

Gainsborough turned toward Bruce, his sword out in front of him, the steel blade trembling in his hand.

Seeing so many soldiers around them, the dogs spread apart, still waiting for Bruce to unleash them.

The soldiers continued to back away slowly. No one had seen a wild dog this close before, not outside of a defensive structure with spears and pikes protecting them. No one wanted to provoke the two massive beasts as they would tear them into pieces. It seems they realized how tenuous Bruce's control was over the monstrous animals and didn't want to risk upsetting that balance. The slightest move could incite the dogs to attack.

Gainsborough dropped his sword, sinking to his knees.

Bruce stepped forward, pulling his sword out of its scabbard. He held the blade to the general's throat, raising the old man's chin with the cold steel so he could look him in the eye. James understood what he was doing. Bruce was mimicking the exact manner in which Gainsborough had intended to kill him.

"No," Lisa cried. "Please, don't."

"Dad, no," James said.

"It has to end," Bruce replied, his sword outstretched. "It has to finish here, tonight. There can be no more war among us. Life is too precious. Don't you see? Men like this are the real monsters."

"It has ended," James said, pleading with him. "We've won."

Bruce never took his eyes of Gainsborough. For his part, the old man didn't flinch. He never begged for mercy or sought leniency. In that moment, James knew Gainsborough would accept his fate, whatever that may be.

"Don't do it," James added. "You're better than this. You're better than him."

"You don't understand, son. We thought all this ended on Bracken Ridge, but it didn't. There's only one way this can end. He cannot be allowed to live."

"Dad." James spoke softly. He had staggered over beside his father and had his hand resting on his shoulder. "I understand what you're feeling. I understand the loss of your brother all those years ago. But times must change or we have no chance at a new future. Don't you see? Look in his eyes. He is a defeated man. No one will follow him. Not anymore."

One of the soldiers standing beside McIntyre raised a crossbow, pointing it at Bruce. Simon raised his crossbow as he walked over to the soldier, touching the sharp tip directly against the man's forehead, daring him to fire.

"You want to think carefully about what you do next," he said coldly.

McIntyre intervened, putting his hand out and gently pushing the soldier's crossbow down toward the ground. He said, "He's right. Let the madness end. There has been too much bloodshed."

McIntyre was looking at James as he spoke, not at either Bruce or Gainsborough. Somehow, James understood. For all the tension there had been between him and McIntyre, James knew this wasn't more posturing on his part, this wasn't some ploy simply to displace the general. Somewhere, deep within, that sense of honor James had first sensed while on horseback to Richmond still shone through. McIntyre was the right man caught on the wrong side of history.

Bruce spoke to Gainsborough.

"Do I have your unconditional surrender this night?"

"Yes."

Bruce then spoke to McIntyre, recognizing his authority from his uniform.

"You will withdraw your men. You will depart from the south, never to return. Is that understood?"

"Yes," McIntyre replied. Gainsborough mumbled consent as well.

Bruce put his sword back in its scabbard. With brute force, he ripped the stars from the General's shoulder boards, causing the old man to rock back and forth with the violence of that act.

"You are witnesses," Bruce cried, casting the bronze stars on the ground before the soldiers gathered around. "You will bear this testimony, that this man shall never again hold the rank of an officer."

No one spoke.

Apart from the distant cries, the night had grown uneasily quiet.

The dogs held their ground, staring down the soldiers, still growling softly.

"Now, be gone," ordered Bruce. "Depart and never return."

Gainsborough lowered his head. McIntyre walked over and helped the old man to his feet. His shoulders were slouched. He no longer moved with the arrogance he'd once held.

Slowly, the remaining soldiers disappeared into the swirling mists, their forms fading from sight until only Bruce, James, Lisa and Simon remained.

The dogs sniffed at the air.

Bruce raised his fingers to his lips and let loose a loud wolf whistle, calling off the other dogs.

Out of the mist, the dogs appeared, seven of them, bloodied and torn.

Two older men approached, walking in through the haze. James didn't recognize them. They introduced themselves as Shakespeare and Sherlock.

Bruce tended to the dogs, giving them a friendly pat, looking at their wounds as he thanked them for their service, talking to them as though they understood him.

Simon was in awe of the huge dogs, keeping a wary distance, but impressed by how the readers worked with them. Shakespeare called Simon over, letting the dogs smell him and encouraging him to pat them.

James smiled, understanding Shakespeare was passing the torch to yet another generation.

"What now?" Lisa asked, rolling her arm in its shoulder socket, trying to work out the pain. Blood dripped from around the cuffs still hanging from her wrist.

James was aware his father could hear him. Bruce made out like he was more interested in the dogs, but he was within earshot, and James could see his father wanted to say something but was deferring to him.

James walked over to Bruce as his father gave one of the massive beasts a good, hard rub under the neck.

"Dad?"

"It's your life. It's your call, son."

James could see they were all waiting for him to speak his mind, especially Lisa.

"We can't stay here. We need to go back to Richmond. In the morning, we'll meet up with Anders and the others, and return to the north."

"But why?" Bruce asked. "What is there for you in Richmond?"

"There's unfinished business, Dad." James was looking at Lisa. "There can be no more north and south, no more war between the tribes. We will never rise above the monsters if we continue fighting with ourselves. There are no differences between us, none but those we imagine. The old general was right about one thing: It's time to write a new future."

"What will you do that is any different?" Simon asked.

James held Lisa's hand as he spoke. She squeezed his fingers, signaling her support, and that made him feel confident. In the midst of the exhaustion and pain, he felt strangely at peace.

"We will do the one thing that has made a difference throughout all time, we will teach. We'll teach people to read and write. We'll teach people to value knowledge, teach them to rediscover the science of old."

"How?" Lisa asked with tears in her eyes.

"We will open a school. And we will do it together, for those from the north and the south, from the east and the west. Understanding shall be our banner. Wisdom shall fly as our standard. And when knowledge prevails, the reign of monsters will be at an end."

The End

Interview with the author

Where did the idea for Monsters come from?

2012 was the National Year of Reading in Australia, and that got me thinking about how easy it is to take reading for granted.

Literacy is a relatively modern phenomenon. For most of history, reading has been a privileged act, something reserved for priests and monks.

Access to written knowledge was pivotal to each of the great revolutions of the modern era, the scientific revolution, the reformation, industrialization and enlightenment. Reading brought mankind out of the dark ages. And that got me thinking, what would life be like if we lost the ability to read?

Few realize how free, open access to knowledge is the cornerstone of civilization, but what if that knowledge was taken away from us? Would people fight to restore knowledge within a crumbling society? I think the answer is, yes.

Could monsters like this exist in real life?

Monsters similar to those depicted in this novel this have existed at various points in time, right up to the present day.

Haast's eagle of New Zealand went extinct in the 1600s. It had a wingspan of 10 feet and is rumored to have snatched Maori children.

Ligers are a cross between a male lion and a female tiger. Ligers can reach 800 pounds and 12 feet in length, which is roughly the size of the dogs described in this story.

Brutus is a wild crocodile found in the Northern Territory of Australia. At 5.5 meters (18+ feet), Brutus has been known to feed on full-grown Bull Sharks.

The Giant Golden-Crowned Flying Fox has a wingspan of 1.7 meters (5'4")

Friesian cows can stand 6'5" in height and weigh in at over a ton.

Male polar bears regularly reach nine feet in length and up to 1,500 pounds.

The Japanese Spider Crab is long and lanky, reaching up to 12 feet in length, while the Bobbit worm is 10 feet long and venomous.

In 2014, a hunter killed a nine-foot grizzly with a skull bone half an inch thick.

The Blue whale, the whale shark and basking shark, along with elephants and rhinos are all examples of megafauna (large animals) that have survived to modern times.

In Monsters, a combination of Natural Selection and the fallout from Comet Holt allows the outliers in the animal kingdom to become the norm and dominate the food chain.

If the animals became enlarged, why weren't humans also bigger?

The history of life on Earth shows us that Natural Selection doesn't favor one particular size. Even such giants as dinosaurs ranged in size from that of a cat to a three-story building.

During the age of the Megafauna some 10,000 years ago, carnivorous sloths reached sizes larger than an elephant, and yet the humans alive then were roughly the same size as we are now.

What is your favorite Monster within the novel?

Ah... that's a bit like asking me, who's my favorite child? I love all of them. In writing Monsters, I wanted to show that monsters aren't simply dark, foreboding creatures of the night. Some of the scariest monsters in this book are bacteria, or the loss of medical knowledge that costs one of the characters her life. Then there's us, people. Humans can be monsters every bit as scary as a giant, blood-sucking bat.

Will there be a sequel to Monsters?

I hope so, but that depends on how well the book is received. I've got enough material for a sequel, appropriately titled Monstrous.

Are you active on social media?

Yes. My twitter handle is @PeterCawdron, and I can be found on facebook, tumblr and pinterest. I also keep a science fiction blog, called thinking scifi http://thinkingscifi.wordpress.com/

What books do you read?

I enjoy reading a wide variety of books, and I'm never short of someone suggesting another good read. My problem is, I'm a slow reader. The more I enjoy a book, the slower I read, savoring each moment, so I don't get through as many books as I'd like.

I often struggle to finish books. I've been reading Rendezvous with Rama for about five years now. Anyone that follows me on Goodreads will know I have half-a-dozen books I'm reading at any one time, but they can sit on my virtual shelf for quite some time before I finish them. I chop and change between them as my interest grows and wanes.

In particular, I enjoy the classics: Mary Shelley's Frankenstein, H.G. Wells War of the Worlds, Charles Darwin's The Descent of Man, Benjamin Franklin's autobiography. But I also enjoy Michael Crichton, Alistair Reynolds, Hugh Howey and Stephen Baxter.

In our day, there's so much competition from newspapers, the internet, blog posts, video games, movies and TV, that it easy to lose sight of reading books. And yet reading a good book achieves a level of immersion these other, quick-fix mediums lack.

In five years' time, what will you remember about the TV show you watched last night? Or the news report you read online this morning? Books are formative. A good book can stay with you for a lifetime. Most evenings, I'll read with my two girls. My son's a little old for reading with dad these days, but he'll wander past and hear us reading out loud to each other. At the moment, we're reading Inkheart, James and the Giant Peach and The Magic of Reality.

Do you watch much television or movies?

Reality TV was the best thing that ever happened to my writing, it got me off the couch and in front of a keyboard. I love a good science fiction or action/adventure movie. I try not to pick apart movies, but plot inconsistencies throw me out of a story quite easily.

What hobbies do you have?

I enjoy running in the forest most weekends. It's a nice way to unwind and leave a hectic week behind. Here in Australia, it's common to see wallabies and kangaroos in the early morning. I've seen goannas and snakes, and even a wild koala.

Having grown up in New Zealand, I enjoy watching rugby and rugby league. If you've never seen either game, imagine a bunch of grown men acting like mountain goats in the rut, running hard at each other and butting their heads together. Throw in an inflated pig skin along with a few white lines on the grass and you get the gist of it.

Do you get help writing your novels?

I do. My wife and close friends help by reviewing early drafts, but there's a lot of input from fans as well. As a writer I've "met" people from around the world without ever actually meeting them in person. This is a wonderful part of publishing eBooks. I've had the opportunity to "meet" university professors, physicists, surveyors, doctors, aerospace/astronaut instructors, other indie authors and indie book reviewers from as far afield as Florida, well, at least that's far from Australia.

Sometimes they'll have some scientific input, correcting technical mistakes, other times they'll pick up on plot inconsistencies or typos, or problems with a particular stylistic approach. Sometimes they'll just provide a kind word of encouragement, all of which is deeply appreciated.

Is it hard to write an independent book?

Yes.

Well, I guess that answers the question, but do you have any advice for aspiring authors?

* Writing is an art.
* Don't underestimate the effort involved.
* Never stop learning.

If I seem a bit withdrawn on the subject, it's because I could waffle on for hours about it, but I think those three points sum things up nicely.

Independent publishing is tough. Big name authors are, well, big names. If you look at their book covers, their name is the most dominant aspect of the cover. Think about Stephen KING novels you've seen. Often, the actual title of each book will be quite small, because books sell on his reputation. And, to be fair, that's understandable, as how can anyone purchase a book based on its contents before they've read it? Independent authors, generally speaking, haven't developed a name for themselves and so sell almost solely on word-of-mouth.

In this regard, reader reviews are the lifeblood of indie writers. Is Monsters a good book? That's a question I can't answer. Well, I can, but no one will believe me. They'll believe you, though, the reader. In my experience, less than one percent of readers will leave a review on

Amazon, GoodReads or Smashwords, etc. But that one percent will carry absolute authority in the mind of other potential readers.

Is Monsters based on any personal experience?

None of the characters or monsters are real, but several of the scenes are loosely based on some of my personal experiences.

I once went mountain climbing in the Colorado Rockies. With snowshoes strapped on our boots, my wife and I hiked up to a peak at just over 11,000ft and I was fascinated by all the dwarf trees on the summit. I wanted to get my photo taken by them, but our guide told us the trees were in fact 30-40 feet high, buried by snow drifts. He explained that because of the conical shape of the trees, it was quite dangerous to stand next to them as you could fall through the branches to the ground so far below. I never did get that photo, but I drew on that moment for one of the scenes in this novel.

Oh, and the section where James paints a harvest bin "the same" is another loosely true story, although the farmer I was working for was quite kind and laughed at the misunderstanding. He'd wanted the bin painted the same as it was originally, red and green, but I painted it the same, all red.

One final question. Where did you get these questions? Did you make them up yourself? Hey, wait. Come back... You haven't answered the question...

~~~

Thank you for supporting independent science fiction. I hope you've enjoyed Monsters.

Please take the time to provide a review on Amazon. Self-published authors like myself don't have big budgets for advertising and rely on word-of-mouth to find new readers.

You've read the book, now get the shirt!
http://www.cafepress.com/thinkingscifi

Other books by Peter Cawdron

You might also enjoy the following novels also written by Peter Cawdron.

MY SWEET SATAN

The crew of the Copernicus are sent to investigate Bestla, one of the remote moons of Saturn. Bestla has always been an oddball, orbiting Saturn in the wrong direction and at a distance of thirty million kilometers, so far away Saturn appears smaller than Earth's moon in the night sky. Bestla hides a secret. When mapped by an unmanned probe, Bestla awoke and began transmitting a message, only it's a message no one wants to hear: "I want to live and die for you, Satan."

SILO SAGA: SHADOWS

Shadows is fan fiction set in Hugh Howey's Wool universe as part of the Kindle Worlds Silo Saga.

Life within the silos follows a well-worn pattern passed down through the generations from master to apprentice, 'caster to shadow. "Don't ask! Don't think! Don't question! Just stay in the shadows." But not everyone is content to follow the past.

THE WORLD OF KURT VONNEGUT: CHILDREN'S CRUSADE

Kurt Vonnegut's masterpiece Slaughterhouse-Five: The Children's Crusade explored the fictional life of Billy Pilgrim as he stumbled through the real world devastation of Dresden during World War II. Children's Crusade picks up the story of Billy Pilgrim on the planet of Tralfamadore as Billy and his partner Montana Wildhack struggle to accept life in an alien zoo.

THE MAN WHO REMEMBERED TODAY

The Man Who Remembered Today is a novella originally appearing in From The Indie Side anthology, highlighting independent science fiction writers from around the world. You can pick up this story as a stand-alone short or get twelve distinctly unique stories by purchasing From the Indie Side.

Kareem wakes with a headache. A bloody bandage wrapped around his head tells him this isn't just another day in the Big Apple. The problem is, he can't remember what happened to him. He can't recall anything from yesterday. The only memories he has are from events that are about to unfold today, and today is no ordinary day.

ANOMALY

Anomaly examines the prospect of an alien intelligence discovering life on Earth.

Mankind's first contact with an alien intelligence is far more radical than anyone has ever dared imagine. The technological gulf between mankind and the alien species is measured in terms of millions of years. The only way to communicate is using science, but not everyone is so patient with the arrival of an alien space craft outside the gates of the United Nations in New York.

THE ROAD TO HELL

The Road to Hell is paved with good intentions.

How do you solve a murder when the victim comes back to life with no memory of recent events?

In the 22nd century, America struggles to rebuild after the second civil war. Democracy has been suspended while the reconstruction effort lifts the country out of the ruins of conflict. America's fate lies in the hands of a genetically-engineered soldier with the ability to move through time.

The Road to Hell deals with a futuristic world and the advent of limited time travel. It explores social issues such as the nature of trust and the conflict between loyalty and honesty.

MONSTERS

Monsters is a dystopian novel set against the backdrop of the collapse of civilization.

The fallout from a passing comet contains a biological pathogen, not a virus or a living organism, just a collection of amino acids, but these cause animals to revert to the age of the mega-fauna, when monsters roamed Earth.

Bruce Dobson is a reader. With the fall of civilization, reading has become outlawed. Superstitions prevail, and readers are persecuted like the witches and wizards of old. Bruce and his son James seek to overturn the prejudices of their day and restore the scientific knowledge central to their survival, but monsters lurk in the dark.

FEEDBACK

Twenty years ago, a UFO crashed into the Yellow Sea off the Korean Peninsula. The only survivor was a young English-speaking child, captured by the North Koreans. Two decades later, a physics student watches his girlfriend disappear before his eyes, abducted from the streets of New York by what appears to be the same UFO.

Feedback will carry you from the desolate, windswept coastline of North Korea to the bustling streets of New York and on into the depths of space as you journey to the outer edge of our solar system looking for answers.

GALACTIC EXPLORATION

Galactic Exploration is a compilation of four closely related science fiction stories following the exploration of the Milky Way by the spaceships Serengeti, Savannah and The Rift Valley. These three generational star ships are manned by clones and form part of the ongoing search for intelligent extra-terrestrial life. With the Serengeti heading out above the plane of the Milky Way, the Savannah exploring the outer reaches of the galaxy, and The Rift Valley investigating possible alien signals within the galactic core, this story examines the Rare Earth Hypothesis from a number of different angles.

This volume contains the novellas:

- Serengeti
- Trixie & Me
- Savannah
- War

XENOPHOBIA

Xenophobia examines the impact of first contact on the Third World.

Dr Elizabeth Bower works at a field hospital in Malawi as a civil war smolders around her. With an alien space craft in orbit around Earth, the US withdraws its troops to deal with the growing unrest in America. Dr Bower refuses to abandon her hospital. A troop of US Rangers accompanies Dr Bower as she attempts to get her staff and patients to safety. Isolated and alone, cut off from contact with the West, they watch as the world descends into chaos with alien contact.

LITTLE GREEN MEN

Little Green Men is a tribute to the works of Philip K. Dick, hailing back to classic science fiction stories of the 1950s.

The crew of the Dei Gratia set down on a frozen planet and are attacked by little green men. Chief Science Officer David Michaels struggles with the impossible situation unfolding around him as the crew are murdered one by one. With the engines offline and power fading, he races against time to understand this mysterious threat and escape the planet alive.

VAMPIRE & WE ARE LEGION

Bram Stoker wrote Dracula over the course of a decade, researching historical figures and compiling notes from scattered diary entries. What was supposed to be a work of fiction holds far more truth than he realized. Dr. Jane Langford is investigating a murder-suicide unlike anything she's ever encountered before. Sleepy Boise, Idaho, is a haven to an evil that has passed unnoticed down through the centuries.

ANTHOLOGIES

In addition to these stories, Peter Cawdron has short stories appearing in:

- The Telepath Chronicles

- The Alien Chronicles

- The A.I. Chronicles

- The Z Chronicles

- Tales of Tinfoil

Coming in 2016

THE COLONY

The colony on Mars is the first step in humanity's long walk out of Africa and into the stars. Mars Alpha is heavily dependent on resupply from Earth. Where possible, colonists use 3D printing and locally grown food, but they still rely on Earth for complex medicines and electronics. The colonists are prepared for every eventuality but one. What happens on Mars when nuclear war breaks out on Earth?

WELCOME TO THE OCCUPIED STATES OF AMERICA

Seven years after the invasion of the grubs, 110 million Americans have been displaced by the war, with over 50 million dead. Ashley Kelly was crippled by a cluster bomb. While the world crumbled, she spent seven years learning to walk again, and she'll be damned if she's going to lie down for anyone, terrestrial or extraterrestrial.

Subscribe by email to hear of new releases

39136148R00197

Made in the USA
Middletown, DE
05 January 2017